THE REBEL BRIDE

THE REBEL BRIDE

Catherine Coulter

Severn House Large Print
London & New York

This first large print edition published in Great Britain 2003 by
SEVERN HOUSE LARGE PRINT BOOKS LTD of
9-15, High Street, Sutton, Surrey, SM1 1DF.
First world regular print hardcover edition published 2002 by
Severn House Publishers, London and New York.
This first large print edition published in the USA 2003 by
SEVERN HOUSE PUBLISHERS INC., of
595 Madison Avenue, New York, NY 10022

British Library Cataloguing in Publication Data

Coulter, Catherine
    The rebel bride - Large print ed.
    1.   Love stories
    2.   Large type books
    I.   Title
    813.5'4 [F]

ISBN 0-7278-7239-7

Except where actual historical events and characters are being described for
the storyline of this novel, all situations in this publication are fictitious and
any resemblance to living persons is purely coincidental.

Printed and bound in Great Britain by
MPG Books Ltd, Bodmin, Cornwall.

To my wonderful sister,
Diane Coulter,
The second time around for this Baby

Thus in plain terms; your father hath
consented
That you shall be my wife...
And, will you, nill you, I will marry you.

Now, Kate, I am a husband for your turn;
For, by this light, whereby I see thy beauty,
Thy beauty, that doth make me like thee
well,
Thou must be married to no man but me...

—Shakespeare,
The Taming of the Shrew

1

Julien St Clair, earl of March, flicked a careless finger over her white belly, lay back on the large canopied bed, and gazed beneath half-closed lids at the dancing patterns cast by the firelight on the opposite wall. He felt a sort of lazy satisfaction that, for the moment, relieved his boredom.

"I have pleased you, my lord?" She twined her fingers in his fair hair, her own body languid from the pleasure he had given her.

"Of course, Yvette," he said, annoyed that she disturbed the silence he wanted.

There was a flash of anger in her doe-brown eyes. She knew full well she had pleased him but a short time before, and it galled her now to see him again remote and withdrawn. But from her long experience with noblemen, she realized that reproaches would gain her nothing. She let her face soften into an inviting expression and lowered herself onto his chest, pressing her breasts against him. She slid her arms around his neck and gently tugged until he turned his face to hers. She smiled knowingly as he brought his arms lazily from behind his head downward through her chestnut hair and began to

7

explore her back and knead her hips.

To Yvette's surprise, she soon felt a quiver run the length of her body, and she sighed, a low moan of pleasure.

In a graceful motion Julien rolled over on top of her. He took her mouth. He would give her what she wanted. His hands stroked her body, teasing, caressing, feeling the soft flesh of her buttocks.

He watched her eyes widen when his fingers found her. Her lashes fluttered and her mouth worked, making her look very real, very human. A dull flush began to creep over her cheeks, and her body trembled. She urgently willed him to enter her, and he drew up so she could guide him into her.

Though his body responded with rhythmic motion, Julien felt strangely detached from the very soft, giving woman beneath him, unable to let himself feel the passionate intensity of her need. Yet he felt his breathing quicken as she reached her final tensing. He drove deep, heard her cries of release, and let his body respond.

He allowed himself to be locked to her for one long moment before falling full length on top of her, his head beside her face on the pillow.

Yvette calmed, becoming relaxed and still beneath him. She was certain this time she had pleased him. Her own pleasure she discounted. She waited for him to utter some slight words of endearment, but he lay quiet above her, his breath becoming even.

Her body began to protest against his weight, but she didn't move, for fear of disturbing him.

"Yvette, what is the time?" he asked, his voice muffled by the pillow.

"It lacks but a few moments until ten, my lord," she said with definite edge to her voice.

"Be damned." He rolled away from her. Yvette watched him rise from the bed and briefly stretch his tall, muscular body. As always, she was unable to look at him without admiring him. For months she had called him her golden god. But now, she thought bitterly, he was a fickle god, leaving her with scarce a backward thought.

Her frustration grew as she racked her mind for a charmingly turned phrase to catch his attention. Finding herself unequal to the task, she sighed and raised herself up onto the pillow, pulling a cover over her body.

He drew on his white ruffled shirt and turned to look at her. "I must leave, Yvette. I am promised to meet Blairstock at White's and am already late."

"When am I to see you again, my lord?" she asked with controlled sweetness, half-rising to go to him.

He halted her progress with an impatient wave of his hand and replied with only casual interest, "That is difficult to say. I'm meeting friends in the country for hunting and shall be absent from London for some time."

She sucked in her breath, now wary. He had not told her of his imminent departure

9

from London.

He shrugged himself, not without some difficulty, into a coat of superfine blue cloth that was molded exquisitely to his broad shoulders, and strode over to her.

"I trust you will find sufficient to amuse you during my absence," he said, and she could hear the warning in his voice. "I only ask that you not be too indiscreet while you are still in my keeping." A faintly sardonic look passed over his handsome face, making his gray eyes cold and hard.

"I don't know what you mean." Her face drained of color even as she spoke.

"Oh, don't you, Yvette? How very strange. I had thought you would know exactly what I meant. In any case," he continued with careless emphasis, "we shall discuss the matter upon my return."

He picked up his cane and pulled his many-caped cloak around his shoulders and walked to the door. As he let himself out, he said over his shoulder, "Don't, whatever you do, underestimate your value, my dear. You're as fine a possession as any man could wish."

He closed the door quietly behind him and was gone. Yvette could hear his retreating footsteps as he took the stairs two at a time.

"Damn you," she shouted at the closed bedchamber door, wishing for something to hurl. "All those fine lords, damn them, arrogant crowing peacocks."

As her anger lessened, a frown creased her white brow and she pursed her lips, now

10

annoyed at herself for her own carelessness. She should have guessed that her capitulation to Lord Riverton would send his boasting, vain lordship to proclaim his triumph. It was a mistake she should not have made, a stupid, ill-timed blunder that had lost her, she was forced to admit, a very generous protector.

She pushed back the covers and rose slowly, her body aching from her exertions. She sat at her dressing table and began to brush out her tangled chestnut hair. She paused a moment to examine the undeniably alluring face and felt cheered. Lord Riverton was a rich man and appeared to enjoy her lisping English and her views of life in England, as well as the voluptuous attractions her body offered.

She sighed, momentarily cast down. She was fond of Julien, and he was after all an earl. And dreadfully rich. She found herself gazing wistfully at her elegantly furnished room. She would miss this charming apartment and also, she reflected, a man very nicely skilled in the art of lovemaking—and only a few of those skills had she taught him. No, when she'd first come to him, he was already a man of pleasure, a man who wasn't selfish in the giving of pleasure, despite the fact that she was his mistress. He could still surprise her by his ability to make her forget herself, make her forget all her own wiles for giving him pleasure.

She rose from her dressing table, blew out the candles, and took herself back to bed. As pragmatic as she was passionate, she realized

11

that it was just as well that Julien was leaving for the country. It would give her time to assess Lord Riverton's intentions.

It did not take her long to devise a plan which pleased her, and she fell asleep confident that she could part the pinch-penny Lord Riverton from some of his precious guineas.

Outside the red brick house on Curzon Street, Julien hailed a hackney and directed the driver to make all haste to White's. He sat back against the rather worn cushions and stretched his long legs. The old wooden cab swayed precariously as the horse clip-clopped on the uneven cobblestones, and Julien had to steady his position by holding the frayed leather strap. He felt now only slightly irritated that he'd shared Yvette with another man while she was under his protection. In all honesty, he knew that he had given her scant attention these last few months, his visits infrequent and for only one purpose. He had used her body to escape for brief periods of time from his growing restlessness. Yvette had been his choice recently over the lovely Lady Sarah, as he had found it increasingly difficult to speak with any sincerity at all the words of endearment and affection required of such a liaison. With Yvette he could behave exactly as he wished, for it was her duty to please him. He thought of her unsuccessful attempt at perfidy and felt faintly amused. He had no doubt that she would take care of herself; like a cat, she was, soft, purring, and quite able to land on her feet. He sighed and closed his eyes. He wished Yvette luck in her pursuit of Riverton.

When the cab drew to a halt in front of White's on St James Street, he alighted quickly, paid the driver handsomely, and gave Yvette not another thought.

"Good evening, my lord." He was greeted at the door by one of White's renowned retainers, who, after straightening from his low bow, deftly relieved Julien of his cane and cloak.

Julien nodded briefly. "Is Sir Percy here, Henry?"

"Yes, indeed, my lord. I believe him to be in the card room."

Julien made his way through the dark, wood-paneled reading room, his steps muffled by the thick plush carpeting. Rich vellum-bound books lined the walls—books scarcely ever opened, truth be told—and well-read London papers lay in neat stacks on the heavy mahogany tables. He stopped a moment and thumbed through the *Gazette*, his eye caught by the latest bit of news of Napoleon's incarceration on Elba, an island he now ruled as he had France, the little bastard. At least now he was a tin god, his power stripped away.

"It is shocking, is it not, my lord, that the pompous Corsican held Europe so long in the palm of his hand?"

"Indeed it is," Julien said, as he turned and

proferred a slight bow to the arthritic duke of Moreland.

The duke looked pensively down at the paper and continued in his slow, painstaking way, "It is quite beyond me how that upstart little toad achieved such power." He gave an eloquent shrug of his shoulders that brought a grimace of pain to his face. "But the French, you know, have always suffered from political untidiness. Yes, they've always been an unsteady race."

Julien said gently, "Perhaps it isn't so unfathomable a turn of events, your grace, when one considers the terrible plight of the French people even after the beginning of the revolution."

"I hope you are not becoming a republican, my boy. That is surely something your late father would find most abhorrent. He was a stern, perhaps overrighteous man, though, as I suppose you know very well."

"Yes, your grace. My father was those things and, naturally, more. And, being an Englishman in a country where all men are treated with at least a modicum of justice, I don't think myself at all republican to comment with truth on the stupidity and blatant greed of the past French monarchs. Surely they were more than simply untidy."

"Well said, my boy, well said." His grace beamed, having forgotten his earlier criticism.

"If your grace will excuse me—" Julien said, as he took the old duke's hand in his.

14

"Off with you, my lord. Do not forget to pay my compliments to your dear mother. I do hope her fragile health hasn't faltered." The duke added more to himself than to Julien, "It is difficult to keep up with one's friends nowadays, so many of them gone, either dead or just, well, gone."

"My mother will be pleased, your grace." Julien smiled, not without a good deal of affection, at the duke before turning and continuing his way to the card room.

He made his greetings to other acquaintances in his casual, easy manner as he progressed the length of the reading room. But he didn't stop, reflecting with a grin that poor Percy would in all likelihood be mad as hell at him for having his dinner so very delayed.

A footman opened a great paneled oak door to the card room and quickly closed it behind Julien so as not to disturb the more sober club members in the reading room. The card room was ablaze with candles, in marked contrast to other, more sedate rooms in White's. It was a glittering company, loud and boisterous. Footmen seemed to be everywhere, scurrying from group to group bearing silver trays laden with quantities of drink that would bring many aching heads on the morrow.

Julien gazed around the room at the various tables until his eyes came to rest on Sir Percy, sitting slouched with one elegantly clad leg swinging to and fro over the leg of a delicately wrought satin-covered chair.

He stood quietly for a moment behind Percy, noting with a shake of his head the small pile of guineas stacked in front of him. As Percy shoved most of the remainder toward the faro bank, Julien dropped a light hand on his shoulder.

"I see your luck is quite out tonight, Percy." He seated himself in a momentarily vacant chair next to his friend.

Sir Percy Blairstock turned a pair of pale-blue eyes to Julien and said with a grunt, "Well, Julien, what other choice do I have but to game away my fortune? I suppose you were in the arms of one of your fair Cyprians and quite forgot our dinner engagement."

Julien smiled broadly, even white teeth flashing. "Quite accurate, old boy, but as you see, I did not forget. Just a bit late, that's all. Your humble servant."

"You conceited dog. You aren't anyone's humble servant, March. Bedamned, I'm nearly done in." Sir Percy pushed back his chair and gathered up his few remaining guineas, stuffing them into his coat pocket.

"It appears that I've saved you from total ruin. Perhaps you owe me some words of thanks." Julien grinned and at the same time shook his head in refusal at a footman who offered him brandy.

"Ho, March! You do not play tonight?"

Julien turned away from the footman and Percy and calmly surveyed the dissipated face of Lord Devalney, who appeared to be already deep in his cups. He had never liked the man, but he had been a friend of Julien's father's, and therefore, in Julien's code, deserving at least of civility.

He gave a rather thin smile and said easily, "As you see, sir, I am otherwise engaged with Blairstock here."

"And I for one am famished," Sir Percy broke in. "Do come, Julien, let us try some of Pierre's delicious fish."

Julien shrugged his shoulders, rose, and bowed to Lord Devalney. "You will forgive me, sir, I must see to the pressing needs of Blairstock before he takes me to Hounslow Heath at dawn. Your servant, sir."

Lord Devalney waved a thin, darkly veined hand and returned his attention to the faro bank.

"What a reckless old fool. Never liked him above half." Sir Percy looked back over his shoulder as he spoke. Julien merely tugged on his sleeve, and the two friends made their way from the card room.

"Tolerance, Percy, tolerance."

"But that wig, Julien ... and he still paints his face. Did you see that ridiculous patch by his mouth?"

"A relic, Percy, just a relic who still breathes and still walks. Just imagine how he must regard us with our elaborate cravats and artfully disheveled hair."

"My father used to tell me that wigs were full of lice," Percy said, stubborn as a goat chewing on a boot.

Julien laughed but said only, "I fear if you

dwell on that thought, Percy, you might well lose your appetite."

It was well after midnight when Julien and Percy left White's. There was a full moon. Since the night wasn't overly cold, Julien cajoled Percy into walking to Grosvenor Square to the St Clair town house. Their comfortable silence was broken only by the clicking of their canes on the cobblestones until Julien said pensively, "You know, Percy, I grow quite tired of the fair Yvette. Can I depend upon Riverton to take her off my hands?"

Percy turned his head with some difficulty above his high starched shirt points, to gaze wonderingly at his friend. "She is a tidy morsel," he said only, trying to gauge Julien's mood. As Julien's countenance remained impassive and he offered no response, Percy said with some exasperation, "Good God, Julien, she has been in your keeping for but, what is it? ah, only five or six months?"

"Why don't you take her then, Percy? Cut out old Riverton. Surely she would enjoy you more than that bag of wind."

"Quite above my touch, as you well know, March. Unlike you, I am cursed with a father who holds a tight rein on the purse strings."

"Come, Percy, you know very well you could afford to maintain the fair Yvette if you were not so careless with your guineas at the gaming tables."

"That's quite easy for you to say, Julien,"

18

Percy said, allowing himself some bitterness. "In control of your own fortune and rich as Midas at eighteen—good God, it makes my dinner churn at the thought."

"As you will, Percy, but if you change your mind, you must move quickly, for I intend to dispense with her favors upon my return to London."

"Well, it is thoughtful of you to offer, March. But for the moment I and my pocket-book are quite content with less expensive pieces of enjoyment."

They fell into silence once again, and Julien's thoughts were drawn back to the years he'd spent learning to manage his vast estate after his father's early and unexpected death in a hunting accident. And, of course, there had been his ever-complaining mother. It was with profound relief that he had installed her, according to her wishes, in a cozy house in Brook Street to spend her days and evenings with an assortment of dowagers in equally comfortable circumstances.

"I say, Julien, when do you go to St Clair?"

Julien pulled himself out of his memories. "Tomorrow, I think. I will expect you and Hugh toward the end of the week."

"And what kind of sport do you offer besides hunting and fishing?"

Julien looked down at Percy's expectant face and said gently, "Fresh country air, Percy, nothing more. But it is exceedingly fresh."

"That's too bad of you, March. Surely you

know that fresh air is bad for the lungs. All know that's the case."

"Of course, we shall enjoy François's excellent cooking to maintain our spirits in the evenings." Julien poked the head of his cane into Percy's expanding stomach.

"A concession that meets my approval. Do you mind if I give François a recipe for cod with capers in black butter? My man is quite unable to get it just right."

Julien laughed, picturing such a confrontation between Percy and his emotional, artistic chef. "You certainly may try, but be prepared for the most comprehensive of Gallic oaths. He really does them well, perhaps even better than some of his dishes."

He reflected on François's past tirades and added, "Perhaps you had best not, Percy, for I have known the good François to brandish his butcher knife with manical intentions. I remember a poor scullery maid who chanced to make a face when she ate one of his scones. She ran screaming for her life."

Percy suddenly remembered his father's constant harping on the instability of the French. He decided it best to forget any improvements in his cod and changed the subject abruptly. "I trust we will play at cards. I expect to lose a fortune to you, you know."

"I keep telling you, Percy, be more careful with your discards. You stake too much on the chances of winning a big hand. It's your head you must use, not that elusive entity you call intuition."

Percy ignored this advice, for he'd heard it too many times before, and said with a good deal of satisfaction, "Well, I know that Hugh will put you in your place, for a better card player I have yet to find. Then we will see how well you practice your own advice."

"You're right. We shall see." Julien grinned, his calm unruffled. "I just might prove you wrong this time. There will be nothing to disturb my concentration at St Clair."

Percy refused to be drawn, his thoughts turning again to the epicurean delights he would enjoy at Julien's estate.

2

Julien's journey to St Clair occupied the better part of two days. As he tooled his curricle at a smart pace on his way north, with only his tiger, Bladen, for company, he felt again an unsettling restlessness that even the promise of excellent shooting and the thought of comfortable evenings spent with his friends did not lessen. A faint crease on his forehead was the only visible sign that anything disturbed the earl of March. Had Bladen seen his master's face, he would have probably thought him displeased with a new hunter or perhaps with a wager lost at cards. But he did not have an opportunity for such speculation, for the earl kept his gaze fixed on the road ahead, over the heads of his beautiful matched bays.

As Bladen handled the payment of tolls at the various stages, brooking no nonsense from the toll takers, Julien was left to his thoughts, undisturbed.

He hadn't traveled to St Clair for some months, and his visit now was prompted not by the cares of the estate but by motives he himself could not define to his satisfaction. He thought to break free of the admittedly comfortable restraints that were binding him to a round of activities that held little pleasure for him, for there was a growing emptiness that nagged at him whenever he slowed his frantic pace.

Perhaps, he reflected, as he flicked the thong of his whip over the head of his leader, he would be able to speak to Hugh. Unlike Percy, Hugh Drakemore, Lord Launston, was an older, settled man who seemed to know his way. In their long years of friendship, Julien had never known Hugh to react with anything but an amiable equanimity to the vagaries of his fellow man. But then, what would he say to Hugh? Certainly he could not complain that he was tired of his wealth and title, for he most assuredly was not. No, it was something else, something elusive, just out of his reach.

He had found himself looking searchingly at Percy the night before, noting the small yet obvious signs of dissipation about his eyes, the once-athletic body that was now running to fat. Percy had quizzed him often about being a fixture at Gentleman Jackson's boxing salon, a pursuit, however, that kept Julien's body hard and muscular. Percy seemed to devote his energies, indeed his life, to gaming, women, and drink. Now it occurred to Julien that he was being a hypocrite, criticizing his friends. How was he different from the pleasure-seeking ton, flitting about brightly in the evenings, hurling themselves into the gaiety? Surely his head ached just as abominably as his friends' heads did the mornings after evenings spent in consuming quantities of brandy.

Beyond making this silent observation, Julien found that this train of thought was inordinately frustrating and inconclusive. Perhaps, he thought, this visit to St Clair was just what he needed. But his lips twisted ironically at this wishful conclusion. He was still seeing St Clair as the place of happiness and innocent adventure of his boyhood, with dragons to slay and fair maidens to rescue, though in all truth, there hadn't been any maidens, fair or otherwise, to rescue.

He urged his horses to a faster pace. Fine-blood cattle, they jumped forward, a well-trained extension of his arm. They forced him to concentrate on his driving, for the road was narrow, even dangerously so.

The slightly built Bladen hung on tightly, shaking his head. His master always drove to an inch, but he had never seen him increase his horses' pace on such a winding, narrow road. He thought fleetingly that his master was driving as if demons were after him. He paused, alarmed by this thought, and swung his head around quickly to search the road behind them. Seeing nothing but clouds of dust raised by the curricle, he shrugged his shoulders and wondered whether demons were invisible. He turned his attention on the road ahead, thankful now more than ever that his master was an excellent whip.

Late in the afternoon, three days after leaving London, Julien drove his curricle through the village of Dapplemoor, which lay but a few miles to the west of St Clair. The village seemed practically empty save for a few ducks that swam lazily in a small pond at the center of the green.

"Everybody be home having their dinner, milord," Bladen said, surveying the quiet village.

"And you'll be having your own dinner soon enough, Bladen," the earl said over his shoulder. "We'll be at St Clair in but a short time now."

"Aye," Bladen agreed, reflecting with some pleasure on the meal that would be ready for him. He tightened his grip once again as his master passed out of the village and spurred his horses forward.

Julien felt a quickening within as they entered St Clair park. Giant oak trees lined the drive, forming a lush green ceiling of leaves. Only slight beams of sunlight penetrated the dense covering. He mused that these giant oaks would remain as they were long after the St Clairs were dead and forgotten.

The oaks came to an end when the curricle burst onto the graveled drive that wound around in circular fashion in front of the mansion. Julien drew his horses to a halt in front of the great stone steps.

The last rays of sunlight cast their gold hue on the thick stone walls that rose up two stories, extending at the four corners to form round Gothic towers. Julien was seized by a feeling of agelessness, of being drawn back in time, away from the modern society of London. As he gazed at his home, he could not but respect his hard-willed ancestors who had ensured his birthright. St Clair had been gutted on two occasions, the last being over one hundred and fifty years ago, during the interminable battles between Charles I's Royalist troops and Cromwell's Roundheads, but the earls of March had simply scrubbed down the smoke-blackened stone walls and rebuilt the interior. Julien knew as a simple fact that if war again ravaged England he would do just as his ancestors had done. St Clair must never be allowed to fall into ruin.

No sooner had Julien alighted from his curricle than the great doors were thrown open and Mannering, the St Clair butler for over thirty years, made his way down the ancient stone steps to greet his master.

Julien's eyes lit up at the sight of his old retainer. He knew full well that the smooth running of St Clair resulted in great part from the competence of the faithful Mannering.

Mrs Cradshaw, St Clair's housekeeper, followed closely on the butler's heels, her plump, simple face alight with pleasure.

"Ah, welcome home, my lord," Mannering boomed in his rich, deep voice, bowing low.

"It's certainly good to be home, Mannering. I trust all goes well with Mrs Mannering?"

"As well as can be expected, my lord, considering the years are making us all a bit rickety."

Mannering beamed at the young earl, pleased that his lordship was never too high in the instep to be concerned about those in his employ. It was true that Mrs Mannering had hidden the earl once years before when he'd unloosed all his father's hunters into the formal St Clair gardens. He could still remember the countess's hysterical screams.

"Master Julien!" Mrs Cradshaw bustled forward and swept Julien a deep curtsy.

Julien encircled the small, plump woman in his arms, a wide smile on his face.

"Your prodigal has returned, Emma. Is it too much to hope that there will be some blueberry muffins beside my plate this evening?" He gave her a gentle hug and released her.

"Fancy that, Edward," she said, turning to

26

Mannering. "Master Julien never forgets his blueberry muffins. It's a good lad you are."

"Indeed this lad would never forget. Moreover, François will not be arriving until well after dinner tonight. Far too late to turn up his artistic nose at my tastes."

"What can you expect from those Frogs? Why, I had it on the best information that the Frenchies are so ignorant the ladies crush up blueberries and rub them on their eyes."

"Why, Mrs Cradshaw," Julien said, "I have it from my best sources that the French think blueberries fit for only pigs and Englishmen. And perhaps as coloring for the ladies' eyelids."

She laughed and laughed, lightly tapping him on his arm.

"Now, Emma," Mannering said, "his lordship looks worn to the bone and it's time we got everything ordered away for his comfort."

He turned to Julien and continued formally, servant now to master, "Your rooms are all ready, my lord, and since I do not see your valet—" he paused slightly to leave no doubt that he found Timmens an unnecessary encumbrance "I myself will attend your lordship tonight."

Julien was amused by the rivalry between his two households but managed to maintain a serious expression. Poor Mannering. If he only knew that Timmens considered himself quite put upon to be dragged into the wilds of the North, into the company of persons he considered to be outlandishly uncivilized.

27

Julien gave a brief moment's thought to the dusty state of his normally gleaming Hessians. He could almost hear Timmens's high, reedy voice reproaching him. It was remarkably irritating.

Julien nodded his agreement to Mannering and made his way through the great front doors, past several footmen and two giggling maids who had peeped around a corner to peer at him.

"I always feel that I should be removing my armor rather than a meager cloak and hat," Julien remarked, as Mannering gently removed the many-caped greatcoat and the beaver hat.

"Indeed, my lord, isn't it just grand?" Pride rang in his voice, perhaps as much as in the earl's.

Like many great houses of its age, St. Clair opened its oaken doors directly into a magnificent hall, whose walls were covered with ancient tapestries and brightly lit flambeaux. Suits of highly polished armor stood upright around the great room. Julien had always the impression that at a moment's notice they would spring forward into action to defend St Clair, and as a boy he had joined them in many an imaginary battle. A wistful smile played over his lips, and it was with a conscious effort that he turned his attention to Mrs Cradshaw.

"I find myself quite famished. Could I have my dinner, with, of course, the blueberry muffins, in about an hour?"

"Certainly, my lord." She gave him a sideways glance as if to remind him that he was no longer among that rackety pack of good-for-nothing servants in London, who could not be trusted to take proper care of his lordship.

Julien strode to the main staircase, a dark oak affair that dominated a goodly portion of the hall. He touched the ornately carved railing, aware that it glowed shiny and bright under the careful ministrations of Mrs Cradshaw. He slowed his step halfway up the stairs, turning his gaze for a moment to the portraits of past earls and their wives on the wall beside him. They had been a prolific line, he thought, mentally adding to this number of portraits the scores of others that hung in the gallery. The portraits reminded him that the St Clairs had inherited father to son in an unbroken stream of earls from the mid-sixteenth century until the present, an unusual occurrence in itself. Julien could readily imagine his father hurling abuse at his head for all eternity should he not marry and produce the necessary male child. It had seemed rather absurd to trouble himself with such thoughts, for he was young and quite healthy, certainly more so than his nominal heir at present, a distant sickly cousin who would become the eighth earl should Julien depart this world without a son.

On his next birthday Julien would be twenty-eight, a reasonable enough age to take a wife and beget a future earl of March.

29

He was certain that this decision would please his Aunt Mary Tolford, sister to his mother, who had been voluble on the subject of his marriage from the moment he had passed his twenty-fifth birthday. He could always count on her, after all formal amenities were done, to look at him with narrowed eyes and inquire after his plans to modernize the nursery wing at St Clair. Over the past three years whenever he had crossed the portal of her rather dark and airless house in London he knew that in the drawing room he would face a nervous young miss, elegantly clad, pale with anxiety, awaiting his inspection.

Julien looked up, surprised that he had reached his room. A footman appeared and quickly flung open the massive door. Like the hall below, the master bedchamber was amazing in size and filled with heavy furniture that dated from Tudor times, when that particular St Clair had been the second Viscount Barresford and the fifth Baron Hedford. It had crossed his mind to wonder how the diligent Mrs Cradshaw managed to move the ponderous pieces in order to sweep beneath them. But it was the huge canopy bed that Julien most appreciated. The Tudor St Clair responsible for its construction must have been a giant of a man, for the bed was nearly seven feet long and almost as wide. Julien could not be displeased at this, for he himself was six feet tall and suffered unending discomfort at inns and at his friends' houses.

While Mannering directed footmen in the preparation of the bath, Julien walked over to a brightly burning fire and eased himself into a large leather chair. He negligently loosened his cravat and with a sigh of comfort stretched his long legs out before him.

What more could a man wish for? he wondered lazily. Somehow the thought of a wife's domestic chatter intruding on the majestic silence of this ancient chamber was unimaginable to him. In any case, he thought with a grimace, its sole purpose would be to grate on his nerves.

Having done justice to Cook's innumerable dishes, Julien rose, sated, and walked from the formal, rather somber dining room to the sixth earl's library. Julien never felt quite at his ease in this room, for it was uniquely his father's. All Tudor influence had been swept away, replaced by pale-blue-satin hangings and light, delicately carved French pieces from the last century. Lush, light-blue-patterned Aubusson carpets covered the cold stone floor, and even the massive carved mantelpiece had been removed and replaced by a light-colored Italian marble one. He could still picture his mother, a descendant of a long, proud heritage of drafty castles in the North, casting scathing comments at her husband's folly. Since his father's death some ten years ago, this room, and indeed all of St Clair, was Julien's alone, to do with as he

31

pleased. But he had vowed long ago that the library would remain just as it was, the only tangible expression of his father's taste at St Clair.

An overly large wing chair stood near the fireplace, quite out of place with the other exquisitely wrought pieces. It was his father's chair, and Julien always found himself grateful that his sire had made this one exception to the room's decor in the name of comfort.

It was in this chair that Julien sat himself, stretching his Hessians to the glowing fire.

Mannering approached him, coughed slightly to gain his attention, and turned inquiring eyes upon the plate of Mrs Cradshaw's blueberry muffins that he had carried with him from the dining room.

Julien said, "Good God, Mannering, those damned muffins are still here on their plate and not in my belly. Will Mrs Cradshaw refuse to serve me my breakfast?"

Mannering said, unbending a bit, "Mrs Cradshaw will understand, my lord."

Julien waved his hand at the small table at his side. "No, Mannering, I don't want to brook her displeasure my first evening home. I promise you, I shall do them justice before the evening is out."

Mannering set the plate of muffins at his side and made his way to the sideboard to fetch a decanter of claret. A smile flitted over Julien's face as he recalled Mannering's herculean struggle to help him into his form-fitting coat. He had shown unbounded relief when Julien divested himself of his own boots, a task that most certainly would have shaken Mannering's dignified image of himself. Perhaps, he thought, Mannering would not now think his valet, Timmens, a bad sort after all.

"Will that be all you require, my lord?"

Julien, aware of his old retainer's fatigue, said quickly, "Yes, Mannering. Do retire now, I will snuff all the candles when I go up."

Mannering turned and strode in his stately manner out of the library, softly closing the double doors behind him.

Julien leaned forward and poured himself a glass of claret. He took a sip and sat back, savoring the quality. He began absently to twirl the stem between long, slender fingers, his thoughts turning to Percy and Hugh, whom he expected to arrive the next evening. He discovered now that he regretted having invited them to join him here. Aside from the fishing and shooting, the time he would spend in their company promised to be no different from his activities in London.

Julien frowned. He decided after a long drink of claret that he was simply becoming hermetic.

A ghost of a smile played over his lips as he pictured Percy's boredom at being incarcerated in the country. He found himself concluding, without much regret, that in all likelihood Percy and perhaps even Hugh would leave St Clair after just a few days.

The claret curled about warmly in his

stomach and he began to grow drowsy. He eyed the muffins with a marked lack of enthusiasm and admitted that he couldn't manage even a nibble. He decided to take them to his room and down several the next morning before breakfast.

He fell asleep not long thereafter, comfortably stretched at his full length on the large Tudor bed, his head clear of the effects of too much drink. It was a pleasant condition, one he had seldom experienced in the past several months.

3

Julien awoke later than intended the following morning. Upon opening his eyes, he found himself looking up into his valet's perturbed face.

"Good God, Timmens, what a face to be greeted with after a pleasant night's sleep. Go wash it or something."

"Good morning, my lord," Timmens said, his voice as stiff as Julien's malacca cane. He gave an audible sniff of displeasure and helped his master into his dressing gown.

"Come, man, surely things are not so bad as all that. I assure you that even though my Hessians and coat have suffered in your absence, you won't find them quite beyond repair."

"They were awful, my lord. I have already expended a goodly number of hours endeavoring to restore your Hessians, and it was an experience that I would not care to repeat."

Julien paused a moment, now fully awake and aware that the sensibilities of his stiff-lipped valet were ruffled in the extreme. He said with perfect seriousness, "Of course I have missed your fine service, Timmens. You are a grand valet, a gentleman's gentleman of exceptionable ability, whom I find invaluable and—"

"I quite understand, my lord, indeed I do. Do allow me to assist you now in the renewed quiet of the morning."

Finally dressed, Julien was at the point of escaping to his breakfast when he chanced to see the plate of muffins beside his bed, still untouched. He eyed Timmens, who was arranging his hairbrush and shaving gear in too-neat rows on the dressing table. A small punishment, just a bit of revenge, he thought, would be just the thing—ah, but subtle, that was important. He cleared his throat and said, "Timmens, you see the muffins here by my bed?"

"Yes, my lord, they are indeed muffins."

"As a reward for your excellent service this morning, I require you to enjoy at least two of them before allowing the maids to enter the room."

Timmens darted his rheumy eyes again to the muffins, bemused by this ambiguous token of praise. He realized that his master was awaiting his answer and said, "Yes, my lord. Thank you, my lord. It is a fine reward for my invaluable services, if one doesn't think of other rewards which would be perhaps even more tasty to the palate."

Not more than an hour later, in fine good humor, Julien mounted his Arabian mare, Astarte, and rode out of the park at a comfortable canter to inspect his lands.

Bright sunlight poured down through the crisp morning air, as if bending all of its brilliance on St Clair. With a great sense of well-being, Julien turned Astarte into an open field and gave her her head. His body moved smoothly with hers, swaying in rhythm to her firm stride. The chirping of birds and the gentle rustle of leaves and foliage were a welcome change from the everpresent noise of the London streets.

Julien quite lost track of time, and some time later, realizing that Astarte was blowing hard, he reined in, straightened in the saddle, and looked about him. A short distance ahead lay a large wood, forming a near-circle around him. He saw with vague interest that he was no longer on St Clair land.

"Come, Astarte, let us see what lies ahead. Perhaps we'll find a leftover dragon from my boyhood still lurking in those woods, waiting for me to stick him with my sword."

Julien made out a small path just to his left that led into the woods and click-clicked Astarte forward. The floor of the woods was green with spongy moss that deadened the sound of Astarte's hooves.

All too soon the trees began to thin and Julien could make out a small clearing a few yards ahead. Suddenly he knew he wasn't alone. He wasn't certain how he knew, except that his ears had grown used to the sounds of the forest.

He allowed Astarte to move slowly forward toward the clearing. His vision no longer blocked by the trees, he stiffened at the strange sight that met his eyes.

There, in the small clearing not twenty yards away from him, stood two men, pistols raised properly in front of their faces, standing back to back. There were no dragons to slay that Julien could see.

Good Lord, he thought, appalled, they're going to duel. He thought blankly that surely that wasn't right. Dueling was for dawn on a foggy morning with seconds standing about slapping their hands together for warmth.

There were no seconds—no one but the two duelists, who now began to pace away from each other, one man's voice calling out the paces in a loud, clear voice, "One, two, three... "

Julien gently dug his heels into Astarte's side, and she obediently moved forward, making no sound until they reached the edge of the clearing.

Fascinated, Julien stared fixedly at the two men. Surely it was just some sort of practice, surely the pistols weren't loaded. Surely.

"Eight, nine, ten!"

The men turned in quick, smooth motions and faced each other. One of them pulled up his pistol in a quick, jerky movement, stiffened his arm, and fired.

The gun's report rang through the silence of the woods. The pistols were most certainly loaded.

The bullet missed its mark, for the other man remained standing, and now, in what seemed an endlessly cruel delay, he slowly raised his pistol and aimed it at his opponent's chest.

Julien found himself frozen into inaction, his hands clutching the reins, simply disbelieving. The man stood proud and stiff, waiting, without a sound.

With a nasty laugh the man fired. To Julien's horror, he didn't raise his pistol skyward and delope. No, he fired straight at the man. His opponent grabbed his chest, gave a loud moan of pain, staggered forward, and finally fell heavily to the ground, arms and legs flung wide.

The spell broken, Julien dug in his heels, and Astarte leaped forward. He pulled her up short not ten yards from where the man lay, and jumped from his horse. With unbelieving eyes, he saw that the man who had committed this dishonorable murder was leaning against a tree, holding his sides in laughter.

Ignoring him, Julien strode quickly to the fallen man and knelt down. He was small, slight of build. Julien gathered the scrawny body in his arms, and suddenly, overwhelmed with fury, yelled at the murderer, who now stood in shocked silence, as if aware, finally, of the enormity of what he had done, "You damned idiot! What in God's name have you done, man?"

The man raised his hand in a helpless gesture, but seemed unable to come forward and speak.

To Julien's shock, the slight figure in his arms began to struggle violently, and he gazed down for the first time into the face of the fallen man. A startled pair of the greenest eyes he'd ever seen stared up at him.

Those moss-green eyes didn't waver from his face, but they did blink in rapid succession. Pale lips parted in surprise and then two dimples peeped through on white cheeks.

"Good grief, it's a stranger. Why, sir, I think you have much mistaken the matter."

"My God," Julien said, so taken aback he nearly dropped her. "You're nothing but a damned girl."

"Well, I am a girl, that is true enough, but I've never thought of myself as nothing. Also, I don't believe you need to damn me for it." Her damned dimples deepened.

Finding himself without a word to say, Julien instinctively dropped his arms from about her shoulders. With the utmost unconcern she pulled herself away and came up to her knees, her hands resting lightly on her breeched thighs.

"Harry," she called, laughter lurking in her voice, "I do believe we've given the gentleman something of a shock. Stop standing there like a half-wit and come here. Thank the Lord he didn't interrupt our duel. That would have been beyond what I could have accepted."

Julien, finding that his addled senses were returning to normal, looked up to see a young man coming toward them, a sheepish grin on his cherubic face. He rose slowly and turned to look down at the girl. He was not happy. He was beginning to feel very much the fool, a condition that made his innards cramp. His eyes narrowed on the girl's face, and he said in a voice colder than the St Clair lake in January, "Are you in the habit, my girl, of playacting at such deadly games?"

The dimples quivered and his indignation grew. She turned to him and said, calm as a nun at her prayers, "When you have recovered from your very slight embarrassment and obvious mortification, dear sir, you will realize that it was not we who interrupted you. This is Brandon land, and how my brother and I wish to spend our time is certainly no concern of yours, whoever you may be."

"Now, Kate," the young man said, "Don't get yourself into an argument, else you just might find yourself fighting a real duel. The gentleman was understandably worried. I did fire at you straight on. It would scare the devil

40

out of any man." He planted himself neatly in front of the girl.

To Julien he said, "I do beg your pardon, sir. Kate here must needs know all the masculine sports. I must say she did overdo it a bit, died much too lavishly this time, with much too much drama and flourish. Come on, Kate, don't bounce around and pretend you're angry. Stand up here and pretend rather that you're a lady, if you can even begin to manage it in those wretched breeches."

The girl, who had jumped to her feet with more speed than grace, now turned on her brother. "Dammit, Harry, there's no reason for you to apologize or explain anything. The gentleman was trespassing, clear as the wart on Aunt Mildred's face. I believe he should explain his presence here. And I wasn't too dramatic this time. I thought flailing the arms a bit was a nice touch."

"I do beg your pardon, ma'am," Julien said easily now. "Who the devil are you two?"

Harry cast a quelling glance at his sister and quickly extended his hand to Julien. "Harry Brandon, sir. And this is my sister, Katharine."

Julien grinned down at the young man and extended his own hand. "I'm St Clair, you know. My lands lie not far distant from yours."

"Goodness, what an honor for us. So you're the absent landlord, the most noble earl of March."

He instinctively disliked her snide tone. His

41

hackles rose a bit, but he drew on the sang-froid for which he was renowned. He raised his brows and gave her a mocking bow. "Why, yes, I do have that honor."

It was a well-delivered snub, but Julien quickly realized that Katharine Brandon didn't recognize that she'd just been slighted, or should have been, by a renowned gentle-man. Her head remained cocked pertly to one side as she said, "Yes, I suppose it could be regarded as an honor to some. Perhaps to a few who wouldn't know any better."

A silver glint came to his gray eyes. So she wanted to cross verbal swords with him, did she. He said swiftly, enjoying himself sud-denly, "It is a particular honor to ladies of breeding."

He maliciously eyed those very tight-fitting breeches of hers. He expected her to blush to the roots of her hair at the very least, perhaps even to stammer incoherently until he would graciously excuse her, for he had many times achieved this result with but the mildest of set-downs.

He didn't receive even the very least, for she said in a revoltingly cheerful voice, all the while brushing leaves from her breeches, "I suppose it is difficult to evince breeding when one is engaged in a duel." She raised those green eyes to Julien's face and added as brazenly as a hussy in Soho, "But you must admit, dear sir, that breeches are much more the thing when one must fall down and play dead. Imagine what a gown would do. Why,

42

petticoats would be spilling all over the place. You would be quite horrified, being so very proper and so dreadfully well bred."

Before Julien could come up with words, rather than just boxing her ears as his hands itched to do, she added, seeming to ponder the problem, "Perhaps it is a sad trial to gentlemen of your breeding and, er, advanced age, and *nobleness*, to accept with any degree of composure such trifles as ladies dueling."

For the first time in his life, Julien Edward Mowbray St Clair, earl of March, found himself with a tongue dead in his mouth.

"Kate, really," her brother said, grabbing her shoulders and giving her a good shake, but not nearly a hard enough shake, Julien thought. "Sir, she's overzealous in her insults. She usually is, however. She truly doesn't mean half of what she says, particularly if she's intent on besting anyone, which she is more times than not. She cuts me up with her tongue better than the cook wields her knife."

"Overzealous. What a thing to say, Harry. I see it all clearly now. Just because he's a *man* and an *earl*, you're ready to spring to his side and leave me here alone in a ditch."

Julien looked back and forth between the pair and felt a muscle twitch at the corner of his mouth. Although he found the manners of this hoydenish girl deplorable, the situation was ridiculous in the extreme, and he could not help breaking into a grin.

"Miss Brandon," he said gravely, gazing into her upturned face, "please accept my profound apologies. You look most charming in breeches, though I confess that seeing swirling petticoats would doubtless be an equal treat."

She shot him a look of pure mischief and said in a demure voice, "But, sir, I could not look more charming in breeches than you do."

Julien would have liked to take his hand to her breeched buttocks, but realizing in all truth that this pleasure must be denied him, he threw up his hands and gave up the battle. He forgot about an earl's consequence, threw back his head, and gave way to a shout of laughter. "Where, Miss Brandon, have you and your brother been hiding yourselves? I count it my misfortune not to have met the pair of you before."

Harry replied quickly to prevent any further impertinence from his unpredictable sister, "It's not so strange, my lord. You are not often here."

"As I said, an absent landlord," she said, and robbed the words of insult by grinning impudently up at him.

Julien felt a quite odd sensation, equally as vague and undefined as the nagging thoughts that had pursued him from London to St Clair. He turned slowly to Harry and said thoughtfully, "No, Harry, I believe you're right. My visits have been infrequent and of rather short duration, up until now. It doesn't do to be absent from one's home for too long. One never knows just what might pop up

44

in the meanwhile. Strange and wonderful things, perhaps."

"Do you plan to stay long this time, my lord?" Harry continued, lightly poking his sister's arm to keep her quiet—no mean feat.

Julien was silent for a moment. He found himself looking at Katharine and felt again the odd sensation that was now, without his conscious wish, spreading deep within him, filling him, making him feel quite odd, but it was a miraculous feeling, one that he didn't want to lose. She had removed her tight-fitting hat, and clouds of thick, rich auburn hair fell about her shoulders in deep waves nearly to her waist. She was oblivious of him and didn't look up, being occupied with braiding her hair into long plaits and tucking them under her hat.

Julien forced himself to look away from her and said easily, "It is a possibility, Harry, an excellent possibility. It is a lovely time of year, is it not?"

"Oh, damnation, Mannering, I had clean forgot Sir Percy and Lord Launston are to arrive for dinner." Julien gave his butler a harassed look, all the while peeling off his riding gloves and wishing both of his impending guests to the devil.

"It is nothing to concern yourself with, my lord," Mannering said, all dignity and re-assurance as he smoothed invisible creases from the tan York gloves Julien handed him. "It is merely, my lord, that Mrs Cradshaw is hesitant to accord their lordships chambers without your approval."

Julien felt a tug of impatience. "Very well, Mannering, have Mrs Cradshaw allot our guests the Green Room and the Countess's Chamber. I'll tell Percy that if he eats too much, our touted ghost of that long ago countess will come and torment him."

Mannering nodded, then gave a discreet but quite audible cough, clearly indicating to his master that this was not his only concern. Julien, well aware of the butler's roundabout ways of securing his attention, fixed his eyes on him. "Out with it, Mannering. I promise you I shall not fly into a great rage. Just a minor one, at the most."

Mannering gave another cough and gazed at a point just beyond Julien's left ear. "It is the *Frenchman*, my lord," he said with mournful finality. He brought his focus back to his master, as if to ask instructions, his point clearly made.

"The Frenchman? You refer, I presume, to François, my chef."

"Of course, my lord."

A sense of foreboding descended upon Julien. He didn't want to ask, but he knew he had to. "You may tell me the truth, Mannering. Has a scullery maid fled St Clair in terror of her life? Did he try to kill the kitchen cat?"

Mannering drew himself up and said with dignity, "It is not our staff, my lord. As I said, it is the Frenchman. He swears that he cannot be expected to be an artist in such a

46

backward, barbaric kitchen. I believe he also called our kitchens *squalid*, but I may have misunderstood him, what with that ridiculous accent of his. That, I think, my lord, is the gist of it." He did not add that in his opinion it wouldn't be at all a bad thing if his pretentious, utterly revolting excuse for a chef were to fling out of the kitchen and remove his voluble presence elsewhere, preferably far from St Clair.

Julien knew, of course, even from the restrained account Mannering had given, that François was on a rampage. "Squalid" was the key word. If Percy and Hugh were not to sit down to an empty dinner table, he must soothe his chef's outraged sensibilities. Damn, he should never have ordered François to accompany him here. He'd done it primarily for Percy, who always proclaimed a violent dislike for sturdy English fare. Julien recalled that he wouldn't be overly displeased if Percy and Hugh found St Clair quite a bore and departed posthaste for London. Perhaps, his thinking continued in fine Machiavellian style, it would not be such a catastrophic occurrence were François to leave in a huff.

Having reached this happy conclusion, Julien favored Mannering with an indifferent shrug of his shoulders and said with the greatest unconcern, "Mannering, please inform François that if he finds his accommodations here not to his liking, he will be paid his quarterly wages and driven to Dapplemoor to catch the mail coach back to

London. And, if you please," Julien continued, "have a footman fetch Stokeworthy and ask Cook to send me a light luncheon. I will be in the library."

Mannering's jaw dropped. In that instant, his respect for his master soared to heights heretofore unknown. "Fancy," he repeated in awed tones later to Mrs Cradshaw, "his lordship was as calm as a lord admiral. Quite ready he was to let that repulsive Frenchman go without a blink of an eyelash. He just shrugged, that's all, just a wonderful shrug."

As Julien partook of cold chicken and crusty bread, he was informed by Mannering, who was unable to contain the news, that upon hearing of his master's undisguised sentiments, François had abruptly ceased his French ravings and in a burst of enthusiasm declared that his lordship and his guests would have the finest, most exquisite repast his culinary skills could achieve, a dinner more *formidable* than anything these peasants who surrounded him and clearly didn't appreciate him could ever imagine.

Julien received this news with mixed feelings. He shrugged, deciding that at the very least, he would suffer no more tantrums from the fellow.

4

After he finished his luncheon, Julien made his way to the estate room, for generations the account room of the earls of March. As he awaited his agent's arrival, he let his mind wander back to his curious encounter that morning with the Brandons. "What an impertinent girl," he said half-aloud, but without an ounce of displeasure. Though he had openly derided the girl's clothing, he could not help dwelling briefly upon that quite nicely shaped figure of hers, emphasized by the tight breeches. And the long, thick russet hair. Lovely hair. He had never seen hair like that before. He tried to remember freckles. Perhaps there'd been a light dusting across her nose. His fingers itched now to trace over them. He was mildly surprised he hadn't until now made her acquaintance, nor that of her brother, Harry. But then, since he was at least six years Harry's senior, it was no wonder that their paths hadn't crossed in his youth. They would have been but children when he left for Eton.

Brandon ... Brandon. Of a certainty he knew the name, but until now there had been no faces to attach to it. He wondered with a questioning frown why his father had never spoken of the family or, for that matter, seen them socially.

Well, he planned to see them now. Indeed, he couldn't wait.

Julien called out, "Enter" when there came a knock on the door.

Stokeworthy, the St Clair agent, appeared in the open doorway, his long, thin face (rather like a horse's, Julien had always thought) wearing an apologetic look.

Julien rose. "Ah, do come in, Stokeworthy. It is certainly good of you to come on such short notice. I do hope it did not inconvenience you."

He took the older man's bony hand in his and gave it an enthusiastic shake.

"I wish to apologize, my lord, for my tardiness, but you see, Mrs Stokeworthy's niece has come down with a chill and the house is at sixes and sevens. Very unsettling, everything is." Stokeworthy fastened his watery eyes on his master's face, hoping to see no displeasure. There wasn't any, but Stokeworthy, being conscientious, continued quickly, "Perhaps the house is even at nines and tens. Such noise and commotion. It would drive me to the brandy bottle, if I had one."

Unknown to Julien, he would have preferred to spend much more time than he did here in the estate room at St Clair, and had welcomed his summons, albeit on short notice, with profound anticipation. He found

50

invariably after his visits with the earl that Mrs Stokeworthy quite fell over his words. The folk of Dapplemoor would pay his household unexpected visits, listening with avid attention to any tidbits of gossip he chose to relate about the earl of March.

"Given your niece's illness, perhaps you would rather return home. We could meet again in several days, when you have no other worries on your mind. Nines and tens are difficult, I know."

"Oh, goodness gracious, no, my lord," Stokeworthy exclaimed, sorry that he had ever mentioned his niece. "I assure you, my lord, a man's presence is never the thing in the sickroom. Or anywhere near a sickroom, perhaps not even in a room that is downstairs from a sickroom."

Julien was hard put not to laugh. "If you're certain, sir."

"I am very certain, my lord, beyond certain even." He quickly pulled a sheaf of papers from his timeworn case and poked them beneath his master's nose.

Julien and Stokeworthy spent the next several hours poring over accounts and calculating the sums that the estate's tenants' crops would likely fetch at market. It had been a good year at St Clair, not too much rain and not too much snow. The county had fared well, and the St Clair coffers would prosper, as would the pocketbooks of the tenants.

Julien trusted Stokeworthy implicitly, as his

father had before him. He was pleased, even more so than usual after Stokeworthy's glowing account of St Clair's prosperity, that his father had brought this man into his employ. Many people had been surprised at his father's choice, Julien had learned not many years past. It seemed that the garrulous Mrs Stokeworthy bore a striking resemblance to Julien's grandfather, and if the rumors were true, Mrs Stokeworthy was but one of his grandfather's by-blows.

It occurred to Julien that his father, a man of unwavering moral standards—indeed, nearly depressing moral standards—must have found it unnerving to be in contact almost daily with the several men and women who so closely resembled him. Julien had asked his father once about his grandfather's vagaries, but he had received such a stern, uncompromising set-down that he quite vowed to take his inquiries elsewhere. Although Julien had never known his grandfather, he had believed all the stories since he first looked closely at the portrait of his grandfather that hung in a darker corner of the gallery. He could almost picture his bewigged grandsire, with his full, sensual lips and the lewd twinkle in his gray eyes, swooping down from astride a great black charger upon unsuspecting village maidens.

Julien was unaware that his grandfather's exploits had become romantic legend in Dapplemoor and that the locals continued to embroider upon the facts to pass the time in the long winter months. Nor would it have pleased him to discover that they compared him more often with his righteous, moral father than his dashing, amorous grandfather. It would have been the deepest of blows had he only known about it, and doubtless if he had known about it, he would have hurled himself into an orgy of depravity.

After sharing a glass of sherry with Stokeworthy, he saw the good man off, consulted his watch, and deemed it time to change into evening apparel.

A few minutes after Julien descended the staircase, the exquisite folds of his neckcloth perfectly placed, Mannering informed him of the imminent arrival of Sir Percy and Lord Launston.

"It appears, my lord, that their lordships have journeyed together." He motioned a footman to open the great oak doors to admit them.

"Good Lord, Julien, what an outlandish place," Percy said the minute he entered. "I forget how in the very middle of nowhere at all you live. Ah, but it's a grand house, just nowhere, if you know what I mean."

Mannering relieved him of his cloak and hat and stood in tolerant silence as Percy stepped forward to shake Julien's hand.

Hugh appeared but a moment later, a calm smile of pleasure on his intelligent face. He bade a polite good evening to Mannering, who unbent a trifle at this gentleman's welcome sobriety, and removed his cloak and hat.

"Feel as if I've stepped back into the pages of my history books," Percy continued, letting his gaze travel about the hall. "Not, of course, that I ever read many of the bloody things, but rest assured that I've seen pictures, pages of pictures."

"I know just what you mean, Percy," Julien said, grinning. "I too have seen many of those same pages, I daresay."

He turned to greet Hugh Drakemore, who remarked in his well-bred voice, "A beautiful estate, Julien. We should visit more often. As you know, my great-aunt Regina lives not twenty miles to the west, and I count this like a visit home."

"It's always a pleasure to have you here, Hugh. I trust this madcap here did not over-turn you on your way north."

"Dash it, Julien," Percy said, "damn Hugh's eyes, he wouldn't let me take the reins until we were on the widest roads with the fewest turns. He is cowhearted. I didn't come even near to overturning him." Percy looked point-edly at Hugh.

Never one to let his friends down, Hugh said with unruffled composure, "Quite true, all of it, Julien. When Percy was handling the ribbons, why I believe I took a nap and dreamed of the green hills of Ireland."

"Enough of your bloody insults, Hugh, even though they're smooth as honey. Dash it all, Julien, it's later than you can begin to imagine, at least to my stomach. I'm near to fainting with starvation."

"Quite right, Percy. Why do not you and Hugh repair to your rooms and change? You see, I can't allow guests to dinner in their traveling clothes. It would be a great disservice to my consequence."

"Humph," Percy said. "You're a damned dog, Julien. You wish us to change simply because you do not want to feel foolish alone in your evening clothes."

Julien laughed his agreement. "True it is, but bear with me."

Hugh said, "We shan't be long, Julien, unless"—he cast a quizzing glance at Percy—"our exquisite here must needs dandify himself."

Julien could not resist a rueful grin, thinking of the half a dozen neckcloths he had ruined before achieving his own elegant appearance. He turned to Mannering. "Lord Launston and Sir Percy will go to their rooms. If you will, please have a footman escort them."

"Very well, my lord." Mannering bowed in his most formal manner, as if to impress upon Sir Percy that St Clair was indeed an earl's establishment.

"Mannering tells me that the lake has abundant trout," Hugh said, as he walked with his friend across the east side of the lawn toward St Clair lake.

Julien inhaled the fresh morning air and hiked his fishing gear more securely over his shoulder. "Yes, so full that those trout might just jump into our baskets."

"It's a pity Percy can't rouse himself, for the country air is quite invigorating." He turned his dark eyes to Julien, a smile breaking his usually composed features.

Julien laughed. "What? Watch what you say, Hugh. Percy up and about before noon? Why, it's unheard of, something to be devoutly avoided. And you know that Percy can't stand to see the beasts wriggling around on the string when you haul them in."

Hugh grinned, then paused a moment to look about him. "I own you must be proud of your lands and home, Julien."

"Yes, I suppose I am proud. It's so very permanent and lasting." Like Hugh, he turned momentarily to gaze back through the trees to the sun-bathed east tower, which commanded a magnificent view of the lake and the vast meadows and hills beyond. He turned back to Hugh and added, "When I am here, I scarce ever miss the racket of London. Particularly this time."

"Why this time in particular?"

Julien pulled the branches of a bush from their path before he turned to Hugh, a silent smile on his face that did not reach his gray eyes. It was strange, he thought, but he did not at all have the inclination to speak frankly to Hugh. As a matter of fact, he realized with a start, the vague, unsettling feelings had quite vanished. He felt content and would have preferred to be striding to the lake by himself, enjoying the quiet and peaceful surroundings. But Hugh was here, and he must be a gracious host.

"Do forgive me, Hugh. I'm a sorry host this morning. What did you ask?"

Hugh cocked an eyebrow and gazed intently at his friend. Never one to pry, he stayed his curiosity, saying only, "It was nothing, Julien. I hope our baskets are large enough to hold all those jumping trout."

At that moment they broke through a small circle of trees, and the unruffled blue water of St Clair lake greeted them.

"A magnificent prospect, is it not, Hugh?"

"Yes, indeed."

As Julien gazed about him, he chanced to see something move to his left, close to the water's edge. "Who the devil can that be?"

"Perhaps Mannering has informed others of the abundant trout," Hugh said, shading his own eyes.

"The devil," Julien said. "This is certainly private land, and I intend to find out just who thinks he has the right to fish in my lake." Julien turned swiftly and strode in the direction of the trespasser. He called over his shoulder, "Stay here, Hugh. I shall be back shortly."

Julien walked rapidly and quietly, the dewy, thick grass cushioning any sound his boots might have made. He drew up short in surprise, for the intruder was but a lad. The boy was sitting cross-legged, a rude, homemade fishing pole held firmly in his somewhat dirty hands. He was gazing intently at the water, completely absorbed.

Concentrating on my trout, Julien thought, ready to grab the boy by his collar and shake him.

There was something faintly familiar about the lad, but Julien couldn't quite put his finger on it. He strode up behind the boy and said in a voice that was exactly like his father's at his grimmest, "And just who, my lad, gave you permission to fish in my lake?"

The boy jumped in surprise, and the fishing pole fell from his hands into the water. As he tried frantically to retrieve it, he yelled, "How dare you give me such a fright! Now look what you've done. I've a good mind to box your ears, you miserable—" The words died abruptly as the boy whirled on his heels to face the earl of March.

Julien found himself gazing into the face of Katharine Brandon, dressed again today in her boy's breeches, her hair tucked under an old leather hat.

"You... " she said, quite as surprised as he.

Julien was the first to recover his wits. "I wish you good morning, Mistress Kate." He bowed low in front of her. "I trust you find the fishing good here on St Clair land."

She scrambled to her feet. At his thrust, she had the grace to look momentarily flustered, but quickly recovered, curse her eyes. "Your agent, Stokeworthy, gave me permission to fish here. You know," she confided easily now, "it is quite the best spot in the area. So many trout are running now. It is quite remarkable. Sometimes I feel that I could merely call out to them and they'd leap from the water and land at my feet."

"St Clair is honored by your accolades, Miss Brandon." Oddly, he found himself somewhat put out by her confidence. Had she no maidenly shyness? He chanced to see her fishing basket and said, "And just how many of my trout are now at this very moment snug in your basket?"

"It appears to me, sir, that you are quite tight. After all, what can a few fish mean to the great earl of March?"

"No more tight than your breeches, madam."

He should have guessed that he wouldn't be able to discomfit her. Indeed, she replied in a confiding tone, "Quite right of you to notice. You see, I have had to wear this pair for the past two years, Harry's breeches being now too large for me. They are, I assure you, a bit confining."

She turned toward the water, shaded her eyes with her hand for a moment, searching intently, and then brought her gaze back to Julien's face.

"It's a pity you gave me such a start. You see," she explained, "it took me quite two weeks to whittle that pole so that it was just right. Harry thinks himself far too grown-up and wouldn't help me. Now it is gone. Well, I can only hope that you're satisfied."

There was nothing else outrageous that she

could say. Julien shook his head. "Miss Brandon, you will, of course, allow me to make reparations. In fact, my friend over there—" he turned and waved to Hugh to come to them—"has equipped himself with several very finely whittled fishing poles. It is likely he can be convinced to part with one of them."

"Why, that is quite handsome of you." Those damned dimples of hers were clearly evident. He wanted to trace them with his fingertips. He contented himself with saying, "What an unaccountable girl you are, Miss Brandon. You must be quite a trial to your family."

It was a jest, only a simple jest, but at his words she seemed to freeze. She looked away from him, and he saw her lips draw into a tight line.

What the devil had he said that upset her? He stretched his hand out in an unconscious gesture. "Miss Brandon, I did not mean to—"

He didn't finish, which was probably just as well, for he had no idea of what he would have said. Hugh approached and stood beside him, gazing in some surprise at the breeched boy.

He raised an eyebrow at Julien.

5

With an effort, Julien turned to Hugh and said, "Hugh, I would like you to meet Miss Katharine Brandon. Her family lives somewhat west of St Clair."

She stretched out her hand to Hugh, who, for want of something better, extended his own hand and clasped her slender, albeit dirty, fingers.

Her green eyes twinkled, for she realized full well what he was thinking. Julien was relieved to see that whatever had made her unhappy was for the moment forgotten.

She gave Hugh a winsome smile and said simply, "Do forgive me, sir. I fear that curtsying in breeches is quite beyond my abilities."

Calling on the great aplomb and polish that he'd acquired over the years, Hugh said easily, "Do not disturb yourself, Miss Brandon. I quite understand. Though I have, myself, never endeavored to curtsy in breeches, I do think it would be an awkward and unpleasing sight."

Julien said now, "All that, Hugh? Good God, that speech much have taken at least four breaths. Now, unfortunately, I startled Miss Brandon, and she dropped her fishing pole in the lake. I've handsomely offered one of yours if one of them suits her. She's quite a stickler, you know. I doubt she'll accept just any offering. She tells me she's quite the angler."

Hugh, a gentleman to the tips of his well-manicured nails, said quickly, "It would be my pleasure, Miss Brandon. Please make your selection. I have but three poles with me, but I have been assured by Julien that they are of the finest quality."

Kate glanced at Julien with a gleam of amusement before bending over the three poles laid out by Hugh. After careful inspection, she rose, quite enthusiastic over her choice.

"How very fine it is, and such balance. Now I shall be able to pull in every trout that takes the veriest nibble, that is, if his lordship here doesn't kick me out."

Julien gave a shout of laughter. "Be my guest, Miss Brandon, be my guest. I'll do no kicking. Consider the meager contents of my lake at your disposal."

She joined wholeheartedly in his laughter. "How very *noble* of you, my lord earl."

Even before Mannering handed him the *London Times* on a silver tray, Julien's nostrils quivered at the unmistakable scent of Lady Sarah's exotic perfume. It usually amused him that he could smell her heavy musk scent at a soiree before actually seeing her, but today he found himself a bit put out. Even the letter from his mother, who found perfume an irritant to her nerves, was tinged with the cloying scent. He remembered the attar of roses he'd given her once, but she hadn't liked it, claiming it was too discreet a perfume. He had rather thought discreet was the point of the business.

Julien tossed the letters on an elegant French writing table and stopped Mannering as he turned to go. "Mannering, do stay a moment."

"Yes, my lord?"

"I find myself abominably ignorant about some of our local gentry. The Brandons, to be exact. The name is, of course, familiar to me, and I have but recently met for the first time the Brandon offspring. Quite a charming pair, incidentally. What can you tell me of the family?"

Mannering's eyes lit up for a brief instant, and his thin lips curved into a smile. "Ah, yes, Miss Katharine. A most delightful young lady, if you will pardon my saying so, my lord. And, of course, Master Harry, too."

Julien was intrigued by his normally staid butler's praise of any person not directly connected with the St Clair family or household.

"But who are they?"

Mannering, who prided himself on his intimate knowledge of every noble family within two days' ride of St Clair, cleared his throat ceremoniously. "Sir Oliver Brandon, Miss Katharine's father, is a baronet who is considered quite an outsider here, having arrived only in the last thirty years. His family lives, I believe, in the Lake District, near Windermere. His lordship's late wife, Lady Sabrina, was the only daughter of the McCelland laird, a most powerful lord whose grandfather fought for Prince Charlie in '45. Unfortunately, my lord, I am unable to recount how the Lady Sabrina met Sir Oliver.

"Notwithstanding, my lord, I have been given to understand that the McCelland laird forbade the marriage, and the Lady Sabrina and Sir Oliver actually eloped." Mannering's nostrils flared at the very mention of such an action. "Sir Oliver also was cast out by his family, his father, as I understand, being none too fond of Scots."

"You mean, Mannering, that the McCelland laird considered the Brandons beneath his touch?"

"Quite beneath, my lord. As you know, their union produced Miss Katharine and Master Harry. Lady Sabrina was never a strong lady, it was said. She died some six years ago, from an inflammation of the lung, most say."

"Most say, Mannering?"

"Well, if you will forgive my saying so, my lord, it is my opinion that Lady Sabrina died of misery, pure and simple misery." Mannering quickly added, "Sir Oliver isn't a very generous or compassionate man, my lord, and Lady Sabrina's years with him were not contented ones. How she came to elope with him eludes everyone's reason."

Mannering's story of Lady Sabrina brought

to Julien's mind Kate's unhappy look when he had mentioned her family. But he merely nodded and said, "Then why haven't I met the Brandons? If they have been here thirty years, well, I have been here nearly twenty-eight years myself."

A sense of foreboding descended over Mannering as his master fixed him with a hard stare, reminding him forcibly of the late earl. The young earl had drawn him out about the Brandons, and he had already said far too much to avoid answering this question. He had been silent for so many years, in keeping with the late earl's wishes, that he found himself quite at a loss as how best to proceed.

He gave his characteristic cough and began with painstaking slowness. "As your lordship knows, the two Brandon children were too young for your notice when you lived at St Clair. Master Harry was barely out of short coats when you left for Eton." Mannering paused, hoping for a reprieve, but the earl gave him the eye and said impatiently, "Yes, yes, I know all that, Mannering. Get to the point, man."

"Yes, my lord. You see, my lord, your late esteemed, very *upright* father did not deal well with the Brandons—rather, with Sir Oliver. It seems that your lordship's grandfather was regarded by the Brandons as being of questionable reputation where females were concerned."

Julien laughed. "A rake and licentious womanizer is what you mean, is it not,

Mannering, until he dropped dead of over-indulgence at sixty?"

Mannering fixed Julien with an offended stare, the like of which Julien hadn't seen since he was a boy.

"One hesitates to speak ill of the dead, my lord, particularly when the person is one's late master and an earl of March."

"I stand corrected, Mannering." He had to remember that he wasn't in London, where such colorful curses about persons living or deceased were mundane and expected. "Please continue, Mannering. You say my father and mother had a falling-out with Sir Oliver over Grandfather's questionable reputation?"

"If I may venture to say so, my lord, Sir Oliver Brandon is a staunch Methodist and overly rigid in his moral views. It seems that Lady Sabrina's personal maid was found to be in the family way. The girl swore it was your grandfather, the earl, though it hardly seems likely, as your grandfather had quite a number of years already on his plate. Sir Oliver, so I was informed, beat the girl soundly, cast her out, and never again spoke to your grandfather. As you know, my lord, your own father was a very proud man, as is, of course, proper. Although his late lordship did not always agree with your grandfather's conduct, he thought it disgraceful that a mere baronet should dare to condemn an earl of March, much less cut the acquaintance."

"The light dawns brightly, Mannering."

Julien could picture without much difficulty how his father and mother would react to such an impertinence. It took him but a moment to shrug off his irritation at not being told all this, as he realized that Mannering would in all likelihood be able to tell him more about Katharine.

"As you know, Mannering, Miss Brandon is a somewhat unusual young lady. The two times I have met her, she was dressed in breeches, quite like a boy. As a matter of fact, she is forthright in her manners and speech, very unlike the daughter of a rigid Methodist."

"Perhaps I have acted precipitately, my lord, but I pray you will not believe that to be true. During the past several years, your lordship being rarely here, Mrs Cradshaw and I have become well acquainted with the young lady and have let her spend much time here. Mrs Cradshaw and I have a liking for Miss Kate. As you can imagine, my lord, a young lady of her high spirits is sadly out of place in Sir Oliver's household, particularly since the death of Lady Sabrina, her mother. She is certainly not an encroaching young lady, my lord. It is just that she is much alone. She, er, needs friends other than her brother, who now isn't often here. Also, I would say she needs friends closer to her own age than Emma and I."

"You are quite certain she's not an 'encroaching' young lady, Mannering?"

"Quite true, my lord."

To Mannering's relief, his master gave a little chuckle and placed his hand on his shoulder. "You have acted quite right in this matter. I only regret that my presence here prevents Miss Katharine from fully enjoying herself on St Clair land, though she was quite at home pulling one trout after another out of the lake."

Julien dropped his hand and turned his view toward the large French windows that gave a brilliant view of the front lawn. He said under his breath, "As you say, she is in need of friends, perhaps friends closer to her age."

"I beg your pardon, my lord?" Mannering asked, thinking his master's low-spoken words meant for him.

"It's nothing, Mannering. Don't mind me. I become as meandering as a lake in my talk. Thank you for telling me about the Brandons."

Left alone, Julien again gazed out into the peaceful summer scene. So Kate had made friends with his staff, had she? Quite a feat, he thought, considering Mannering's strict adherence to propriety. A lady in breeches. A lady with the sunniest smile he'd ever seen in his life. A lady who could charm a snake right out of its skin. She was a lady, in short, who was fascinating. He realized he was smiling, not a lazy, mocking smile as was his habit, but a tender smile. It scared him witless, but just for a moment. Then he grinned at himself. "I must be becoming a half-wit," he said aloud to the empty room. "Taken with an impertinent, outrageous—"

He turned and walked slowly back to the center of the room. He wondered if Kate had ever been in his father's library. He could picture her pouring tea dressed in a gown of, perhaps, green velvet, her beautiful thick auburn hair piled high on her head. Unaccountably, he found this picture of domesticity not at all alarming or repugnant. Indeed, he was loath to let it slip from his mind. He shook his head, bemused at himself. He very much wanted to see Katharine Brandon again.

The next several days passed pleasantly enough for Julien, though he and Hugh did not come upon Katharine Brandon on their outings. For the most part, he and Hugh rode, hunted, and fished together. Percy seemed quite content with this arrangement, planning the evening's menus with François each morning, perusing the London papers, and napping in the afternoons.

Had Hugh told Julien that he wasn't particularly good company, Julien would have been frankly surprised. He was an excellent host; he was known for being an excellent host. But Hugh, long accustomed to Julien's quickness of wit and good-humored cynicism, found it quite odd that his friend seemed distracted, his responses vague and not at all to the point. He regarded Julien covertly on several occasions and speculated on the cause of his preoccupation. Finding no likely answers, he concluded that since Julien seemed not to wish to speak of what was bothering him, his as well as Percy's presence at St Clair was not at all what Julien needed.

And so it was Hugh who announced at dinner one evening that he really must return to London. He bent a stern eye on Percy and began to enumerate various reasons why Percy, also, should accompany him.

"After all, my dear fellow," he said to Percy, over his goblet of claret, "we have enjoyed Julien's hospitality for quite long enough. And you, Percy, have a horse running at Newmarket next week. Since I have wagered on your horse to win, I feel it only right of you to return with me and see to his training." He absolved himself of this harmless lie, for his motives were, after all, only the purest.

Percy, who had a bite of creamed artichoke heart in his mouth at that moment, paused in his chewing and said with all the candor of a friend who knows that anything at all can and will be forgiven, "Don't take me for a damned idiot, Hugh. You know very well that Julien wishes us miles from here. Your paltry reasons have nothing to do with my bloody horse, whose name, I suspect, you can't even remember." He turned his light-blue eyes on his host and added with a shrug, "Although I can't imagine why."

"Why what?" Hugh asked. "What the devil are you talking about, Percy?"

"I can't imagine why Julien doesn't want us here. You're right, Hugh. He does indeed
70

wish us to Jericho. He pays us attention, but he isn't really here, if you know what I mean."

"Hold, both of you," Julien said, looking from the one to the other. "I assure you that nothing could be further from the truth. As for Percy's horse, Hugh—why, the nag hasn't a chance of winning. There's no reason why either of you should think of leaving so soon."

Julien would have said more, but he suddenly became aware that Percy was merely staring at him with disbelief. As for Hugh, he became preoccupied with the dissection of a leg of broiled chicken.

"Must be a woman," Percy announced. "Yes, no other reason for all this wretched excess of excuses on both your parts."

Julien felt a dull-red flush creep over his face. He had to smile, for Percy was exceedingly acute.

Percy took another bite of the creamed artichokes and pondered the problem. Upon swallowing, he said, cordial as a mother who'd just received a wonderful offer for her homely daughter, "Can't imagine where you met a woman in such an outlandish place, but no doubt you did. You were always a dog with women, St Clair. Not one of them, if she's toothsome enough, can escape your eye for very long. Just fancy, a woman here who has quite besotted you."

Oblivious of Julien's heightened color and a puzzled look from Hugh, he concluded imperturbably, "Do hope that Riverton has taken the fair Yvette off your hands, old boy.

Ah, and poor Lady Sarah, all low in the brow because you've not shown her enough affection. What is the chit's name, Julien?"

"Really, Percy," Hugh said, seeing Julien's appalled discomfort. "You go too far. How Julien wishes to conduct himself on his own lands is certainly none of your concern, or mine. We're off to London tomorrow. And keep your mouth closed and chewing on those bloody artichokes."

Percy once more bent his gaze on Julien's face and said a trifle glumly, "Must be serious, Hugh. Never have I seen him make such a cake of himself over his mistresses. Good Lord, he's been miles away from us for the past three days. He didn't even blink an eyelash when he lost twenty pounds to you in cards last night. Yes, it's a damned woman, and he's ready to have her in his bed."

Julien found himself at a loss for words, a condition he was becoming rapidly used to. Lord, had he been so obvious? He quickly picked up his glass of claret and downed it in one gulp. He met Hugh's eyes over the rim of the glass and saw the light of comprehension spread over his serious face. Only Hugh had met Katharine.

At that moment, Hugh seriously questioned the powers of his own intellect, which he had always considered more than tolerable. He felt somehow that his ability to comprehend his fellow humans had grossly betrayed him. Good God, Percy was right and he hadn't even known, blast his heathen's eyes. A woman—Katharine Brandon to be exact, that winsome, smiling, utterly outrageous girl—had somehow turned Julien's head? He could not believe he had been so blind. He consoled himself with the fact that in his long acquaintance with Julien he had never seen him treat any of the endless bevy of charming girls making their come-outs with anything but polite indifference. Why, it was not long ago that he had confided to Hugh that he found the chatter of young females quite beyond his limits of endurance. He had always taken his pleasure with older women, who were experienced in the games of flirtation and love, and were, above all, married. Or with his mistresses.

Hugh blinked. How could such a change be wrought by a mere girl in the country? All he could actually remember of her person was that she was quite pretty and had remarkable large green eyes. She also had a dash of summer freckles across the bridge of her nose.

But she wore breeches and that wretched old hat pulled down over her ears. He gazed up at Julien, a frown furrowing his brow. His friend had always been fastidious in all things, and in particular, in his choice of women. All knew it.

What the devil was going on here?

6

Percy was quite satisfied with himself, as his devastating pronouncement had reduced his friends to silence. Having had the last word, he returned his attention to his dinner. What Julien chose to do with his women was no concern of his. He merely hoped that his friend had not been ensnared by some ill-bred, conniving wench. But then, Julien was such a proud, arrogant man. He would never besmirch his noble lineage.

Julien pushed his plate aside and eyed his friends with wry good humor. He wondered if they thought him mad. He found to his own surprise, however, that it had never occurred to him to deny Percy's comments. If he tried to do so now, he would only appear the more ridiculous. He would also be a liar. He broke the short silence and remarked in a creditably calm voice, "Have I been such poor company, Hugh? Come, Percy, you cannot say that you wish to leave François's cooking. Haven't you enjoyed testing his culinary abilities?"

Percy lost all patience and waved an empty fork at Julien, "Dammit, man, I, like Hugh, have no desire to remain and watch you

74

mooning after some girl. It's unnerving, it's unworthy of a man of your reputation. Maybe it's something in the country air. What do you think, Hugh? Is it the damned lazy warm air here? You're silent as a grave, Hugh. Well, if that's it, I, for one, certainly do not wish to catch it."

"Percy," Hugh began.

"Now don't you try to insult what little intelligence I have, Hugh. Wasn't it you who suggested leaving in the first place?" He sat back in his chair and regarded Julien and Hugh with an owlish stare.

Hugh reddened, and a sharp set-down was on his tongue when Julien threw up his hands, his sense of humor overcoming the absurdity of this situation. "Leave him be, Hugh. It's quite the first time he is able to crow, albeit he resembles more a stuffed peacock than a lean scavenger."

The tension was broken, and both Hugh and Percy grinned at him good-naturedly.

"I wondered when you'd get your wits back, Julien. Damned glad that you haven't quite lost all your senses," Percy said and loaded his fork once more.

"I strive, Percy, I strive." Julien looked down at his glass and swished the claret from side to side. The deep red reminded him of her luxurious auburn hair. She has bewitched me, he thought, his pulse quickening. He thought of her green eyes and the dimples that danced outrageously. Lord, he was completely besotted. Strangely enough, he found that he was not at all distressed by his condition. It struck him forcibly that he wanted Katharine Brandon not simply as a summer idyll, to end with the coming of fall. No, he wanted her, all of her. He wanted those dimples of hers, and he wanted to take her and hold her and keep her. He wanted her by his side until he cocked up his toes.

He raised his face to his friends and said matter-of-factly, "Perhaps it is better if you return to London. I would find it unnerving to go a-wooing with the two of you smirking behind my back." Ignoring the startled looks, he concluded with quiet determination, "I intend to return to London with my bride. Oh yes, Percy, her name is Katharine Brandon, and she brandishes pistols and foils and fishes and doubtless will lead me a merry chase. Hugh has met her. You, Percy, will meet her in London."

Percy's eyes grew round with wonder and disbelief. Hugh chewed meditatively on his lower lip.

Percy said suddenly, "Now, Julien, you haven't lost your wits over a simple country maid, have you? No, I can see from the blood in your eyes that you haven't. Katharine Brandon. A reasonable name, quite charming, really. What does she look like? Shall I like her?"

"I believe so, Percy. She's really quite—" He paused, frowning into the deep red of his claret. "She's refreshing and different and utterly charming. Do you not agree, Hugh?"

76

"Of a certainty she is all those things and much more. You will find her immensely likable, Percy. She is quite lovely."

"It's a dashed shame that I had to spend so much time directing François. If Julien hadn't needed my culinary advice, I could have judged her as well. Well, nothing for it. I suppose I'll have to trust your taste in this matter, Hugh."

"Thank you," Hugh said, his voice as dry as his dinner sherry. "Yes, I have yet to see her equal. An altogether unforgettable young lady."

He was aware that Julien was regarding him with an amused grin.

"Hmmm," was all that Percy said to this glowing, albeit ambiguous description. He stroked his chin and sighed deeply. Julien being leg-shackled was in itself an appalling thought, for it meant that their gay bachelor evenings would come to an end. But perhaps, he thought, the new countess will be fond of entertaining, and that will mean many delicious dinners prepared by François. Percy's blue eyes brightened at this prospect, and in sudden good humor he rose and thrust his glass forward.

"Come, Hugh," Percy said, "let us congratulate Julien here. A toast to the new countess of March. May she meet all of our expectations, as well as Julien's."

Hugh was quick to follow Percy's lead, and the two men turned to Julien, clicked their glasses together, and drank deeply.

Julien rose slowly. The last week and a half compressed itself into but a moment. A toast to the countess of March. He silently bid farewell to a life that now seemed inordinately boring, downed his own glass, and in a burst of excitement demanded another toast.

Two vintage bottles of St Clair claret were consumed before the three men finally separated and shakily departed, each to his own room.

It was quite late the following morning when the three friends finally emerged, their eyes blurry and their heads heavy.

Under the efficient command of Mannering, mountains of luggage were assembled in the hall and strapped onto Percy's great carriage.

"An altogether unforgettable stay, Julien," Hugh remarked lightly, as he shook his friend's hand.

"Lord, Hugh, you are never to the point." Percy brushed a speck of dust from his immaculate sleeve. "I'd say it was a deuced unsettling experience. Women can find you anywhere, even in the damnable bowels of the country."

"Rest assured, Percy, that the next week will be far more unsettling for me," Julien said, a confident grin belying his words.

Percy leaned out of the carriage window and shouted to their receding host, "Wish you luck, old boy. If you need help, Hugh and I will be more than willing to serve as your faithful emissaries."

A ghost of a smile flitted over Julien's face as he stood watching the carriage rumble down the graveled drive and disappear into the park. He had no doubt that the most difficult part of entering into the married state would be surviving the jokes of his friends.

He retraced his steps and made his way to the library. As he passed by several portraits of past earls of March, he chanced to look up. Their painted eyes seemed to regard him with approval, their faces no longer accusatory. If he had been wearing a hat, he would most certainly have proffered them an elegant bow. As it was, he merely grinned and let his thoughts turn most willingly to Katharine. Katharine St Clair, countess of March.

His footstep was light as he entered the library and eased himself comfortably into the large chair beside the fireplace. He pursed his lips and formed a sloped roof with his long, slender fingers, tapping them thoughtfully together as he contemplated his strategy.

It was but a short time later that he uncoiled gracefully from his chair, tugged the bell cord, and ordered that Astarte be saddled.

"I do wish you didn't have to leave so soon, Harry. You know how wretched it is here without you." She was plainly unhappy and her shoulders dropped pitiably.

"Now, Kate, it will not be long, only until

Christmas. I'll come and we'll enjoy ourselves, you'll see." Harry clumsily patted his sister on her shoulder.

"Aye," Kate said, reverting to her Scottish mother's tongue, "but it's still over four months away, Harry. Four months with just Sir Oliver. It's an eternity."

Harry searched his mind for sage words, reassuring words, for he was, after all, her elder brother. He could think of nothing except the warning that he had given her many times before. "Don't forget to take care that father does not find out about your escapades during the day. You know as well as I what he would do."

It gave Harry a start to see her woebegone expression vanish and a curiously cold and hard look take its place. "Do you take me for a simpleton, Harry? Of course I know what he would do. He would beat me within an inch of my life. We both know it is quite a habit with him."

Harry was appalled that she could speak with such hardness. The picture of Kate as a child rose in his mind; her laughter, her openness, Kate tugging on his coattails, begging to be included in his games.

"Lord, Kate, why does he hate you so?"

His voice shook with impotent fury. He had argued with his father on several occasions, in an attempt to draw Sir Oliver's anger onto himself. He felt a miserable coward, for he seldom succeeded, and when he did succeed, it never lasted long. Just until Sir Oliver again recalled the existence of his daughter.

"When Mother was alive, he was not so cruel," he said, to himself more than to his sister.

Kate cut him short, her voice grim. "No, Harry. He became so toward me before mother died. Of that I am certain. But why does he hate me? I don't know. Nor do I believe I really care now, not anymore."

Harry grasped her shoulders and in a sudden protective gesture pulled her against him. She was alarmingly stiff. He thought back to his mother's funeral and felt a stab of pain. He had been at Eton that year and had been home rarely, savoring his freedom and his image of himself as being quite grown-up. It was after the funeral that he had sensed a change in his father.

Kate relaxed against him but didn't speak. It had been many years since Harry had held her, and he became aware that he was holding not just his little sister, but a woman. Maybe that is the reason, he thought. Maybe Sir Oliver finds it painful to be with Kate because she so closely resembles our mother.

Kate drew back from the circle of Harry's arms and looked out over the poorly kept lawn. She despised herself for her weakness, such damnable weakness. If she lost her pride, she would have nothing else.

"It's that damned religion of his," Harry said between clenched teeth. "I wish I could burn all those ridiculous musty books. They've rotted his brain and turned him into a monster, at least where you're concerned."

To his surprise, Kate turned back to him and gave a mirthless laugh. "Do not curse his religion, Harry, for I, in truth, find it many times my salvation. You know, he is scarce aware of my existence, at least during the day. Even Filber dares not disturb him in his theological studies."

Harry's lips tightened in disdain as the memory of the stern lecture he had received from Sir Oliver only an hour earlier came back to him.

"Damnation, the only thing he can think about is his infernal wages of sin. And adjuring me to be a son worthy of his father's honor, whatever the devil that means. What claim does he have to any honor?"

Kate's eyes brightened for a moment in tender amusement. "What, dear brother, do you mean that you don't intend to become a Methodist?"

Kate was rewarded, for Harry gave her a twisted grin, the frown fading from his forehead.

"Hold a moment, Marcham," he called out, seeing his valet emerge from the stable with their horses.

At that moment Kate felt immeasurably older than Harry. She looked at his blond curls, brushed and pomaded into what he had stiffly informed her was the *latest style*. His breeches and waistcoat were of severe, somber color, but she knew that before he arrived at Oxford he would change into the

82

florid yellow patterned waistcoat he had shown her one evening after Sir Oliver had retired.

"My dear, poor Marcham is sadly weighted down. Are you certain that you intend to be gone only four months?" Her voice was sweet and light as she tugged on his sleeve.

Harry replied to her jest with a perfunctory smile. Despite his best intentions, he was impatient to be gone, and in truth, he didn't know what to say to her, nor what he could do about her future. He knew that Sir Oliver was encouraging the suit of that provincial oaf, Squire Bleddoes. It was altogether ridiculous, for Kate was far too well born for such a marriage, and besides, she had told him she would have nothing to do with that "miserable, boring windbag." This he had understood, but when she had blithely informed him that remaining her own mistress did not seem at all a bad thing, he was frankly shaken. She knew very well that his fondest wish was to join a crack cavalry regiment; she must also realize, he thought despairingly, that it would be impossible for her to accompany him.

Lord, what a mull. What a miserable situation. Perhaps when he returned for the holiday at Christmas, he and Kate would think of something.

Harry drew on his gloves and leaned over to kiss Kate lightly on the cheek. It occurred to him that there might be danger from another quarter.

"Kate," he said earnestly, his blue eyes narrowing, "don't forget the earl of March. You can't be sure that he won't tell Father of our escapade. Most probably he's prouder than Wellington himself and thinks very highly of himself. Lord, we can't tell what he might do."

Kate looked at him and smiled, saying in a reassuring voice as if talking to a child, "I'll be careful, Harry. Don't worry yourself about it. I don't think his lordship would ever stoop to such paltry and petty behaviour."

Harry was a bit put out by her calm assumptions about the earl of March. It was at times like this that Harry wished Kate were more docile, more accepting of her older brother's advice and counsel. He had the nagging doubt, grown stronger in the past several years, that he was no match for her quick tongue, that it was she who had the stronger will.

Harry shook himself free of this not-altogether-pleasing image of himself. After all, it was rather stupid of him to regard his sister, a mere girl, as a possible superior to him. Was he not to be Sir Harry Brandon of Brandon Hall someday? And if Kate had not yet married upon the demise of Sir Oliver, it would be he, Sir Harry, who would arrange her life and give her direction.

Seeing the rather benign smile on her brother's boyish face, Kate thought that she had succeeded in keeping their leave-taking as unemotional as possible. She said, "I think the horses grow impatient, my dear. You may rest assured that I shall avoid Sir Oliver assiduously, as well as that alarmingly persistent suitor of mine."

Harry was immeasurably relieved. Kate was acting her usual self again. He quieted his conscience with the thought that before too many more months passed, he would find a solution to her problem.

She added, green eyes twinkling up at him, "Do read at least one book this time, and not, I pray, one of those young gentlemen's turf books."

"Well, don't you kill anyone with your dueling pistol."

There was a sudden sound behind them, and Kate whirled about. It was only Filber, the Brandon butler, come to wave good-bye to Harry. She breathed a sigh of relief, knowing that Sir Oliver would openly condemn brother and sister spending too much time together. It was strange, she thought suddenly. It was as if their father thought her a bad influence on Harry.

"You did say good-bye to Father?" she asked nervously, still expecting to see his tall, gaunt frame appear at any minute in the open doorway.

"Oh, yes, not to worry, m'dear. Now, I must be off. Do keep out of trouble, old girl."

She watched Harry swing himself onto his horse and signal Marcham to do the same. He kissed his fingers to her and whipped his horse about. He turned and waved once again before disappearing from sight.

Kate raised her own hand in silent reply. She had certainly succeeded in cheering him, and she supposed now that she should feel quite noble. After all, it was not his fault that he was a male and therefore free to go and do as he pleased. But it seemed a cruel twist of fate.

She turned away, feeling sorry for herself.

7

She stood unmoving, striving to control such uncharitable thoughts. A gentle breeze ruffled her hair. Unaccountably, she found that her thoughts turned to the earl of March and the delightful morning she had spent fishing with him and Lord Launston at St Clair lake.

Her depression unaccountably eased. In an unconscious gesture she pulled at her outmoded gown. His lordship had shown himself to be witty and entertaining, his descriptions of the sights and activities of London stirred her imagination. She had jokingly told Lord Launston that the earl might as well be telling her of the Taj Mahal, for London, to her, was just as remote.

The corners of her mouth lifted. She remembered his laughter when she spoke whatever was on her mind. He was a delightful companion, willing to cross verbal swords with her. Perhaps she had found a friend. But for how long? The earl of March never stayed at St Clair for any extended period of time. She knew from Mannering and Mrs Cradshaw that this was his first visit in five months. As a matter of fact, even now he might have already returned with his friends to London.

She turned slowly and walked back into the hall. Her spirits plummeted. She wondered if she would ever see him again. Probably not. She was a provincial dowd, nothing more, as unsophisticated as the trout she'd pulled enthusiastically from his lake with his fishing pole. He was simply amusing himself. Ah, but she did want to see him again.

That very afternoon, as she sat disconsolately at her piano doing great injustice to a Mozart sonata, Sir Oliver unceremoniously interrupted her. He stood over her, his hot breath fanning on her face, his voice filled with cold suspicion

"I am informed, daughter, that the earl of March is calling." He pursed his thin lips, and his rather close-set eyes drew closer together. "He calls ostensibly to visit with me, a fact I have difficulty crediting. Would you be so kind as to tell me where you have made his lordship's acquaintance? And be quick about it. Men of his rank do not like to be kept waiting. Tell me the truth, girl, all of it, for I do not like to play the ignorant fool."

Though Kate trembled inwardly, she was long used to her father's peremptory attacks, and her expression never changed. Her mind worked furiously. She could certainly not tell him the truth, for his retribution would be swift and unpleasant. She calculated rapidly that there was at least a slim chance to come through this unscathed, and if her attempt failed, the result would be the same in any case.

She looked at her father, who looked about as pleased with her as the worms on her fishing hook, and said calmly, "Last week Harry and I were riding through the village. His lordship, as it happened, was visiting his agent, Mr Stokeworthy. It would have been unforgivably rude of us not to introduce ourselves, given the circumstances. His lordship mentioned that he might call, as he had never made your acquaintance, sir," she added, embroidering the lie because it would perhaps serve her. Sir Oliver was vain; he believed himself stalwart and upright. He saw himself as a model of rectitude. Even the Regent himself, were he to ride by, would surely stop.

As her eyes didn't waver and her improvised story sounded plausible to Sir Oliver, he merely grunted and said sharply, "Well, then, girl, you might as well come along with me and perform the proper introductions. I only hope that the present earl is not the dissolute arrogant sinner that his grandfather . was. Probably a disdainful nobleman like his hypocritical father."

He strode out of the room, Kate following on his heels, her mouth suddenly gone quite dry. She did not have time to ponder the earl's intentions for visiting Brandon Hall. She ran her tongue nervously over her lips and, in an unconscious gesture, pulled on her gown to make it longer. Not only did she look provincial, she looked quite outmoded.

At the door of the drawing room, her father had the good manners to allow her to enter the room first.

The earl stood by the fireplace, elegantly dressed in riding clothes and gleaming Hessians, looking quite at his ease.

Kate forced her leaden feet to move forward. She extended her hand and said as calmly as she could, "How very kind of you to call, my lord. It's very nice to see you again, and unexpectedly, even though you said you would perhaps call, for you are so very busy and have so little time for other matters."

Julien clasped her slender fingers in his hand. Before he could make a suitable response, she added quickly, "I have been telling my father how Harry and I met you at Mr Stokeworthy's house in the village. I told him," she hurried on, not meeting his eyes, "that you expressed a wish to pay us a visit. It is delightful that you have come."

Julien gave only an infinitesimal start at her story. She looked up at him then, and he saw the fear in her eyes. No, surely not fear, that made no sense, but nonetheless, he gave her hand a slight squeeze before releasing it, and turning to greet Sir Oliver.

He extended his hand and said with exquisite good manners, "A great pleasure, sir, finally to meet you. I count it provident that I met Harry and Katharine so conveniently in the village, for I have long wanted to reestablish good relationships with the Brandons."

Kate gazed with something akin to awe at her father, who had received the earl's suave and fluent speech with an almost obsequious deference. His hard eyes softened, and he clasped the earl's outstretched hand with the greatest alacrity.

"Indeed, my lord," he breathed in a voice full of awe, "I am greatly honored that you have deigned to call." He gave a slight cough that reminded Julien forcefully of Mannering, and added in an apologetic voice, "I presume your lordship is aware of the rift between our two families. An unfortunate affair, and if your lordship is willing, best now forgotten."

Julien executed the most elegant of bows and replied smoothly, "I count myself grateful that you wish it to be so, sir."

Kate cast a furtive glance at the earl. She had the strangest feeling that what had just transpired between her father and the earl had not—indeed, could not—have really happened. Why, her father's very attitude was one of a condemned criminal being pardoned by royal command. It was unnerving. It made

90

her feel inferior. She felt even more gauche and provincial. She became acutely aware of her old dress and the scuffed sandals that were all too visible beneath her hemline.

Sir Oliver turned to his daughter, who was standing literally openmouthed. He ground his teeth but managed to moderate his voice. "Katharine, my dear, won't you see that Filber brings in the sherry? His lordship is undoubtedly needful of refreshment. Don't dawdle now, my dear."

Kate nodded and hurried to the door. In all likelihood, she thought, Filber had already heard his instructions through the closed door and was probably even now fetching the sherry and glasses.

"Yes, Miss Kate, right away," Filber said, before Kate had time to speak.

She walked quickly to a mirror and regarded her messed hair with vexation. She was trying to smooth down errant curls when it occurred to her to wonder if the earl were here merely to mock her and her father. She felt a new wave of humiliation at her father's toadying behavior and at the thought that the earl had seemed to find nothing amiss with such deferential treatment. She paced the floor in long, boyish strides waiting for Filber to bring the blasted sherry.

Sir Oliver rubbed his hands together and asked the earl to be seated. Kate was only partially right in her assessment of his attitude. Certainly he was impressed at his lordship's courteous condescension to visit

91

Brandon Hall, but more than that, he was aware that the earl was as yet unwed. It did not take him long to see the earl as a possible answer to the number of bills that lay piled on his desk.

Julien would not have been at all surprised had he known what Sir Oliver was thinking. In fact, he found himself watchful of Katharine's father, hoping that he had made a favorable impression, that the natural desire of a parent to see his progeny well placed in the world and, he thought cynically, to line his own pockets would work to his advantage. He hadn't been deceived by Sir Oliver's deferential treatment of him. Having read the fear—and yes, he knew now that it was fear he'd seen—in his daughter's eyes, he realized that to his family Sir Oliver was an altogether different man.

The thoughts of neither of the men were at all perceptible on their faces or in their painfully polite and mundane conversation. Bonaparte was always a safe topic, and Julien, in his most respectful manner, elicited Sir Oliver's opinion.

"It has now been nearly three months that Napoleon has been on Elba," he began. His choice of topics seemed at first an excellent one, for Sir Oliver immediately sat forward in his chair, his eyes blazing.

"Would for the safety of all men's souls, that the Allies had not allowed the monster to live. For years I trembled for fear that an invasion of those degenerate French Catholics would throw our land back into the hands of the papists."

Papists. Good Lord, Julien thought, as he tried not to blink with surprise, didn't he realize that Napoleon was an atheist? Evidently not. Sir Oliver was suddenly moved to explode in religious fervor. "I would have sought them out and destroyed them and all their loathsome, filthy idols."

"Ah, you are doubtless quite right. An England returned to Catholicism after so many centuries wouldn't be acceptable to Englishmen." He wondered, now more worried than ever about Katharine, wondering if Sir Oliver were not a bit mad.

Sir Oliver gave a start. Perhaps he'd been a bit too dogmatic in stating his view. He said in a more moderate voice, "We must pray that the Allies are able to keep Bonaparte on Elba."

"As I understand," Julien added gravely, "the French people have welcomed back the Bourbons with open arms. Louis seems quite firmly planted on the throne."

Julien was greatly relieved to see Katharine return, followed by the butler bearing a rather discolored silver tray. He rose quickly, and she seated herself on a small sofa facing him.

While Filber served the sherry, Julien was freed for a few moments to regard his future wife. He wasn't at all disappointed by her appearance. He'd wondered how she would look dressed in something other than her boy's clothes, and although the gown she wore was rather out-moded, her grace and bearing were clearly evident. And her poise delighted him. The rich auburn hair hung long down her back, secured with a simple ribbon. Tendrils curled over her ears. He wished he could lightly trace his fingertips over the freckles on her nose, a very nice, thin nose. He wondered how she would react to her new station. As his countess, she would have anything that she wished. And he would have her.

He frowned as he saw her hands twisting nervously at the folds of her gown. She wouldn't meet his eyes, and gazed alternately from her lap to her father. There was no vestige of the spirited, self-assured girl who had crowed when she caught many more trout than either he or Hugh. There was no more poise. He felt hesitant to address even the most innocuous of comments to her for fear that her answers would draw the wrath of her father after he left. He contented himself with simply enjoying her presence until he would have the opportunity to speak with her alone.

"It is a pity, my lord," Sir Oliver said jovially as he toasted Julien, "but you have just missed my son, Harry. He left but this morning to return to Oxford. A brilliant young man, if you'll forgive a father's natural pride. He has the makings of an accomplished scholar. Doubtless he will someday make his mark in some area, perhaps in science or mathematics."

Harry, a scholar? Mathematics? Julien repressed another blink of surprise, but said easily enough, "Yes, a fine young man. You say he excels at scholarly matters? He enjoys history, or perhaps religion, in addition to science and mathematics?"

Kate choked on her sherry, and Sir Oliver cast a look of ill-concealed dislike at her. He remarked with some reluctance, "No, it would be, of course, my wish, but Harry is intent on being in a cavalry regiment. You know boys, my lord—they wish for adventure. I hope and pray he will return to a calling for which he was meant. If he doesn't choose to—why, then, he is still my son and the future Sir Harry Brandon of Brandon Hall."

"I see," Julien said pleasantly. "Yes, Harry would become that eventually." He took a sip of sherry, which was not nearly as good as the St Clair sherry. It occurred to him again that perhaps Sir Oliver's finances were in need of a healthy settlement, given the rather frayed appearance of the furnishings here in the drawing room.

Not at all a stupid man, Sir Oliver had seen the earl's eyes on Kate as Filber served the sherry. Had his lordship already fixed his interest in her? The thought seemed preposterous to Sir Oliver—indeed, absurd—but nevertheless he decided to test his observation. After all, stranger things had been known to happen. He briefly saw his long-dead wife in his mind's eye. Ah, she'd been so

95

beautiful, beyond beautiful really, and he'd wanted her more than anything in those first months, been wild to have her, until he realized she was weak and not of his level in religious faith and scholarship. She'd also hated him in her bed after but a few weeks. She'd suffered him, damn her, when he insisted. And then Katharine had been born and she'd refused him. And he'd watched his daughter grow up and look what she'd become, despite all his efforts.

He cleared his throat and said, "Perhaps your lordship would like to see the Brandon gardens. They are not, of course, at their full beauty, but still they are not to be despised." He turned and trained his gaze full upon his daughter. "Kate, conduct his lordship to the gardens. Show him the roses, which will improve their appearance in but a few months."

Kate looked at her father with blank surprise. Whatever could he be thinking of? The gardens? The mangy roses? They were a mess, beautiful to her but overgrown and wild. Surely the earl would feel abused were he forced to walk amid the tangled vines and rosebushes.

Julien rose, placed his glass on a table, and said with no humor whatsoever in his voice, "I would enjoy seeing the gardens, Miss Brandon, if you would not mind."

Kate rose somewhat unsteadily, nearly knocking over the small table beside her. She could almost hear her father cursing her for her clumsiness. She raised a pale face to the earl and replied in a small voice, "I would be delighted, my lord. Please come with me."

Sir Oliver also rose and extended his hand to the earl. "If your lordship would deign to take dinner with us, say tomorrow evening, I would count it a great honor. We can seal our new coming together, if you like."

A slight smile hovered on Julien's lips as he shook Sir Oliver's hand. "The honor is mine, sir. A new beginning it is, sir."

"Then I bid you good afternoon, my lord." With those words Sir Oliver darted a sideways glance at his daughter, then removed himself from the drawing room, nearly lightheaded, he was so pleased with himself. It was all he could do not to rub his hands together.

Kate frowned after her father, gave her head a tiny, perplexed shake, and walked to the side door beside the windows. As she opened the door, she said over her shoulder, "The gardens are wretched. I cannot imagine why my father would wish you to see them. Truly, you don't have to risk your beautiful Hessians if you don't wish to."

Julien smiled at her naïveté and declined to comment. It had been quite some time since he had been treated to such blatant tactics as Sir Oliver's.

8

"Lead the way, ma'am," he said.

Kate said nothing more as they walked through the overgrown, ill-kept bushes and brambles. She finally drew to a halt and seated herself on a stone bench that stood in the middle of what must have been at one time a lovely rose bower. Her mother had loved the roses and had taught her daughter to tend them along with her. But when she died, something had died in Kate too, and she'd grown to hate touching the now-straggling wild roses.

She was certainly no gardener, Julien thought. He sat down beside her and gazed at her lovely profile. He very much liked the straight, proud nose and her firm chin. Tendrils of soft hair blew gently against her cheek, and he felt a fleeting urge to smooth them away, to touch her cheek, to feel her soft, warm skin under his fingertips. He felt other urges as well, but held himself well in control.

She turned to him suddenly, and he saw the dimples deepening and readied himself to be charmed, which he was indeed when she said in a wondering voice, "However did you

98

manage to turn him so sweet? I have never seen anything like it in all my life. He unbent so far, I feared he would fall at your feet."

Julien arched an elegant brow and said in his father's haughtiest voice, "My dear Miss Brandon, would you accord any less treatment to the great earl of March?"

She gave a crow of laughter, the dimples he found so endearing making her whole face alight with amusement.

"Great? Surely it is more infamous than great. But you know, truly, my lord, he was positively toad-eating you. I found it intimidating. Actually, I didn't like it at all. I also thought for a moment that you were perhaps mocking us, but then I realized that couldn't be so."

"Perhaps I was mocking your father, just a bit, but never you, Katharine, never you."

"I should cosh you were you ever to try it."

"Ah, then you tempt me to be outrageous just to see what you would do."

She just shook her head, her dimples still in full force. She continued with undisguised wonder in her voice. "And dinner tomorrow evening—Cook will be in such a flutter of nerves. I shall probably have to spend the greater part of my day tomorrow polishing silver so our noble neighbor will not be disgusted."

"I trust you will do a good job, for I will have you know that I am very aware of what is owed to me and won't lower myself to eat if the silver does not sparkle."

"You are quite horrid, and I haven't laughed so much in a very long time. I thank you, my lord."

He grinned at her, trying not to look at her mouth, trying not to imagine what she would taste like, how she would feel to his tongue, how she would shiver when he kissed her and began to caress her. Good God, he had to stop this or he would drive himself mad.

Quite at her ease now, she said, "Have your guests left?"

"Yes, Hugh and Sir Percy departed just after lunch to return to London."

"Why did you not go with them?" she asked, utterly without guile.

Julien was jolted for a moment, for he hadn't expected her to be so completely ignorant of the intent of his visit. He pulled himself together and managed to say smoothly enough, "I do have quite an estate here, and there are matters which require my attention."

He added in an easy voice, "It is also possible that I wish to further my acquaintance with Katharine Brandon. You know her, that pert chit who thinks she's such a great and skilled angler?"

"That she is, my lord. Still, I can't imagine why you'd want to waste your time with her. That girl is nothing but a graceless provincial, quite unworthy of the attention of the great earl of March."

"Don't ever say that again." His voice was so harsh that she jumped. She couldn't

100

imagine why he was so incensed by the simple truth. With disarming candor, she said, "One should never be blind to what one really is. I don't see why it should anger you, my lord. After all, it is I who am the subject of my own stricture, not you."

Julien found that he was losing rather than gaining headway. She relieved him of the burden of finding suitable words to express his feelings by smoothly changing the topic.

"Harry will be sorry to have missed you. He thought you a great gun, you know. Well, perhaps not all that great, and now we're getting into that *infamous* area again. He did think you might be arrogant and conceited, but, of course, he didn't have the benefit of fishing with you." She chuckled. "Harry was afraid that you would expose me and thus kindle Father's wrath. And I must say, I did find myself rather on tenterhooks when Father asked me where I had met you. Thank you, my lord, for your kindness."

She smiled, reaching out her hand to lay it lightly on his arm.

Julien took her hand in his and pressed her fingers. He looked into those incredible green eyes, and saw only openness and, yes, trust. She didn't yet understand, nor did it appear to him that she felt anything for him but friendship. It rankled a bit. For all her independent ways, for all her outrageous hoydenish behavior, she was innocent of the ways of the world and even more innocent of the ways of men. He curbed his impatience, realizing that he would have to give her time.

He rose and helped Kate to stand. "I must be going now. I've kept you overlong as it is."

"Well, you haven't really, but perhaps it is best if you leave. I never know how Sir Oliver will react." He said nothing to that, afraid that if he did, it would come out harsh and angry and serve only to upset her. He was extraordinarily pleased when she looked up at him, all her disappointment in her eyes, just like a child who was going to lose a coveted treat.

"I have the best of ideas. Will you ride with me tomorrow morning, Miss Brandon?"

"Miss Brandon? Surely, my lord, you can call me by my first name now. After all, we have shared a very personal attachment—we have shared fishing poles." She laughed when he grinned down at her, then she frowned. Seeing that he waited for an answer, she hurriedly said, "Oh, yes, I would very much like that. It is only that I must have my father's permission. Sometimes he isn't all that one would expect or prefer."

"Don't fear on that score. Sir Oliver won't mind." Mind, ha! The damned bastard would probably kick his heels in the air.

"How true. I had forgot how you have quite won him over. But sometimes he changes his mind. I never know, but I will ask him."

"He won't say no this time, I promise you."

As the remnants of the frown still furrowed her forehead, he asked, "What else troubles you, Kate?"

The frown vanished, and she turned laughing eyes to his face. "It will be such a bore. Oh, it has nothing to do with you, my lord. It is just that I will have to wear a riding habit and not my breeches."

"I am most honored that you're willing to make that sacrifice, ma'am."

"Ah, I'm not all that willing, but I must, for you will come to Brandon Hall and my father will be there, and, I assure you, he would be quite upset upon seeing me in breeches. But the problem is that my riding habit is much outdated and quite tight. I do but pray that I will not pop my buttons."

Julien laughed aloud and in an unthinking swift movement brought his hand up and cupped her chin. She made no resistance whatsoever, merely looked up at him, her eyes shining with innocent humor.

"You are an outrageous chit, Katharine." He drew her arm stiffly through his, and looking straight ahead, walked back to the hall.

Kate awoke slowly from a dreamless sleep. She stretched luxuriously under a mound of covers, savoring the warmth of the August sun upon her face. Her body felt light, and as she turned to look at the clock on the table beside her bed, as she had each morning for the past week, her lips curved into a smile of anticipation. She would be riding with the earl in but two hours.

She slipped quickly out of bed, wincing

slightly as her bare feet touched the cold wooden floor. Hurriedly she stripped off her nightgown and bathed in the basin of cold water, scrubbing and splashing the water over her body until her skin tingled. She shivered and looked at the empty grate with displeasure. It was a chilly summer, and she wished that her father would break his rule, just once. As far back as she could remember, he hadn't allowed fires in the bedrooms until after the first snow.

She was tugging on her stockings when a light knock sounded, and a moment later Lilly peered in. She said with an arch expression, "Squire Bleddoes is downstairs and wishes to see you."

"Good Lord, whatever can that wretched man want at this hour? Oh, Lilly, can't you tell him that I've come down with the plague, remind him how very virulent it is? He is very sensible and quite terrified of catching any illness at all. Perhaps it will send him directly back to his doting mama."

"He is probably here for the usual reasons, my lady," Lilly said, eyeing her mistress.

"Well, I suppose that means you won't lie for me. Ah, well, then I will see Robert, curse him for his rude timing. Do help me into my riding clothes, Lilly. The earl will arrive in little more than an hour, and I want to be ready."

Lilly's face took on a look at the mention of the earl, a rapturous expression fit to rival that of an actress on Drury Lane.

"Oh, Miss Kate, whatever will you do if the two men meet? I would swoon, I would."

"Don't be a goose, Lilly," Kate said sharply. "That expression you're wearing is really quite professional."

She sat herself at her dressing table and began vigorously brushing her hair. In the mirror she saw that Lilly was still in blissful contemplation over this imaginary scene. She put down her hairbrush and said matter-of-factly, "Lilly, let me be serious. The earl honors us with his friendship. That is all. Indeed, he probably simply has more time on his hands than he's used to, and thus he wants for diversion. We are the diversion. As for Robert Bleddoes, well, you know as well as I do that the idiotic man expects all females to swoon at his feet. Why he must continually pester me, and with no encouragement, is more than I can fathom, curse his hide."

She turned back to her mirror and continued brushing the tangles from her hair. She'd not been exactly forthcoming with Lilly, but it was none of her maid's affair in any case.

Lilly shot her mistress an incredulous look. If only she knew the servants' gossip. It was plain as a pikestaff that the earl was smitten with Miss Katharine Brandon, daughter of a mere baronet—and a daughter also despised by her father. Why, he had called at Brandon Hall no fewer than four times during the past week. Everyone knew it, save, it seemed to

105

Lilly, her mistress. As for Squire Bleddoes, that pompous windbag, Lilly would be quite content to see him routed. Quite a nuisance he'd become, presenting himself at the hall on only the flimsiest of pretexts.

Kate harbored very close to the same opinion of Robert Bleddoes as her maid did. She'd met him by accident nearly six months before, when she'd ridden a far greater distance than she had intended. She thought him at first to be a rather overserious young man but quite unexceptionable. She soon realized that his prosaic opinions, invariably uttered with monotonous precision, masked a feeling of vast self-importance that made her grit her teeth and talk herself out of smacking his face. After his first visit to Brandon Hall, she was convinced that he was a total bore.

She said as much to her father and stared at him with disbelief when he rounded on her in fury. "You discourage him, my girl, and you'll feel my walking stick on your back." He added with such blatant derision that she flinched, "You think yourself so puffed up, my little lady. Let me tell you, if Bleddoes offers for you, it will be much more than you deserve. That any man would want you is more than I can imagine."

Mindful of Sir Oliver's warning, she didn't openly discourage Robert. She forced herself to learn tolerance and tried to treat him as kindly as she treated Flip, the pug. She'd played a dangerous game the past three months, holding Robert off as best she could

106

with soft, vague words, and skirting the issue of marriage whenever Sir Oliver tried to broach it.

Sir Oliver, happily not aware that Robert had declared himself on several occasions, blamed her for her failure to bring the squire up to scratch. He commented to her sourly one evening at dinner, "I might have known that you couldn't attract a man. You are a witless, unnatural girl."

Kate didn't think of herself as being witless or unnatural, but she remained wisely silent. She kept her head down and concentrated on forking a lone pea that lay in the center of her plate.

It occurred to her now, as she handed Lilly a ribbon with which to secure her hair, that Sir Oliver hadn't mentioned Robert Bleddoes for the past week. She tapped her fingers on the tabletop. No, it was true, there had been no mention of the squire since the earl of March had come to call. She went pale at this realization. Dear God, Sir Oliver couldn't possibly think the earl was interested in her.

Kate rose somewhat unsteadily and raised her arms for Lilly to slip the riding skirt over her head.

"Draw a deep breath, Miss Kate. The buttons won't meet elsewise."

Kate sucked in her breath and felt the buttons dig into her skin through the thin material of her chemise.

Her jacket followed, but as it didn't meet over her breasts, she was forced to leave it open, revealing a well-worn white blouse.

"I'm not exactly the height of fashion, am I, Lilly?" She stepped back and regarded herself ruefully in the mirror, making a moue at herself. "Well, no matter, it's not that important just so long as I don't gain enough flesh so the buttons won't meet."

Lilly felt a stab of indignation. It was disgraceful how Sir Oliver treated his daughter.

"You look just fine, Miss Kate. Now, just let me twitch this pleat in place. There."

"You are quite kind to say so, Lilly. But so untruthful. However, a compliment shouldn't ever be turned away. I'll savor this one fully, I promise you." She gave Lilly an affectionate hug, picked up her riding gloves, and made her way with a light step downstairs.

She took a deep breath, planted a smile on her face, and squared her shoulders.

9

Robert Bleddoes rose with alacrity and hurried over to greet her. He was dressed in his usual brown broadcloth, eminently suitable for country wear, as he had once informed her. Harry, who now affected the "windblown" fashion made stylish by Lord Byron, had sniffed disdainfully at Robert's close-cropped brown hair, declaring him to be the complete flat, which, truth be told, he was—a conceited, arrogant, complete flat.

"Good morning, Robert," she said, extending her hand. "To what do we owe this unexpected pleasure?"

Robert bowed ponderously and clasped Kate's proffered hand in his longer than necessary, but she pulled it firmly away.

"Good day to you, Miss Katharine. May I say that you are in great looks today."

"I would prefer that you did not say something so utterly untrue, Robert, but since you have already, I suppose it would be inhospitable of me to cavil." She watched him closely as he blinked in an effort to understand her words.

He brightened. "Ah, my dear lady, you have such a ready wit. I see that you are jesting with me. Jesting is suitable for a young girl, so it doesn't bother me at all. A few more years and you will grow more properly reserved, I doubt it not, particularly with kindly superior nurturing."

She wanted to hit him on his head with a fireplace poker, then kick all his superior nurturing to York, but she managed to contain herself. She pictured her father's reaction and forced a very false smile. "Do take a seat, Robert. What news of Bonaparte do you have for me today?" With Napoleon's defeat and his subsequent departure to Elba, Robert, for the past six months, had never arrived at Brandon Hall without some bit of news to give credence to his visits.

He cleared his throat, beaming at her with approval. "I had thought that you and Sir Oliver, of course, would find it of great interest that the Allies will convene this fall in Vienna to determine the fate of France."

She didn't tell Robert that the earl had already discussed this interesting topic with her and that as a result, she found his news to be not entirely accurate. "It's a critical step in restoring a balance of power," the earl had told her. "Lord Castlereagh, our ambassador, has a mighty difficult task facing him, particularly after the bad will resulting from the Czar's visit to England in June."

"Actually," she'd said with a laugh, "it was more the Grand Duchess Catherine who nearly flummoxed the Regent."

He laughed and ruffled her hair, the braid coming unbound beneath her old hat. Just that one afternoon, she'd sneaked out of Brandon Hall wearing her boy's clothes and they'd gone fishing.

She answered Robert now with only a ghost of humor in her voice. "How very kind you are to ride such a great distance to so enlighten me. Why, I wish I could pack my bags this instant and accompany our ambassador to Vienna. I do wonder, though, how much diplomacy will actually be conducted, with all the routs and balls and soirees."

Robert pondered her words with great seriousness and finally announced, "Ah, you are attempting to jest with me again, my dear. You would, of course, have no desire to travel

110

out of England. Foreign travel is not at all the thing for well-bred English ladies. And your jests about our men of power, well, naturally they are not quite the thing. These men will comport themselves with high propriety."

Kate forced a smile and a nod, allowing the veil of boredom to close over her. She listened politely as Robert regaled her with the happenings of the past week. His mother was in fine health, barring, of course, her anxiety over the chill he had contracted.

Kate, knowing her duty, said, "Nothing serious, I hope, Robert. You seem to be quite well now."

Robert was delighted with her expression of concern. Though he thought the Miss Brandon to be a bit too vivacious upon occasion, he had always dismissed it as girlish spirits. Now, for instance, the true womanliness of her nature would be apparent to anyone.

He expanded most willingly upon the topic of his health, anxious to allay her concern about his illness.

Kate was near to screaming with vexation when Robert's commentary was halted by the entrance of Filber, announcing the earl of March.

She nearly leapt from her chair, a radiant smile on her face. Rescue was at hand. She walked swiftly to the earl and stretched out her gloved hand.

Julien lifted her hand to his lips and murmured softly so that only she could hear

111

his words, "My poor Kate. My timing is exquisite, is it not? What have we here? Dare I take it for a suitor?"

She bit her lip to keep from laughing aloud and raised her eyes to him in silent warning.

"Humph!" Robert had risen and stood alarmingly redfaced, his eyes narrowing upon the unwelcome intruder.

"Oh, do excuse me, Robert." She pulled her hand slowly from the earl's. Somehow she hadn't noticed that the earl had held her hand overlong, much less kissed her fingers lightly.

"Mr Robert Bleddoes, this is the earl of March, our neighbor." She added smoothly, "The squire has been good enough to bring us news of Napoleon this morning."

A strange transformation came over Robert. He appeared to shrink visibly, and he was able to murmur only a strangled greeting to the earl.

Julien seemed not to notice the stumbling phrases that were proffered and performed his greetings with his customary grace. He found himself being scrutinized, from his exquisitely tied cravat to his polished Hessians. He bore up under this well, quelling the set-down that rose automatically to his lips for such behavior. He thought with well-concealed amusement that much could be forgiven a man who was so obviously smitten and hiding it so poorly.

Julien was glad that he'd remained silent, for a chance glance at Kate's face showed her to be in an agony of apprehension.

Robert managed to recover a modicum of self-assurance and observed in a tight voice, "I did not know that your lordship was acquainted with Sir Oliver." He realized that he didn't show to advantage next to the earl, that somehow his serviceable brown breeches and coat seemed perhaps a bit bland, perhaps a bit too serviceable, as if he and his clothes were fading slowly and inexorably into the wainscoting. His lordship wore a superfine light-baize coat that fit so well it seemed a part of him.

Robert cast a surreptitious glance at his near-conquest to see if he could read her feelings about her noble guest. What he saw sent red flashes of danger shooting through his mind. He reluctantly pulled his eyes away when he became aware that the earl was answering him.

"Yes, Miss Brandon and her brother were riding in the village. We met there."

"But Harry isn't here any longer."

"True, but I contrive to make do with his sister. She is, upon occasion, sufficiently charming. And she fishes well, for a female, of course. Do you not agree, sir?"

"Well, naturally, certainly. Of course I agree. She is all that is charming and modest and demure. I say, do you really fish, Miss Katharine? Surely not."

"She tries, sir, she tries. Perhaps some years from now she'll come close to my skill." To his surprise, she seemed to have lost her

113

tongue, and Robert was tugging unconsciously at his cravat, even while he reddened with anger. Julien felt laughter bubble up but sternly held his amusement in check. He shifted his attention back to the squire, who looked fit to slay him, and asked easily, "What news have you of Napoleon?"

Robert drew himself up at this opportunity, knowing that his brilliant mind would now be admired and duly appreciated. His mother had assured him that he was brilliant, that he should himself be traveling to Vienna. "I was telling Miss Katharine that Bonaparte is safely secured on Elba and that the Allies will convene in Vienna this fall to determine his fate."

"How very interesting. Is there nothing else going on?"

Thinking that he had impressed the earl, Robert proceeded to favor the company with his opinions on Napoleon, Tallyrand, and the Restoration of the Bourbons. It didn't occur to him to halt because, after all, his mother had always assured him that his political knowledge was unrivaled and that she could listen to him for simply hours. It had never occurred to him to doubt her assessment.

"Why, Robert, you constantly amaze me." Kate couldn't bear it another moment and threw herself into the breach. She was well aware that the earl's forbearance was stretched to the breaking point and that soon he would tell Robert what a toad he was, all in very smooth verbiage, but he would do it and she would understand, and Robert would come to as well, perhaps after he'd had a week to think about it. "It's amazing how you never lose yourself in a tangle of words. How you contrive to remember so much is astounding. You must be very pleased with yourself."

Robert's chest expanded under this ambiguous praise, and he seemed quite content to take her words at their face value.

Kate eyed Robert for a moment and said, not unkindly, "I regret, Robert, that his lordship and I must leave now. I have promised to inspect a new hunter and must indeed keep my word. I know you will understand, for you are so sensible." With those words Kate firmly shook the bewildered squire's hand, turned quickly, and rang the bell cord. Filber entered in only a moment. She hoped he'd been vastly entertained at the keyhole. She didn't fault him for this habit. Life here was normally grim, so any enjoyment to be found should be savored.

"Filber, do show Squire Bleddoes out. He must be taking his leave now." She propelled him straight to the door, her hand on his arm.

Robert found himself in a quandary. He wouldn't have minded leaving were it not that Miss Brandon would be left alone with the earl. Though he knew his own worth, he had heard that females were highly impressed by a man's rank and fortune. The earl was undoubtedly a dangerous marauder. But for the moment there seemed to be nothing he could do about it. As he reached the open doorway,

115

he turned and said with as much calm as he could muster, "A pleasure, my lord." He executed a quick bow and followed Filber from the room.

Kate waited until she heard the front door close. She then closed the door to the drawing room and leaned against it, heaving an undisguised sigh of relief.

Julien said in a meditative voice, "I do hope that he will not call me out. I have no one available to act as my second."

"Perhaps Filber ..." She giggled.

Julien continued in the same meditative voice, "I suppose that now I must purchase a new hunter and make you promise to inspect him."

"Oh dear, I hope I haven't put you in an unhandy situation, but what would you have had me do? Tell him he is a prosy bore and demand that he leave?"

"Something of the kind," Julien said. "You are, after all, Kate, quite gifted with words and never one to draw in the clutch. The powers above know you've pinned my ears back a goodly number of times in the short time I've known you."

"It is something I cannot do," she said slowly.

"Why the devil not?"

"My father would not like it."

Good Lord, he thought, had Sir Oliver envisioned that country bumpkin as a suitable husband for his daughter? The thought was appalling, yet he wasn't really surprised.

He stepped forward and gently placed his hands on her shoulders. "Forgive me. I shouldn't have spoken so. I wouldn't for the world cause you discomfort."

She raised her eyes to his face and saw a good deal of kindness and concern written there.

She broke the power of the moment by giving her head a tiny shake and said, "You might well wonder why Robert is allowed to run free in Brandon Hall. But now he is gone, and I don't wish to think any more about him. That is, my lord, if you do not mind."

"As if you would care if I minded or not." With some effort he forced himself to remove his hands from her shoulders. Actually he wanted very much to kiss her, to hold her close to him, to feel her breasts against him. He wanted her to kiss him back, to put her arms around him and squeeze him to her.

He noticed the shabby riding habit, the same one she had worn on the several occasions they had gone riding together. Damn Sir Oliver.

Kate caught the brief look of anger in Julien's gray eyes. Perplexed, she asked, "What's wrong? It can't be something I've said, for I know I've been most guarded in my every word to you. Do you not agree with Robert that I'm demure and modest, even though he's shocked to his toes that I, a female of supposed decent breeding, actually indulge in fishing?"

"No, none of that. You're a hoyden and

utterly without guile and really quite clever. Now, I can't seem to think of a place in the neighborhood that would have a hunter for sale."

"I can see that from now on I must be more careful in my choice of fibs," she said, giggling.

"Particularly when it involves my pocket-book."

She felt instantly contrite. "Oh, dear, now I've been grossly impertinent. I do beg your pardon, Julien. Are you short of funds?"

10

Her ingenuous question, so ridiculous to anyone with even the slightest knowledge of the earl of March, left him speechless for a moment.

She misread his silence and said in a voice so filled with sympathy that he could only stare at her, "I can truly commiserate with you, for we are forever short in the pocket."

"Kate, how dare you so insult my importance? You unman me, you pauperize me, in short, you reduce me to laughter."

Words of apology died in her mouth. She kicked several small stones with the toe of her slipper, and he wondered if she wished she could be kicking him instead. "I might have

118

known you're disgustingly wealthy. As if you would care about buying a new hunter. It would mean nothing to you, less than nothing."

"Before I'm forced to give you a full reckoning of my holdings, curious Kate, let's go for a gallop."

She shot him a grin, dimples dancing on her cheeks.

As was her custom, she patted Astarte's silky nose and whispered endearments that were quite unintelligible to Julien but not, apparently, to his mare. Astarte nodded her great head in seeming agreement with the compliments and gave a snort of impatience.

"She's such a beautiful creature." She sighed, turning to mount her own mare, a docile swaybacked bay that was known to all at Brandon Hall as the Ladies' Hack.

Julien cupped his hand and tossed her into the saddle. He looked forward with great anticipation to the day he could provide a suitable mount for her. His own Astarte, he thought, would suit her to perfection. He pictured her fleetingly in a rust-colored velvet habit and a riding hat with gauzy veils to float behind her in the wind.

"Come, my lord, Astarte grows impatient. As to poor old Carrot here, why she's growing older by the minute, and the good Lord knows, she's already a relic."

He spoke without thought. "What, Katharine, a shrew already?"

She blinked at him, then said, "Why, how

119

dare you call me a shrew. A shrew, as in a termagant or a fishwife? Really, my lord, it isn't what I'm used to. No, not at all. I am quite used to being toadied and complimented until my eyes cross."

He appeared to consider the matter with great seriousness as he turned Astarte about. There was laughter in her voice and it pleased him, even if her jest against herself didn't. He said, grave as a bishop, "My apologies, ma'am, I fear that I've read my Shakespeare quite recently and was unjustly influenced. In the future I will contrive to compliment your fingernails rather than comment on your character."

She puzzled over this for a minute, mentally dusting off the bard's innumerable plays. Then her eyes widened and she declared, very much incensed, "It isn't gallant of you to compare me to Shakespeare's Kate. Furthermore, I did not like at all the way she ended up. Can you really imagine her falling at her husband's feet and vowing that she lives only for him? It quite makes my stomach turn."

"Being irreparably a male, I must confess that I don't find the idea entirely repulsive." He flicked Carrot's rump with his riding crop, and both horses broke into a comfortable canter.

As they turned their horses into the country lane just beyond the park to Brandon Hall, he shot her a sideways glance. Much to his relief, her attention was drawn to the brilliant riot of leaves. She seemed not to have noticed that his comment to her had given away his amorous intentions, for which he was profoundly grateful.

He was painfully aware that it was far too soon for him to propose marriage to her. He was quite certain that when he entered the drawing room that morning that her eyes lit up at the sight of him, but he could not be sure that her obvious joy denoted a more serious sign of affection or merely relief at no longer being alone with Bleddoes. Just the day before, when they sat fishing on the soft grass beside St Clair lake, she'd confided to him in her open, unaffected way, "It's so very nice to have a friend. You know, someone you can feel perfectly at ease with and say whatever comes to mind without worrying that the other person will think less of you or become angry or bored."

He didn't say a word, and she'd continued, happy as a lark and just as oblivious, "You're the only person that I can laugh with, save, of course, for Harry. But he's different, of course. He's only a brother, and alas, I am just a little sister."

He had looked at her searchingly for a moment, hoping to see something more in her words. A friend ... He was momentarily taken aback, but upon brief reflection he found, much to his own surprise, that she'd spoken the truth. Indeed, she was also his friend, an experience that he hadn't known with a woman until now, with Kate.

"It's a new experience for me as well," he

said, carefully choosing his words. "You see, I've never before met a woman with whom I didn't have to..." He paused, biting his tongue, for he had been on the point of saying "offer absurd compliments in exchange for her favors."

Kate, having no idea why he'd faltered, waited patiently for him to finish. Somehow she wanted very much for him to agree wholeheartedly with her.

He looked at her, and his mouth curved into a twisted grin. She was gazing at him expectantly, like a child waiting for a long-treasured treat. He said simply, "I've never met a woman who is so excellent a companion. You're a treasure."

Her eyes sparkled happily. She took his words at their face value and was quite pleased at his response. It didn't occur to her that no other woman in the earl's acquaintance would be too pleased to be called an "excellent companion."

Now, as they rode for a time side by side in comfortable silence, each thinking private thoughts, Julien chanced to look up and gaze around him, unsure of where they were.

"Let's go down this path, Kate," he said, giving Astarte a gentle tug on her reins.

She nodded her agreement, and their horses continued in an easy canter for some time until they emerged in a small meadow, bordered on one side by a wooded copse. The full, lush green foliage gave Julien the inclination to spend some time exploring.

He dismounted and called to her, "Come, this is a lovely spot. Let's commune with nature for a while, perhaps contemplate the glory of all those bees buzzing about those hydrangeas, and discuss Squire Bleddoes's immense charm."

It was several moments before he realized she hadn't moved to dismount.

"Kate... ?" He stopped abruptly at the sight of her face. She sat rigid in the saddle, her face suddenly gone very pale. Her eyes were riveted on the small copse.

He strode quickly to her. "Good God, what the devil is the matter?"

Her lips moved, but there was no sound. As if with great effort she tore her gaze away from the copse. "I don't like this place."

Her voice was so low that he could barely make out her words. She was trembling visibly, and she looked at once frightened and bewildered. "I don't like this place," she said again.

Before he could say anything, she whirled poor Carrot about and dug in her heels fiercely. Carrot gave a snort of surprise and plunged into an erratic gallop. Kate didn't look back.

Julien swung himself into the saddle in one swift motion and urged Astarte forward. Good God, what had upset her so? Had she seen something that he hadn't? He felt at once perplexed and fearful for her. In but a few moments he drew alongside her panting horse. She seemed not to see him; her eyes

123

were fixed on the road ahead.

His first thought was to grab her reins and forcibly pull the horse to a halt. But she appeared to have her mount well in control. Thus he contented himself with keeping pace with her.

She swung off to the left to another path that Julien hadn't noticed on their ride. Without hesitation she soon veered from the path and skirted a large meadow. Several minutes later, Julien saw that they were quite near to Brandon Hall. He would never have thought they could return so quickly.

The instant her horse's hooves touched the gravel of the drive, she pulled to a halt and blinked rapidly, as if awakening from a dream.

He reined in beside her, his arm stretched out to touch her shoulder. "What the devil is the matter? What did you see back there?"

She turned a pathetically white face to him. It was a moment longer before she answered him. "I don't know. It's simply a place that makes me very uncomfortable." Her voice was surprisingly calm, almost devoid of emotion.

"Don't tell such bald-faced lies, ma'am. If that is your notion of discomfort, you have need of verbal education. You were terrified back there. That or you saw something. What did you see?"

She flinched at his harshness, and he eyed her with mounting frustration. "I'm sorry," he said at last. "I didn't mean to shout at you.

But I would like to know what upset you so. I saw nothing out of the ordinary, nothing at all. Please speak to me."

"No, it's really nothing, my lord. I've behaved quite foolishly. Indeed, I was more of a ninny than I was three years ago when I managed to fall from an apple tree right on my head. It wasn't anything, truly. If you wouldn't mind, I would like to forget it."

He looked searchingly at her, trying to probe her mind. She returned his gaze almost defiantly.

"Very well, if that is what you wish." But it wasn't at all what he wished. However, she didn't yet belong to him, and until she did, he had no right to demand the truth from her, in any and all things.

She fanned her hands in front of her in a helpless gesture. She realized that he wanted her to confide in him, but how could she explain something that she could not even now understand herself? She had the lingering certainty that the place was evil. Just exactly what the evil entailed, she didn't know, for it seemed closed behind an impenetrable wall. For a moment, she'd probed at that wall, but something black and deep was behind it and she was too afraid to continue. She backed away.

Julien curbed his frustration at her silence and lifted his arms to help her down from her horse. It was a gesture he normally proffered, and one that she usually ignored, alighting unassisted, as would a man. This time she responded and touched her hands lightly on his shoulders as he circled her waist. He swung her down but didn't immediately release her. To his infinite joy, she didn't draw away but gazed up at him, an unfathomable expression on her pale face. Without thought and with great gentleness, he bent down and kissed her. And he knew he wasn't mistaken in her response. She parted her lips ever so slightly. He felt her hands press against his shoulders. But the brief moment was over as quickly as it had begun. She tore herself free of his arms and jumped back, her breath coming in short, jerky gasps. She raised her hands to her lips in a protective, bewildered gesture. Her eyes grew larger and darker. Then she just stood there, staring up at him in the most innocently provocative way he'd ever seen.

He took a quick half-step forward, his hand outstretched to her. He said her name very quietly.

She seemed to snap back to attention. She backed away, shaking her head, her hands spread toward him to ward him off. "No, I don't, I can't... " She turned on her heel, grasped her riding skirt, and fled without a backward glance.

This time he didn't attempt to follow her. He stood motionless, watching her, feeling not at all disconcerted by her abrupt, confused flight. On the contrary, he was glad that he was obviously the first man who had kissed her. He touched his fingertips to his mouth. He could still feel her, warm and soft, so very tentative. He smiled confidently. She was an innocent girl, a virgin, and her maidenly display of confusion pleased him immensely. Surely she had to care for him now, surely. He'd wooed her slowly and easily, giving her what she wanted, what she appeared to need, and it had paid off. He had her now.

He turned to see her horse lazily chewing some errant blades of grass at the side of the drive. "Well, you old relic, you know your way to the stables." With a lighthearted laugh he flicked the animal's rump with his riding crop and aimed the horse in the direction of Brandon Hall.

Astarte nuzzled his shoulder with her nose, as if she were jealous of his attention. He patted her nose and swung up into the saddle.

"An excellent morning's work, Astarte. You may offer me your congratulations."

Obligingly, she neighed and, at the light tug on her reins, broke into a canter.

He'd not ridden far when her strange behavior at the copse came again into his mind. She'd been afraid of something, yet strangely confused. What could have bothered her? But his buoyant spirits wouldn't let him long dwell upon the unusual incident. In all truth the experience paled beside her response to him when he'd kissed her. As her husband, he would, of course, have her trust and her confidence. She would willingly tell him whatever he wished to know. She would be his wife. She would be his, all of her.

He willingly let his mind race ahead. This very afternoon he would draw up an exceedingly handsome marriage settlement, a settlement that Sir Oliver could not refuse.

Filber tapped softly on the door and entered the small, rather airless book room where Sir Oliver spent the greater part of his day. His master sat hunched over a large tome, oblivious to his presence.

Filber cleared his throat. "My lord."

"Yes, yes, what is it, Filber? You know I don't like to be disturbed."

Sir Oliver wheeled around in his chair and glared at his butler, but to his surprise, Filber didn't flinch or embark on a round of apologies. Sir Oliver's bushy brows snapped together as he noted the rather smug, complacent look on Filber's face.

Filber stood his ground, even under the frowning scrutiny of his master, and said, "His lordship, the earl of March, is here to see you, my lord."

This information carried a wealth of meaning. Sir Oliver eyed Filber for a moment before replying. Filber noted with satisfaction the myriad emotions that crossed his master's face, particularly the speculative glitter that finally narrowed Sir Oliver's eyes. He knew that he hadn't been mistaken about the importance of his announcement. Miss Katharine had obviously succeeded in capturing

128

the wealthy and powerful earl of March. Undoubtedly Sir Oliver was at that moment busily calculating some vast sum of money that he would try to extract from his future son-in-law. Filber couldn't help but feel pleased with himself, for it had been he who'd announced to Cook and Lilly, not long after the earl's first visit to Brandon Hall, that the earl was taken with Miss Kate, as sure as Sir Oliver would yell at one of them before sunset. Not altogether surprised by this revelation, Cook and Lilly had given free rein to their condemnation of Sir Oliver, whom they thought a vicious, despicable man despite his puritan ways, and then heartily toasted Miss Kate's good fortune from Cook's bottle of cowslip wine.

Filber shifted from one foot to the other as he watched Sir Oliver expectantly.

Sir Oliver's mind reeled at the implied nature of the earl's visit to him. He had been very much aware of the earl's constant attention to Kate during the past week, and simple avarice had led him to nurture some fantastic notions that the earl might offer for her. But the earl was here, now, and wanted to see him. He cursed himself, remembering how he had forced Kate to receive the attentions of that oaf, Robert Bleddoes. But how could he have imagined that the miserable little creature would do better for herself? Good God, she would be a countess. The countess of March. It was fortunate that his need for money was greater at the moment than his abhorrence of his daughter, for the mere thought of her queening and pluming herself about him was nearly enough to dampen his enthusiasm.

He became suddenly aware that Filber was covertly observing him and quickly decided on what he considered to be a suitable settlement from the earl. He rose from his chair. "Filber, tell his lordship that I will be with him directly. And don't tarry, man."

Filber obligingly scurried from the room, and Sir Oliver stepped to a small mirror on the mantelpiece and adjusted his cravat to a more acceptable shape. His face was pale with suppressed excitement, and he shook his head in sheer wonderment as he left the book room to greet his future son-in-law.

11

When Julien was informed by Filber that Sir Oliver would join him directly, he asked quietly, "Is Miss Katharine about, Filber?"

Filber noticed the softening of his lordship's voice at the mention of his mistress's name, and allowed a slight conspiratorial smile.

"No, my lord, she isn't here inside the hall, but I fancy she's walking in the grounds. She enjoys walking. It is possible that she is by the small fish pond behind the gardens. It's one of her favorite places."

Julien nodded. On the brink of making his first offer of marriage, Julien found himself unusually calm, for which he was profoundly grateful. He felt at his ease, and confident, particularly about the interview he would shortly have with Sir Oliver. He'd taken the man's measure and had determined that despite his officious, sanctimonious ways, Sir Oliver was eager to see Harry well placed and Kate off his hands as quickly as possible. Since he seemed as solitary as he was cheerless, and appeared to nurture for some curious and inexplicable reason a profound dislike for his own daughter, it wasn't likely he would thrust himself upon them after their marriage—surely a blessing.

"My lord, welcome, welcome." Sir Oliver executed a formal bow and advanced toward Julien with his hand outstretched.

Julien returned his greeting, aware instantly that his purpose was quite evident to Sir Oliver.

"Please do be seated, my lord."

Julien obliged, easing his long frame into a worn leather chair next to the fireplace. Sir Oliver seated himself opposite and looked expectantly at him, for all the world like the pug Julien had had as a boy.

"I would imagine, sir, that you can easily guess the nature of my visit."

Sir Oliver could not repress the gleam of anticipation in his eyes, and Julien realized that he could dispense with any further formalities.

He said smoothly, "As you know, sir, I have developed a great regard for your daughter and cherish hopes that she returns my affection. I've taken the liberty to have a marriage settlement drawn up." He paused for a moment and pulled a folded sheet of paper from his pocket. "You'll notice, sir, that I've included the promise to buy Harry a pair of colors and see him admitted to an elite cavalry regiment."

Julien was pleased with himself that he had thought of this, for the pleasure was evident on Sir Oliver's face. "As you see, the sum to be presented to you, sir, upon my marriage to your daughter, is named, I believe, in the third paragraph."

As Julien had anticipated, Sir Oliver's eyes widened and he was voluble in his expression of gratitude. "Very, very generous of you, my lord. Indeed, it is good of you, for I detest haggling over something as odious as money, and you know my daughter's beauty and accomplishments, not to mention her immense charm and kindness—ah, yes, all of those things, surely. I count it a rare privilege that our two families will be united. Naturally Katharine is worthy of the exalted position your lordship offers and if she isn't, well then, you will instruct her."

Julien felt a stab of anger mixed with relief. He didn't care if Sir Oliver didn't like his daughter. It didn't matter. She would be out

132

of this house just as soon as Julien could arrange the matter. He rose and sealed their bargain with a handshake. Sir Oliver thought to ask, "I presume your lordship has already spoken to my daughter?"

"No, sir, I felt it would be proper to secure your permission first."

"Very proper, and quite right, my lord." Sir Oliver sounded worried. But that was ridiculous, surely. He said, clearing his throat, "I suppose your lordship would like to speak to her now?"

"Yes," Julien said, as he walked beside Sir Oliver out of the shabby drawing room.

Julien strode from the hall into the overgrown gardens and shaded his eyes with his hand from the bright sunlight. He scanned the landscape and, not seeing Kate, walked toward the pond.

He found her seated on the mossy bank, her arms clasped around her knees, a pensive, faraway expression on her face. Her hair was unbound and hung down her back in soft waves, reaching nearly to her waist. His calm assurance didn't falter as he approached her. He knew exactly what he wanted to say, and he'd spent much of his day visualizing her response. She would be surprised at how soon he was declaring himself, but she would be prepared, for his feeling for her was obvious. Her face would flush slightly, and she would softly tell him that she cared for him as well. Perhaps she would even tell him she loved him. The altogether delightful vision ended with a discreet, yet promising kiss.

As he drew nearer, he could hear her singing a Scottish ballad. He grinned, for she had a small, wooden voice. He rather hoped she didn't play the pianoforte, for he'd had to endure the painfully accurate performances of too many nervous girls out to impress him.

She didn't notice his presence until he dropped down to his knees beside her. She looked up, not at all startled, and said cheerfully, "Good morning, sir. You are up and about quite early."

"What is this? You think me a lazy sluggard, Kate?"

"Well," she said slowly, the irrepressible dimples peeking through, "not exactly a sluggard. Being one of the—what is it you fine gentlemen call it—ah, yes, being a Corinthian, you would naturally be expected to be at your dressing table until at least noon."

"Little baggage." He lightly buffeted her shoulder and she laughed.

He looked at her searchingly for a moment, thinking suddenly of the way they'd parted the day before, of her fear at the copse and her undeniable response to him. Neither of these incidents appeared to be disturbing her now. She was perfectly at her ease, the pensive expression he'd observed on her face vanished.

She saw that he was looking at her very seriously. "What, my lord, can't you find a suitable hunter to buy?" She laid her hand on the sleeve of his light-blue-broadcloth coat, thinking fleetingly how very exquisite he looked. His cravat was snowy white and arranged with such subtle perfection that she wished Harry could see it.

Julien looked down at her hand and clasped it in his own. She made no move to pull away, but simply cocked her head to one side and gazed at him inquiringly. With supreme confidence, emboldened by her gesture, the earl of March set course on his first proposal of marriage.

"I've spoken to your father. In fact, I've just come from meeting with him."

"Good heavens, whatever would you have to say to Sir Oliver? I hope he didn't annoy you."

A bit daunted by her naïveté, he hesitated a moment, carefully choosing his words. "I of course wanted to make a suitable agreement with Sir Oliver before speaking with you. I have always believed this is the way it is done."

"What is done?"

"You do not ease my task, do you? Very well, in short, Kate, my dearest Kate, I asked his permission to pay you my addresses. I want you to be my wife. I care very much for you. Will you do me the honor of marrying me?"

"Marry you," she repeated blankly. "You want me to marry you?"

"That's right." He wasn't dismayed, not really, for she was quite innocent. Her

135

uncertainty, her charming guilelessness pleased him, for it fitted to perfection the reaction he'd expected to see from her at his declaration. He could almost imagine now the softness of her lips and the feel of her silky hair in his hands. He wanted to stroke his hands down her back, cup her and bring her up tightly against him, let her feel how very much he wanted her.

"You're not jesting with me, my lord?"

It occurred to Julien that perhaps she couldn't quite believe that she would become a countess. "It's a serious matter, Kate. I can't imagine any man ever living has jested when he's proposed marriage. I've already spoken to your father, as I said, and he gives us his blessing. It just remains for you to say yes to me and it is done. Then we'll select a date and everything will go forward."

"My father has agreed to this?" Her voice was a whisper, and he had to strain to make out her words.

"Yes, of course. Actually I had few doubts that he would."

With an effort she wrenched her gaze from his face, terribly aware at that moment of his nearness to her. The day before, when he'd kissed her, she had known an instant of tingling excitement, an altogether new sensation that had been actually quite pleasurable. But the brief moment had passed so quickly that she wasn't now certain it had happened at all. What she remembered was that she had felt at once so consumed with the unexpected deadening fear that had caused her to run from him. She hadn't been able to understand either the unwanted feelings that had surged through her when he'd touched her or her sudden fear. She'd decided later that she had behaved foolishly, that the earl had merely given way to a moment of capriciousness. She realized now that she had been mistaken not only in her final dismissal of her own feelings, but in the earl's motives as well. His had not been the action of a capricious nobleman. He wanted her. She felt the strength and possessiveness of his hand, knew the power in that hand, and jerked hers away. Her chest tightened painfully, as it had the day before. She felt an overwhelming desire to run, but she didn't move. Her body seemed leaden, weighted down by a strange lethargy. Her mouth went dry and she licked her lips nervously. Without wishing to, she pictured his powerful man's body barely held in check by his elegant clothing. The inexplicable terror that had consumed her at the copse now descended, cloaking her mind in a pervasive and dreadful blackness.

"Kate." His voice penetrated the darkness.

Her mind cleared at the sound of his voice. The full realization of what he wanted broke over her like a massive wave of freezing, numbing water. *Marry him.* He would be her husband, a man who would rule her life just as her father did now. Her husband. She would belong to him. He would own her. She would have nothing, no escape, no freedom, nothing. Her father had given him his blessing.

A bitter fury gripped her and she encouraged her rage, for it gave her mind direction. How could he be so presumptuous, so very sure of himself? "How dare you? You bargain with my father for me like stocks on the 'Change. Did it never occur to you that I would find your sly maneuver despicable?"

She paused for breath, and to find more words, hurtful words to drive him away, to keep him away, to give him a lasting disgust of her.

"I don't understand you," he said, staring intently at her, doubting her words even as she spoke them, not understanding her, not understanding any of it now.

She fanned her fury, searching out more painful words, more insults, anything to make him hate her, to make him leave her alone. "How odd. To this moment, I have always found your understanding to be quite superior. What's wrong, my lord? Don't simple words make sense to you? Are you so sure of yourself and what you are and what you want that you refuse to listen to a contrary opinion? Truly, your arrogance and conceit pass all bounds."

He gazed at her, stupefied, and suddenly she couldn't hold to her anger. Brokenly she whispered, "I thought you were my friend, that you held me in equal esteem. I can't believe you've done this."

He'd been incredulous at her sudden fury,

and was now appalled at the pain in her voice. He leaned close to her and said, "Kate, surely you must see that it is only proper for me to seek out your father first. That you are angered by my action, I am sorry. No, don't look away from me. Of course I'm your friend. My esteem and respect for you are surely obvious. That won't change. It's just that I wish to be much more to you. In truth, I want to be your husband, the man with whom you will spend your life, the man who will make you happy."

She closed her eyes tightly as each of his words burned deep into her. She knew of a certainty that she couldn't escape him as she'd done the day before, that he would pursue her and demand an explanation. But she had no such explanation, even to herself. She drew a deep breath. "Pray forgive my anger, my lord. I was unprepared and therefore am shocked by your proposal. I'm aware of the great honor you do me." To her own ears her words sounded stilted, and she finished in a rush, "But I don't wish to wed you, nor any other man, for that matter."

He grabbed her arm, his own gray eyes darkening with anger. "What game are you playing? Surely you can't expect me to believe that you are indifferent to me, that you don't care. By God, I've waited until I was certain of your feelings. Don't you remember opening your mouth to me yesterday?"

She looked down dispassionately, thinking it strange that she felt no pain, for he was holding her arm in an iron grip. She replied calmly, "What you wish to believe is your own affair, my lord. That I don't wish to wed you is a fact."

"Surely you cannot wish to marry that bumptious ass Bleddoes." His grip tightened more.

"If you would like to beat me, my lord, my father finds a cane to be much to his liking, the results giving him immense pleasure." She stared at his angry face, her chin thrust up. She had nothing left but defiance, nothing at all. Please God, let him believe it.

It was as if she had struck him full in the face. Appalled at his lack of control, he released her abruptly.

She didn't move or attempt to back away from him. "There is no one else, my lord, nor will there ever be. I don't wish to be any man's possession, any man's chattel."

He looked at her blankly and repeated vaguely, "No one else, Kate?" This gave him rational direction, and he asked slowly, "Then what is it you want? I offer you all my wealth, the protection of my name, I offer you a safe haven with someone who will place your wishes over all others', and above all, I offer you the chance to escape from the intolerable life with your father. That I love you is without question. I've never loved a woman before in my life, but I know I love you and it will last. I'm a loyal man, if that worries you, faithful to my toes. Never will you know infidelity from me."

Kate looked down and unconsciously began to rub her arm. What he said was true, though she could not fathom why he should possibly profess love for her. As to his faithfulness, she didn't want to think about that. She knew a brief moment of doubt before the strange fear gripped her. She knew she couldn't marry him. Not ever.

She raised her eyes again to his face and saw that he clearly expected an answer from her. His gray eyes were clouded with confusion. He was her friend, her only friend save Harry, and now she would lose him.

"What you say is true, my lord. It would be absurd to deny that my father and I do not deal well together. But I cannot, indeed, I will not marry you for such reasons as you have listed."

"I see." Julien's voice was flat, emotionless. His eyes bore into hers for one long, silent moment. He wanted desperately to see some change, some hesitance in her, but she met his gaze without flinching or turning away. He didn't know the effort it cost her, for absurdly, she wanted to cry.

He had no more words, no more arguments to present to her. He had only a shred of his pride. He executed a brief, ironic bow and strode away from her. He turned back after a few steps and flung at her over his shoulder, "Pray forgive me, madam, for assuming feelings you obviously don't share with me."

He turned again and hastened away from her. He did not again look back. In an unconscious gesture, she raised her hand toward his retreating back. The overgrown garden soon blocked him from her view. Slowly she lowered her arm, and finding herself quite unable to support her own weight, she sank down onto the mossy bank. There were no tears, only a deep sense of loss.

12

Mannering was aghast when he opened the great oak doors to admit his lordship. The earl said not a word. His face was pale, his eyes a blank gray. Words of congratulation died on Mannering's lips, and he stepped quickly aside. He watched his master walk the length of the hall, fling open the door to the library, and slam it behind him.

A sense of unreality seized Mannering. Good God, he thought, Miss Katharine refused him.

Mrs Cradshaw, who had been waiting impatiently in the parlor for the earl's return, came bustling out. Her smile vanished as she approached Mannering and saw the pained expression on his face.

"Oh dear, Edward, what's happened?"

Mannering drew a deep breath to steady himself. "I fear, Emma, that there won't be any congratulations for his lordship. It would appear that Miss Katharine has turned him down."

Mrs Cradshaw drew back in stunned surprise. "No, Edward, surely not. Why, she loves St Clair, she knows she would be happy here. His lordship is a fine young man, kind and ever so handsome. Oh, no, surely not."

Mannering seemed not to have heard her. She was suddenly indignant. "How dare Miss Katharine serve his lordship such a turn. I wouldn't have thought such a thing possible. Does she believe herself too high for him? That's nonsense, Edward, utter nonsense. It's disgraceful, that's what it is, and I've a mind to go to Brandon Hall and tell that young miss a thing or two. Turning down my boy. I'd like to smack her."

Mannering felt beyond tired. It was with an effort that he pulled himself up straight and squared his shoulders. He patted Mrs Cradshaw's arm in a soothing gesture. "I'm very much afraid, Emma, that there is little we can do about it, save wait and see what will happen. We will have to be very understanding with his lordship," he added, realizing that it was his duty to protect the earl from the curious glances of the servants and any embarrassing questions that Mrs Cradshaw might take it into her head to ask. He began to silently rehearse his speech to the staff, who were all waiting for his announcement that a new countess was to come to St Clair.

Mrs Cradshaw nodded slowly. That such an unbelievable turn of events should happen to

143

the St Clairs. Arm in arm, the two old friends walked across the hall to the servants' quarters. Mannering thought fleetingly of the vintage champagne that he'd unearthed from the wine cellar. It was chilled, the beautiful crystal flutes waiting. He must remember to return it and put the glasses away.

Julien stood in the middle of the library, staring blankly ahead of him. His body felt curiously detached from his mind, and neither seemed capable of functioning. He'd managed to nurture anger at her for the greater part of his ride home, only to find that he couldn't sustain it. A great sense of loss had descended over him.

He flung himself into the large chair and sat brooding for a time before a deep sense of humiliation stung him to action. God, what a fool he'd been. He mocked himself bitterly as he remembered how he'd been so certain of her, how he'd even gone so far as to envision her every response to his gracious offer of marriage. And he'd been mortally insulted when she flung his declaration in his face. He realized he'd never been denied anything he really wanted in his entire life. He would set his eyes on something, and sooner or later it would be his. Or a woman. He would see a woman he wanted, and it wouldn't be long before she was in his bed. God, was he such an officious sod?

He could find no excuse for himself. Though he'd never believed himself such a wondrous specimen of manhood, a bloody paragon, for God's sake, it was painful to realize that he'd behaved in the most reprehensibly conceited manner possible. And now he would pay for it as he'd never paid for anything in his entire adult life. He wasn't used to pain or disappointment. Now, he feared, he would gain retribution in full measure.

"Dammit to hell. If ever a demented man needed a drink—" He grabbed a bottle of brandy from the sideboard, carried it back with him to his chair, and hurled himself down again.

Mannering hurried to the library when he heard the ring of the bell cord. He hoped that his lordship would be wanting his dinner, for it was growing quite late. The sight that greeted his eyes when he opened the door made him wince. The earl was sprawled in the large stuffed chair, his late father's chair, an empty bottle dangling in his outstretched hand. His cravat was askew as if he had unsuccessfully tried to pull it away, and his fair hair was decidedly disheveled.

"My lord. Oh, dear." Mannering was shocked. He'd never before seen his master so obviously foxed.

Julien turned his blurred vision on his butler. "Get me another bottle of brandy, Mannering. And don't give me one of your looks. There are times in a man's life when brandy is not at all a bad thing. Trust me, this is one of those times. Indeed, this is probably the only real time. Do be quick, man. I've no intention of losing my hold on a world that is for the moment altogether tolerable."

"Yes, my lord. As you wish, my lord." He left the room with dragging steps to do his master's bidding.

As he closed the library door, he heard a curse and the sound of glass breaking. He glanced hastily around, hoping that none of the servants, particularly Mrs Cradshaw, were within hearing.

Upon his return, he saw that the earl had thrown the empty bottle, shattering it against the marble fireplace.

"My lord."

"Don't you dare even think about preaching to me, Mannering." Julien rose drunkenly from his chair and grabbed the bottle. "And don't stand there gaping like a black crow. Get out of my sight. I'll call you if I have further need of you."

Mannering stiffened at the harsh words but almost instantly forgave his master. He bowed, and with as much dignity as he could manage, walked out of the library, closing the door softly behind him.

With considerable effort Julien forced his eyes open and looked about him. He was lying in his bed, fully clothed, a cover pulled over him. He winced at the bright sunlight and turned his head away, only to find that this simple movement brought on excruciating pain. He lay very still until the pounding in his temples lessened. He had no memory of how or when he had left the library to come to his room. He gave a loud groan upon seeing a half-empty bottle of brandy standing precariously on the night table, and wondered how much he had consumed before falling into a drunken stupor. He didn't know. He didn't want to know.

Too soon he remembered the events of the previous day, and he found himself almost welcoming the physical pain in his head, for it forced his attention away from less pleasant thoughts. He lay quietly in the silent room until finally, with a determination born of despair, he rose unsteadily. He glanced at the clock on the night table and was surprised that it was quite early, in fact, only seven o'clock in the morning. He began to feel disgusted with himself, for he had always scorned those gentlemen in his acquaintance whose sole purpose for getting drunk was to escape their misery. And here he had done exactly the same thing, weak sod that he was.

He cursed long and fluently, and it made him feel better. He wanted to cleanse himself, to clear both his mind and his body of the effects of the brandy. He hurried from his room, not even thinking of the odd appearance he presented, made his way downstairs, and flung open the front doors. He strode past two startled footmen, who had barely enough time to bow, and broke into a run across the front lawn toward St Clair lake. The rapid movement made the pain in his head near to unbearable, but he gritted his teeth and never broke his stride until he reached a large rock that formed a cliff about six feet above the water. He quickly pulled off his clothes and poised himself naked on the edge of the rock, panting a moment from his exertion, then dived, gasping with the shock of the icy water.

His pounding head felt like it would split open and his skin tingled as if jabbed by sharp needles, but he ignored all of it and set out with long, firm strokes. He swam at a furious pace until he reached the opposite shore and then turned himself about and swam back. He found his footing and waded through the water reeds to the grassy bank. His heart pounded with the exertion, but he felt exhilarated, somehow renewed. He stretched out his arms and embraced the cold air against his wet skin.

He turned and gazed out over the lake, a strange smile flitting over his face. Enough of being a sniveling fool. He said half-aloud to the calm blue water, "What a fool to think of giving it all up, a damned weak fool. I'll wed her, just as I planned. And I won't pay her court as does that half-wit Bleddoes."

As he dressed himself, he let his mind nurture the idea until it burst forth. He announced again to the silent lake, "Damn, but I'll have her. I'll use my brain this time, not drown myself in bottles of brandy. Damn, but I'll make her love me."

Not bothering to tie his cravat, he strode with confident steps back to the mansion.

Sir Oliver's arm ached. He considered himself a pious man, and it angered him that this wretched daughter of his had made him curse to vent his spleen. "Damn the girl." He sought fiercely for more curses, turning to his Bible for epithets that would fit what had come to pass. "I've nurtured a viper to my bosom, an unnatural, willful child. God, why didn't she die? She should have, the damned little slut." He massaged his arm. He'd been fair. Of course he'd been fair.

When she'd calmly informed him that she didn't want to wed the earl of March, he controlled his immediate outrage and presented her with innumerable advantages to such a match. But she just stood stiffly before him, in that contemptuous silent way of hers, saying nothing, but he knew she would never agree. And when he threatened her with Bleddoes, she told him quietly that she'd already refused the squire. Obstinate, that's what she was, unnatural and stubborn as the devil who spawned her. The little slut didn't even cry, nor did she beg for mercy when he raised his cane and shook it in her face. She pulled her long hair away from her back and covered her head with her arms. When he stopped beating her, she rose unsteadily to her feet, gazed at him with hatred in those sinful green eyes of hers, and staggered to the door. He realized full well that the beating hadn't made her change her mind. At least, he reflected, it had made him feel better.

As he sat pondering his ill fortune, he was informed by Filber that the earl of March was here, asking to see him. A flicker of hope widened his eyes. "Well, don't just stand there like an idiot, Filber. Show his lordship in."

Hastily he rose and removed the cane. There was dried blood on it, and it did not seem politic for his lordship to see it.

Filber returned to the earl and took his riding crop and cloak. "Sir Oliver will see your lordship in the book room, my lord."

"Filber, just a moment. Is Miss Katharine here?"

Filber's calm facade nearly broke, and as he replied he was aware of the hardness of his own voice, "Miss Katharine, my lord, is physically unable to see anyone at this time and for some time to come."

Julien asked, his words so softly spoken that Filber had to strain to hear, "Has he hurt her, Filber?" To anyone who knew the earl well, the quietly spoken words would have been an instant signal that his lordship was in a deep rage. Filber, who didn't know this, felt emboldened to say, "Yes, my lord, he hurt her very badly. She is in bed, her maid Lilly attending her. He wouldn't even allow a doctor to see her. He beat her more savagely than he ever has before. It's possible that he's scarred her this time. Lilly will see that she remains still and quiet until she heals. She has always healed before, at least on the outside."

There was an infinitesimal pause before Julien said in a deceptively cool voice,

150

"Thank you, Filber, for your honesty."

Julien stopped him again as he turned to go. "You may be certain that Sir Oliver will never touch her again."

Filber gazed at the earl with a thoughtful, arrested expression. He realized that he had been wrong about his lordship. The servants had been surprised at Miss Katharine's refusal of the earl, but that Sir Oliver had dared to try to beat her into submission had left them all enraged. The baronet had suffered sullen looks and indifferent food prepared by Cook since that time.

Julien was closeted with Sir Oliver only briefly. He stated his business in a concise, controlled voice. Sir Oliver stammered and fussed, but naturally he agreed to the earl's demands. They were, after all, in his own best self-interest. Julien rose as soon as they had reached an agreement. "Very well. I will expect to see Katharine installed with Lady Bellingham in London within two weeks. Not longer, mind."

"As you say, my lord, within two weeks. But why not sooner? Surely I can have the girl off to London within days if you wish it."

"You miserable bastard," he said, so calm that Sir Oliver didn't at first realize the depths of the earl's rage. "She is in bed, doubtless in great pain. You will see that the physician attends her. I care not if he tells the world of your treatment of her. He will attend her, and he will give her laudanum for her pain. And he will see her within the next hour. Do you understand me?"

Sir Oliver nodded slowly, smart enough to keep his mouth shut. It didn't occur to him to question how his lordship knew of the beating.

"If you dare harm her again, you can be assured that she will be an orphan before the day is through. Do you understand me a second time?"

Sir Oliver paled. He tasted real fear for the first time in his life. He nodded his head. "I quite understand you, my lord."

"If I discover that you haven't done exactly what I've told you to do, I will take my own cane to your miserable hide and leave you in a ditch for all to see."

It was some moments before the hammering of fear lessened and Sir Oliver was able to walk slowly to a chair and sit down. He sagged against the back and closed his eyes. He could see her bloodied back, her dress shredded as she staggered away from him. Fleetingly he wondered if he had scarred her. He brightened as he realized that the earl, the autocratic, arrogant sinner, would perhaps not be so pleased with his bride. Indeed, he reflected with satisfaction, there would be much to displease the earl.

Kate chewed absently on her thumbnail as she sat gazing out her window overlooking Berkeley Square. She marveled that the peaceful scene below was yet another face of London. The Pantheon and Bond Street, where she'd shopped with Lady Bellingham, were filled with the clatter of carriages and horses, the shouts of coarse vendors in words that she barely understood, and the bustle of linkboys clearing the way for their masters and mistresses. It had been difficult to believe that so many different kinds of people contrived to make their way in one city.

There was a light knock on her door. Eliza stepped into the room and swept Kate a slight curtsy. Kate rose slowly from the window seat, mindful of the red weals on her back. They were healing, but still brought pain if she moved suddenly. She was yet unable to face her maid without embarrassment, since Eliza had attended her first bath and without a word produced an ointment and gently rubbed it into her tender skin.

"Yes, Eliza, what is it?"

"It's Lady Bellingham, Miss. Some of your gowns have arrived, and she requests you to come to her sitting room."

"That is good news indeed." Her embarrassment was momentarily forgotten in her excitement. "But Eliza, good heavens, it's only been three days. There was so very much to be done."

"Lady Bellingham is never one to be put off," Eliza said as her mistress straightened a flounce in her old gown and patted her hair into place. She thought fleetingly, and with no regret, of Harry's old breeches folded out of sight at the bottom of her trunk. Her disreputable leather hat she had carefully

153

hidden with her fishing pole in a dark recess of the stable.

Kate made her way down the carpeted hallway to Lady Bellingham's sitting room and tapped lightly on the door. She heard a muffled "Come in!" and opened the door to see her hostess pacing back and forth in obvious agitation, her brow puckered and her plump, beringed hands clasped to her bosom.

"Ma'am? What's the matter? What can I do?"

"Oh, my dear Kate. Do come in, child, yes, come right in and sit over here on this chair. That's right. Your new gowns have arrived. Madame Giselle has performed marvels with the materials we selected. Just look at the evening gown, my dear."

Kate was perfectly willing to be distracted at the sight of all those wonderful boxes. She opened them with great enthusiasm, tossing the silver tissue paper about as she unearthed her clothes. There was a severely cut gold-velvet riding habit with a plumed, high-poked hat to match, a morning gown of soft yellow muslin with laced frocking, and the most beautiful dress she had ever beheld, a pale-blue-velvet evening gown, fashioned high in the back in the Russian style, with plunging neckline and long, fitted sleeves sewn with tiny seed pearls on the cuffs. Kate drew the gown from its silver tissue paper and held it in front of her.

"My love, it suits you to perfection. How very elegant you will be tonight, to be sure."

154

"Tonight?" Kate ceased her exuberant pirouette and looked at her hostess.

Lady Bellingham refused to meet her eyes. "What is happening tonight, ma'am?"

Lady Bellingham sat heavily down on a settee and began to wring her hands.

"My dear ma'am, whatever is the matter?" Kate quickly sat down beside her and captured her fluttering hands in her own.

Lady Bellingham embarked on a somewhat tangled explanation of what she had unwittingly let slip, "Oh, dear, I hadn't intended—that is, dear child, of course I was going to tell you. The earl, you know—"

Slowly Kate pulled her hands away. So that was why Lady Bellingham appeared so very upset. The good lady didn't have to finish, for Kate knew that tonight, dressed in her beautiful new gown, she was to be escorted by the earl of March to some occasion. Did Lady Bellingham think her dim-witted? From her first day in London, when her hostess had begun making oblique yet complimentary references to the earl of March, she had realized that it was he who was responsible for her presence here. She'd cursed her stupidity for not understanding from the first, when her father had been so adamant that she visit the fashionable Lady Bellingham, whose relationship to her own family was so tenuous as to be laughable. She hadn't even known of the relationship until Sir Oliver brought it up. She had passed from shock at the earl's sly maneuvering to outrage when

155

she discovered that even the lowest scullery maid considered her all but betrothed to the earl. She felt even now, as she gazed with a hard look at Lady Bellingham's crumpled features, that he had taken ruthless advantage of her. She had known that it was just a matter of time until he came to pay her court, and there was absolutely nothing she could do about it.

"Kate, my dear, I realize that you and the earl have had some sort of misunderstanding. But surely you must see that your marriage to him would bring you the greatest advantages. Come, child, don't be so upset." Lord, how had she ever allowed Julien to embroil her in such a wretched tangle? She'd always had a weakness for the boy, and look where it had landed her.

Kate turned away, angry at herself for being such a fool and at the earl for placing her willy-nilly in such an untenable position. It was on the tip of her tongue to unleash her anger and frustration at Lady Bellingham, but she realized the good woman really had as little to say in the matter as she did.

At the sound of Lady Bellingham's pained breathing, she turned quickly back.

"Please, ma'am, I'm sorry you're so upset by this matter. Here, let me fetch you your vinaigrette."

Lady Bellingham closed her eyes and leaned back against the pillows Kate had carefully placed behind her head. She managed to say with some semblance of calm,

156

"Kate, I vow you will much enjoy yourself. We are to see John Philip Kemble perform *Macbeth* at Drury Lane. The earl will arrive at eight o'clock this evening, and after the play we shall have a late supper at the Piazza, a most delightful place, my dear, I promise. It will be enjoyable, fascinating, really, and the earl is so very, well, manly and really rather charming."

Lady Bellingham halted her monologue, for Kate was staring blankly ahead of her, seemingly oblivious of what Lady Bellingham was saying.

Drat Julien. Why couldn't he have chosen a girl to wed who was at least not averse to his suit? Why must he have a girl who positively loathed him?

"At eight o'clock, did you say, ma'am?"

"Yes, my dear." Her hostess smiled. Finally, she thought, relieved, Kate is coming around to accepting the situation. And although she was quite pale and her green eyes looked strangely blank, she seemed now, at least, quite composed.

"Very well, ma'am," She bundled the gowns in her arms. "I do suppose I shall very much enjoy seeing Kemble."

Lady Bellingham didn't notice the bitterness in Kate's voice and silently congratulated herself on her deft handling of the situation.

13

Julien rose from his dressing table, satisfied with the exquisite result he'd achieved with his cravat, and allowed Timmens to remove an infinitesimal speck of dust from his black-satin evening coat.

"Does my appearance meet with your approval, Timmens? Ah, before you answer, please remove that Friday-face. It will make my cravat limp. Perhaps it would be a fine idea if you never married."

"There can be no one to outshine your lordship," Timmens said, eyes straight ahead. He'd discovered long ago that if he attempted to respond to his master's little jests, he fell into such a floundering tangle of words he was quite discomfited for days afterward. It appeared to him that the earl was quite amused if he simply pretended ignorance at his lordship's humor and treated his every utterance with the utmost seriousness.

"Let's hope you're right, Timmens," Julien remarked as he drew on his evening gloves. "Oh, yes, and don't wait up for me." Even though his valet dutifully nodded, Julien knew he would be waiting no matter the lateness of the hour, but he never failed to remind his valet not to do it.

It was with a light step that Julien descended the carpeted stairs to the elegantly marbled front hallway. He looked about him for a brief moment before nodding to a footman to open the front doors. It wouldn't be long now, he thought with satisfaction, before he would know if Kate found his town house to her liking.

Bladen, elegantly clad in the St Clair scarlet and white livery, hurried to open the door of the carriage for his master.

"Bladen, I find that I'm somewhat early. Pray inform Wilbury that he need be in no hurry." Julien sat back comfortably against the red-velvet cushions, stretching his long legs diagonally to the seat opposite him.

Wilbury was surprised by this instruction, being used to driving at a spanking pace no matter the occasion. He shrugged his shoulders and gently urged the magnificent matched bays to move slowly forward.

Julien smiled in anticipation of his long-awaited meeting with his future wife. It had been with some difficulty that he'd forced himself not to pay her a visit immediately upon her arrival in London. He realized that he must give her time, time primarily to discover that it was he who was responsible for bringing her here, and time to adjust to the idea that he had no intention whatsoever of letting her go. He knew full well that he'd placed her in a situation where her choices were very limited. She couldn't return to

Brandon Hall. He guessed that she was far too well-bred to behave in an openly churlish manner toward Lady Bellingham. He knew she would be furious at his treatment, but he quelled any pangs of conscience, certain that he was acting in her best interest and, of course, in accordance with his own wishes. He didn't like the taste of failure. He would make certain he never tasted it again.

He did, however, reproach himself momentarily about his devious maneuver of placing Eliza in Lady Bellingham's household to act as Kate's personal maid. He smiled in the dim light of his carriage at what Eliza had told him about Kate's behavior after her meeting with Lady Bellingham. Kate had been a caged tiger, Eliza had informed him, pacing her bedroom, hurling invectives at his head, until finally, her anger spent, she had grown quiet. "Too quiet, if you know what I mean, my lord. She's smart, is Miss Katharine, and she's no coward. She's madder at you than my ma ever was at my pa, even when he was drunk."

Actually, Eliza's description had fit well with his own prediction of Kate's reaction. Well, he would soon see. He had chosen Kemble's *Macbeth* deliberately for their first meeting, fairly certain that Lady Bellingham would drop off to sleep by the second act, leaving Kate for all practical purposes alone with him. She wouldn't be able to yell at him for fear of waking her kind hostess, nor would she be able to leave the box, for she was well

160

aware that such behavior would cause endless speculation. Besides, if she left the box, where would she go?

He grinned quietly to himself, remembering the speculation he himself had caused when he had invited Hugh and Percy to dine with him upon his return to London. That they had thought his scheme a little mad, in fact, became obvious as the evening wore on.

Hugh had finally said, "You must forgive us, Julien, for appearing to think your behavior strange."

"Beyond damned strange, if you ask me," Percy said.

Hugh said, "It's just that we've never seen you go to such lengths over a lady."

Hugh's mildly spoken observation brought a quick smile to Julien's face. "Do not trouble yourselves," he said cheerfully, "for believe me, I've quite given up trying to explain my damnably strange behavior. But I will have her, and I plan to do whatever necessary to get her. I fear that's all there is to it."

Hugh grinned. "Well, it appears that we must again offer you our congratulations."

Both men raised their glasses and Percy said, "To a well-fought and successful campaign. May the best man—or lady—win."

"The chit doesn't stand a chance," Hugh said. "No matter that red hair of hers."

"I hope she serves you up some nasty turns before you nab her, Julien. It would be good for your character."

Actually, he thought she'd given him

enough of a nasty turn already. He wondered how many more she'd give him.

Julien roused himself and pulled the white-satin curtain away from the carriage window. Lord, he thought, Wilbury was certainly taking him at his word. He settled back again against the luxurious cushions and let his mind wander to Yvette and Lady Sarah, reflecting with a certain degree of relief that he had no more to worry about in regard to either of them. He had most willingly given his blessing to Lord Riverton in his pursuit of Yvette. But the Lady Sarah had been a more serious matter.

"Julien, my dear, I'd quite thought that you'd decided to immure yourself forever in the country." Sarah had greeted him in her high, breathless voice. Always aware of gos-siping servants, she had led him to a small parlor on the second floor of Lord Ponson-by's mansion in Portsmouth Square. She was elegantly dressed in a riding habit of blue velvet and looked to be on the verge of leaving.

"You're going out?" He said, as he took her small hand for a brief moment and raised it to his lips.

She made a small, fluttering gesture, fanning her hand in front of her, and gave him an arch smile. "It will do Lord Daven-port no harm to wait half an hour," she said softly.

Julien realized that she hoped to provoke him to jealousy, but he felt only relief at the

162

mention of Lord Davenport. A man of great address was Sir Edward. Julien had never before thought of the affected viscount with such fondness.

Sarah moved away from him and sat down gracefully on a small sofa, patting the place beside her.

"Come, Julien, sit down. You make me quite nervous standing there like a great silent bear."

"Good Lord, Sarah. A bear?" He grinned at the unlikely simile. One of the lady's greatest charms lay in her ability to make peculiar, yet delightful, comparisons.

"That isn't at all important. Come, my dear, what's on your mind? Surely you're not here for an afternoon tryst?"

Julien didn't answer immediately. He was rather taken off guard when she filled the silence in a rather flat voice, saying, "My God, so that's it. You've met another lady."

How the devil could she possibly tell? Did women have special powers that enabled them to see through a man instantly? It was unnerving. "You're astute, Sarah. Indeed I've come to tell you, and hope that you will wish me happy."

Her blue eyes widened and she stared at him open-mouthed. "You... you plan to marry? *You*? This isn't just another flirtation?"

"Surely it isn't as great a surprise or shock as all that." He saw what he thought was hurt in her eyes before she turned her head away.

163

He didn't wish to admit it, but he knew that this abrupt ending of their liaison was not only a blow to her pride but also to her heart. At least he believed so. But who knew with women?

"Sarah, I'm indeed sorry, but that's the way of it." He spoke gently but was aware of a great impatience to be gone. Although Sarah tended to become romantically involved with her lovers, she had known as well as he that their affair would end in time. He was only sorry, knowing Sarah as he did, that it was not she who broke off their relationship.

"What is this remarkable girl's name?"

"You don't know her. She has lived all her life in the country. In fact, her father's estate lies near to St Clair. She will be coming to London to stay with Lady Bellingham. Ah, yes, her name is Katharine."

She heard a new note in his voice, deepening it, making it somehow tender. She turned back to him. Wonder and a goodly dose of incredulity were written on her face. "My God, Julien, you are in love with a girl from the country? An innocent? Good heavens, no one will believe it. Not you, my lord, who fancy your pleasures from ladies who know what's what and what they're about."

He frowned at that, disliking to see himself in such a light, but said, "Yes, I suppose I am in love with a girl from the country who is very innocent. But she isn't stupid or ignorant or boring."

"And you have come to end our affair," she stated flatly.

"Yes."

She rose abruptly and pressed her fingertips against her temples. "It won't last, you know. You'll tire of her as you do all your women. She might be a perfect saint, but it will happen. And when you're bored? You'll have a wife, and a wife isn't tossed aside as is a lover or a mistress. Well, you'll do as you please no matter what I say. It seems, my lord, that we have little else to say to one another."

Julien also stood up. In a swift motion he leaned down and kissed her gently on the forehead. He gazed deep into her china-blue eyes and said quietly, "I hope you will be kind to Katharine. She knows no one in London."

That wasn't bloody likely, she thought, but forced a very charming smile. "Of course I shall be kind to her, Julien. I wish you the best, you know that. And your Katharine. You had best go now before I become the fool."

It wasn't lost on Julien that she glanced covertly at the clock as she spoke.

Julien sat up with a start and saw Bladen patiently holding open the door of his carriage for him to alight.

"Thought you'd fallen asleep, my lord," Bladen said.

"Very nearly," Julien said, as he stepped down on the flagstone in front of the Bellingham mansion. He called to Wilbury, "Walk the horses, Davie, I can't be certain how long

165

I will be."

Julien was quickly admitted and shown to the drawing room.

"Oh, Julien, dear me, you have arrived, and quite none too soon. Oh dear, yes, come in, come in." Lady Bellingham straightened her dowager's lavender turban over the small, crimped curls and turned distractedly to him.

"I hope I find you quite well, Lady Bella," he said, his voice and expression at their charming best, crossing to where she sat and lightly touching his lips to her gloved fingers. He raised his eyebrows in question.

"Don't stare down your nose at me, Julien. I vow I can't help it if Katharine must needs spend hours getting dressed. And I thought that she'd changed her mind toward you. I should have known the two of you would cut up my peace. What can she be doing?"

Julien laughed and moved over to stand next to the fireplace. "Tell me more."

"A more ill-matched pair I have yet to see. Do help yourself to a glass of sherry. Lord knows what the girl is doing. Probably plotting to poison your supper."

Julien did as he was bid, careful to pour a very full glass for Lady Bellingham. She was fond of her sherry, particularly when she was undergoing an agitation of the nerves.

He handed her a glass and eased himself into a chair opposite her. "Have you been waiting long, ma'am?"

"Stupid question, my boy. You were expected at eight o'clock. It's now eight-thirty, and

166

I feel at least two years older."

"The performance doesn't begin until nine-thirty. We've lots of time."

"That is not the point, as you well know, young man. Whatever your mama would say to your antics I don't know. Why must a man be so perverse as to pick a chit who wants to see him with his throat cut?" She quickly downed a sizable gulp of sherry.

"Actually, I haven't yet spoken to her." He added quickly at the look of surprise in Lady Bella's eyes, "Never fear, ma'am. I shall pay her a visit as soon as our engagement is to be announced in the *Gazette*."

"At the rate you're proceeding, your hair will be as gray as mine." She heaved a deep sigh and swallowed the rest of her sherry.

When Julien had paid Lady Bellingham his unexpected visit almost three weeks ago, she had been eager to fall in with his plan. She had proudly seen her dear Anne, the last of her numerous brood, wed to the young Viscount Walbrough during the past summer and had grown quite bored resting her bones at home in the evenings. She had known Julien's mama before her marriage to Julien's papa, and she'd watched Julien over the years politely but disinterestedly turn away from each new season's crop of girls making their come-outs, including her own dear daughters. The thought of again being involved with a courtship, and particularly the idea of meeting the girl who had finally managed to bring his lordship to heel, had made her quite animated. As for the tenuous connection she shared with the Brandon family, that bothered her not at all. Indeed, she wasn't at all certain that Julien was right, that there was indeed a connection. Her only concern had been that Katharine would speak with that horrible northern accent and thus make both of them a laughingstock among the ton.

When Katharine had arrived on her doorstep, clad in the most horrid and outdated of clothes, she had groped for her vinaigrette, believing that the worst of her fears had been realized. The girl spoke in a soft, cultured voice, which was somewhat of a relief, but Lady Bellingham didn't set aside her vinaigrette until Kate proudly announced that she had a thousand guineas with which to purchase a new wardrobe. Her enthusiastic response was catching, and Katharine herself unbent considerably. But what a surprise it had been to Lady Bellingham when at every mention of the earl's name, the girl's magnificent green eyes had flashed red.

Julien asked Lady Bellingham matter-of-factly, "Has Katharine been a sad trial to you, ma'am?"

"Good gracious, no, Julien. It's just that, well, she's quite independent, but a dear girl, so bright and smiling—at least most of the time, when you're not the topic of conversation. She will lead you a merry chase, Julien, that's for sure. I only hope I am still alive to see it when it finally happens, but I'm not at all sure it will happen, given the way things

168

are going now—or not going."

"Believe me, ma'am, she's been confusing me, leaving me to twist and turn in the wind since the first time I met her, when she died at my feet."

"I beg your pardon, my boy?"

Upstairs, Eliza was in an agony. She said again, "Miss Katharine, his lordship and Lady Bellingham are awaiting you. Really, you must go downstairs."

"Yes, Eliza, I am aware of that fact. Pray inform his lordship and Lady Bellingham that I will be down directly. Perhaps not quite directly, but it will do."

"Yes, Miss, but do make it happen somewhat directly this time, all right?" Eliza sped toward the door, thought better of it, and turned. "Perhaps I can help?"

Kate cut her off. "No, no, I have just to fetch my gloves and cloak."

She didn't move from her dressing table until Eliza had closed the door behind her. Kate stared for a moment into the mirror at her pale, set face. She didn't look at all like herself, with her hair fashionably dressed, and the blue-velvet gown plunging low over her bosom and revealing, she thought, far too much white flesh, plump white flesh that was surely too much to show.

She knew she was purposely dallying, knew it was a childish thing to do, but she wasn't able to think of a more comprehensive revenge at the moment. She'd decided only a

169

short time before that she would suffer the earl's presence, for she appeared to have no other choice in the matter, but she wouldn't give him the satisfaction of showing overt distress or anger. She would face him with the coldest of dislike. She would be indifferent to him. She would ignore him. That would show him what she thought of him, and keeping him waiting was a very good beginning. She just wasn't certain how to achieve the coldest of dislike, but it would doubtless come to her soon enough.

Damn him, he'd turned from being her friend to being now more in the nature of an enemy, and she would see him in hell at the devil's right hand before she would give in to him.

She picked up her gloves and cloak and slowly made her way down the curving staircase. Smithers, the Bellingham butler, stood awaiting her at the door of the drawing room. Kate forced herself to halt a moment, schooled her face into an impassive expression, and waited for her heart to stop banging against her ribs.

Kate finally gave Smithers leave to open the door, and he observed that her nose rose a good three inches as she sailed past him into the drawing room.

It was with a distinct effort that Kate maintained her imperious pose, for the earl stood quite at his ease, leaning negligently against the mantelpiece. She wanted to hit him when she realized that he was amused by her.

She remarked, without wishing to, that he looked his usual elegant self, his black-satin evening clothes fitted to perfection. Damn his eyes, she thought, laughing at her even though he wasn't doing so out loud.

Julien didn't immediately move toward her but watched her closely as she swept into the room, the train of her velvet gown trailing behind her. How very beautiful she looked, not that he was surprised. The gown fitted her very nicely, but he wished her lovely breasts weren't so very visible to every gentleman's greedy eyes. Beautiful breasts, white, full, delicious. His fingers curled and his palms grew warm. He wanted very much to pull that gown to her waist and touch her and taste her. Her thick auburn hair was piled artfully on top of her head, and two long tresses lay gracefully over her bare shoulder.

"Oh, there you are, my love, at last, at very long last." Lady Bellingham's voice was a mixture of relief and reproach.

Kate swept what she hoped was a cold curtsy to the earl, at least she hoped it was cold and quite indifferent, then proceeded to pay him no further notice. She turned to Lady Bellingham and gave her a warm smile.

"I do hope, ma'am, that I'm not too late. Eliza had some difficulty with the buttons on my gown." Surely that was a nice touch, she thought, standing there in the middle of the room, hoping she presented a very stiff, very proud figure.

Lady Bellingham wished she had another

171

glass of sherry. Julien hadn't poured her enough, drat him.

Julien, however, seemed to think nothing was amiss and moved gracefully toward Kate.

"Good evening, Mistress Katharine. It is indeed a pleasure to see you again. I hope that you had a pleasant journey to London and have been enjoying the sights." He took her hand and brushed his lips lightly over her fingers.

14

A dull flush spread over her face. She snatched her hand away. "Indeed."

"I trust your buttons are now adequately arranged?"

"I said I was sorry that I was a trifle late."

"I don't recall asking you for an apology. In fact, I quite understand."

She wanted very much to cosh him on the head with a poker that was negligently set by the fireplace. He looked very calm, very much in control. She felt stupid and vulnerable and she wanted to scream at him, yes, perhaps even shoot him. "Do we continue this nonsense, my lord, or do we leave to see the play you have so graciously chosen?"

He leaned close to her and said softly, "Cold Kate. Indifferent Kate. Surely there must be something written somewhere about such a Kate."

Julien turned before she could answer and said to Lady Bellingham, "If you've finished your sherry, ma'am, perhaps we should be leaving. I'm certain," he added, glancing at Kate, "that you wouldn't want to miss the first act of *Macbeth*."

Julien helped Lady Bellingham to her feet and arranged the silk paisley shawl around her plump shoulders.

Lady Bellingham watched Kate turn on her heel and sail from the room, her chin so high she'd trip if she chanced to run into anything. She turned a troubled countenance to Julien. "Oh, dear. Perhaps I should speak to her, Julien. She's being quite provoking, you know."

"Oh, no, she's behaving admirably, I assure you. She's young, she's in a situation she can't control, and she's just learning to fence verbally. Already she does it quite well. On no account, ma'am, I beg of you, say anything to her." He took her arm and steered her after Katharine.

As they walked through the front door, Julien leaned down and said, "Believe me, Lady Bella, I have the situation well in control, and that, naturally, is what irks her to wishing she could strangle me and hurl my body into the Thames."

She saw the calm look of self-assurance on his face, and thought that perhaps he did. She felt a momentary twinge of concern over

173

Katharine. Although she was an ambitious mama, well versed in the art of matchmaking, she would never have dreamed of pushing her offspring into marriages that were distasteful to them. She shook her head in wonder. How any breathing cogent female wouldn't wish to marry the earl of March was more than she could fathom.

As Julien helped her into the carriage, she cast an uncertain glance at Kate, who was sitting ramrod-stiff, gazing out of the carriage window. She would have given up her medicinal dosage of sherry for a week to know what was going on in the girl's head.

Julien swung himself into the carriage and seated himself opposite Kate and Lady Bellingham. He tapped his cane on the roof of the carriage, and Wilbury whipped up the horses.

"So we are to see *Macbeth*," Lady Bellingham said brightly.

"Yes, ma'am. I do hope you approve my choice."

She wasn't particularly enthusiastic about seeing a Shakespearean play, for she found the dramatic lines, delivered with wild gesticulations, beyond her comprehension and thus rather boring. Her thoughts leaped ahead to the sumptuous supper they would enjoy after the play. Even Katharine at her most glacial wouldn't spoil that part of her evening.

Though London was rather thin of company this time of year, many of the ton having

174

followed the Regent to Brighton for the summer, there was still a sizable crowd to attend Kemble's performance. Lady Bellingham was able to wave to several acquaintances as they took their seats in the elegant box that Julien reserved each season.

Kate wasn't quite sure how it happened, but she found herself seated between Lady Bellingham and the earl. She turned her shoulder toward him, fastening her eyes on the stage. Despite her best efforts, however, she quickly became quite involved with Kemble.

When the curtain fell after the first act, Kate was dismayed to see that Lady Bellingham was gently dozing in her chair. She was uncomfortably aware of how close the earl was sitting to her. She tried to draw away, for his leg was but an inch from hers, but Lady Bellingham's ample figure prohibited it. She felt his eyes upon her, and she paled, hating herself even as she felt herself go white. He was big, too big, and she knew that he'd set himself upon a course and would do his best to bring her to heel.

"Are you enjoying the play, my dear?" he asked, leaning close to her.

She could feel the warmth of his breath on her cheek and was uneasily aware of something insidiously warm deep inside her. Her heart was pounding loudly; surely he must hear it. Without turning to him, she said, low and vicious, "It's quite tolerable, if only I could enjoy it fully. That is, if you were absent."

"Only tolerable? You surprise me, for I thought you quite animated over Kemble's performance, despite my presence. Know too, my dear, that you couldn't attend the theatre without a gentleman at your side. Since I am the devil you know, don't you prefer me?"

"A devil is a devil. I wish all of you in hell, where you belong, certainly not here with me."

"I really do wish you would face me. Although you have a lovely back, I would much prefer conversing to your face."

She didn't move.

He said, his voice ruminative, "I hadn't thought you a coward. It's a disappointment to have so misjudged your character."

She turned quickly in her seat, her mouth open, doubtless to shoot him verbally. He said quickly, "That's much better. You really must cultivate that look of innocent outrage, it makes your green eyes sparkle quite attractively, you know. Please don't turn away again, for I'll think you're afraid of me."

"Afraid of you? I'd just as soon split your gullet, my lord. Afraid, ha! Your perfidy passes all bounds. If I had you alone I would surely make you sorry for what you've done to me."

"Done to you? Surely I've done naught but very acceptable things for you. You're out of your father's house and with Lady Bellingham, surely a gracious hostess, though I imagine that you torment her quite enthusiastically when the poor lady happens to mention me."

She gave him a long, bitter look. "I wish you would go away, my lord. I told you very nicely that I wouldn't marry you. I meant it. I wasn't being coy. Please, just leave me alone."

"That's much better, though you're still not up to your former repartee. I feared that your wit had grown dull during my absence. Poor Bleddoes, he had not the wherewithal to keep pace with you. Rest assured, my dear, that I will keep you properly amused, when it pleases me."

She'd never met his like in her life. He was so different from the kind gentleman, nay, the kind *friend*, at St Clair. Here he was the ruler; here he commanded, he ordered, and everyone obeyed without a blink. She couldn't begin to understand him, nor could she seem to hit upon a strategy to reduce him to rubble. He was deliberately provoking her, taunting her, letting her know quite clearly that he was the one in control. Well, she couldn't let him succeed. She shrugged her shoulders as if in only slight irritation and turned to look at the elegant audience. She was immediately diverted.

"I do wish you would tell me who that oddly dressed man is who is waving at us. How very curious he is wearing a yellow-and-green-striped waistcoat."

"That's Mr Fresham. He's always fancied himself Brummell's greatest rival. You must see him walk, his heels are so high one fears to see him to topple over at any moment. One

177

fears or waits with gleeful anticipation, myself included."

"How altogether ridiculous. Men should appear as men, and not as painted peacocks. Someone really should take him in hand."

"Shall I take that for a compliment?" he said, humor and a good deal of satisfaction in his voice as he returned Mr Fresham's wave.

She raised her chin, managing to keep her mouth shut.

"You must take care, else you won't see the view of the world that we ordinary mortals have. Ah, my manners. Would you care for refreshment? Perhaps some champagne?"

"No."

"A lady who is not demanding. What a nice change. Now, what was I going to say? Oh, yes, I believe you told Lady Bellingham you wanted to enter the hallowed doors of Almack's. I have secured vouchers, and will escort you, and, of course, Lady Bella, tomorrow evening."

She trembled with indignation. She'd needed to be in London less than a week to know that his escort to Almack's would be tantamount to announcing their betrothal. Indeed, an announcement in the *Gazette* would be expected to follow but a few days after such an appearance.

She turned on him, all thoughts of pleasant indifference gone. "How dare you. I wouldn't dream of going to Almack's with you. Never, do you hear me? Never. You can't force me to go."

"I beg your pardon?" he asked, the picture of bewildered innocence, but he found he was looking at her breasts, pushed up by the tight banding beneath, very white and full breasts, beautiful breasts. His hands clenched. Dear God, he wanted her. He swallowed and shifted his position in his chair. He wanted her too damned much.

She was furious, he knew that, and he found it amusing, at least he did when he didn't want to rip her clothes off her and make love to her right here in his theatre box, perhaps against the curtained wall. Ah, and those beautiful breasts of hers were heaving with fury.

She was hissing now, not wanting to wake up Lady Bellingham. "My lord, I don't recall ever having evinced a desire to attend the dancing at Almack's. And you know quite well what your escort would imply, indeed promise, to all present."

It seemed to Kate at that moment that flickering lights shaped like tiny devils danced in his gray eyes. Her hands fisted. She raised her right hand, only to feel his fingers close about her wrist and pull her hand back down on her thigh. He held it there. She felt the heat of him, and that made her feel other things too, strange things that were frightening yet oddly tantalizing, but just for an instant. She tried again to free her fist from his grip.

He leaned close to her ear. "Now, my dear Kate, it wouldn't be seemly for a lady to strike a gentleman in so public a place. I might have to exact retribution if you did. Besides, you don't wish to embarrass your kind hostess."

"I'm not your dear Kate, damn you."

"Such language. However, I will accustom myself to it. Perhaps if you're with me enough, we'll improve upon your rather mild curses. And, dear Kate, you will soon be whatever I want you to be, very soon now."

She felt the strength of purpose behind his words. She was very afraid.

She bit her lower lip and turned away from him. With an effort she forced herself to say in a calmer voice, "Why won't you leave me alone? What is it you want of me?" A stupid question, she thought, hating herself, and quickly added, "I've told you I have no wish to wed anyone, not just you. I don't ever wish to wed. Please, my lord, believe me and leave me in peace."

He answered her in a low voice, without hesitation, "I care for you, Kate. If I really believed that you didn't care for me, I would withdraw, though unwillingly, for it would mean a continued life of unhappiness for you with your father. But I can't and I won't believe you're indifferent to me. I've watched you when you weren't aware of it. Your eyes give you away, that and your response to my kiss. You quite enjoyed my touching you, caressing you."

"I don't wish to wed you, Julien, no matter the assumptions you have dared to make

180

about my feelings."

"But you will wed me." His voice was very quiet, very firm.

"Your choice is a foolish one, Julien. You lie to yourself. It is only because I rejected you that you now want me. It is only your wounded man's pride. Stop looking at me like that. How can you want a wife who doesn't want you?"

He pulled her hand unwillingly from her lap and held it in an iron grip. "You must wed me, if for naught else than to escape the cruelty of your father."

She looked down at his long fingers closed tightly around her wrist. A man's hands, strong and hard. A man's hands, which could easily wield a whip. She heard her own voice as if from a great distance, "I don't wish to marry any man, Julien."

"That is unfortunate and, I think, untrue. But you now have no choice in the matter."

"You can't bend me to your will, Julien. You have evidence that my father has tried."

"My God, do you think I would ever hurt you?"

"You've humiliated me, Julien. That is worse than the physical pain of my father's cane."

His grip loosened on her wrist. She quickly pressed her advantage. "You must beware, my lord, that someone doesn't place a higher bid with my father. Then your investment in this charade of yours would all be for naught."

He wanted at that moment not to kiss her and fondle her but to shake her until her teeth rattled. She'd made him lose his control, and since he realized that he had lost it, he didn't put a guard on his tongue. "Damn you, don't be a fool, Katharine Brandon. I've borne with your bloody antics quite long enough. If you push me further, I'll forcibly drag you out of here, perhaps to my yacht in Southampton. After several days in my company, my dear, you'll be quite willing to accept me as your husband."

"Since you're a licentious rake, I suppose that would be your style. Well, I won't let you do such a thing, so you can just forget your threats. They won't work with me."

Julien took a firm grip on himself. She was good, she'd gotten him to lose every shred of his control. She wouldn't ever bore him, that was certain. He had failed to intimidate her. It was both irritating and exhilarating.

She took his silence for defeat. At last she'd bested him. Unaccountably, she found herself swallowing convulsively, tears very near the surface. Her victory seemed a hollow one, which was surely strange.

"Good evening, Julien, Miss Brandon. I hope you're enjoying the play. And you, Miss Brandon, I trust you're enjoying London?"

She stiffened and Julien cursed silently under his breath at Hugh's unfortunate interruption. He forced a smile of welcome though and said easily, "Good to see you, Hugh. Won't you please join us?" He shot her

182

a look of pure mischief. "Katharine and I have just been discussing the merits of yachts."

"Ah, yes, your lovely *Fair Maid* down at Southampton. A very elegant yacht, Miss Brandon." It was then that he noted her flushed face and realized that both of them wished him to be far and away from here. He said quickly, backing away, "I believe I see someone waving to me. I will take my leave now. Indeed a pleasure, Miss Brandon, to see you again."

He took a step backward, freedom within his reach, when, to the chagrin of the entire company, Lady Bellingham jerked her head up, blinked her eyes, and announced in a flurry, "Oh, dear. I declare, I must have dropped off for a moment. Lord Launston, how charming to see you, dear boy. Have you been keeping Julien and Katharine company?"

Hugh took a deep breath, cast an apologetic glance at Julien, and bowed low to Lady Bellingham. "Your servant, ma'am. Actually, I was just about to take my leave."

"He noticed a friend waving to him," Julien added, eyes laughing.

Kate turned to Hugh and said with the sweetest voice Julien had ever heard from her, "We would count it a great honor, sir, if you would stay awhile with us. Surely your friend will understand."

"I agree," Lady Bellingham said. "Come, my boy, sit beside me and tell me all the latest gossip." She patted the empty chair beside her, and Hugh, defeated, sat down.

Kate knew but a fleeting moment of victory, for the box was small, and although Hugh was slender, they were forced to move their chairs even closer together. She felt Julien's thigh pressing against hers, and the gentle pressure sent again that strange tingling sensation coursing through her, landing deep in her belly. She looked at him, frowning. She didn't like it. She didn't want him near her. Fortunately, many of the huge branches of candles were extinguished at that moment, the light became quite dim, and the curtain rose for the second act.

Julien had felt her reaction and now he sat back, a self-satisfied smile on his face. For the remainder of the play he indulged in various pleasurable fancies, having to do most of them with her naked, sprawled on her back, her glorious hair fanned about her head, and him above her, caressing her, coming deeply inside her. Ah, and there was a smile on her face and her arms were about his back.

Had anyone later asked him to discuss the merits of Kemble's performance, he would have been quite unworthy of the task.

Kate didn't awake until nearly noon of the next day. She felt surprisingly well rested and alert despite the fact that she'd not fallen into her bed until well after two o'clock in the morning. She rose, eased her feet into slippers, and pulled on a wrapper. She thought of Julien and jerked the bell cord with more

184

violence than was necessary.

Eliza appeared but a few moments later, carrying a tray with crunchy rolls and hot chocolate. "Good morning, Miss Katharine. Cook just baked the rolls for you. Piping hot they are."

"Thank you, Eliza."

"Your new green-velvet gown has just arrived, just in time for you to wear to Almack's this evening. I went around to Madame Giselle's myself this morning to fetch it, Lady Bellingham being in quite a taking that it wouldn't be ready in time."

The crunchy roll seemed to revert to dry dough in Kate's mouth. She lowered her head so that Eliza wouldn't see her fear and her anger. Almack's. She could easily imagine the curious stares and the smug glances, the whispered comments behind gloved hands.

"Then you know that Lady Bellingham is planning to attend Almack's this evening?"

"Oh, yes. Walpole is in quite a tizzy about how best to arrange her ladyship's hair." She picked up a brush to comb out the tangles from Kate's messed hair. She fancied Walpole was jealous of her attending Miss Katharine.

Damn him, Kate thought furiously, thumping down her cup of chocolate on the tray. He'd told her himself about their attendance at Almack's this evening so that she wouldn't have the opportunity to refuse Lady Bellingham, were the good lady the one to suggest it.

Still glorying in Walpole's supposed jealousy, Eliza brushed her long, thick hair, quite

185

oblivious of her mistress's anger. "If you wouldn't mind, I'd like to dress your hair high on top of your head, in curls. You will be the most beautiful lady present, for I am quite good at it, you know."

15

The day was already half gone, and the remainder passed much too quickly for Kate. She paced restlessly back and forth in her room, alternately shaking her fist in the direction of Grosvenor Square, and cursing herself for her inability to find a solution to her most immediate problem. She felt that she might as well be an actor on the stage saying lines and going through motions provided solely by the earl. If only there were a way she could best him, if only—

Eliza interrupted her mental rantings to announce that a young gentleman was downstairs asking to see her.

"He didn't give his name, just said that you'd want to see him. He's a nice-looking young gentleman, if you don't mind my saying so, quite jolly too."

Puzzled at this, Kate quickly patted some strands of hair into place, smoothed her gown, and hurried downstairs to the drawing room.

"Harry!" She stood poised an instant in the doorway before running into her brother's arms. "Oh, my dear, it is so good to see you. Whatever are you doing here? I had no idea, oh, dear, it's so good to see you." She buried her head against his shoulder and wrapped her arms tightly around his neck. At last. An ally who would help her escape.

Harry hugged her briefly, but it was obvious he was embarrassed. "Lord, Kate, of course it's me."

He firmly took her shoulders and pushed her back. He looked down into her glowing face and said cheerfully, "What looks you are in, little sister. I see that town life agrees with you. You must be cutting quite a dash. I'm proud of you." He held her at arm's length and critically surveyed her modish yellow-muslin gown, an appraising gleam of appreciation in his eyes.

"Oh, the gown, it's nothing. Of a truth, Harry, I would much prefer my breeches and my old hat."

"Now, old girl, stop squeezing me like an orange, you'll ruin my new waistcoat."

Kate laughed and stepped back to look her brother. "Well, I say, Harry, it is you who are looking terribly smart. Those yellow stripes quite dazzle the eye."

Harry beamed at her. "I always knew you had good taste, my dear. Now, don't sidetrack me. You certainly know why I'm here, you sly puss. My congratulations to you, little sister. I must say, though, I was surprised to hear from Father that you had attached the earl of March. Quite a feat, yes, indeed. How proud I am of you." In truth, Harry had been very nearly speechless at the news. His Kate getting married, his little sister. But now as he looked down at her, he realized that she was quite beautiful, certainly lovely enough for an earl. Dressed in the height of fashion, she already looked grand enough to be a countess.

"Father wrote you?"

"Don't look so surprised. Of course he did. Quite right of him to do so, you know. Come, let's sit down. You can't leave a guest standing in the middle of the room. I will tell you all about it, and then you must tell me how you managed to attach the earl."

She gritted her teeth. She gazed at her brother's open, smiling face for a moment, bit her lower lip, and held her tongue. Neither of them talked of anything of consequence until she'd served Harry a glass of sherry and sat herself down beside him.

"Now, Harry, tell me what our father wrote and why you are here." Her voice was a trifle hard, but she couldn't help it.

"I got a letter from Father just last week. Told me in great detail how the earl wanted you to gain some town polish before your wedding."

Town polish. The lying, perfidious sod. She made a choking sound into her sherry.

"There, there, Kate. I know you must have difficulty believing your good fortune."

188

"Yes, yes, Harry, certainly, please continue. Tell me all that Father told you."

"I must say, Kate, the settlement the earl made to Father made my head spin. Father wrote that the earl is not only settling his debts but that he also wished to buy my colors. Lord, I never hoped for this." She could easily picture what was in her brother's mind. Harry astride a magnificent black charger, dressed in a dashing hussar's uniform.

Indeed, she was very nearly right, and Harry pulled himself away unwillingly from his delightful vision. He continued in happy ignorance, "Father also sent me some money. So I got myself rigged up and came to London. I got here just this morning."

"Morning? But it's now afternoon, Harry. Why didn't you come to see me when you arrived?" Harry as an ally, as a rescuer, was fast fading as a possibility. Damnation, did the earl think of everything? He had bought her father, and now he had made Harry's fondest wish come true. It seemed that she was quite alone, but that was, in truth, something she was used to.

Harry leaned over and patted her hand with brotherly affection. "Now, old girl, don't be miffed. You must know that it was only proper that I pay my respects first to my future brother-in-law."

"You what?"

"I went to see the earl," Harry repeated with great patience. "Lord, what a mansion he has in Grosvenor Square. But of course you've been there, probably more times now than you can count."

As Kate didn't deny this, being quite unable to fit two words together at the moment, Harry continued serenely, "You know, Kate, I was certainly wrong about his lordship. Dashed nice fellow, not at all cold or conceited or patronizing. Why, we spent quite two hours together discussing the regiment I wanted to be in and, of course, other things."

Harry paused and looked at his sister. She was no longer the wild hoyden, dressed in boy's breeches, ready for any lark. She looked positively regal. He wondered at her quietness, for it was quite unlike her. But having spent the entire morning with the elegant and very charming earl of March, he decided that her silence was properly due to her modesty.

"You're in favor of this match, Harry?"

"Good God, girl, do you have bats in your mental belfry?" He eyed her warily for a moment. "All right, out with it. What's wrong with you? I've never known you to ask stupid questions before."

She saw the happy flush on her brother's handsome face and gave her head a tiny shake. Harry would think her mad if she were now to tell him that she found the very idea of marriage to the earl abhorrent. No, more than that, frightening. And even though she didn't understand it, it was nonetheless true. And how could she tell him? The earl had swooped down into Harry's life and granted him his greatest wish.

"This is deuced odd, love. I've never seen you succumb to womanish vapors. Lord, Kate, you will make the perfect countess. Here now, you're not thinking you won't be up to his weight, are you?"

Kate clutched her hands together in her lap and gazed at her brother, the only person she loved in the world. She would not—indeed, she could not—risk losing his affection. She forced a smile. "You know I'm up to any man's weight, Harry. Why, didn't I kill you regularly at our early-morning duels?"

To forestall further comments on her marriage to the earl, she said, "We go to Almack's tonight. Will you accompany us?" She'd spoken lightly, with no real interest, but in that moment, she realized that if Harry also were to be her escort, it might perhaps lessen the impact of Julien's presence with her.

Harry stared incredulously at her and exclaimed in a voice of loathing, "Almack's? Good God, what a repellent notion. It isn't at all my style. No, don't get all down in the mouth. I'll come by tomorrow and we'll go riding. The earl offered me one of his hacks. We'll go riding in the park and rub shoulders with all the ton."

It was the final blow. "Oh no, you wouldn't use one of the earl's horses, Harry. No, surely not."

"Don't be a half-wit. It's quite proper, my dear. After all, he will be my brother-in-law in

191

a week's time."

A week's time? By all that was holy and unholy, the earl had already set a date and announced it to her brother?

Harry clasped her hand and exclaimed happily, "Good Lord, my hoydenish little sister a countess. You deserve it, Kate, don't ever think you don't. Only one more week, my dear, just one more week."

Kate had not yet been to King Street and she found the rows of buildings, including Almack's, not to be as grand as she'd supposed. Almack's had been so touted that she had half expected to see a structure as impressive as Carlton House. She had to admit, though, once they entered the enormous entrance hall filled with branches of glowing candles and lined with very superior-looking footmen, who gave the impression that they were conferring a favor by admitting guests, that she seemed indeed to be stepping into the very inner sanctum of society. As Julien divested her of her cloak, she heard strains of a waltz coming from one of the rooms that branched off the hall and wondered with a sinking feeling in her stomach how many people would be there to witness her arrival on his damned immaculate sleeve.

She knew she looked particularly fine this evening in her high-waisted green-velvet gown that hung straight to the floor, accentuating her slender figure. The yards of green muslin were broken by rows of white

Valenciennes lace delicately sewn to fit snugly under her breasts.

She unconsciously fingered the exquisite emerald necklace with its intricate gold setting that circled her neck. It was indeed kind of Lady Bellingham, she thought, to have lent her the beautiful emerald set. There were also a bracelet and earrings. The jewels sparkled with mysterious green lights, seeming to enhance the whiteness of her skin and matching perfectly the color of her gown.

As Julien turned back to her, she was aware of the open expression of admiration on his face, and she felt a moment of power over him. She met his gaze with a cold stare. Let him admire her as much as he wished, she thought with an elegantly indifferent shrug.

She graciously gave him her arm, and Julien guided her and Lady Bellingham down the long hall and into a noble, high-ceilinged room where the glitter of the candles was rivaled by the sparkling gems and bright-colored apparel of the assembled company, who were dipping and bowing in the steps of a country dance. Rows of chairs covered in burgundy brocade lined stark-white walls, and were occupied for the most part, by turbaned dowagers, who formed small, chattering groups.

It seemed to her when the portly white-haired announcer cleared his throat and called out each of their names that the music grew softer and many eyes turned in their direction. Julien leaned toward her and said close to her ear, "Well, my beautiful shrew, didn't I tell you that you would outshine all the lovely ladies present?"

"If I'm such a shrew, my lord, then you must be quite mad in your intentions."

"Oh yes, quite mad. I've known it for some weeks now. We're well matched, you and I."

In a calculated gesture, Julien drew her arm through his and escorted both ladies to the far side of the room to the spot where the patronesses of Almack's held their court. He realized that his party's arrival was causing an instant sensation, as the rumors of his imminent marriage to an unknown girl from the country had provided polite society with choice conversation for the past week.

Of the four patronesses, only the Countess Lieven and Mrs Drummond Burrell were present this evening. The raven-haired Countess Lieven, wife to the Russian ambassador, raised her dárk eyes and gazed at Kate with open curiosity. Lady Bellingham, long acquainted with both patronesses, greeted them and moved aside for Julien to present Katharine.

Himself a favorite with both ladies for some years, Julien said with easy familiarity, "Countess, Mrs Burrell, I would like to present Miss Katharine Brandon. She is new to London, and this is her first visit to Almack's."

Kate repeated polite words to the Countess Lieven, who made a rather startling picture in pink satin and gauze. The countess smiled at her, not unkindly, and Kate turned to Mrs Drummond Burrell. The lady was appraising her coldly, her hawklike nose thrust upward to a height that even Kate had not achieved. An idea burgeoned in her mind, and she executed it without further examination.

Proffering only an infinitesimal curtsy, she observed to Mrs Drummond Burrell in her coldest and most distant voice, "How very odd. Almack's is not as elegant as I was led to believe."

Lady Bellingham froze in shocked silence and stared aghast at Katharine. She would have been thankful had the floor opened beneath her feet and dropped her into oblivion.

Julien gave no sign of having noticed anything extraordinary in Kate's remark and stood quite at ease waiting to see what would happen. If only she realized that he didn't care if she insulted the Regent himself. If she created a scandal, why, he was powerful enough in society to dampen it. Or even if he wasn't powerful enough, he didn't care if the both of them were pariahs. Let her play her games.

The Countess Lieven gasped aloud and darted an expectant glance at Mrs Drummond Burrell. Mrs Drummond Burrell, however, didn't move a muscle in the tense moment of silence that followed.

Kate thrust her chin higher and waited to see the result of her outrageous comment. Surely Julien must be acutely embarrassed at her behavior. Well, she would show him that she wasn't a helpless female, a puppet to be dangled willy-nilly on his string. Perhaps he would realize that he was mistaken in her character and pack her back to the country.

To the infinite surprise of all present, the haughty mask Mrs Drummond Burrell presented to the world loosened and her thin lips parted in a slight smile. Reputed to be the most insufferably proud lady in London society, which indeed she was, she realized in a flash that at last she had found a kindred spirit. She dismissed the scathing set-down that had instantly come to her lips. Long used to simpering young girls and ladies of her own rank who were openly terrified of her scathing tongue, she saw with something of a shock that here was someone, indeed a mere girl, who wasn't in the least afraid of her. A girl, in fact, who was openly provoking her.

What a novel occurrence. A sense of humor that she had thought long dead was resurrected, and she replied with a hint of amusement, "Indeed, you are right, my dear, but you see, Almack's is considered almost a shrine, an old revered meeting place for society. Though the rooms aren't as elegant as one could wish, we hope that you won't quite disdain it, and turn your attention rather to the people you will meet here."

Kate, who was quite unaware of the terrifying rule over society held by Mrs Drummond Burrell, decided after a brief moment of disappointment that the lady was but another supporter of the earl's. Thus she did not unbend and flush to the roots of her hair at her rudeness, as those present expected. Rather, she turned and gazed briefly, with a distinct air of boredom, around the room. Very slowly, she raised incredulous eyebrows, turned back to the lady, and said, "Indeed, ma'am, I suppose that you could call this place a shrine. Or perhaps a relic would be more fitting. It appears that many of the people also fit that category."

She would have said more, but she chanced from the corner of her eye to see Lady Bellingham's face. She looked ready to collapse, her face as red as the ruby on her right hand. She didn't want her own social ostracism to descend on the hapless Lady Bellingham. Thus she merely stared with complete indifference at the two patronesses, shrugged carelessly, and turned away.

16

Mrs Drummond Burrell found herself vastly entertained by this unconventional girl, though perhaps "unconventional" was a bit too tame a word for her. She herself had just been blatantly insulted, as had many of the other ladies and gentlemen present. But she couldn't bring herself to dash down the girl. She smiled, making the Countess Lieven, the silly woman, gasp with surprise. She said to Kate in a not unkind voice, "Stay for a moment and converse with me, my dear. The earl will, I'm certain, not begrudge me your company for a few moments."

Julien wanted to laugh aloud at the look of utter bewilderment on her face but managed to bow deeply and say easily, "Miss Brandon finds herself honored, ma'am. I gladly relinquish her to you."

"My dear St Clair, I am quite certain that you don't relinquish your betrothed willingly, but five minutes with her vastly interesting and unpredictable company shouldn't leave you quite downcast."

Julien met Mrs Drummond Burrell's eyes with a distinct gleam in his own, turned to Lady Bellingham, who stood with her mouth unbecomingly open. "Come, ma'am, we will leave Katharine and refresh ourselves with a glass of orgeat."

Lady Bellingham promptly thrust her arm through his. It was she who bore him off.

Kate felt completely at sea. It didn't seem possible that she'd not managed to disgrace herself. She was being asked to enjoy a civilized conversation with a forbidding lady whom she had grossly insulted. It was impossible, but it had happened. She'd been done in, and she had no idea how it had come about. Defeated, she dropped her cold disdain and seated herself gracefully in the chair next to Mrs Drummond Burrell. As she felt no fear of the lady, she spoke openly and, had she but realized it, quite charmingly. She noticed the look of awe on the Countess Lieven's face, but not understanding, she dismissed it and gave her full attention to the questions of Mrs Drummond Burrell.

It was like a dousing of cold water when Mrs Drummond Burrell remarked, "The St Clair emeralds look as if they had been made especially for you, my dear. They always reminded me of heavy green stones on Caroline's unprepossessing neck. Caroline is, of course, to be your mother-in-law, the late earl's wife," she added, turning back to Kate. She didn't notice that Miss Brandon's color had mounted, and continued to enthusiastically enumerate the shortcomings of the dowager countess of March, a weak ninny she'd always despised.

It was just as well that Mrs Drummond Burrell didn't expect any interruptions in her monologue, for Kate was so furious at the earl's latest underhanded maneuver that it took all the control she could muster to cloak her anger from the patronesses. How very devious of Lady Bellingham to conveniently forget to mention that the emeralds belonged to the earl. She looked down at her reticule, wishing it was a club.

Mrs Drummond Burrell smiled with great understanding at Miss Brandon's distraction.

She looked up to see the earl approaching and leaned over and patted Kate's hand. "Your betrothed approaches, my dear. Although the earl of March has been the object for many years of matchmaking mamas and indeed is a charming young man, I confess that I think him more the lucky one. You will make a fine countess, and I look forward to many more meetings with you. Your observations are most unexpected."

Julien heard her last words and smiled with undisguised affection at Kate. The look was not lost on the two ladies, and for a brief instant they were drawn back in time, dusting off such magic moments of their own.

"I am, of course, in absolute agreement with you, ma'am. I count myself the most fortunate of men."

Julien offered Kate his arm, and she rose and stood beside him.

Mrs Drummond Burrell nodded her dismissal and said to Kate as she turned to go,

"After you return from your wedding trip, I expect to see you, my dear."

Kate didn't realize it, but from that moment, her success in the ton was assured. Her intimate conversation with Mrs Drummond Burrell was remarked by all present, and as Julien led her on the rounds of introductions, she was treated with a respect bordering upon awe. Because she was seething with anger, she responded with the most brief and clipped of phrases. Ladies and gentlemen vied to meet the seemingly proud but, of course, interesting Miss Katharine Brandon, even though she was only the daughter of a mere baronet and, rumor had it, utterly without a dowry.

When the band struck up a waltz, Julien turned in the direction of the two patronesses and arched his brow upward in a silent question. Mrs Drummond Burrell waved her hand and nodded, a benign smile on her face.

"Come, Kate, dance with me. As you have observed, it's mandatory for you to have the consent of the patronesses to dance the waltz. I have just secured that permission."

He whirled her around to the fast German music and felt her body slowly relax against him as she gracefully followed his lead. He bent down, and her soft hair tickled his chin. "What, little termagant, no words of abuse this evening?"

Her head jerked up. "Damn you, my lord, this isn't a play, I'm not so easily won as Petruchio's Kate. Indeed, I believe her to have been an utter coward with no spine at all."

His response was to tighten his grip about her waist. He was pleased to see a dull-red flush creep over her pale cheeks.

"You see, Kate," he whispered close to her ear, "though you are but a girl, innocent in the ways of men and women, we both know that you are all fire and passion beneath that cold facade. Admit this to yourself, my dear. Stop fighting me. You must not be afraid, Kate, I will teach you. Never be afraid of me or the pleasure I offer you."

Never before had he spoken to her with such ill-disguised intent. She suddenly felt very weak, and she could sense the color drain from her face. She tried to pull away from him, but he held her fast.

"Don't give the world cause for comment. We are betrothed and in their eyes the happiest of couples. I'll be gentle with you and easy and slow. You'll be crying with pleasure before I come into you. Trust me in this. Don't be afraid of me or what I will give you as your husband."

"You bastard, I wish I had a whip. You shouldn't speak to me in such a way."

"When we're married, I will give you that opportunity," he said, bending his head close to hers. "Ah, a whip in your hands. How I shall enjoy wresting it from you. Will you still fight me? I shall enjoy that as well, for a while at least."

"I hate you, Julien. Don't think I'm such a

fool, I know now that these are the St Clair emeralds. Oh God, I hate you."

"You must take heed, my dear, not to become repetitious in your conversation. You wouldn't wish to bore your husband."

He sounded calm as a clam, almost indifferent, as if he were instructing a student of very backward intellect. Bereft of speech, she narrowed her eyes and looked over his left shoulder. He merely shrugged and looked amused.

"Do allow me to congratulate you on your most unusual performance for Mrs Drummond Burrell. Unfortunately, you picked quite the wrong person on whom to try your antics. Ah, yes, you hoped to disgrace yourself, didn't you? Let me tell you, my dear, that the good lady finally met someone more cold and haughty than herself. A strange coincidence, isn't it? Ah, yes, let me make something very clear to you. Even if you had managed to enrage the lady and she had sent both of us from Almack's with loud curses, it wouldn't have gained you anything. I don't care if society turns its back on me. All I want is you, and you I will have."

Kate wondered at that moment if she had been born under an unlucky star. Everything seemed to go awry. She looked up at him, her eyes filled with misery. "Why do you torment me?"

In that moment, he was sorely tempted to throw his masterful stratagem to the winds and comfort her, perhaps even to plead his case with her again. But he caught himself, realizing that it would be a fatal mistake.

"What would you, Kate? Shall I languish at your feet like that fool Bleddoes? Let you treat me as you would a fractious puppy?" He shook his head, his strong white teeth flashing. "Oh no, my dear, it's a strong hand you need, and I'm the only one to suit you."

"I will surely make you sorry for this."

He merely arched an elegant brow and whirled her faster and faster until she was panting for breath.

When at last the interminable waltz ended, Kate looked up to see herself being regarded with shy admiration by a young man clad in colorful regimentals. He reminded her of Harry. She smiled most beguilingly at the young man and watched him begin a hopeful approach.

"Another Bleddoes, Kate. I pray that you don't break his heart to spite me." He enthusiastically waved the young man forward.

The young man said shyly, "If you don't mind, my lord, may I dance with Miss Brandon?"

"Not at all. My betrothed is very much taken with young men in uniform, as her brother is shortly to join the cavalry."

"I believe, sir, that it is from me you should seek your permission."

"Don't lead him a merry dance," Julien said, as Kate took firm hold of the young man's arm and led him away.

He stood quietly for a moment as he

watched her look with the most appealing expression at her young gallant. She was flirting outrageously to spite him. His mouth curved into a rueful smile. He could not imagine ever being bored by this one girl who had managed to capture every feeling inside him, even creating new feelings he'd never known before, and he knew that there would never be another woman for him, ever.

"So that's the dashed girl you're going to marry, eh, Julien?"

Julien turned to see his aunt, Lady Mary Tolford, standing at his elbow.

"Good evening, Aunt. You look charming tonight. Yes, that is Miss Katharine Brandon. Have you ever seen a more beautiful girl?"

"Well, I'll say this for you, Julien. Your taste in women, like that of your grandfather, is impeccable. Yes, my boy, certainly she's pleasant to look at, but you know, the girl doesn't look much of a breeder to me. Far too slender. Look at those long legs, like a boy's. Now her hips, it's difficult to tell. What do you think? Will she give you as many children as you wish?"

He looked down at her. "Surely you know you're shocking me, Auntie. I'm not even married, and you're contemplating the room necessary for my betrothed to carry a child. Good Lord, you're already planning to fill my nursery with future earls."

Lady Mary tapped her fan on his sleeve. "The St Clairs are a long, proud line, Julien. You've picked a lady of quality, no doubt

205

about that, but there are heirs too, my boy. It's your duty, and about time, too, I might add."

"My dear Aunt, you need have no fears. Even though I can't yet confirm or deny the exact width of her hips, I promise you an heir within the year. Does that suit you?"

"Yes, it suits me, I suppose. Have you informed your mama that she is about to become a mother-in-law? I'll wager she became hysterical."

Fortunately, Julien had just that afternoon paid a long-overdue visit to his fond parent and informed her of his imminent marriage. She did resort to her smelling salts upon hearing he was to wed a Brandon, and it had taken him a good half-hour to soothe her from tears and sighs and little quivers, at which she excelled.

"Yes, Aunt, I have seen Mama, and no, she didn't have hysterics. She did rely, however, on very strong smelling salts and numerous soothing murmurs from me."

Lady Mary, quite his favorite relative, gave a crow of delight, envisioning with some satisfaction the look of shock on her sister-in-law's face. She had always thought Lady Caroline a fool, and now that the dowager countess was getting older, she had taken to quacking herself with every conceivable medicine. As the state of her health was also Lady Caroline's favorite topic of conversation, Lady Mary had found her own nerves near to the breaking point, and thus, recently, had paid fewer and fewer visits to Brook Street.

"Now, my dear Aunt, if you will excuse me, I must detach my betrothed from that gay young buck. It's my duty, as you said, and before I do anything of a siring nature, I must first wed the lady."

Lady Mary gave Julien a light rap on the arm with her fan. "At least you want to marry her. That has to be a miracle indeed. Be off with you, rogue."

Julien was careful to ensure that he danced three waltzes with Kate. Two waltzes between an unmarried couple caused wild speculation. Three placed the gold band on her finger. He wondered when Kate would discover this fact and curse him straight to hell. He hoped she did. He would find it vastly entertaining.

Evidently she was not informed, for the remainder of the evening she maintained a stony silence in his presence, pointedly ignoring even the most provoking of comments. Even when he informed her matter-of-factly that he had procured a special license so they could be wed within the week and that her trousseau would be arriving at the Bellingham mansion on the morrow, she kept her eyes downcast and refused to favor him with a reply. He thought at first that she was employing a new tactic, but as the evening continued, he wondered if she was finally coming to her senses and had given up her losing battle with him. It was very late when he deposited Lady Bellingham and Kate at the Bellingham mansion.

Only later, as he lay comfortably in his own bed, did it occur to him to worry about her behavior. She'd been too pliant, too docile, her surrender almost too immediate and complete. He'd not known her long. But he *knew* her. Something wasn't right, he knew it, but didn't know what it was. He didn't sleep well that night.

As for Kate, she didn't sleep at all. She was far too busy packing her portmanteau and making her plans. Had the dashing young officer in his colorful regimentals, whose name she couldn't remember, known of the daring idea he was giving the beautiful young lady, he wouldn't have been so forthcoming in his praise of Paris. Kate was but half listening as they danced, too aware of Julien's eyes following her around the dance floor. But she smiled prettily up at the young man, and he felt emboldened to speak of his adventures in a Paris now freed from Napoleon's influence. He'd been astounded at the gaiety of the French people, the prosperity that was restored under Louis, and above all, the enthusiastic attitude of the Parisians toward the English, whom they now regarded as their liberators.

It was a short time later, as she stood drinking a glass of orgeat, that the promise of the young officer's words struck her forcibly. She'd done naught but fail. The earl had outdanced her at every turn, not just on the dance floor. She, in turn, had danced to his tune quite long enough. It was time she took matters into her own hands.

Why shouldn't she go to Paris? She'd always told herself that she wished to be her own mistress. Surely she would be the most despicable of hypocrites if she didn't jump at the chance to be free forever not only of her father but also of the earl. It didn't take long for her to convince herself that only a coward would let such an opportunity slip by.

As she sat now in her darkened room, she recalled the earl's last words to her about her trousseau. Let him speak smoothly and make his damned plans. Let him do whatever he wanted. He could obtain a dozen special licenses for all she cared. It didn't concern her. He could, in short, go directly to the devil. She would be far away, free of him.

But to do what, to be what? A vision of herself in a foreign land, alone, rose in her mind. She felt a wave of apprehension and a taste of fear. "No," she said aloud to her shadowed bedchamber. "I'll find employment and be quite comfortable. I'm not stupid. I can work and work hard. I'll survive, and I'll be free." She spoke French passably well and had sufficient accomplishments to make a position of governess not out of the question.

She folded a pair of stockings and stuffed them into the portmanteau. She remembered the thousand pounds, obviously given to her father by Julien to pass on to her for a new wardrobe. If only she'd had the knowledge then that she did now. His damned money and she'd spent nearly all of it. She lit a candle and searched methodically through her dresser and reticule. After some moments she scooped up what money she'd found and sat cross-legged on her bed. Uncertain what it cost to reach Paris, she decided it best to be overgenerous in her estimates. This deduction made, she was left staring with some dismay at four guineas. She frowned, but held hope nonetheless. She would simply have to find employment very quickly. And was she not an Englishwoman, one of the liberators of the French, who now loved the English and welcomed them with enthusiasm?

She drummed her fingers and thought of how she would travel to Paris. Though she knew nothing of coach schedules from London to the coast, she reasoned that surely there were such vehicles leaving early in the morning. Once at the coast, she should have no problem finding a packet to take her to France. And how long would that take? She hadn't the foggiest notion. And once in Calais, or wherever she ended up, how would she get to Paris? Another question to which she had no answer. She refused to worry about it.

She thought of the scandal that would descend from her disappearance. And Julien. He would finally receive his just deserts. He would no doubt despise her and curse her soundly for making him look the fool. But a fool he was for thinking he could snap his fingers and she would docilely submit to him.

Ah, but her dear Harry was quite a different matter. For him, her marriage to the earl meant his colors, a career in a crack regiment. It would be a severe blow. Perhaps he would never wish to see her again. Tears stung her eyes. She was letting him down, and for a moment she faltered. But then she thought about her own life, how all choice had been wrested from her. Sir Oliver would manage somehow to buy Harry his colors, for Harry was, after all, his favored son.

Just before dawn she slipped quietly out of her room and sped lightly down the stairs. The front door groaned in protest, and the sound was so loud to her own ears that she stood frozen, waiting for the servants to descend upon her.

The house was silent. She pulled her cloak closely about her shoulders and the hood over her head and stepped out into the night. She gazed a moment up and down the empty square, clutched her portmanteau tightly, and walked quickly away from the Bellingham mansion.

17

Kate Brandon made her way with forced enthusiasm to the Luxembourg Gardens after quitting her rather dismal room at 47, rue Saint Germain. She sat down on a wooden bench and drew the *journal* from her pocket. Her attention was drawn to the sound of a child's voice. She looked up to see a small boy skip past her, with his nanny in pursuit. A gentleman and lady strolled by, their heads close in intimate conversation. There was a small gleam in the gentleman's eye and a shy look of confidence on the lady's face. She silently cursed the romantic gardens, heaved a deep sigh, and forced herself to turn back to her unopened *journal*. She thumbed her way through the pages until she found the advertisements for positions. It seemed to her that no one ever filled the various posts, for the same ones appeared day after day. A butcher's assistant, a linkboy—ah, a blasted governess. A dark look came over her face on seeing the listing.

She'd applied for it with alacrity a few days before, feeling hope surge through her. Outfitted in her most subdued gray high-necked gown, her hair drawn into a severe bun at the nape of her neck, she sounded the brass knocker at the solid brick residence in the heart of a very respectable bourgeois area of Paris. The front door swung open, and she confidently faced a rather pinchfaced butler who demanded without preamble what the Young Person wanted. The Young Person wanted a job, she wanted to shout at the man, but she didn't. Upon being informed in rather halting French, punctuated with gestures to the governess post in the *journal*, the butler allowed a flicker of surprise to pass over his cadaverous face and cast Kate a look that made her feel as if she were some sort of oddity. He said quite unnecessarily, "Mademoiselle is English. It is of an oddness, that. I will see if Madame wishes to see you."

She bore this with fortitude and was admitted not many minutes later into a large *salle* that struck her as being furnished in less than the first stare of elegance. Like the salle, the large, somberly dressed Madame Treboucher looked to be a bastion of respectability.

"You are an English Young Person," Madame announced, her eyes on Kate's hair. "Your hair has much too much redness."

Finding both these statements to be unarguable, Kate replied simply and proceeded to inform Madame of her aspirations. Madame was silent for a moment, her thick lips pursed. She looked Kate up and down and finally announced with the utmost disdain that Mademoiselle was far too young for such

213

a responsible position, and furthermore, she wanted no red-haired Englishwoman running free in her house to seduce her son and her husband. Kate stared at her openmouthed, and finding herself unable to vent her outrage in the French tongue, rose stiffly and stalked out without a word. Once outside, she raised her fist to the heavens and demanded that God strike down the wretched woman, and the young gentleman she'd danced with at Almack's who'd assured her that the French considered the English their liberators.

She sat back on the bench, the *journal* lying open on her lap, and stared for a moment ahead of her. Her flight to Paris had been so utterly undramatic that she had quite decided that her luck had changed, that perhaps she'd not been born under the wrong stars after all. But now, after more than a week in Paris, her small hoard of coins practically gone, she felt near to panic. A growl of hunger in her stomach reminded her sharply that panic over her situation wouldn't buy food, nor would it pay the rent for her room for another week. She scanned the remainder of the positions on the page with fierce intensity. A milliner's assistant on the rue de la Bourgoine. What a paltry wage, barely enough to maintain the small room. But her alternatives were rapidly dwindling. She set her mouth, and with a determined effort repeated aloud the street number.

When she looked up, the street address on her lips, she saw a tall, elegantly dressed gentleman walking purposefully down the hedged walk toward her. Her eyes widened in disbelief. Julien! All her careful planning, for naught. No, surely it couldn't be he, no, certainly. She was just tired and hungry; the sun was in her eyes.

Of course it was the earl. "Damn you," she yelled toward him. She jumped to her feet, the *journal* gliding unnoticed to the ground, and took to her heels in the opposite direction. Her breath came in quick gasps and her violent exertion on a very hungry stomach made her dizzy. She pulled up short, weaving back and forth. The gardens blurred before her eyes. She took another uncertain step forward, only to find that two strong arms were around her and her head was against his shoulder.

Julien held her against him none too gently and said in a hard, uncompromising voice, "How very coincidental to see you here, Miss Brandon. Don't you find it strange? First I meet you lying dead at my feet and now in Paris. Well, no matter what you think, truth be told, for your little game is quite over."

She looked up unwillingly into his set face and, to her own chagrin, felt tears of frustration spill onto her cheeks.

She got hold of herself, but it was hard. She even managed to say calmly enough, "There is no coincidence. You've never been involved in a single coincidence in your bloody life. Why are you here? How did you find me? Damn you, let me go."

"No, I like you here, against me, my arms around you. Just hold still. I don't wish to fight with you more just yet." His features softened, and a look of great warmth came into his eyes. He tightened his arms about her and gently touched his cheek to her hair.

Finally, completely wearied and exhausted by her hunger and by her unwelcome relief at being here with him, she flattened her fists and stood willingly against him.

After a few moments she drew her head back from the circle of his arms and gave a watery sniff. She said in a matter-of-fact voice, "I'm a ninny. This isn't me, this watering pot. It's just that I'm hungry."

A smile lit his eyes, and he raised a gloved hand to brush away the tears from her face.

"That, at least, is something I can remedy to your satisfaction."

"If you will simply disappear, that will be more to my satisfaction than food."

Julien arched his eyebrows and regarded her with mild surprise. "I won't leave you. Come now, I'm merely offering you breakfast. Cry peace, Kate, cry peace, at least until after you've stuffed yourself. You're hardly a worthy opponent on an empty stomach."

She would have liked very much to yell at him, to curse him in Harry's most colorful epitaphs, but she couldn't think of any that she hadn't already called him too many times. It dawned on her with a good deal of force that she had finally lost.

"I should have gone to India."

Julien bit back sudden laughter, relieved and charmed, as he always was by her. "No, not India, I think, my dear. There you would serve many men, being a beautiful woman without protection. Indeed you're fortunate, my love. You need to serve but one man, namely me. Come, I'm not such a bad fellow. I have all my teeth, I'll never gain flesh, and I've been told I'm rather an excellent lover. Also, I plan to be faithful as a hound by the hearth."

She looked ready to quite literally spit on him, and he quickly released her, took her arms, and said, "Come, let's find a café and feed you properly."

She fell into a stiff step beside him. As they emerged from the gardens, they passed once again the lady and gentleman and Kate saw the lady gaze at Julien coyly from beneath her lashes.

"Why, that disloyal ninny, she quite deserves to be whipped. Eyeing you and all the while simpering up at that other fellow."

"On that point, ma'am, we find ourselves in complete agreement."

"Not that I care, you understand. It's my hunger that's making me say stupid things. The lady could have thrown herself on you for all I care."

"I quite understand. What more could a man ask for? I presume you will be a fiercely loyal and faithful wife, that you will guard my virtue with uncompromising vigilance." He squeezed her arm.

"You're a damned toad. You know very well what I meant. You can't force me to wed you, Julien. These aren't medieval times, when outlaw barons captured their brides in raids. No, this is a quite civilized time, and it's absurd."

"Ah, so very sure, are you? Well, we'll see, won't we?"

She shut her mouth, though he guessed it required strong resolution on her part. He looked down at the beautiful face beside him. She was so very proud. He admired her greatly, truth be told. Even when he'd wanted to shake her for being so damned obstinate and blind to her own needs, he could not help respecting her.

When Eliza had come panting into his breakfast room the morning of her flight, he at first wanted to beat her soundly the moment he got his hands on her. But then he grinned, for he'd suspected—nay, he'd known deep down—that her docile behavior was anything but an indication that he'd finally brought her to heel. She had certainly succeeded in making him feel the fool. He told Eliza not to say a word to Lady Bellingham, then immediately dispatched several of his retainers to the posting houses in London. He was informed within two hours that a young lady answering Kate's description had taken the mail coach to Dover. So she was off to France, was she? Were he not certain in his own mind that she cared for him, he would have readily drawn the conclusion that such

218

an outrageous and even dangerous act by a young lady of breeding was an evident sign of loathing. But he was certain that she did want him. After her miserable existence with her father, it was no wonder that she looked askance at a man who wanted to be her husband. He looked impatiently toward getting this damned marriage over with. Then he would show her once and for all that she could trust him, that he would never hurt her, that she could *believe* him.

He'd met briefly with Percy, Hugh, and Lady Bellingham. By that evening, the announcement that he and Miss Katharine Brandon were to meet in Paris and there to be wed was being circulated to all the appropriate quarters. He himself dispatched an elegantly worded announcement to the *Gazette*.

As he now guided Kate down the boulevard, his steps shortened to match hers, he wondered when she would figure out how much she'd simplified his plans.

When he first arrived in Paris, he had thought to bring her to heel immediately. Upon reflection, however, he decided to give her free rein, hoping, perhaps foolishly, that when he came to her she would joyfully welcome him. Actually, he thought, she had, in her own way, welcomed him. Her eyes always betrayed her, and for a fleeting instant her pleasure and relief at seeing him were obvious. Had he truly wished to break her spirit, he would have held away from her longer. But he knew too well of her straitened circumstances, and he couldn't allow her to be alone any longer. He smiled as he thought of her honest admission to being hungry. Lord, she was stubborn, but he didn't want her to change. No, not that.

He guided her into a small café off the boulevard. He quickly dismissed the idea of taking her to his lodgings. She had to eat, else she would never have the strength to go through the activities he'd planned for the day and evening. He didn't wish to chance her throwing the food at his head, and thought it less likely that she would refuse to eat in a café than in his rooms.

The owner, observing that Quality had entered his modest establishment, bustled forward to provide his best service. He assisted the lady into her chair at the choicest table and hovered as the gentleman disposed himself gracefully across from her.

Julien ordered her a very liberal breakfast and a cup of coffee for himself. Kate seemed to find the checkered tablecloth of great interest. She removed her gloves and began with the greatest concentration to trace the red checks.

"The design is most fascinating," he said after she'd been engrossed in this activity for some time.

"Is it not? Why, I've always loved checks. My mother was a Scot, you know, and there were red and white and green checks in her clan's tartan."

The owner returned shortly, laden with covered dishes. Julien applauded his decision to bring her here, for her eyes rested longingly on the plates of eggs, toast, kidneys, and the rasher of bacon. She ate quickly at first and then more slowly as the gnawing in her stomach eased. Abruptly, she laid her fork down, sighed in obvious satisfaction, and leaned back in her chair.

"You would have an instant friend in Sir Percy Blairstock, a friend of mine who very much enjoys his food."

"If he's one of your friends, it's likely he eats quite regularly, probably stuffs himself until the buttons on his waistcoat pop."

"Actually, you're quite right. I was merely indulging in light conversation. You'll meet Sir Percy when we return eventually to London. I trust you will like him, for he is a good friend, with no malice."

Her confidence had returned with each bite of food, and now she felt strong and self-assured. How could she have been such a weak fool as to cry? How could she have let herself actually lean against him? She was an idiot, three times a nitwit.

She daintily passed her napkin over her lips, took a final sip of coffee, and made to rise. "I thank you, my lord, for the excellent repast. Perhaps when you're in Paris again, we can breakfast together."

His hand shot out and he grabbed her arm. "Do be seated, my dear." He tightened the pressure on her arm until, finally, she had no choice but to seat herself again.

"It appears I must starve you if I wish a docile wife."

She tried to pull away from him again, but he held her fast.

"If you try such a stunt again, little shrew, I shall apologize to our good owner, throw you over my shoulder, and carry you out. Do I make myself clear?"

Would he? No, he couldn't. He was a peer of the English realm. Surely he had standards of gentlemanly behavior. Surely. Ah, but he was himself and not one of these faceless peers. She believed him. She sat rigid as the chair back, waiting to see what he would do.

"That's better. Now, my dear, I have something of the utmost importance to say to you, and you will attend me or it will be much the worse for you. For over a week now I have watched you try to make your way and have seen you fail time after time. Don't look so startled. Did you truly imagine that I would have difficulty in locating you? In any case, I didn't come to you immediately because I wished you to discover for yourself that a young woman with no money, regardless of her breeding and talents, has little if any chance of earning an honest wage. I had hoped that after your experience with Madame Treboucher you would come to your senses, but you didn't."

She could only stare at him. "You know of Madame Treboucher? But how? Ah, that horrible woman. She told me I was obviously

222

English and that my hair was too red."

"You are English, and I would say rather that your hair is more auburn than red, but who am I to quibble with such a stout lady? Don't be a fool, Kate, I had you followed."

18

"That is more than a lie, Julien. Surely you couldn't have done that. Why, it's—"

"It's what? Do you believe I would leave my future wife alone, without protection, in a city like Paris? As a matter of fact, I myself observed you leaving that woman's house."

She was humiliated. He'd stood by and watched her fail. Unaccountably, the fact that he hadn't come to her sooner made her strangely furious. To think that he'd had the gall to wait and watch while she made a total and utter fool of herself day after day was too much to bear. "How could you?"

"How could I what?" His voice was soft as the butter beside her plate. He was looking at her intently.

She turned away quickly, swallowing the absurd lump rising in her throat. She couldn't think of a reasonable thing to say.

"You don't want to answer me?"

"I don't want to do anything with you. You watched me, you saw how I failed and

223

failed—and you knew I would, you knew."

Damnation, he thought. If only she would admit to herself that she cared for him, that she had wished wholeheartedly that he would indeed have come to her in Paris. If only she would but realize the deep intent of what she was saying, if only.

Now she was frozen in her chair, for she'd spoken the truth, even if she couldn't grasp why it was the truth. He let it go. "I believe that's enough about your employment endeavors. Let me return to what I have to say to you. We will presently go to Mademoiselle Phanie's, a most elegant milliner's shop. Then we will purchase the proper shoes for you. I have already acquired your gowns and other personal articles, but I found it quite beyond my ability to recall your size in shoes and to determine what kinds of charming confections look best on your auburn hair, or perhaps it is red, or even titian. It depends on the light, you know. This morning I do believe it's as red as all the heathen's sins."

"What do you mean, you've bought me clothes?"

"You don't have that many with you. I do hope you approve my choices. The morning dresses, evening gowns, riding clothes, chemises, ah, let me see, wrappers, night-gowns, and the like—all of them are quite charming."

"But why?"

"I can't have you being Lady Godiva, can I? I bought you the clothes because after we've

224

suitably finished furnishing your wardrobe, we shall proceed to my rooms, and there you will be dressed in your bridal clothes. Don't look so surprised, my dear. Could you doubt that I wouldn't bring at least your wedding gown with me? Promptly at five o'clock we are expected at the embassy, where we will be married by an English divine."

He'd imagined her screaming at him like a demented fishwife, perhaps cursing him until their French host came scrambling out of his kitchen in alarm. But she didn't say a word, just sat there, staring at him, her face as pale as her collar, her fingers clutching her butter knife.

She couldn't look away from him now. He looked completely in control, his power over her limitless. She saw no signs of affection for her, no gentleness, merely a man who had run her to ground as if she were a fox in the hunt. He'd shamed her, lied to her, humiliated her. He probably only insisted upon wedding her because she'd refused him. He wished to own her, to add her as one of his possessions. He was utterly ruthless.

She gathered her scattered remnants of pride together and raised her face to his. She even managed a dollop of contempt. "I'm not a piece of property or a possession to be sold to the highest bidder, my lord. I fear you've made a sorry bargain with my father and are now out some guineas. You act as though I were some sort of prized animal, a wretched horse to be sold."

"Surely not. You're anything but a horse, but if the simile pleases you, then you must make it accurate. A filly, Kate, a filly."

He leaned toward her in a conciliatory gesture to take her hand in his, but she snatched her hand away and drew back away from him as far as she could in her chair.

"It was a jest, no more. Come now, at least give me a smile to reward my effort, paltry though you found it."

She was as silent as her silverware.

"Very well. I have no intention of prostrating myself at your feet. Now, it's time we got on with your shopping. You wouldn't wish to be late for your own wedding, now, would you?"

"Damn you to the devil. I won't go with you, Julien. And you can't force me, surely you can't. This is a very public place. Surely if you tried to coerce me, someone would stop you. There are gentlemen in this world, there must be."

He only sighed. "Very well. Let me outline the alternative for you. If you don't come willingly with me, I shall take you forcibly to my lodgings, or if you prefer, I shall simply render you unconscious and carry you there. If our host appears at all interested, I shall say that you've fallen ill. If you choose to continue in this obstinate manner, I'll force a certain drug that I now have in my possession down your white throat. It's very efficacious, I assure you, and will make you very pliant, Katharine, as pliant as a puppet, so pliant and agreeable that you'll probably take your clothes off in front of me and do a little dance."

He paused a moment to ensure that she understood his threat.

"Then I'll dress you myself in your wedding finery and take you unresisting to the embassy."

"Surely even you wouldn't do that."

"Most assuredly I shall, if you force me to. I've been remarkably patient, considering what you've put me through, but I find now that I've had quite enough of your antics."

Perhaps Hugh and Percy were correct, he thought, I am quite mad. Had someone told him even a month ago that he would force a young lady of quality to marry him, he would have thought it a ludicrous joke. Damn her for forcing him to go to such lengths. Or damn him for wanting her more than he'd ever wanted anyone or anything in his adult life. Why the devil wouldn't she simply admit she wanted him, even if she had to dredge down to her very being to find that caring, it was quite time she did it.

"Damn you, if I were but a man—"

"That is the stupidest thing I've ever heard you say. If you were a man, this conversation would never take place. Now, will you or will you not obey me?"

She felt suddenly very tired. She felt empty and beaten down. Even her fear of marriage to this man, never far away from her thoughts, was now effectively quelled. She raised her eyes to his, perhaps hoping to find some weakness, some uncertainty written there. But there was none. He was implacable and she knew it.

"Very well. I don't wish to be knocked unconscious nor do I wish you to drug me. The thought of willingly taking off my clothes with you anywhere around at all makes me quite ill. Let's get it over with."

He merely nodded, rose, pulled on his gloves, and helped her to rise from her chair. He drew her unresisting arm through his and led her to the door of the cafe.

The owner was rendered almost incoherent with gratitude when the gentleman pressed a louis into his outstretched hand. He stood in the doorway of his small establishment and watched the lady and gentleman step into a hackney. He had thought their behavior odd but, not understanding a word they'd said, had shrugged his shoulders in expressive indifference. The English were, after all, quite mad.

She spoke scarce a word as Julien guided her to various milliner shops and booteries throughout the remainder of the morning and into the afternoon. She appeared un-interested, coldly withdrawn, and acquiesced to whatever he directed her to do. It was he who chose the dainty kid slippers and the colorful assortment of bonnets. He decided her hair was auburn, a rich, brilliant auburn, at least in the soft afternoon light. He retained a certain degree of skepticism at her seeming capitulation but allowed himself, for the moment at least, to let his nerves enjoy their first respite in over a week.

Later in the afternoon, their shopping completed, he led her, still unresisting, to his lodgings.

"This is your room, Kate." He led her inside, felt her stiffen suddenly beside him, and watched her eyes as she stared at the large bed in the center of the room. She took a step backward, but he stopped her with his arm against her back. He chose for the moment to ignore her gesture. "Ah, here's your maid, Anne. She'll help you bathe and dress. If there's anything you require, you have but to ask."

He turned to the maid and gave her instructions in a low voice. He nodded to Kate and left her room through an adjoining door.

He stood quietly for a moment in his own room. He wasn't displeased by the fear he had seen on her face. He knew he was a skilled lover, and he felt confident that he would make her forget her natural virgin's fear. He had, after all, felt the quickening response of her body whenever he was close to her. His main problem would be not her fear but her pride. In all likelihood she would view pleasure at his hands as a final capitulation to his dominance over her. And that was the sticking point, he thought. He supposed he could always challenge her to a duel. He imagined that if he won, then and

229

only then would she consider being reasonable.

Kate forced herself to turn away from the bed. She felt sweat on her forehead and rubbed her damp hands on her skirt. She watched the maid Anne bustle toward her after giving Julien a deep curtsy as he left the room. In sudden panic she started toward the door, only to realize that she wouldn't get beyond the stairs.

With a dragging step she returned to the waiting maid, who was regarding her with some astonishment. She stood silently as the maid helped her out of her dress and into her bath.

It seemed that but a moment had passed when she heard Anne say with a good deal of enthusiasm, "How beautiful you are, my lady."

"I'm not a lady."

"I'm French, you know, and my English is excellent, but I understand you not at all. You will soon be a countess. Isn't that a lady? What matters if you are not the real lady until five o'clock?"

"It doesn't matter." For the first time that afternoon, she focused her attention on the maid's words and looked to see herself in the long mirror. She stared at her reflection as the maid smoothed an invisible wrinkle from the skirt of the white-satin-and-lace wedding gown. She wasn't a vain woman. On the other hand, she'd never seen herself gowned so exquisitely, her hair fashioned with such elegant style. She had to admit that she looked quite nice, and her fear grew. Julien too would think her beautiful.

She thought of the drug he had in his possession. She now had no doubt that he would use it if she again attempted to escape from him. Tears welled up and rolled unheeded down her cheeks. She turned her back to the mirror, hating herself for the weakness, but unable to stop the damnable tears.

"Give me a handkerchief."

Julien entered just as Kate finished dabbing the tears from her face.

He turned to the maid. "You may go now, Anne. You have done very well."

He strode to where she stood. He saw the wadded handkerchief in her hand, wet with her tears. He smiled at her gently and held out his arm to her.

"Come, it's time. We're expected at five o'clock."

As she raised her pale face to his, he said, "My love, you must trust me. I do what is best, you must believe that. Please, Kate, give me, give us, a chance."

Her expression didn't change, and without a word she placed her hand on his arm.

They were welcomed at the English embassy with all the deference accorded a peer of the English realm. Mr Drummond, the English divine, was properly effusive in his

231

compliments to the bride. He was well aware that his consequence would be enhanced by officiating at the wedding of such prominent personages. He hoped the earl would remember him in the future.

As he had been led to expect, the earl of March was indeed an elegant and charming nobleman. He seemed to radiate an aura of quiet confidence. The priest wondered, however, at the pallor and unremitting silence of the bride. She appeared withdrawn, even uninterested in the proceedings, surely a very strange reaction to such a momentous event.

As Mr Drummond reached his final words, he gave the earl a signal, and Julien turned to Kate. "Give me your hand."

Mr Drummond felt growing alarm as the lady hesitated for what seemed an eternity before finally extending her hand. He watched with relief as the earl withdrew a narrow gold band from his pocket and slid the ring onto her third finger. It was a very tight fit, and it took him several moments to work it over her knuckle.

With dramatic emphasis Mr Drummond pronounced them man and wife. Julien leaned down to kiss his bride. Her lips were cold, but she was unresisting. He wondered fleetingly if such a drug as the one he had threatened her with really existed. If it did, he couldn't imagine that it would render her any more deadly cold than she was now.

Katharine St Clair, the countess of March,

nodded silently to the footman, gathered up the train of her wedding gown, and seated herself across the table from her husband. They were in the small sitting room that adjoined Julien's bedchamber, waiting for the sumptuous wedding dinner Julien had ordered.

The renowned chef Monsieur André, a rather startling vision all in white, was seen to follow closely behind his creative efforts. Consigning a flunky to serve less important persons, Monsieur André served the earl and his countess himself, his voluble presence preventing any conversation between them.

She observed with a feeling of vague ill-humor that Julien seemed to be enjoying himself, his fluent French blending with that of the small, dark, mustachioed chef. She didn't particularly find favor with the innumerable references to *la belle comtesse* and remained silent and aloof, her lips curled disdainfully. The two men laughed. In all probability, they were exchanging ribald jokes. No, she thought quickly, Julien would never do that. Somehow she simply knew that.

When Monsieur André finally bowed himself out of the room, an undisguised knowing look in his black eyes, Kate felt the urge to fling her delicate fillet of fish with wine sauce in his face. Damned foreigner. She should have refused to eat, but she was so very hungry.

Julien looked across the table at his wife.

She looked exhausted, the shadows beneath her beautiful eyes emphasized by the white satin of her wedding gown. As he savored a bit of the light, flaky fish, he said, more to himself than to her, "It would be interesting to pit Monsieur Andre's skill against that of François."

"Yes, it would be a fierce competition. I would hope they'd poison each other, for they're both French and unbearably conceited. François tried once to kill the kitchen cat at St Clair when poor Tom stole one of his lamb chops."

"So, you know about my temperamental chef?"

"Yes, but only through the colorful pictures painted by Mannering and Mrs Cradshaw. Mannering was most upset about Tom. Didn't you notice that he's missing a good inch of his tail?" She lowered her head quickly again to her plate. Surely it was a betrayal of herself even to speak to him, to feel even the slightest enjoyment in the kind of banter she'd enjoyed with him so long ago, when he'd pretended to be her friend.

"When we return to London, François can prepare the same dish and you can judge the winner. I didn't see Tom on my last visit to St Clair. He always was an ugly bugger, though. Perhaps missing some of that swishing arrogant tail of his improved his appearance."

She made no answer.

He began to think of how he would approach lovemaking with her. He could not

234

but dismiss the thought after only a moment of weighing her evident exhaustion against his ardent desire for her. Ardent, he thought. What a milquetoast word. What he felt was consuming lust. He wanted her more than he himself could begin to imagine. He wanted to bury himself inside her, to wrap her so tightly against him that they would be as one. Ah, but she was a virgin, an unwilling bride, truth be told, and he imagined that she would likely try to slit his throat if he tried to make love to her.

As if she read his thoughts, she raised her face, and he saw such apprehension in her eyes that any faltering in his determination was effectively stilled.

Once the covers were removed and a bottle of chilled champagne was set in front of Julien, he dismissed the footman.

Kate looked up as the door closed and warily met her husband's eyes. She simply couldn't believe she was now married to this man. It seemed as though the footman had locked the door to her prison cell. She had little knowledge of lust and desire, her experience having been confined primarily to the stilted declarations of love proffered by Squire Bleddoes. But she was certain that she read both of these on Julien's face. Unconsciously her hand stole to her neck.

"Here is your champagne." Julien handed her a flute. As he could think of no toast that would not in all likelihood upset her, he simply clicked his glass to hers.

She took a long, deep drink of the champagne and barely managed to restrain a sneeze from the spuming bubbles. Julien refilled her glass. She was beginning to think that champagne was not at all the nasty sort of drink she had once believed, and confirmed her new opinion by quickly downing the second glass. The third glass gave her a certain sense of warmth and light-headedness that dissolved the gnawing fear and the shaky feeling in her stomach. She grew quite warm, both inside and out. Her once-taut nerves began to loosen, and the room, indeed even Julien's face, took on a pleasant blur.

Julien had never before seen her take more than a few sips of any drink, including the mild orgeat at Almack's, and as he watched her finish her fourth glass, he grew concerned that she would make herself ill. He gently leaned forward and removed the glass from her fingers.

"Surely you've had enough. It's time for you to retire. It's been a long day, at least for me and my nerves."

His nerves. She very much disliked being disturbed in her foggy haze, and he'd had the gall to say something about *his* bloody nerves. Then he was at her side, his hand firmly gripping her arm. He pulled her to her feet. She weaved uncertainly from the effects of the champagne and, to her horror, leaned heavily against his chest.

"I can see that you are in need of some assistance. I hope I've not married a wife

236

who's a tippler." He ignored the slight flutter of protest and swung her up into his arms.

"I'm not drunk. It's *my* nerves. Your nerves indeed."

He smiled at that, as he carried her through the adjoining door to her room and sat her down on a chair. "Try not to fall off the chair," he said over his shoulder as he pulled the bell cord.

She huddled in the chair and watched tensely as he spoke in a low voice to the maid. But a moment later she curtsied and Julien left the room.

A small voice deep within her told her that now was her chance to escape. She could render the maid unconscious and flee. But her mind seemed strangely befuddled, and the door seemed such a great distance away. But it didn't matter. She forgot the maid, lurched to her feet, grabbed up the train of her wedding gown, and dashed to the door.

19

The damned maid yelped.

Julien was in the bedchamber in an instant, and behind her in the next, his hands firmly against the door over her head. "If you wished to take a stroll, you should have told me." Slowly he turned her about and studied her upturned face. "No, I believe you're too tired for a walk. I wouldn't want the French watch to arrest you as a drunken bride and whisk you away from me. Come, my dear, let Anne put you in your nightgown. I won't harm you, I swear it. Nor will I come to you tonight. Will you contrive to trust me in this?"

"I don't believe you. You're a man and you do anything you wish to do. I don't want you near me. I—"

"Believe what you wish to. Now, can I trust you not to try to snaggle off again? If you don't promise me, I myself will stay here and put you in your nightgown. What do you say?"

"I think you're a bastard."

"And?"

"I'll stay."

He looked at her for another too long moment, patted her cheek, and left.

She stood quietly as the maid, Anne, began to unbutton the many tiny hooks of her wedding gown. The dress dropped to the floor. Next came her petticoats, stockings, slippers, until finally she stood with only her chemise. As if from a great distance, she heard the maid ask her to sit at the dressing table. Her body obeyed the request, and she sat down. The maid unfastened her long hair from its pins, and it uncurled down her back. As the maid brushed out the tangles, she thought that this was the strangest wedding night she'd ever seen. The young lady had acted odd this afternoon, but now, goodness, she acted as if the devil himself were after her. She was drunk, that was it. She was drunk and she was afraid of her bridegroom, the silly girl. With her French common sense, Anne could see no reason why the lady shouldn't be excited about the prospect of being bedded by such a handsome gentleman. But the lady was quite young, and in all likelihood innocent. Her maidenly display of modesty was probably just what the English gentleman would wish. She wondered what the groom thought of his bride's drunkenness.

Anne finished brushing the lady's hair, slipped the chemise off over her head and found herself staring for a moment at her body. She was delectable, no doubt about that, even though she was very English. All long and white and slender, a nest of auburn curls between her thighs to match the thick hair on her head. The gentlemen would lose his head when he saw her, no doubt about that. At least he would once he got the night-gown off her. *If* he managed to get the night-gown off her. She thought it far more the thing for the lady to await her husband naked in her bed, but the English gentleman had given her explicit orders to put the lady in her nightgown. This she did, fastening the rib-bons around the new countess's throat and straightening her long hair. Finally, according to her instructions, she walked to the adjoin-ing door and lightly tapped on it.

She turned and curtsied to the lady, who was standing, still as a malacca cane, in the middle of the room where she'd left her, seemingly oblivious of her presence. At first the maid had believed her to be only drunk, but now she saw her fear. She felt a stab of pity and quickly sped to her, whispering, "It won't be of a badness you won't like, my lady. Your husband, he has that air about him, he knows, that beautiful man, he knows how to do these things you will like. Do come now, and put on a good face to him, a little smile, eh? You might even enjoy yourself once you have the understanding of it." Yes, he should be kind, Anne thought, wondering if she would want any kindness from him if she were going to be bedded by him. No, she'd want him urgent and rough, his hands every-where. She heard his approaching footsteps, darted one last glance at the lady, and left the room.

Julien pulled up short at the sight of her, standing still as a tombstone where the maid had left her, covered from her chin to her feet in the fine white-lawn gown. Her hair fell like soft clouds of rich auburn down her back and over her shoulders. The nightgown was a bit large for her, and it made her appear more like a frightened child than a bride.

He strode over to her, cupped her chin in his hand, and forced her to look up at him.

"You're beautiful, more delectable than I'd ever imagined, and believe me, I've imagined you every which way. But you're tired, my dear, are you not? And I'm not a pig."

She nodded mutely, her eyes huge and dark against her white face.

"Come, then, I'm the gallant tonight. You may call me Lancelot, or was it Galahad? Either one will do, I daresay. I won't get into that bed with you, but know that it tests me, Kate, tests me more than I've been tested in my life. But alas, I'm not a monster, nor am I a randy boy. I want you utterly sober and well rested when I come to you. I want you to want me."

She didn't move.

"Come, sweetheart," he said again, and pulled her arm through his.

She was trembling, although the room was quite warm. She tried to still her shaking body, but to no avail. She thought inconsequentially that his brocade dressing gown was very soft to the touch. Her fingers twitched nervously on his sleeve.

He wondered what thoughts were going through that drunken mind of hers. Her face was pale, far too pale, and he felt her fingers clutching at his arm. He gently disengaged her hand and lifted her onto the bed. Lord knew he didn't intend it, but just lifting her, just feeling her through the batiste of her nightgown made him want her so much he thought he would die from it. She turned her head away from him on the pillow, and without intending to, he sat down beside her, his hand reaching out to touch her hair, to feel it. Perhaps he even wanted to crush a handful of her beautiful hair against his cheek. He reached out an unsteady hand and stroked the rich auburn hair. It felt like silk, smooth and soft in his hand. She didn't move. He saw the outline of her full breasts, made more prominent by their rapid rise and fall.

He didn't think, just acted. She wasn't too drunk or too tired, no, she couldn't be, she hadn't moved, had she, when he'd touched and stroked her hair? Perhaps she was just shy, just waiting for him to take charge. He laid a hand on her breast and began to caress her.

She rolled suddenly away from him, a low cry of panic escaping from her throat. She jerked about and stared at him, her hand out to ward him off, him or the devil, he thought, freezing, his hand still outstretched. He took a deep breath and with a strong effort drew back his hand. "I've wanted you too much and for too long. I'm sorry to frighten you.

Go to sleep now. Everything will be different in the morning."

He forced himself to rise. Mechanically he pulled the covers over her. He couldn't think of a thing to say to reassure her. All he had on his mind was stripping off that bloody night-gown, caressing her breasts with his hands and with his mouth, and feeling her, all of her, those long white legs of hers spreading for him. He shook himself. He said only, "Sleep now. I'll see you in the morning."

He had meant his words to be calm, but even to his own ears there was a tremor of lust. He drew a deep breath, turned from her bed, and walked slowly to his own room, disbelieving that he'd left her, actually left his bride on their wedding night, that he hadn't taken her, made her his wife.

Long after she heard him close the door behind him, she drew her knees as close to her chest as she could and burrowed into the covers for warmth. Her hand stole to her breast, the breast he'd touched. For the first time in her life she became aware of her own womanliness, of the softness of her body, of her differentness, of what she was to him, a man. She could still feel his hand upon her, caressing, wanting her, his fingers stroking through her hair.

A shock of fear ripped through her, and she gulped down a sob. The sound of her own voice brought with it a certain calm, and with forced detachment she tried to examine her fear. She knew that men took total possession of women's bodies, that they had this long thing between their legs that they stuck into a woman. She saw his hands on her hair, her breasts, and then moving elsewhere on her body. He would touch her everywhere. He would see it as his right as her husband. There was nothing he couldn't or wouldn't do to her. She pressed her thighs tightly together.

Strangely, she thought about Julien's French mistress. Lady Bellingham had let her name slip. What was it? ... Yvette. How many other women had Julien touched and caressed? How many other women had he possessed? Unbidden, innumerable faceless women rose in her mind, and she pressed her fists against her temples to blot out their images. There was an unaccountable bitter taste in her mouth, and for the moment she encouraged a contemptuous disgust of him, a man, a lecher. She didn't understand herself, but the contempt was there, deep inside her, for him, for herself, ah, yes, particularly for herself. Hadn't she allowed him to do just as he had wished with her? Even forcing her to wed him against her will? She saw herself as weak and despicable, capitulating to a will stronger than hers. In vain she tried to excuse herself on the grounds of Julien's physical threats. She should have fought him, forced him to rely on the drug. Anger at herself welled up within her. She'd been contemptible, a gutless, worthless female, and now she hated herself for it.

She forced herself to be calm again. She sought to understand why she'd lost all will to fight him, why indeed she had executed his every command. The thought that he'd been right, the thought that she had wanted him to force her gained a foothold in her mind, and anger surged through her again. She forced herself to relive the moments when Julien had carried her, unresisting, and laid her on the bed, when he had stroked her hair, when he had caressed her breast. She sat up in her bed and shook her head in blind confusion.

Her thoughts flew again to Julien's French mistress. How was she different from that woman? After all, Julien had bought her just as he had Yvette. He would tire of her, just as he had tired of Yvette. That he had married her did not count to his advantage, for she wasn't so naive as to believe that even the powerful earl of March would attempt to seduce an unmarried lady of quality. No, he'd been forced to wed her. Her own destiny, whatever that might have been, had been wrested from her control the moment he had decided he wanted her. He'd won, and she wondered bitterly how long it would be before he left her to preside alone over his household and search out his next quarry.

She smiled, a mean smile. Undoubtedly Julien now thought her cowed and submissive. Her jaw set itself into a stubborn line as she resolved never again to show weakness. He had compared her to Shakespeare's Kate.

Very well, that's just what she would become.

Possession of her body would be his next object. She fought back the sudden unreasoning fear that accompanied this thought. Damn him, no. He had made a very expensive purchase, but she would see him in hell before she would allow him to enjoy it. Her life had been a constant battleground since she met him, and it didn't seem likely to her now that anything would change. Nay, she wouldn't let it change.

As Julien lay in his own bed, his head propped up on his arms, he reviewed the day's events with some satisfaction. He was pleased that he had forced Kate to wed him as soon as he had, for he had allowed her to hold on to her pride. He could have waited another week, but he'd not been able to bring himself to do it. He hadn't wanted an admission of failure from her. No, he hadn't wanted her on those terms. In all truth, to Julien their marriage was not a victory over her but rather a natural course of events.

He raised himself on one elbow and blew out the candle beside his bed. He lay back, wondering how long it would be before she would admit to her love for him. At least now she appeared to be more reasonable, and he felt confident that being at his side continually, she would learn to trust him. He planned to begin by explaining his high-handed treatment of her. He would become her friend again. He would speak openly to her of

246

lovemaking, for they were, after all, now man and wife. He had acted precipitately this evening. He had to remember that she was young, innocent, and quite vulnerable, despite her independence, her bravado.

Before dropping off to sleep, he decided to quit Paris on the morrow and remove immediately to Switzerland, to the villa he'd hired in the mountains near Geneva. They would be alone, save for two servants. There they would have time to come to an understanding.

He awoke the following morning light of heart and full of confidence. He patiently bore with a valet provided by the hotel, having given Timmens a congé until his return to England. His coat, at least, was properly pressed. He was impatient to see his bride, and so contented himself with the first result achieved on his cravat. A hotel lackey arrived just as he finished dressing, bearing the hearty English breakfast he'd ordered, hoping to please his new wife.

With a light step and a gleam of anticipation in his eyes, he tapped on the adjoining door. Receiving no immediate answer, he opened the door and stepped into the room.

She was seated at the dressing table, engrossed in the coiffure the maid had achieved. She didn't turn immediately, but rather patted her hair here and there, straightened the collar of her gown, all in all making a fine show of ignoring his presence.

He approached her and stood behind her chair so that she could see his reflection in the mirror.

"Good morning."

She turned slowly in her chair, gazed at him with great indifference, and said, "Good morning to you, sir. I trust you slept well."

She silently congratulated herself, for even to her own critical ears she had spoken with a marked lack of concern, as if his presence were a mundane occurrence, not at all above the commonplace. She held his gaze and noticed with satisfaction that his brows arched in fleeting surprise. Oh, yes, he'd expected her to behave quite differently, perhaps with docility, perhaps with fear, but certainly not with sublime indifference.

After a moment he said, even as he brushed a fleck of nothing in particular from his sleeve, "Yes, I slept quite well. I would have preferred to have you in my arms all night, but my dreams were passing good. And you, sweetheart? Did you miss me during the night?"

Kate patted her hair again, quite unnecessarily. "My dreams passed as well as yours, no doubt. Now, give me but a moment longer, sir, and I shall join you for breakfast. It does seem to be a very lovely day, does it not? That is very fine, Anne, you have performed wonders with my hair."

She rose and shook out her skirts, all the while watching him carefully. She was rewarded with a frown on his brow, for instead of wearing one of the elegant gowns he had bought for her, she had insisted on donning her own gown. It was sadly in need of pressing, and she delighted in each wrinkle.

Julien turned abruptly to the maid. "You may go now. I think you've done quite enough for her ladyship."

He didn't turn back to Kate until he had carefully schooled his features and gotten control of himself. She had wanted to anger him, and he had most willingly obliged her. Gentle, reasonable treatment from a loving husband was not, at least for this morning, what his dear wife would tolerate. Would she always surprise him? He hoped so, he surely did. However, this morning, he would have preferred a kiss, perhaps even a word of endearment.

He offered her his arm, saying, "How very charming you are this morning, my love. Marriage obviously agrees with you. Come, your breakfast will get cold. As you said, it's a lovely day. I know you and your enthusiasm for all things outdoors. Surely you don't want to waste it."

Once seated at the table, she gave her full attention to her breakfast. After eating her fill, she spent an extraordinarily long time pushing her cold eggs back and forth on her plate. Bored with this pastime, she chanced to look up and saw Julien gazing at her, his eyes alight with amusement.

She felt a bolt of panic, then anger, then she calmed herself. Lightness, she was all sweetness and light. "Do forgive me, sir. I was raised to think it rude to stare at others who haven't yet finished their meal, but then, perhaps you are in a hurry to quit these rooms and think that I am much too slow at my breakfast. Do allow me a moment longer." She gave the eggs another couple of shoves.

He laughed, he actually laughed. "As to the urgencies of your breakfast, I fear that your toast is by now like dried leather and your bacon stiff with age. Those poor eggs have long since plummeted over the precipice."

"Perhaps they have. Now, I long to hear what delights you've doubtless planned on this altogether lovely day. Any drugs, my lord? Any threats, perhaps?"

She was good, quite good. He drew out his watch and consulted it. "My pleasure, my dear, is that you're packed in an hour. Why the look of surprise? We are, after all, on our wedding trip. We're leaving for Switzerland this morning."

"Switzerland? I've never cared for Switzerland."

"Really? How very curious of you. I wasn't under the impression that you'd ever traveled to that country. Could I be mistaken? Did I completely misunderstand Sir Oliver? Did he give you a grand tour as a child?"

"Very well, I haven't visited Switzerland, that's true enough, but I've been given to understand that it is quite inferior to England."

He burst into laughter.

250

20

He laughed himself silly. She wanted to hurl strips of her stone-cold bacon at him, but suddenly he stopped, drew a steadying breath, and said, even as he gave her a huge, white-toothed grin, "I thought you were singularly undisturbed by other people's opinions, Kate. I must confess that I find myself somewhat disappointed that you don't wish to form your own independent judgment." Then he had the gall to sigh like a martyr. "I'd hoped that, unlike most other women, you would not be content to merely parrot words. I fear I hear the sound of poor Bleddoes's absurd pompous opinions."

"You're a bloody sod, well, perhaps not that, but it isn't true, as you must know. I couldn't bear Robert and his prosing and his prudery and ... all right, so he did say on occasion that Switzerland wasn't—damn you, you are a sod, and I won't sit here and be ridiculed." She jumped to her feet, sending her cold eggs plopping over the edge of the plate, her cheeks so flushed it looked as if she had the fever.

He sat back in his chair, crossing his arms over his chest. "An hour, Kate?"

She flung her napkin on the table, turned on her heel, and strode like an angry boy from the room.

Julien remained seated for a moment longer, looking at the recently slammed door. It had never before occurred to him to bless his quickness of wit. It came to him with something of a shock that she was behaving more arrogantly than he had done himself when trying to bring her to heel in London. That she would ride roughshod over him given the least opportunity, he did not doubt. For a fleeting instant he envisioned his life as a marital battleground.

As he rose to ring for a lackey, he wondered idly how long she would insist upon wearing the same gown.

The post chaise he'd procured for their trip to Switzerland was well-sprung and elegantly furnished with blue-satin squabs and warm blue-velvet rugs. But though the horses stood at over fifteen hands and were blessed with broad chests and powerful thighs, Julien found that they didn't possess the speed of his own bays.

He watched his new wife with some amusement as she tried valiantly not to appear interested in the French countryside. He well understood her dilemma and thought her altogether adorable. He also thought her so appealing that he had to shift position several times for the pain it brought to his groin.

They ate their lunch in the small town of

Brayville, drinking the local cider and feasting on cold chicken, cheese, and crunchy warm bread. Feeling fortified by the heady cider, Julien found himself, not long after their return to the carriage, clearing his throat to gain her attention.

"I ask you to listen to me for a moment."

"Oh?" A brow went up a good inch. "Have you planned a delightful detour from our trip to Switzerland? Are we going to the Barbary Coast? Perhaps you'll be so infuriated with me that you'll sell me to a slaver?"

"Good God, woman. What do you read?"

"I read everything. I'm not ignorant, nor am I stupid."

"I never believed you were—well, perhaps just a bit of both of those things, but not an overabundance. Now, listen to me, for now I'm perfectly serious. My intention is to cease these meaningless hostilities between us. You thought me cruel, perhaps overbearing in my treatment of you in London. No, don't interrupt me, let me finish. When you refused me, I was forced to admit to myself that I had rushed into the matter too quickly, that I hadn't given you sufficient time to judge your feelings for me. I never meant to insult you. Perhaps I am overly proud—arrogant perhaps, as Harry said—but I found I simply couldn't lose you."

He paused for a moment, thinking that no man had ever before so abased himself. He looked at her searchingly. His speech didn't seem to be going as well as he had expected, but he pursued it anyway, speaking more rapidly.

"I knew that I couldn't continue to see you at Brandon Hall, for your father would force you to meet with me and perhaps try to beat you into submission. You must understand, Kate, I couldn't allow you to remain under his roof any longer than necessary. That's why I arranged for you to go to London, to Lady Bellingham. There, at least, I knew I could control the situation. You thought me cruel, hard. I tell you now that I had no other choice in the matter. My intention was and still is to do what is best for both of us. That I forced you to marry me was not a reprehensible act. I had to wed you as speedily as possible after your flight to Paris, for had I not, had I left you alone to your own devices, you would eventually have had to return to England, your reputation ruined.

"As for my threat about the drug, I don't know if such a drug exists. Perhaps opium, but it's nasty stuff and I would never give you such a thing. It's just that I couldn't think of any other way to secure your agreement."

"There was no drug?" She was appalled at her own gullibility.

"No. And I wouldn't have you think me a licentious rake, for I would have never forcibly taken you aboard my yacht."

"You're quite right, I'm both ignorant and stupid. It's also clear that I'm a fool and that you have admirable sangfroid, my lord, for I didn't ever doubt that you were utterly ruthless and implacable in gaining your ends. No drug! Damn you to the Devil."

"Perhaps it was merely that I felt compelled to use whatever tactics I needed to secure you as my wife."

"Nothing has changed. I told you I never wanted to marry any man, not even your magnificent self. But you wouldn't heed me. Well, my lord, you've paid dear for a wife who loathes you. I swear to you that you'll never enjoy your purchase."

She'd gotten to him at last, the damnable shrew. She was illogical, stubborn, ah, but passionate. "Don't rant nonsense at me, Kate. It now does you no credit. We're married and that is the end to it. You speak of my purchase. Let me tell you, madam, you're now the one being arrogant and implacable."

"By God, you dare to criticize my actions? You pass all bounds. You exceed all probabilities, you outrank even the rankest species that now exists on this earth."

"You need to close down that malicious brain of yours." He leaned over and dropped a hand on her shoulder, gripping it for an instant. She tried to pull away, but he grasped both her shoulders, jerking her close to his face. He'd meant to give her a good yelling-at, but found instead that his body went from anger to lust. It was all of an instant, and he hated it, but he couldn't seem to help himself. In a swift motion he cupped her face between his hands and pressed his mouth against hers. Dear God, she was so warm and sweet and he wanted her to open her mouth for him, but she didn't, of course. She tried to twist free of him, but he simply lifted her bodily and held her firmly in the circle of his arms. His hands were on her breasts, kneading her, feeling their weight in his hands, learning her, and he thought he'd die if he couldn't have her now, this very instant. He flattened his hand on her belly, cursing the damned cloth that kept her from him, and his hand went lower, and his breathing hitched painfully.

At that moment the chaise lurched violently, throwing them both to the opposite seat. As they sprawled on the cushions, Julien automatically released her. She scrambled away from him, clutching desperately at the door. He grabbed her hand and pulled her upright opposite him. All desire and anger left him as he stared at her white, shocked face.

Julien turned and looked out the chaise window. They were moving at a comfortable pace again. He methodically straightened his clothes and his cravat. He felt rather irritated at her. For God's sake, she was still fully clothed. If he had his way, she'd be sitting there naked and white and soft and he'd be sweating and heaving with lust just looking at her. Still, he had scared the bloody hell out of her. But she was his wife, she was his and ... "I apologize for being so enthusiastic. I didn't mean to scare you." He was beginning to feel the clumsy fool and thus spoke with a harshness of voice he didn't intend. He saw her eyes darken with sudden anger. Trust her not to hold to calm and control for very long.

He drew a deep breath and continued in a more controlled voice. "The fact is, we're man and wife. Can you not doubt that I wish to consummate our marriage, or, for that matter, that I wish you to bear my children? Although you cannot yet bring yourself to admit it, ours is a love match and not a marriage of convenience."

"I would rather die than let you touch me, do you understand, my lord? Ours is no love match, for I feel none for you, and your treatment of me—well, you speak well, my lord, as fluently as the devil trying to bargain for a new soul. But you cloak your lust with words of love. You disgust me, Julien. Do you hear?"

He curbed his fury. To match her anger would achieve naught. She was overwrought, and his sudden passion for her had made her totally unreasonable. He said with surprising gentleness, "Enough said, Kate. Believe me, though, I will make you my wife, in every way. I love you, and soon you'll come to trust me."

"You dream, my lord, you believe your own fantasies. In truth, I would sooner trust any one of the Carlton House set than you, and Harry has told me that group is reprehensible, dissolute and hardened gamesters."

"Harry doesn't know the half of it," he said. "Actually, I'm not at all a hardened gamester."

She rearranged her bonnet, which was sitting precariously atop her hair, folded her hands primly in her lap, and looked out, unseeing, onto the French countryside.

They arrived in Geneva late in the afternoon three days later. Kate found she simply couldn't restrain her appreciation when Lake Geneva came into view. Though it was early September, the mountains surrounding the lake were snowcapped, and the setting sun cast a fairy-land glow on the water.

"Oh goodness, how lovely it is."

"Yes, it is rather beautiful. I'm delighted you've changed your opinion."

She drew back into the chaise and fastened her eyes on the cushions. "Well, perhaps it is passable."

She couldn't prevent her eyes from going to his face, and she saw his brows rise in ironic amusement. She flushed, mortified at her own churlishness, and wanted to cosh him at the same time for making her so very much aware of it.

Soon, though, she became absorbed with the endless rows of quaint shops that lined the cobblestone streets, each sporting colorful signs and displays. The Swiss themselves, no less colorfully arrayed than their shop fronts, bustled out onto the walkways, apparently hurrying to their homes for the evening.

The Coeur de Lyon was a two-storied, gabled brick building of some antiquity, which stood back from the street, nearly hidden from view by giant elm trees. The courtyard surged with activity, and no sooner did their chaise pull to a halt than two stable lads appeared to grab the reins.

She allowed Julien to assist her from the chaise and was thankful that she had done so, for her legs were weak from their long-cramped position. She looked up to see a very rotund, quite bald little man emerge from the *auberge* to greet them.

"My lord March. What a long time it has been. A pleasure to see you again, my lord, a pleasure indeed." He bowed, all gracious compliance and deference.

"Good evening, Perchon. Your establishment prospers, I see. This is my wife, and it is her first visit to your beautiful country."

Monsieur Perchon beamed, bowed, and turned to give instructions in rapid French to two of his henchmen.

"Now, my lord, my lady, if you will please to follow me. Your accommodations, I assure you, are quite in order."

She was somewhat surprised that Monsieur Perchon spoke English so well. She was soon to discover that he spoke French, German, and Italian with equal ease.

A slender, brown-eyed maid, who reminded Kate of a small, timid doe, was assigned to see to her comfort, and as she prepared to follow the maid up the winding wooden stairs to her chamber, Julien called to her, "Put on a warm cloak, Kate, and we'll

259

explore before dinner."

It was on the tip of her tongue to tell him that she had no such warm cloak, when Julien, apparently guessing her objection, added smoothly, "You'll find such a cloak in your large trunk, my dear. It is, I believe, of blue velvet and lined with ermine."

Ha, he'd bought it for her. She'd see him in hell before she'd wear any of the clothes he'd bought her. "The pelisse I'm wearing will be perfectly adequate, thank you, sir."

She felt rather deflated when he turned away from her and said over his shoulder, "As you wish. Surely you know best. I will appreciate having a hot-blooded woman for my wife. I'll expect you in the parlor in five minutes."

She untied the strings on her pelisse and tossed it, not without some violence, onto the bed. She moved to the small, blazing fire and warmed her hands for a moment before flinging herself down into a chair. Orders, nothing but orders from his lordship. She gnawed at her thumbnail and tried to cool her anger, for she had learned through painful and humiliating experience that such violent emotion dulled her wits and slowed her tongue. She forced herself to relax and settle back into the chair. She looked dispassionately at her chewed nail and thought, not without satisfaction, that the last three days had been more of a trial to Julien than to her, for after their brief and violent scene in the chaise, she'd treated him with a kind of indifferent courtesy. Instinctively she knew it was her best weapon against him. It had, at least, kept him in check.

"Excuse me, my lady, can I help you change?"

Kate jerked her head up, thinking that she had dawdled a sufficient length of time, and rather proudly smoothed her travel-stained gown. She rose, grinning. "No, thank you. I believe I look fine as a five pence. Ah, yes, please give me my pelisse."

There was a rather dubious look in the maid's soft brown eyes, for she'd unpacked many of the lovely gowns. She bobbed a curtsy and handed Kate her worn pelisse.

As Kate swept past the smiling landlord into the private parlor, she rather hoped that Julien would be irritated, since a good half-hour had passed. She pulled up short in the middle of the room to find him seated comfortably before a blazing fire, engrossed in reading a paper.

Julien finally raised his eyes from the paper and said with some surprise, "Good heavens, that was indeed a short five minutes. How very impolite of me. My pardon, my dear. Have you been waiting for me long?"

"You are the most—" She caught herself just in time. She yawned and quickly changed her tone. "If you wish to continue with your paper, it would be quite shabby of me to take you away to what one might consider a boring pastime."

"Ah, but it would surely be ill-bred of me to

prefer the company of a newspaper over that of my charming bride. Do allow me a few minutes to put on my greatcoat and we'll be off."

He rose and drew on his coat and gloves in a leisurely manner. He sauntered over to her and murmured ironicaly, "Do forgive me for making you wait, my dear. It takes such a damnably long time to pull on one's gloves. Shall we go?"

As they stepped from the *auberge*, a gust of cold evening wind whipped through Kate's thin pelisse and chilled her to the bone.

"How selfish of me. If not precisely selfish, then inconsiderate and thoughtless. Perhaps it's too chilly for a stroll."

She stuck her face into the wind. "On the contrary, it's a beautiful evening for a walk. I have always maintained that it's quite ridiculous to curb one's activities when the weather isn't exactly what one would wish. There is but a small nip in the air."

She drew her pelisse closely about her and strode ahead of him like an Amazon going into battle.

He grinned at her back. He hoped she wouldn't catch a chill.

She soon found that she had to suffer another inconvenience. The uneven cobblestones cut into her feet through the soft kid shoes, and she was forced to stop for a moment to pick out an errant pebble that had worked its way to the sole of her foot.

He stopped beside her, but appeared quite

unconcerned with her difficulty, seemingly engrossed in his contemplation of Lake Geneva. She threw the pebble at him instead, but missed.

By the time they reached the water's edge, her teeth were chattering.

"Look over there, Kate." He tugged at her sleeve and pointed her toward the mountains on the other side of the lake.

"That is Mont Blanc—White Mountain. Out of the ordinary, isn't it?"

"Only the top of it is white. The name isn't right. It's obvious the Swiss have no imagination." She would have most willingly traded the view of that awesome snow-capped peak for a pair of stout walking shoes and a warm cloak.

He turned to her in some surprise. "Why, I was under the impression that the racket of towns didn't find favor with you, that you much preferred the openness and solitude of nature."

"That is perfectly true. But as you see, I am to be denied solitude."

He smiled as fervently at her as a priest bent upon saving a soul. "My dearest wife, since you and I have entered the blessed state of matrimony, we must be considered as one in spirit and in all things."

"It must be obvious to you, Julien, that these considerations of marriage don't apply to us. I do wish you'd stop beggaring the question."

"I'm beggaring nothing. These, ah, con-

263

siderations will apply, you'll see. Do you grow impatient?"

"The only thing I'm impatient for is my dinner. I only hope the damned Swiss know how to cook proper English fare."

He didn't answer her, just leaned down and sought out a smooth pebble. Having selected a stone of the quality he desired, he flicked his wrist and sent the pebble jumping and careening wildly over the placid water. Seemingly satisfied with the number of skips he achieved, he turned to her, a thoughtful expression on his face.

"Impatient only for your dinner, my dear? I can and I will give you much greater pleasure than a simple meal."

21

Thank God they were in the open, in a very public place. If she'd been alone with him, she knew, just knew deep down, that she'd have felt unreasoning fear at his words. As it was, all she felt was wonderful anger. "Don't you dare taunt me with your man's threats, my lord."

"Man's threats? I don't recall having threatened you, leastwise in the past few minutes. When you come to know me better, you'll discover that I don't make threats. I

264

make but statements of fact."

"They are one and the same thing coming from you, Julien. I've told you that I don't like you. I can't believe you so unintelligent as to have so quickly forgotten my words."

She'd hoped to provoke him, to put at least a small dent in his armor, but she hadn't. He gazed at her impassively, a gleam of amusement lighting his eyes, and she saw that gleam and was sorely tried by it.

He was finding himself hard to maintain the calm amusement she found so annoying. He'd failed miserably with his carefully thought-out speech to her in the carriage the morning after their marriage, had succeeded only in providing her with more ammunition for her skirmishes against him. He wondered, somewhat pensively, what the devil he was going to do now.

"Come," he said after a moment, "it's time we returned. It will be dark in but a few minutes."

She gave him a clipped nod and, he saw that she was shivering with cold. "Just a moment, my dear," he said.

She stopped and looked at him questioningly, brows raised. He shrugged out of his greatcoat and wrapped it around her shoulders. She drew back, uncertain whether or not to protest.

"No," he said. "Don't. Come now."

Throughout their evening meal in the cozy private parlor, he spoke to her hardly at all,

265

and it seemed to Kate that he appeared rather distracted. She wondered if he was employing a new stratagem. She was soon disabused of this notion, when, after their meal, as the landlord poured him a glass of port, Julien asked, "Would you care to join me?"

She shook her head vehemently, and he grinned at her. "No, don't worry you'll fall on your face. Just one glass, not half a bottle. Trust that I wouldn't allow you to have more than one glass, for in truth, you are no fit companion when you are drunk."

"Very well, one glass. I also think you're unkind to remind me of that night."

Unused to the heady port, she choked on her first sip and fell into a paroxysm of coughing. She quickly downed a glass of water, drew a few sputtering breaths, and leaned back in her chair.

He gave her a pensive look, then sighed his martyr's sigh. "You really must learn to conduct yourself with more grace, dear wife. It befits your new station, you know."

Without thought, she clutched her wine-glass and readied herself to hurl the contents into his face. He read her intent quite easily. "Don't do what you're thinking. I'll give you another statement of fact: If you commit such a childish act, I shall retaliate and treat you as a child."

She clutched the glass tighter.

"In plain words, Kate, if you throw the wine at me, I shall throw you over my knee, bare what I am certain is a lovely backside, and spank you soundly. Who knows what would follow once my hand is on your hips? Surely something quite pleasurable. Surely something you would come to enjoy, perhaps very much."

She set the glass on the table. She'd been made to look very much the fool. Never again would she underestimate him. She rose quickly and strode quickly toward the door.

"Running away? I didn't think you so craven. Come, my dear, I do apologize."

He sounded perfectly sincere, and she stood uncertain, her hand on the doorknob.

Julien said, silently congratulating himself on this sudden inspiration, "I have been given to understand that you play piquet quite well. Do you care to pit your skill against mine?"

She instantly forgot everything. A warm surge of confidence flowed through her. She would beat him into the ground. She was good, very good.

"Perhaps I might be interested. Piquet, you say? I do play occasionally. Very well, if you wish it. It will pass the time." Without thought, she added, "Would you care to lay a wager on the outcome? Say, perhaps a shilling a point?"

She had no sooner spoken the words than her face fell ludicrously, for she realized she had only the pitiful amount of money left from her Paris adventure.

He merely smiled, saying, "Rather than guineas, why don't we set more interesting stakes?"

"What stakes do you have in mind?"

He looked thoughtful for a moment. "Let us say, Kate, that if I win, you will ceremoniously dispose of the gown you are wearing and willingly wear the wardrobe I've provided for you." He felt quite pleased with himself, for the gown she had insisted on wearing for the past three days was in lamentable shape. If she lost to him, which he was quite sure she would, her pride would be salvaged, for she would be merely paying a debt of honor.

"Yes, I will accept that condition, but know that I won't lose, Julien. I never have." She was suddenly aware of the gravy stain that had somehow managed to appear on the bodice of her dress during dinner. "And what is my prize if I win?"

"Have you something in mind, Kate?"

How could she tell him that if she won, she wanted nothing more than to have him vow not to touch her, to quit frightening her in that way? Her tongue seemed to tie itself into knots, and she stood in pained silence. Finally she managed to recall something that she very much wanted. Her words poured out in a rush, "If I win, Julien, I would that you teach me to fence like a man."

"Ho, I was under the impression that you had already learned all men's sports from Harry."

"Ah, Harry, he's a clod with a rapier. I butchered him at the second lesson. You should have seen the look on his face. I thought he would cry there for a while. You,

268

my lord, you are somewhat skilled, are you not?"

"Somewhat, my dear, somewhat."

"You're not exaggerating? As one of the dandy set—"

"Corinthian," he said very gently.

"Are they not the same thing? You are concerned only with your own pursuits, your own pleasures."

"Now that you're my wife, I'm very much concerned with your pleasure as well. But let us cry peace. If you do not mind, ring for our host for a pack of cards."

Once presented with a rather grimy, well-used deck of cards, Julien rose and held out a chair for Kate. She seated herself at the small table Julien had arranged near the fire and began with a good deal of skill to shuffle the deck.

Julien sat down across from her and found that he couldn't help admiring her green eyes, glowing with excitement, and her auburn hair, shimmering with soft lights from the gentle light of the fire. He tore his gaze away from her face, only to find himself acutely aware of the gentle rise and fall of her breasts against the soft material of her gown. He didn't notice the gravy stain.

"Three rubbers, Kate? We will total points at the end to determine the winner."

She nodded in agreement and extended the shuffled cards toward him. "Would you care to cut for the deal, Julien?"

"Yes, certainly."

In a practiced move she fanned the cards on the table toward him. He turned up the jack of hearts. She perused the cards for a moment and flipped over the king of diamonds. Her eyes sparkled. "My king wins, sir."

She played the first several hands carefully, making a concerted effort to assess Julien's skill. As not a great number of points were scored, she found it difficult at the end of the first game to be certain of his abilities.

The rubber went to her, and although there were not much more than a hundred points to her credit, she began to feel more sure of herself. It seemed to her that Julien was an overcautious player, particularly in his discards. She decided that he was much too conservative.

During the second rubber, the luck seemed to run evenly between them, and since Julien didn't give her overt reason to change her opinion of his play, she began to take small chances, risking a gain of substantial points by relying on her instincts. The rubber went to him, but again the points weren't great and she consoled herself that it was only a mild setback. But as she dealt the cards, she was bothered that she couldn't pinpoint exactly why he'd won. He must have held the better cards after all. She allowed only a slight frown to pass over her forehead as she cut the deck to him.

"A glass of claret?"

"No, not for me. I must keep my wits about me. You're playing well, Julien, and I just don't understand it."

"I daresay you will understand very soon now."

During the third rubber, she found, hand after hand, that she failed to defeat his major holdings because of his careful and studied retention of some small card. She quickly changed her opinion of his skill, for he seemed to calculate odds to perfection, curse his hide. He played his cards decisively, no longer ruminating over discards, and it appeared to her that he had the disconcerting trick of summing up her hands with an accuracy that made her wonder bitterly if he could see through the cards. She threw caution to the wind and began to gamble on slim chances, discarding small cards for the chance of picking up an ace or a king. Her confidence plummeted, her nerves grew taut. It annoyed her no end that he appeared so repulsively casual and relaxed. The third rubber ended quickly when, in the final hand, Julien spread out his hand, all save one card, and said gently, "I trust my quint is good."

"Quite good."

"And the four kings and three aces?"

"Also good." She stared down at the impressive array of high cards and then back at the one card he still held in his hand.

"Oh, hell and the devil," she said. "I'll be fleeced horribly if I don't manage to guess this discard. Drat, I have no idea what to keep."

"No, I agree, there's nothing at all to tell

you." He sat back in his chair, turning the long card first one way and then another between his long fingers.

"Very well, a spade." She flung the card onto the table.

"Sorry, but you must lose." Julien turned the card toward her, and she saw that he held a small diamond.

She gazed at the card for a long moment, unwilling to believe that she'd been trounced so thoroughly. How it galled her to lose to him when she had been so certain that she would defeat him. She fought with herself to take her loss gracefully.

"It appears that you've bettered me."

"I had no doubt of the outcome."

She recoiled from his quietly spoken words, and a shadow of hurt and surprise filled her eyes. She couldn't explain why, but it seemed very unlike him to make her feel her defeat more than necessary. "It's not very kind of you to say that."

"You're a fine player. You're weakest in your discards. You don't play the odds as you should. Of course I would beat you, for I have at least ten more years of experience in the game than you do. In time, if you attend carefully, your skill will equal mine."

As she gathered the cards together, she became painfully aware that he was regarding her steadily. She instantly forgot her vow to beat him at cards as she felt a surge of fear sweep through her. She dropped the cards onto the table and quickly squirmed out of her chair, her eyes fixed on the door.

"Surely you don't wish to leave so soon. Wouldn't you like to discuss some of the finer points of the game?" He rose leisurely as he spoke and walked to the closed door, cutting off her only avenue of escape.

"I want to go to bed now." Was that her voice, all thin and sickly-sounding?

"Precisely my idea, my dear. It's encouraging that you begin to read my wishes."

"That isn't what I mean and well you know it."

He walked slowly over to where she stood. She felt like a fox being stalked by only one big hunter.

"But it's exactly what I mean. I've let you have your way for four nights now. A very long time. Far too long for a man to wait to bed his bride. I want you and I want you now. Will you come with me?"

She ran behind the card table, out of his reach. Though she was a scant three feet from him, the small barrier gave her courage.

"No, I won't come with you. Please, don't you understand? I don't want you to frighten me like that."

He walked around the card table.

"No. Stay away from me. I swear I'll fight you, Julien. I'll hurt you. I'm no weakling. I'm strong and I hurt Harry many times."

He found himself torn between exasperation and a physical desire that was fast dying. The situation had gone beyond absurd. He couldn't allow it to continue another night.

Damnation. He drew a steadying breath. "Listen to me, wife. I find it refreshing that in liberal times virginal modesty still exists, but you carry it to an absurd point." He leaned over and spread his hands on the table, his eyes on a level with hers.

"When are you going to accept the fact that I'm your husband? When are you going to face up to the fact that you and I, madam, will be together until one of us cocks up his toes and passes to the hereafter?"

She was trembling. Not wanting him to see her fear, she quickly whisked her shaking hands behind her back. "It's not that, truly. It's just that—"

He waited for her to continue, but she fell silent, her hands knotting the material of her skirt. He was baffled, no other word for it. There she was, his wife, standing there, her face as white as the collar of her gown had been four days ago.

He'd been so certain that her refusal of him was because of her damnable pride, her anger at him for removing all choice from her. He saw fear now, stark and livid in her eyes, real fear so deep and urgent that he couldn't begin to imagine what was the matter. He cudgeled his brain in an effort to figure out what to do, what to think about this situation.

"Kate, help me to understand you. I know your mother died when you were quite young. In fact, you were alone at an age when a mother's advice and teaching are very important." He paused a moment, studying

274

her face, but oddly, she was simply looking at him blankly, as if she hadn't even heard him.

"A father and a brother aren't the same. Did your father warn you against men? Did he frighten you? Did he tell you that men would hurt you, perhaps even harm you? Did he try to make you believe that a physical love between a husband and wife was sinful?"

A fragile image of her mother rose in Kate's mind. She was crooning gentle words to her, somehow consoling her, stroking her hair. She felt pain, then, but it was long-ago pain that no longer existed, at least in her body. It was still there, though in her mind, somewhere, somewhere. The fleeting picture brought with it inexplicable panic.

"Did he tell you that a husband would treat you badly? Did he try to convince you it was disgusting?"

"Oh no, no." She wished she hadn't spoken, for her words dissolved her mother's face and with it the strange memory.

"Very well, then," he said and straightened to his full height. "I must then assume that you're simply thwarting me, for whatever reason I have yet to fathom. I hope you don't choke on your pride, Kate. I am very tired of playing your adversary in a game I can't begin to understand." He waited a moment, sighed, then turned to the sideboard and poured himself a glass of claret.

She looked after him, perplexed, and as he didn't turn back to her, she picked up her skirts and walked slowly from the room.

275

22

Julien sat alone in the private parlor the following morning, his hands curled around a warm cup of coffee, waiting for his bride of nearly a week now who wasn't yet his wife. He wondered idly if she would honor her lost wager and appear in a gown he'd bought for her. He had not long to dwell on this question, for soon the landlord opened the door and she swept past poor old Perchon into the room, dressed in the height of fashion and wearing a militant expression. He silently applauded his taste, for the lavender muslin, secured below her bosom with rosebud lace, became her to perfection. He rose lazily from his chair and proffered her a deep bow. "How charming you are this morning, my dear."

"I'm gratified you think so highly of your own taste." She seated herself at the breakfast table. Secretly she was quite pleased with the picture she presented, and impressed with the style and cut of the gown. She wished only that it had been she who'd chosen it and not Julien.

"Very well. How did you know my size?"

"Would you like a cup of tea before the inquisition begins? No, I see that you want an answer now. Very well. It was a lucky guess. The top of your head comes to my chin. I held out my hands like this and decided your breasts would fill them nicely. I've clasped you about your waist and found it about so." He made his hands into a nearly touching circle, to which she snorted. "As to your hips, I'm fortunate that I've seen you in breeches. Do you wish to know anything else?"

"I don't believe you. Perhaps you bribed my maid for the measurements."

His eyes twinkled. "As you will. Odd that you don't believe the truth when you hear it."

"It's rubbish. I'm not a fool, Julien. It's obvious you gained such knowledge by purchasing such garments for your mistresses." She drew back, flushed, for she hadn't meant to say anything of the sort and was appalled at her shrew's voice. If she thought he'd be a gentleman and ignore her unfortunate lapse, she was sadly mistaken.

"Ho, my dear, do I detect a note of jealousy? Perhaps a quiver of resentment? Don't worry, since my marriage I've given all my mistresses a permanent congé."

"You might very well change your mind about that. It's quite possible you'll soon find yourself wishing for their amiable company."

"Please don't hold yourself in low esteem. You will be all that I could ever desire in a woman. It appears it will just take me a while to bring you to the sticking point."

"I'm not hungry and you look as if you've eaten an entire cache of eggs and drunk an urn of coffee. Shall we continue our journey?"

"Our wedding trip," he said in his best nobleman's drawl.

They bowled out of the courtyard of the Coeur de Lyon not long thereafter, and as Julien wished to reach the villa by late afternoon, they maintained a smart pace throughout the morning, halting only once to change horses. To Kate's relief, she was relieved of his company for the better part of the afternoon, as he decided to take the reins.

"We've a sluggish leader who needs a firm hand. I hope you don't mind being alone, wife."

She raised her brows at him. As he stepped from the chaise, he remarked over his shoulder, "It's a sad trial. It appears my firm hand is needed in so many things. From my bride's clothes to my rented horses."

Her attention was suddenly claimed by a very interesting rock formation by the side of the road. But it wasn't long before she found that she was grinning despite herself, forced to admit that he was very good with the horses—rot his eyes—for the chaise was moving at a smoother pace, with fewer jolts and lurches.

She settled back and enjoyed the beautiful Swiss countryside that unfolded outside her window, trying to forget that she'd condemned it so shortly before. Such a short time before that, it would never have occurred to her even to think so stupid a thing, but so much had changed since the day she had first met the earl of March. As she recalled the shocked look on his face when he realized that his duelist was a girl, her lips curled into a smile. How very pleasant too were the early days she'd spent in his company. She'd been so very comfortable with him, speaking her mind, never mincing words. He'd been the most delightful of companions. She'd trusted him, as a friend, never really seeing him as a man, as a man who would want her.

She sighed and leaned back against the squabs, closing her eyes. He had destroyed those halcyon days and had robbed her of all comfort and peace of mind. She remembered unwillingly the day he'd asked her to wed him, the suffocating fear that had risen unbidden to choke her. She understood her fear not one whit better than she had then. She knew only that it was deep within her, a part of her from which she could not seem to free herself.

She opened her eyes as the chaise lurched its way ponderously up a steep incline that cut through dense, lush forest. A few minutes later the road widened, and the chaise burst out of the forest into a large triangular clearing atop a jutting promontory. In the center of the clearing stood a small, elegantly constructed white-brick villa. Delicately wrought columns supported the overhanging balconies of the second floor. It seemed to Kate that in the fading sunlight the endless numbers of windows glittered like bright prisms.

Snowcapped peaks were visible in the distance, and the well-scythed lawn seemed to melt into the green of the forest, as if blended into it by an artist's brush. It was an exquisite private mansion suited for royalty. She wondered from whom he'd secured this place.

As Julien reined in the horses, her attention was drawn to an older man and woman bustling out of the front doors toward them. Julien opened the chaise door and helped her to alight before turning his attention to the couple, who stood viewing her with lively curiosity.

"Good afternoon, James, Maria. I'd like you to meet my countess, Katharine St Clair. Kate, meet James and Maria Crayton, thankfully here to keep us clean and dressed and well fed."

The woman drew her stiff bombazine skirts into a curtsy, and the man gave a tug to a rather unruly spike of gray hair. "A real pleasure, my lady." He beamed at Kate, revealing slightly protruding teeth.

Kate inclined her head, conscious suddenly of the somewhat strange yet pleasing experience of being treated with such deference.

"We weren't expecting your lordship and ladyship so soon," James continued to Julien. "But Mrs Crayton and I have everything ready for you, my lord, all right and proper, even though we've had to deal with these foreigners."

"Excellent. Her ladyship is quite fatigued from the long journey. Would you be so kind as to show her to her bedchamber, Maria?"

"I'm not at all fatigued, Julien. However, I would very much like to see my room."

"Her ladyship is renowned for her stamina, Maria. Has the weather continued warm, James?"

"Yes, my lord, though the nights are quite chilly. A peaceful place this is. Mrs Crayton and I fancy that we can hear our hair grow, so quiet it is."

Kate ignored Julien's laugh and followed Mrs Crayton into a small entry way. As she mounted the delicately carved staircase that wound in a lazy circular fashion to the upper floor, Julien called out, "Let's dine in an hour. Is that sufficient time for you to perform whatever womanly chores necessary?"

"What womanly chores? No, don't answer that. I will certainly find something suitably womanly to occupy my time. Perhaps an hour won't be sufficient. Perhaps you would like to tool the carriage back to Geneva?"

"And leave my enthusiastic bride? Not a chance. Do strive to please me in this, my dear. An hour." He grinned at her and to her chagrin, she found the corners of her mouth tilting up. As this would never do, she quickly turned, hurrying after Mrs Crayton.

She was shown into a small, delightfully furnished room, dominated on one side by a fireplace and on the other by long windows curtained with pale-pink brocade. The furniture was all white and gold, in the French style of the last century, blending with exquisite artistry into the delicate shades of pink in the carpet. Her eyes alight with pleasure, Kate turned impulsively to Mrs Crayton. "It's a lovely room. How surprising to find such elegance in so remote a place."

"Indeed, my lady, Mr Crayton and I were a bit concerned when his lordship told us to come here and make preparations, but now we quite like it."

"You are part of his lordship's staff in London?"

"Certainly, my lady. Mr Crayton and I were with his lordship's father, the late earl of March. It was quite excited we were, coming to this foreign place and all, even though we were concerned, as I said. His lordship said we needed a change of air, he did. He knew he could trust us to carry out his wishes."

She pursed her lips. A journey from London to Switzerland must occupy the better part of a week, perhaps even more. The Craytons would have had to leave England before Julien had come to Paris. Surely not. "When did his lordship send you here, Mrs Crayton?"

"We've been here nearly a week now, my lady," Mrs Crayton said, quite unaware that her young mistress was now as stiff as the maple tree outside the bedchamber window. "Naturally his lordship told us he was going to be married in Paris. He wanted us to come immediately to have all in readiness for your ladyship. But, of course, you know all of this already." She smiled kindly at her new mistress. "It's pleased we are that Master Julien has finally wed. Ach, but here I go again. Mr Crayton is forever telling me my tongue runs on wheels, begging your ladyship's pardon."

"Yes, yes, of course I knew, Mrs Crayton," Kate said quickly. Though the woman's tongue ran on wheels, they were quite informative ones. Damn Julien anyway. How very certain he had been of himself and of her.

Mrs Crayton read the tightening of her ladyship's lips and the sudden frown on her forehead as signs of fatigue. "You just sit down and rest by the fire, and I'll have Mr Crayton fetch up a nice hot bath."

When Mrs Crayton had removed her garrulous self from the room, Kate yanked off the expensive bonnet and flung it on a chair. The blue-velvet cloak that Julien had bought for her she tossed in a heap on top of the bonnet. She sank down into the soft cushions of the settee that faced the fireplace and idly looked about her for an object to fling at Julien, were he to present himself. She looked fondly at a small gilded mirror that hung over the mantel but thought pessimistically that he would handily duck it were it to be hurled at his head. She found the mental image evoked by such a confrontation so comical that she couldn't long maintain her anger at him and his officious confidence. She even found herself thinking somewhat philosophically that it would have been most unlike Julien to forget so important an item as accommodations for their wedding trip. She wondered, indeed, if he ever forgot any detail. He had even attended to acquiring the perfectly fitted satin undergarments that felt so delightfully luxurious against her skin, so very different from the stout cotton she'd worn until just days ago.

She sighed and said to the crackling fire, "Well, my girl, there is no way of getting around the fact that you're married. I guess once married, one stays married and makes the best of it."

The fire crackled and popped. She instantly took exception to her own conclusions, for they reeked of capitulation, of nauseating submission. Nothing had changed between them. She wouldn't allow him to bend her to his will. As this resolve brought with it an unsettling sense of dissatisfaction, she closed her eyes and concentrated on thinking about absolutely nothing.

When she appeared in the cozy dining room, closer to two hours than one after they had parted, she saw Julien standing in front of the long windows, his back to her, gazing out into the darkness, his hand holding back the dark-blue drapery, an elegant hand with long fingers, a man's hand with strength and power. He turned as her rustling skirts announced her presence, and she was momentarily taken aback by the very serious expression on his face. But in an instant the

284

expression was gone, and he strolled, as indolent as a lizard lazing about beneath a bright sun, to where she stood, took her hand in his, and kissed her fingers.

"How very beautiful you are tonight, my dear. Do you find your bedchamber to your liking?"

"I fear, Julien, that you compliment the gown you chose rather than its wearer. I'm just me, the same me you met in breeches and that old hat."

"I know it well. Know too that I very thoroughly appraised the wearer long before I purchased the gown. Do tell me, do you find your bedchamber adequate?"

"If you had ever seen my bedchamber at Brandon Hall, you wouldn't ask such a question. It's charming, more than charming. It's quite the nicest bedchamber I've ever seen in my life, and doubtless you know that."

"I trust you'll also find the sherry delightful," he said, handing her a glass. "It's really quite excellent. The Conte Bellini's cellar rivals that of St Clair."

"Who is this Conte Bellini person?"

"A friend of mine. We've done business together and, of course, gamed and caroused together in Milan."

No surprise there, but she knew he was baiting her. She managed not to swallow the bait, saying instead, "Ah, something else. Mrs Crayton informed me that not only are she and Mr Crayton in your household staff in London but they've been here for nearly a week. You told them, my lord, you actually *told* them while you were still in London that you were getting married in Paris. That passes all bounds, Julien. Your conceit and arrogance make you a candidate for the gallows, *my* gallows."

A sleek brow shot up in seeming surprise. "What bounds? Me, arrogant? Gallows? I don't begin to understand you, wife. Surely you would wish to have all in readiness for you when we arrived here."

"That isn't at all the point, as you very well know. You told them in London, damn you."

"Had I not told them, how else could they have been here in good time?" Julien drained the remainder of his sherry and looked down at her with mild surprise.

She fidgeted with her glass a moment, realizing that to continue in her argument would only provide him with more amusement at her expense. "Very well, you refuse to acknowledge the justice of my point. I don't wish to haggle further with you. Oh, how nice, here is our dinner."

"Begging your lordship's pardon, but you said dinner was to be served when her ladyship arrived."

"Your entrance was exquisitely timed, Maria. Kate, my dear, would you care to be seated?"

"How very gracious of you, my lord March. Ah, do try the lamb, it looks quite delicious."

"Yes, ma'am," Julien said, grinning at her, and promptly fell to his dinner.

Some minutes later, he said casually, "Oh, I quite forgot to tell you. Harry wrote you a letter and asked that I give it to you."

"A letter from Harry? But how ever did you get a letter from Harry? No, no, please don't deign to give me a tedious explanation. How could I imagine that you would overlook my brother in all your machinations?"

"You begin to understand me, Kate. I do apologize for not giving it to you sooner, but there were so many other pressing matters that I forgot about it. Crayton found it when he was unpacking."

It didn't take her long to decipher the few lines of Harry's familiar sloping scrawl, and she raised a face pale with anger to Julien. She wadded up the sheet, really quite viciously, and clutched it in a tight fist.

"Good Lord, you look ready to hurl your lamb chops at the sofa. Whatever did he write?"

"You miserable sod, you put him up to this." She flung the ball of paper at him. He caught the paper handily and smoothed it out in front of him. He'd expected Harry to simply congratulate his sister, which of course he did, but in such a way that Julien could readily understand why it had raised her hackles, indeed, sent her temper to the boiling point. Harry had advised her in no uncertain terms not to play the shrew and argue and give orders as was her wont, because she was, after all, a very lucky girl to be offered marriage by such a distinguished,

287

amiable, and accomplished gentleman. Even this could have been forgiven if, in his zeal to commend himself to his brother-in-law, Harry had not gone so far as to advise her to forget all her nonsensical notions of playing at men's sports, to toss away her men's breeches as well as her pistols, to become an obedient wife and conduct herself as a countess should. Undoubtedly Harry had meant to do him a favor. Lord, he hadn't meant to impress the boy so. The last few lines were difficult to read, and Julien, after making them out, decided that Kate hadn't read to the end of her letter. Perhaps it would reduce her anger. Probably not, but perhaps.

"Control your ire, my dear. Your brother was a trifle overexuberant in his, er, counsel, but you should forgive him, for he was very excited about joining his regiment."

"Counsel! Is that what you call it? Oh, what do you mean—joining what regiment?"

"The last lines of his letter. He tells you that by the time you read his letter, he will be on his way to Spain."

"Spain," she repeated blankly.

"Of course. You must have known this was his wish above all things—to be a soldier, all dashed out in a white-and-red uniform, a saber at his side, astride a stallion of doubtless noble descent. I made the arrangements before I left London. Don't worry about him, for there are only minor squabbles with the guerrillas since Napoleon's downfall. Trust me, Kate. I even spoke to Lord Hawksbury, telling him that under no circumstances did I want Harry in the midst of any fighting. He's still too green. But he will learn and mature, and I suspect that he will make an excellent soldier in the not-too-distant future."

She said nothing to that, just sat there, her lamb untouched on her plate, her head averted, stiff as a pike. He said, more harshly than he intended, "Good God, Kate, I don't understand you. Harry is a grown man, or very nearly grown. You're behaving as though he is still in short coats and you're his doting mother or great aunt. Let him have his freedom, let him get away from Sir Oliver, who wants to make a scholar of a boy with no more taste for Ovid than Sophocles, who hated his guts, had."

"It's not that," she said, and she was actually wringing her hands. "It's just happened so quickly. Everything's happened so quickly. Everything is different. The changes ... there have been so many changes."

The world she'd known had crumbled about her. Harry had been everything to her after her mother died. Of course she'd known that someday he would leave her, that he would even marry and another girl would take her place in his heart, but it had always been in a misty, vague future. A very distant future. Dear God, he was only twenty-two, and he'd left her without telling her, without a single damned word, without giving her time to reconcile herself to it.

Quite suddenly, her look of unhappiness

was replaced again by thin-lipped anger. She was now dwelling on Harry's other words. Julien waited patiently for her outburst, but it didn't come. Perplexed, he saw the angry look vanish, and to his consternation, she gazed at him steadily and said in a voice that was surely desperate, "So, my lord, I am to be your obedient wife and conduct myself as a countess should. Just how does a countess behave? Does she stick her nose in the air when addressed by those who are beneath her? And who are beneath her? Pray tell me, for these are uncharted seas for me."

23

He stretched out his hand and let his long fingers close over hers. "You are no longer Sir Oliver's daughter. He has no more say about anything regarding you. You're now mine. You're also now a countess, and that means that however you choose to behave is quite the correct way." He spoke easily, smiling, hoping to make light of Harry's ill-chosen words.

To his surprise and dismay, a large tear gathered and rolled unheeded down her cheek. She didn't sniff or blink, merely let the tear and those following it gather and fall, leaving a light streak to mark their path.

"My dear—"

She calmly picked up her napkin, daubed the corners of her eyes, and wiped her cheeks. She said dully, "It seems that I didn't know my brother. He is exactly like the rest of you men. He cares for naught but his own pleasures, his own pursuits, no matter that they may kill him, and expects women to keep to their place, safe and quiet and subservient. An obedient and, yes, undoubtedly, inferior creature, that's what he expects. Of course, it is what you wish also. The rest is all nonsense. Pray don't insult my intelligence or patronize me."

She slipped out of her chair and without another word walked stiffly to the door. She didn't turn when he called out to her, just let herself quietly out of the room, picked up her skirts, and fled up the stairs to her bed-chamber. Ah yes, such a lovely room, a room fit for a countess, which she now was, but what was that, indeed? Surely not she, for she was miserable and unfit and quite stupid.

She looked blindly about her for a moment and then flung herself face down on the bed. She was lost in her own private misery and was roused only when the fire in the grate burned low and she began to shiver. She stood up, automatically smoothing the folds of her beautiful new gown. It was hopelessly crumpled, but she didn't care, for after all, it was Julien's. If he didn't like the wrinkles, let him smooth them.

She walked to the windows, found the cord,

and pulled back the heavy curtains. The night was black save for a few errant stars appearing through the heavy veil of darkness. She pulled the latch and leaned out, the cold night air pressing against her face. A picture of Harry in his yellow-striped waistcoat, proudly pluming himself in front of her, came into her mind. Harry, flinging his arms heavenward, groaning loudly, falling flat on his back when it had last been his turn to be killed in a duel. Harry, now gone from her, now gone to Spain. Harry, no longer a part of her life. Harry, a man like all the rest of them, now gone from her irrevocably. Deep inside she knew that nothing could ever again be the same. For so long as Harry had remained near to her, a semblance of their years together, the happy moments of her childhood, was preserved. But now they had both crossed unalterably into a different life, their past forever lost to them.

She suddenly felt very tired. She drew back into the room and slowly closed the window, but not the draperies. Not without some difficulty, she managed to unfasten the small buttons at the back of her gown. She let the gown slide to the floor and simply stepped out of it, leaving it where it lay. She slipped out of the silk chemise and then walked slowly to the exquisite bed with its canopy of a soft beige-and-pink silk, pulled back the satin counterpane, and slid between the warm covers.

* * *

Long after the covers had been removed by the unobtrusive Mrs Crayton, Julien sat alone in brooding silence. He held a glass of claret in his hand and stared vaguely into its depths. It was smooth, deeply red, and it warmed his stomach. Unfortunately, it hadn't yet spread its mellowing warmth to his mind or his groin. He wanted a woman. He hurt with need. It wasn't something he was used to, this enforced celibacy, this absurd denial. He was a man, dammit, and a man released his passion in a woman regularly and it was the way it was meant to be. And now he was even married—a wife belonged to her husband, and surely a husband could have his wife whenever and however it pleased him to have her, and yet, here she was, still a damned virgin after day upon day of marriage, and he'd allowed it to go on and on and on, because he liked her. He admired her spirit and her independence, her differentness, which had drawn him to her in the first place, like a moth to a flame. He'd seen Sir Oliver and spoken to the wretched, perverted creature; he knew that he'd beaten her regularly, for whatever reason he couldn't begin to fathom, had guessed at what her life had been like under that despicable tyrant's hand, and was trying desperately to understand her, because, dammit, he loved her, and he wanted her to be happy.

Dear God, he hated the situation. He hurt. He felt a cold, impotent frustration. She seemed farther out of his reach than ever before, even though she was now his wife. Certainly he understood that Harry's admonishments galled her. But Harry's commission was another matter entirely. Why couldn't she accept the fact that Harry was ready for freedom? Wasn't he entering his manhood? Wasn't he ready and entitled for the adventures he wanted so badly?

He rose from the table and walked slowly and thoughtfully to the fireplace. He leaned his elbows on the mantel and gazed into the dying flames. In that instant he cursed the woman who had so changed his life, the red-haired witch who had woven her web so completely around him that he no longer desired any other woman. He wanted her, no other woman, curse her white hide. It wasn't fair. If he had stayed in London, he never would have met her. But he *had* met her, dying in her duel with Harry, falling dramatically at his feet. Then she pulled off her boy's cap and he saw her as the girl she was, as the girl he wanted, the girl he desired more than life itself. Damn her stubborn eyes. He wanted to beat her, perhaps strangle her just a bit. No, he wanted her naked and he wanted to kiss her and caress her and—

He strode quickly from the dining room and flung out of the villa into the dark night. Without really realizing what he was doing, he found himself walking to the side of the villa, to where her bedchamber was located. Almost against his will he looked up at her windows. The curtains were open. She was standing in the middle of her room, clad only in her chemise. He sucked in his breath at the sight of her, knew his hands were fisted at his sides, knew that his member was swelling as hard as a rock, knew that his heart was pounding faster and harder and harder still. He stood rooted to the spot and watched her after a long moment pull the straps of the chemise off her white shoulders. The ache in his groin became nearly intolerable as she let the chemise slip over her breasts to her narrow waist. God, he'd pictured her breasts in his mind, filled his hands with her breasts, at least in his fantasies. She was glorious, her breasts as beautiful as he'd imagined, more beautiful than any woman's he'd ever seen, ever caressed, ever fondled, full and high, the nipples a dark pink, oh, God, so lovely, he wanted to touch her, to take each of her nipples in his mouth and suckle her and bring her such pleasure that she wouldn't be able to bear it and she'd moan and whisper how much she wanted him and please, please, give her more pleasure, and more and more.

He forced himself to turn away, cursing his own weakness, cursing his vivid imagination, which wasn't really imagination, for he knew well her flesh would be soft and warm and there would be her scent, only hers, and he would breathe in that scent and it would drive him mad.

Still, he saw even as he was turning, the silken material fall below her waist and he glimpsed her white belly, white as a saint's brow, white as the body of a virgin, which she was. Oh, Jesus. Despite the coldness of the night, he was sweating. With a growl he broke away, forcing himself not to look back. He knew he couldn't look back and see the rest of her, the thatch of auburn hair covering her, the long, white thighs, sleek with muscle, for she was a country girl used to walking and thus fit and strong. He remained outside, until finally, shivering violently from the cold, he was forced to go back into the villa.

"His lordship isn't here?"

"No, my lady. 'Twas quite early his lordship left this morning to go into the village. He said he'll be returning for dinner."

Mrs Crayton thought it strange that his lordship hadn't informed his countess of his plans. Indeed, she wondered at her ladyship's puffy eyes and remembered the crumpled gown she'd picked up from the floor. She decided that they must have had a lovers' quarrel the previous evening, surely unfortunate, but not unusual for a man and wife newly wed. She remembered the arguments during those early years when she and James had screamed at each other, yelling the most ridiculously horrid things, not meaning them of course, at least not ten minutes later.

"I see," Kate said, slipping into a wrapper. Perversely, she felt slighted that he hadn't told her, but then, of course, she'd not given him the opportunity. She'd left both him and that delicious lamb chop quite alone.

She managed to keep herself busy through-out the morning poking her head in and out of the elegant rooms in the villa. After a light luncheon, she donned a shawl and strolled out into the grounds. It delighted her that there were no formal gardens, for she had never enjoyed her mother's pastime of pulling up weeds and putting in her favorite flowers, particularly the rose plants she'd brought from Scotland, carrying them on her elope-ment. The vast wilderness of forest and mountains here gave her a feeling of un-restrained freedom. From the edge of a cliff to the left of the villa she could make out the small village nestled in the valley below. She sat down near the edge and wrapped her skirt about her legs. Although she had gotten used to being alone, particularly after Harry left for Eton, she found that now she didn't enjoy her solitude. She didn't understand herself. It was disconcerting.

She wandered back to the villa, selected a small volume of Lord Byron's poems from the shelf in the well-strocked library, and curled up in the window seat. But her atten-tion wasn't long held by the poet's bold, haunting words, for she couldn't help re-membering Julien's telling her with laughter and a touch of regret in his voice of Lady Caroline Lamb and her flaunted affair with the quixotic Byron.

She had thought then of the excitement of belonging to such a world, of meeting people who cut such a romantic dash through

London society. She sighed and leaned back on her elbows and allowed the thin vellum volume to drop to the floor. Somehow she still felt like the provincial Kate Brandon. She wondered when she would feel like a countess. Julien had said she was a countess, that whatever she did, it was all right, because she was a countess. She couldn't begin to understand him.

Later in the afternoon, bored with her inactivity, she sallied forth, and without any particular destination in mind, began to walk down the single winding road that led to the village. Being used to country life, she found the exercise invigorating and maintained a brisk pace. She didn't see a single soul. She allowed herself to be drawn into the quiet serenity of the ageless forest. She had bent down to stroke a soft fern that had wound itself around a tree trunk when she was startled to her feet by a shrill cry. She wheeled around and, seeing nothing, hurried around a bend in the road. She pulled up short, not believing what she saw. A peasant stood in the middle of the road, flailing a mare with a knobby stick. The horse whinnied and shied, blowing hard, trembling, her flanks rippling, but the man held her firmly, cursing as he rained blows on her head and back.

She picked up her skirts and ran toward the man. He didn't notice her until she grabbed his arm and shouted at him, "Stop it, you fool! How dare you strike that poor animal? By all that's holy, you should be thrown off a cliff. You should be gutted like a trout, you miserable beast, er, fish."

The peasant jerked around, baring blackened teeth in an astonished grimace at the sight of a well-dressed young lady, her face red with fury.

Realizing that she'd spoken in English, she paused and gathered suitable blighting words in French. "Whatever are you doing, you wretched creature? I demand that you stop beating this poor animal."

"You *demand*, my pretty young lady?"

"Just look what you've done." Flecks of foam dropped from the mare's mouth, and ugly red blood streaks criss-crossed on her head and neck. Kate moved to the horse to quiet her, but the peasant blocked her way and shook the stick in her face. "It's my horse, Missie, and I'll give the beast the beating she deserves. Kicked me, she did, the mangy creature."

"You probably deserved the kicking. You probably deserve much more. And if you fed her properly she wouldn't be mangy. You should be shot." From long experience with facing Sir Oliver, ranting and waving his cane at her, she now felt no fear. She, quite simply, wanted to kill him.

The peasant pulled up short at this attack from the foreign lady and narrowed his eyes at her speculatively. He licked his lips and looked meaningfully at the single strand of pearls about her neck. "How strange it is that such a fine young lady is out walking by herself. Maybe I'll not beat the beast if you give me those fine pearls." He reached out a dirty hand, and Kate jumped back out of his reach.

"Don't be absurd, you cruel creature. You can't frighten me. I shall have you whipped, which is less than you deserve, if you so much as lay a hand on me. I'll have you made into bacon, you swine."

"On aye? And who'll do this whipping, Missie? Who'll do the chopping, eh?" He was advancing on her, the stick poised. He looked revoltingly pleased with himself, happy as he could be.

Without thought, she balled her hand into a fist, as Harry had taught her, and struck the man full in the face, right in his jaw, just left of his lower lip. He staggered back, more from surprise than pain. His rough features distorted with rage, he cursed her loudly in words she couldn't begin to understand.

Now frightened, since she wasn't a fool, she began to back away from him warily. She should have kicked him in the groin, the more extreme measure Harry had taught her to use when a man offended.

"I'll show you, you bloody bitch!" The man rushed at her, swinging the stick in a wide arc.

In that instant the mare, now freed, reared on her hind legs and thrust her hooves at the peasant's back, hard. He went sprawling, yelling as he went down, and landed on his face mere inches from Kate's feet.

Kate grabbed the mare's mane and swung onto her back. The mare snorted in surprise and reared again, her front hooves pawing the air. Kate hung on tightly to her mane, disregarding a huge rip in her skirt. She saw only that miserable man, who was rising slowly and painfully from the ground, his eyes as mean now as Sir Oliver's at the most vicious of times. She threw herself forward on the mare's neck and grasped the loose reins. She felt pain shoot through her leg as the peasant's stick struck hard on her thigh. She bit back a cry, dug her heels into the mare's sides, and hung on with all her strength as the frightened horse shot forward in an erratic gallop. She didn't look back, just hugged herself against the mare's neck. She realized vaguely that there was only the single mountain road and that they were heading in the direction of the village.

She heard the peasant yelling after her and looked back in sudden panic, afraid that he had another horse. He was running after her, his fists raised, screaming. She breathed only a momentary sigh of relief, for she hadn't the foggiest notion what she was going to do. She'd stolen a horse—albeit for the purest of motives—and was fleeing toward a foreign village, where, for all she knew, the people were as vicious and uncaring as that horrible peasant.

She wanted to yell with relief when she saw

301

in the distance two horses coming up the road at a leisurely pace. It took her but a moment to recognize Julien, with James Crayton following closely behind him. She urged the mare forward and waved wildly with one hand. As she neared, she pulled back on the reins. To her despair, the still-frightened mare gave a loud snort and plunged her head down, quickening her pace.

"Good God, Crayton, whoever the devil can that be? What foolhardiness on such a winding road. The idiot will come to grief, you can wager on it." Julien reined in his horse. The words died in his throat as he recognized his wife's auburn hair whipping about her surely too white face and saw her torn clothing. He felt colder than ice. He felt fury boiling his innards. Numb rage, that's what it was. He dug in his heels, and soon they drew so close that he could see the flaring of the horse's nostrils. She streaked past him, yelling, "I can't stop her, Julien! Please help me!"

He wheeled his horse about, galloping after her. After what seemed an eternity to both of them, he drew up beside her and grabbed the mare's reins. For a long moment he struggled with the terrified mare to bring her, finally, to a walk. He leaped from his horse and grasped the reins firmly and with infinite care calmed the trembling animal.

"Thank God! For a moment I didn't think you'd catch us. The poor mare, she was so frightened. Oh, forget the mare, I've never been more frightened in my life. Thank you, my lord." She slipped off the mare's back, found that her legs had become curiously boneless, and promptly sat down hard at the side of the road.

"My lord, whatever has happened?" Crayton dismounted and rushed toward them.

"I don't yet know, James." He continued to quiet the trembling horse.

"But all the blood, my lord—"

"Yes, yes, I see. Hopefully, her ladyship isn't harmed, but rather this wretched animal. Here, James, take her reins. Keep talking to her softly, keep calming her. Yes, that's it. Keep her soothed and quiet."

Julien dropped to his haunches in front of his wife, gripped her shoulders, and shook her slightly. "What the damned hell happened? Are you all right? In the good Lord's name, what have you done?"

She stared up at him, so relieved to see him that all she could to was stare at him and smile and clutch at his sleeve and pray that he would understand.

"Hello, Julien," she said. "I really didn't intend this, you know."

"Before I strangle you and then shoot that poor miserable horse, tell me what happened."

24

Julien pulled her to her feet. "All right, what did you do? Damnation, I have this awful feeling I really don't want to know."

"Probably not," she said, as she brought up her hands to clutch at his shoulders. Though she knew now she was quite safe, the enormity of what she'd just done now left her quite speechless.

"Come on, spill it out. Don't try to fob me off with something benign. You've never done anything benign in your bloody life. Now, what happened?" His voice was sharper than he intended, for his fear for her was great still.

Oddly, his tone steadied her, and she drew back and gave him a rather feeble smile. "I fear I'm going to have to face a magistrate, Julien, though I meant it all for the best. You see, I've stolen the horse."

He just stared down at her, realizing he wasn't really surprised. He held her while she gathered together her disordered thoughts and launched into her story. It required several questions for Julien to grasp the facts.

"You do understand, don't you, Julien? I couldn't let that horrid man continue to beat the mare. And he wouldn't be reasonable

304

about the matter, and I did try to tell him to stop, at first quite nicely, well nearly, but I was so angry at what he was doing. I had to be nice because I had to do it in French."

"This peasant, the bastard, tried to harm you?"

"Well, yes, but, you see, I gave him great provocation by hitting him in the face. Surely that would make anyone rather angry. I should have kicked him in the groin the way Harry showed me to do, but I forgot. The mare struck him in the back, and that saved me."

"Where is this man?" He realized that for the first time in his life he was most willingly prepared to commit murder. Her blathering moved him not one whit. Good Lord, he could just see her trying to kick the man in the crotch.

"The last time I saw him, he was standing in the road waving his fists at me. Back up there." She turned and pointed with a grimy finger.

Julien turned abruptly to Crayton. "Take our heroine mare here, James, and let her ladyship mount your horse. Come, Kate, we are going to settle this matter right now. Kick him in the groin? Good God."

She started to argue, but he ignored her, took her firmly by the arm, and tossed her into the saddle. He ground his teeth at the sight of her bloodied, torn gown.

Kate found herself frightened, not now for herself but rather for Julien. That was surely odd, but nonetheless it was there. "Please, I don't want you to particularly murder the man, even though he was vicious and a bully."

He was white with rage. He wasn't listening to her. She held her tongue. She'd started it all, and now it appeared that he was going to finish it.

"Can you manage the horse?"

"Of course I can. I didn't lose my skill, just my temper."

"Very well. Cease your advice and pay heed to not falling off. Kick him in the groin? I don't believe it."

Kate had not much choice in the matter, for Julien vaulted into the saddle and urged his horse into a gallop.

Julien was furious at the man who would dare try to harm her, and he wanted to box her ears for being so stupid as to walk out alone. That she'd been brave and saved the mare he stored away for future consideration. Fortunately, it was not long before his rational self reappeared and he was forced to admit that Kate had, after all, quite unlawfully interfered and stolen the man's horse. His blood ran cold at the thought of what would have happened if she hadn't had the quickness of wit to escape on the mare. Damnation. How could he wring the man's neck, when, if one were logical, the fellow had had just provocation?

She was praying devoutly that the peasant would be gone. But when they rounded a bend in the road, she saw to her despair that

306

he hadn't budged and now stood in the roadway, legs apart, holding the knobby stick tightly in one hand.

Julien drew up some distance from the peasant and turned to her. "You will stay here—"

"No, I want—"

"Bloody hell, woman, you will do as I tell you. You move a muscle, exercise your tongue just once, and it will be the worse for you. Do you understand me?"

She nodded, pale and now quite frightened for him. She called after him, "Please be careful. I don't want us both hauled to the magistrate."

Julien ignored her, saying to Crayton, "Stay with her ladyship, James, and don't bloody let her leave this spot. Jesus, at least she forgot to kick him in the crotch."

She sat huddled in the saddle, wishing that a Swiss regiment would somehow magically appear. She watched tensely as Julien strode toward the peasant. She hunched lower in the saddle and bit her lip as the man brandished the stick in Julien's face and yelled wildly in her direction. At the next moment, Kate blinked in astonishment, for the man lay sprawled in the dirt and Julien stood over him, calmly rubbing his knuckles. When the man finally struggled to his feet, he appeared to have shrunken visibly in size, or so it seemed to her. She wasn't really surprised that her husband could see to himself and to her. It rather pleased her, but then again, she had been the one who initially saved the mare. Julien had come in on the last act, so to speak. This was only an epilogue.

There followed a rapid conversation in French, dominated by Julien. Money changed hands, and to Kate's further surprise, the man bowed to Julien, dusted off his clothing, and walked quickly into the forest.

Kate clicked her horse forward and drew up beside her husband.

"Well, my dear, it seems that you now own a horse." He allowed his features to soften now at the sight of her. She was a mess, very pale, with her hair hanging in tangles about her face.

She gave him a huge smile, and that was lovely, and completely her, full of bravado. "You hit him smartly. I was impressed. Perhaps you could show me just how you did that."

"Not likely. When you meet Percy, he will tell you in the most condescending manner possible that I spend too much of my time sparring with Gentleman Jackson. I fear they wouldn't approve your membership."

"He's the boxer."

"Yes, he is. Now let's go home. Both you and your horse are in need of attention."

For the first time, Kate became aware of her disheveled condition. "I guess I am rather a mess."

"But no worse off than your horse."

"She will be all right, won't she, Julien?" she said, as she looked at the pitiful specimen she had rescued.

"She will forget this experience more quickly than you will, I wager."

Julien's lightness of heart lasted only until they reached the villa. His anger, born undeniably of his fear for her, fanned again as he recalled her utter stupidity. When he lifted her off his horse's back, he looked down at her and didn't bother to cloak his anger at all. "A fine day's work, madam. If you think that I will condone your altogether asinine behavior, you're sadly mistaken. That you would walk out in a strange country, alone, is in itself so stupid I can scarce credit it, even from a female."

She knew she was in the wrong, but she'd rather thought that he'd gotten over his rage at her. What had set him off again? "I think, my lord, that you're expending a great deal too much ire on the incident." She gave him a fat smile.

It had no discernible effect. "Incident? You're calling this an *incident*? Dammit, have you thought what would have happened if your horse hadn't so obligingly helped you? And what if I hadn't stopped your horse?"

"But you did, Julien," Kate said reasonably. "And if you hadn't, certainly she would have gotten tired, sooner or later and stopped all by herself."

"You little idiot, that isn't the point, as you well know. I will strangle you myself if ever you again pull such a ridiculous stunt. Do you understand me?"

"It's impossible not to understand, you are ranting so loudly."

"Oh, the devil. Talking sensibly to you is like trying to convince a fence post to stand tall without pounding it into the ground. Go to your room and try to make yourself presentable. I will see you at dinner, in an hour."

She walked without another word into the villa, trying in vain to hold together the gaping tear in her skirt.

"James, see to the mare. She just looks to need cleaning up, three buckets of oats, and two days of rest." When he walked through the front door, he heard Mrs Crayton give a scream and thought, not without some pleasure, that Kate would receive a good scold from yet another quarter.

Kate begged, cajoled, and threatened Mrs Crayton not to inform his lordship when the woman discovered the swollen, discolored bruise on her thigh. She finally secured her reluctant agreement after assuring her mendaciously that it bothered her not at all.

For the first time, she entered the dining room not even one minute late. She was even a minute or two early. She was beginning to ache all over, as if the peasant had flailed her and not the mare with his stick.

Julien had planned to lecture her at length during dinner, but at the sight of her exhausted face, such intentions vanished. Without thinking, he took her gently in his arms, and to his surprise, she eased her arms behind his back and pressed herself against him. After a few moments he murmured softly, his chin resting against her hair, "Please forgive me for taking strips off your hide. It's just that if something had happened to you, well, I wouldn't have been a happy man."

She drew back in the circle of his arms and tried for a smile. "You were a worse bully than that horrible man, Julien. Do you think we could just say that all's well that ends well?"

He was obliged to laugh. "What, Kate, more Shakespeare? Just as long as you don't try to tell me it's much ado about nothing at all."

"No, I shan't, and Julien, I will tell you again, I'm not a shrew and your veiled references are quite revolting to me."

"Undoubtedly you're right," he said, not wanting to give her reason to leave the circle of his arms. "You now have one task left, my dear, and that's to name your mare."

She didn't move away from him, thank the powers, just grew silent and thoughtful. "You know," she said at last, smiling up at him, "it's too bad she's a mare, for Gabriel would be my choice. You see, I was quite convinced that I had reached my judgment day."

His arms tightened about her, though his voice was light enough. "Then she shall be Gabriella. What do you think?"

She looked up at him fixedly for a moment,

the expression on her face unreadable, and lightly slipped from his arms.

There was a companionable silence between them as Mrs Crayton served their dinner, clucking worriedly each time she gazed at Kate. When she left the room, Kate looked up from her plate. "The way she is acting, I feel as though I should cock up my toes and pass over to the hereafter. Ah, do tell me, my lord, whatever were you doing in the village today? I thought that perhaps you were not pleased here and wished to make arrangements to return to England."

"Why ever should I not be pleased?"

She fidgeted for a good thirty seconds, then managed to pull herself together, saying, "Oh, I can really think of no reason. How stupid of me to say such a thing. Now, do tell me, Julien, what was your errand?"

"I was on a quest actually, a matter of some importance, and I hope, indeed, I am quite certain that the result will meet with your approval."

"*My* approval? Come, stop teasing me. What have you done?" Her lips were parted slightly, and her eyes shone with excitement.

Rather than answer her immediately, Julien swiveled around in his chair, looked at the clock on the mantel, and appeared to give some weighty problem due reflection. He turned back to her, a smile on his face. "Perhaps we should wait until tomorrow. You have had a rather trying day."

312

"How horrid you are. I'm fine as a new penny, I promise. Now, what have you done, do tell me."

"Very well. Go to your room. You'll find a surprise. I will expect you in the library in fifteen minutes."

She had no idea what to expect, but when she found a pair of black-silk breeches, a frilled white shirt, and a pair of elegant black boots set neatly on her bed, she was baffled. In but a trice she was gazing at her trim figure in the long mirror. She quickly drew on the boots, pulled her hair back, and secured it with a black ribbon.

She skipped out of her room and down the stairs, unable to contain her excitement. She pushed open the library door to see Julien standing in the middle of the room, dressed as she was, in breeches and shirt. In his hand he held two foils.

She gasped with surprise. "Julien, you don't mean—you got us foils? One is truly for me?"

His eyes lit up at her evident pleasure, but she didn't notice, her gaze being fastened on the foils he held.

"As I recall, you said you wanted to learn how to fence, it not being one of Harry's sports. So I will teach you." He walked to her and placed a foil in her hand.

"Oh, goodness, yes, oh, yes. You're too good! Oh, my goodness." She clasped the foil in sheer delight and bent it back and forth, testing its flexibility.

313

She looked up after a few moments of this pastime and said with wonder in her voice, "But I lost our wager at piquet, don't you remember?"

"So? What has that to say to anything? It has been a great while since I've had a worthy opponent. I only hope I'm not to be butchered like poor Harry."

"As long as there is a button on the tip, you have no need to worry." She rewarded him with a dimpled smile.

Julien moved swiftly away from her to the center of the room and presented his side, his foil unwaveringly straight, in salute.

"En garde, madam!"

"En garde!" she repeated with great delight and thrust her own foil forward.

Their foils clashed in the silent room with a ring of steel. Since he wasn't sure of her ability, he controlled the speed and power of his thrusts, at least at first. He discovered very quickly, as he parried lunge after lunge, that she was an aggressive fencer. She held herself perfectly straight, her form excellent. She appeared to have no fear whatsoever and executed the most daring of maneuvers. No wonder she had rolled up poor Harry. He smiled as he tested for areas of weakness. Her foil was like her tongue, quick, sharp, and quite spontaneous. He slipped through her guard, drew up short, and pulled back. She merely laughed and in a quick flurry skipped forward and drove him back with rapid steps to the corner of the room. Their foils locked together for a moment before Julien, with a practiced flick of his wrist, sent her foil spinning from her grasp to the floor. She looked momentarily surprised, laughed at herself, and hurried to retrieve the foil. As she bent forward, the bruise on her thigh, to this point not all that painful, sent a flash of pain through her leg. She quickly averted her head and gritted her teeth, cursing the leg and the peasant who had struck her.

Julien saw the tiny furrow of pain on her forehead and instantly drew up and dropped his foil to his side. But then he thought he must have been mistaken, for when she straightened, her face glistening with sweat and her foil held securely once more in her hand, she shot him a dazzling smile and cried gaily, "I do believe you're just a bit better than Harry. And now, my lord," she added, advancing on him, "I defy you to catch me so unawares again with your paltry tricks."

"Better than even Harry? Such praise, it surely warms my cockles. As for my tricks, let's see just how quickly I catch you napping again."

As Kate lunged forward, shifting her weight onto the leg, another surge of pain distorted her face, and she clamped her lips together tightly to stifle the cry that threatened to escape. She drew up and turned about. "It's been a long day, Julien. Though you have soundly thrashed me tonight, I shall seek redress tomorrow. You'll see that I'm not so easily vanquished."

"That I caught you off your guard for a moment doesn't constitute a thrashing. Redress you shall certainly have." He added with undisguised pride in his voice, "I've indeed been granted a most worthy opponent, even though you're naught but a female." He grinned at her.

"You're kind," she blurted out, feeling suddenly strangely inadequate to express what she felt at his praise. She walked with great care to the desk to place her foil in the open case.

He strode to her with the express intent of placing his foil beside hers. To his chagrin, she misunderstood his motive and backed away so quickly that she stumbled into the desk chair. His jaw tightened. His open, confiding Kate was gone behind a mask of fear. He turned his back to her and began carefully to cover the foils with the velvet cloth. He said in a rigidly controlled voice, "It's getting quite late and you have had a rather strenuous day. I will see you in the morning."

There was no response. He turned to see her clutching the back of the chair, her face as white as her shirt.

"Go to bed, damn you!" Why the devil didn't she move? Was she trying to taunt him?

25

"I would, it's just that, well, the fact is that just for the moment, only this particular instant, I can't walk." She lowered her head, near to tears with embarrassment and she didn't want him to see it.

"Damnation, what the devil?" He was at her side in an instant and drew her up against him. She cried out, and he picked her up in his arms and deposited her gently on the sofa. She lay back against the cushions and took a deep breath. "I'm sorry, just give me but a few moments and I shall be fine. It's all the activity. I'm not used to it, and—"

"Enough falsehood. What the hell is the matter? Why can't you walk? No, don't you shake your head at me. I can see even more lies forming on your tongue. If you don't tell me the truth this instant, I swear I'll tear off your breeches and examine you."

"All right. That wretched peasant, he struck my leg with his stick when I jumped onto Gabriella's back. But I assure you, Julien, it's only a bruise, a small bruise, nothing to concern you. I bumped into the chair and made it hurt, but just a little bit."

He struck his forehead with his hand in

disbelief and exasperation. "Woman, you would try the patience of my father, who wasn't at all a saint but believed himself one. And you were foolish enough to fence with me with your leg hurt? I begin to believe your brain would fit neatly into a thimble."

Kate eased herself into a sitting position. "I didn't tell you because I knew you'd not let us fence tonight, and I wanted to so very much. Please, Julien, I'm all right."

"Listen to me, dammit—no, this argument is quite ridiculous." He lifted her in his arms, ignoring her protests. As he carried her up the stairs, she asked in a small voice, "You're just taking me to my room, aren't you?"

"No, and just be quiet. I'm going to see just how foolish you've been. No, don't argue with me. I'm going to look at your leg myself." As she tensed perceptibly in his arms, he added, "I mean it. Just be silent for once in your life."

"Couldn't you simply ask Mrs Crayton?"

"Be quiet."

She was laid very gently on her bed. "Don't move. I will try not to hurt you, just hold still." He unfastened her breeches and pulled them down. "Lift your hips."

She froze, staring at his face, but there was no lust there to be seen, no man's desire, just determination and anger. She lifted her hips. He peeled the breeches to her knees, then looked at her leg. He cursed, long and fluently.

The bruise had swollen and turned a deep purplish black. Gently he probed around the area and slowly moved his fingers to the swollen bruise. She stiffened in pain but made no sound. He straightened and stood quietly in frowning thought. He said finally, "I don't think a doctor is necessary, but you will have to curb your activities for a while. Damnation, I still can't believe this. Are you in pain now?"

"Oh, no, I promise I'm not."

"Of course, I disbelieve you. I'll send Maria to you with some laudanum in water. If you don't drink it, it will go badly for you."

"Damnation, I could have pierced your heart at least five times in as many minutes. You must think constantly and observe me carefully. You aren't fencing by yourself nor with a blind man. Never underestimate the skill of your opponent."

She stood panting with exertion, her face glistening with sweat. "Aye, you're right." It didn't occur to her to take offense.

"Lunge, withdraw! Lunge, withdraw!" She pushed herself until her arm trembled with fatigue.

It was invariably Julien who halted their lessons, not Kate. After one day of enforced inactivity, she'd announced that she was fit as a fiddle and skipped several times in front of him to prove that her leg no longer pained her.

He'd agreed to riding, which was more than

she had hoped for, which she didn't tell him, of course.

During the next three days, their time had fallen into a comfortable pattern. They fenced in the mornings and explored the countryside surrounding the villa in the afternoons. Gabriella appeared to be favorably disposed toward Kate, her former life with the peasant forgotten.

But to Kate, evenings with Julien were a trial. Each time Mrs Crayton helped her to dress in one of her elegant gowns, she felt a sense of wariness descend upon her. No, it was more than that. It was something menacing and black and chill with foreboding. And yet, she felt it was Julien who was different. Dressed in his severely cut black evening clothes, he became a stranger to her, a threatening personage with frightening claims on her. If only their days could have ended after riding. She came to dread the hours passed in the soft candlelight, sensing in him a growing frustration, a barely restrained urgency. She would feel his gray eyes sweep over her, hungrily resting upon her mouth, then moving lower, to her breasts, devouring her. She cursed herself for showing fear, but she couldn't help the disjointed and hasty excuse of tiredness she made every night even as she backed away from him, backed out of the room.

As she lay in bed each night waiting for sleep to come, she would try to shut him out of her mind. But she couldn't. He was there, stark and real within her thoughts, waiting. With him came that coldness, and strange, unexplained images that swept through her, leaving her confused and frightened. She would stare into the darkness and whisper a simple Scottish prayer her mother had taught her.

One day over luncheon, Julien told her that he had business concerns that afternoon in the village and would be unable to accompany her on their daily riding expedition. Her face fell.

"It's very likely I'll be late returning this evening. Do go riding. You know the countryside quite well, and I believe Gabriella could outdistance the peasant if you happened to be so unfortunate as to cross paths with him again."

She was frankly surprised that he didn't order her to stray no further than the front doors, but she wasn't about to say anything about that. "So, then, my lord, you won't be here for dinner?"

"Were I not to be here, Kate, would you miss me?" He looked at her steadily, and although she answered him calmly enough, she wouldn't look at him. "Of course I would miss you. If you aren't back I'll content myself with a tray. Don't worry, I'll be fine, and I promise to be careful."

He fiddled a moment with his fork, then looked at her straightly. "How could I ever doubt that you would miss me at night?"

She tried to look at him, but she couldn't. Even when he was on the point of leaving, she knew she was withdrawing from him, relieved, really, that he wouldn't be here in the evening, to frighten her, to bring that blackness to her.

Before he mounted, he turned to her and gently touched his hand to her cheek. Startled, she drew back. She watched in numb silence as his gray eyes hardened and turned cold, so very cold, a cold she'd never seen in his eyes before when he'd looked at her. He turned quickly away from her, and without another word between them, he mounted, wheeled his horse about, and was gone. He did not look back.

She was still pondering his words and his abrupt departure as she carefully guided Gabriella through the thick woods to the long, open meadow beyond. Freed from the restraint she felt at his nearness, she could not but feel now that his measured words, so calmly spoken, had been meant to taunt her. But how could that be? Ah, but she saw him again in her mind's eye, the coldness in him. Even a week ago she would have known only relief that he would be gone from her, but now, today, she felt confused and uncertain. She shook her head at herself. Nothing seemed to make much sense to her anymore. Nothing.

The wind tugged at her riding hat when she gave Gabriella her head across the long expanse of meadowland. She had always thought it strange that nature had carved this open land, so at variance with the dense forest that surrounded it. She gave Gabriella a flick of the reins and the horse tossed her head, easing into a steady gallop. Kate was a good deal surprised when suddenly her horse pulled up short and reared back on her hind legs. She grabbed at the pommel to steady herself and wheeled around in the saddle in panic, expecting to see the peasant rushing at her. It wasn't the peasant, but rather a man on horseback, enveloped in a long greatcoat, riding purposefully toward her. She drew Gabriella up, thinking that he was perhaps lost and in need of directions. She felt merely curiosity until he drew near and she saw that his face was masked. Kate dug her heels into Gabriella's sides, her mouth suddenly gone dry with fear. The horse needed no further encouragement and shot forward. Too soon the meadow blended back into forest, and after a moment's hesitation Kate realized that she couldn't escape through the thick under-brush. She jerked Gabriella about, driving her in a wide circle, skirting the edge of the trees as closely as she dared. But the man was fast gaining on her, and she realized with a tingling fear up her spine that in a moment he would cut her off. The horse's hooves pounded in her ears, and even as her mind refused to believe that this could possibly be happening to her, a man's arms pulled her out of the saddle and she screamed in blind panic. She found herself held tightly, unable to struggle, so close to the man that she could hear his low, steady breathing.

The man pulled his horse to a halt and dismounted easily, still holding her pinioned against him. She could struggle now, and she did, trying to strike his face, trying to get loose enough so she could kick him. But he just pulled her hard against him, grasped her hands, and fastened them against her sides. She kicked his shin. Her boot connected with bone and flesh, though, and he gave a cry of surprise and pain. In the next instant she was flat on her her back on the ground, the cloaked man out of reach of her flailing legs.

She froze when he leaned close over her and said in guttural, accented English, his voice muffled by his mask, "I won't harm you. Hold still, *liebchen.*"

She forced her numbed mind to alertness, realizing that she must be calm, use her wits. The man had spoken to her, he'd spoken German. What did *liebchen* mean? Something about darling or beloved? Something like that, but surely that made no sense at all. She had to reason with him.

"What do you want? Please, talk to me, tell me why you're doing this." He said nothing at all. "Damn you, talk to me or I will hurt you very badly!"

He remained silent, faceless, now fumbling for something in one of the pockets of his black greatcoat. She tried to squirm away, but his other arm held her firmly. "Please," she

324

said, pleading now, so afraid she was shaking. "What do you want of me? I have no money and I have done you no injury." Dear God, where was Julien? The thought of him brought her new hope. Perhaps this man didn't know who she was.

"Listen to me. I have a husband, he is the earl of March. He is an English nobleman and a very powerful man. You must realize that he will miss me. He will kill you if you don't let me go this instant. Please, I don't speak German. Tell me you understand me. *Damn you, tell me!*"

Her voice was thin as a reed, her fright clear, but still the man didn't say anything. She didn't know if her words made any impression on him, or if he even understood her, for the mask and hat covered his head completely. They made him all the more terrifying, seemingly faceless.

He withdrew a white handkerchief and with it a small vial of liquid.

"What are you going to do?" She was hollow with fear, numb with it. Before she knew what he was about, he leaned his body over her chest and wet the handkerchief with the liquid. He straightened, grasped her shoulders firmly, and brought the cloth over her face. A strong odor filled her nostrils, and she began to struggle frantically. She thrashed her head back and forth, trying to escape the cloth.

Without realizing it, she inhaled deeply and tasted the bitter liquid, felt it raw down the back of her throat. She began to feel light-headed, reason, fight, struggle, all deserting her. The man eased his arm around her head and held her still. She cried out then and fell into blackness.

26

Kate opened her eyes and blinked rapily, trying to free her mind of the terrifying remnants of her nightmare. She shuddered, for the fear was still so very real, and tried to rise, but her body wouldn't obey her. She focused her eyes in an effort to clear away the clinging light-headedness and realized with a start that she wasn't in her own room. She hadn't dreamed the man, the drugged cloth pressed over her face. She made a determined effort to rise, only to find that her arms were pulled above her head and her wrists securely tied to the posts of a bed. She lifted her head from the pillow and tugged with all her strength, but she couldn't free herself.

She lay back, panting, and tried to calm herself. Why had the man brought her to this place? There had to be some mistake, he had to have believed she was another woman, a stranger. She realized in that instant that she wasn't wearing her riding habit. She saw the skirt, blouse, and jacket neatly folded over a chair. Even her boots were placed next to the chair. All she was wearing was her shift. With terrifying clarity she pictured herself half-clothed, the cotton shift coming only to mid-thigh, her arms drawn away from her body. He had tied her down, she was helpless. What did he want with her? Somewhere, deep within her, she knew why she was tied down, knew what he wanted with her, knew exactly what would happen, knew what this man would do to her.

Her mind seemed to snap with the know-ledge, and she was sent reeling to the edge of a yawning gulf of blackness. All she knew was lost to her as the blackness engulfed her, sucking her down farther and farther into its depths. She knew the blackness. At last it had come to her fully. She saw herself, small and cowering, then struggling frantically, trapped by she knew not what. Intense, rending pain tore through her, and above the pain she heard cruel, deep voices, and panting, raw and ugly. Then there were screaming, furious voices that somehow intensified the pain— no, just one screaming voice, and it was a man's voice and she could see spittle flying out of his mouth, but she didn't know who he was. But the screaming and cursing her didn't stop.

She couldn't bring her hands to cover her ears, to blot out the horror of the pain and the voices. She screamed and the images and the voices faded, drawing away from her, becoming as fragments of whispers, strewn as distant echoes to the farthest reaches of another place.

She became aware of the anguished sound of her cries and felt beads of sweat sting her eyes. She thought at that moment that perhaps she was mad, for she couldn't understand what had happened to her. The present righted itself and she saw that nothing had changed. She was still tied down to a bed, wearing only her shift. She tried to regain her calm, forcing herself to gaze about the unfamiliar room, and found the presence of the solid pieces of furniture somehow reassuring.

The sound of a key turning in the lock brought her eyes, fearful, yet hopeful, to the door. The man, her captor, slowly entered the room, his long cloak swirling about his ankles as he turned and grated the key in the lock. He was still enveloped in hat and mask, even wearing gloves on his hands. Kate stared at him, her eyes a darkening green, now wide with fear and the starkness of her knowledge. He stopped beside her, and before Kate could understand what he was about, he leaned over her and in a swift motion drew a length of black cloth from his pocket and folded it over her eyes. She was plunged into darkness. Like a trapped, frenzied animal, she thrashed her head from side to side as the man jerked her forward and tied the cloth in a secure knot behind her head.

In that moment she wondered if she'd been brought to this place to die. Unbidden,

Julien's calm, handsome face rose in her mind's eye. She saw him turn from her, felt his withdrawal from her, saw his eyes become colder than a winter dawn.

She began to tremble violently, and the sickening, jeering voices pounded again in her head, then receded as if they had never existed. Sudden anger kindled within her and burned away her trembling with its intensity. How dare this man bind and blindfold her! She jerked up her head and screamed at him, "You filthy pig, how dare you! My husband, the earl of March, will kill you if you do not instantly release me. Do you understand me?" There was only a deadening silence, save for the harsh ugliness of her own breathing.

She hated the silence, hated him, this unknown man, and she yelled through the darkness, through the silence, "Damn you to hell, you coward, are you afraid that I'll see your ugliness? Damn you, let me see you!"

Still the man said nothing, not in English, not in German, but she heard him move away from her. She fell back against the pillow, drained, so afraid she was numb with it. As the precious minutes passed, she thought that he had understood and was going to leave her alone. Then, to her horror, she felt him sit on the side of the bed beside her. She felt his breath hot on her face. His lips came down upon hers, gentle yet demanding. He'd blindfolded her so he could take off his mask. He didn't want her to see him. Why? She clamped her mouth firmly shut and felt his lips move to her throat, and his hands lightly caress her shoulders.

The warmth of the room touched her skin as he slowly cut the thin straps off her shoulders, pulling the soft cotton down over her breasts. He pushed the shift to her waist, where it lay bunched about her.

The last remnants of what she knew, of what she understood, of what she thought she was, left her in that instant. There was a blankness in her mind, as if suddenly there was a hole and there was nothing inside it, save an undefined dread that mingled with an ugliness she knew was there also—buried, but still there—and it left her nearly senseless. Tiny points of light exploded in her mind, and she realized dimly that she'd been holding her breath. She opened her mouth, and precious air flew past her constricted throat into her chest. She could feel her breasts heaving, but she couldn't stop their deep upward and downward movement. His fingers were on her forehead, gently pushing back tendrils of hair. She tried to evade him, pulling away as far as her bonds would allow. But his fingers were tracing the line of her cheek, her lips, her throat. She wanted desperately to plead with him to stop, but she could find no words.

The man's hands were on her shoulders, firm, strong hands, hands that could and would hurt her, she knew it, deep down inside her, she knew hurt would come from his hands. She grew still, rigid, as his fingers moved to her breasts, now kneading her, caressing her, lifting her breasts in his hands, holding them, gently squeezing, then lightly flicking his fingertips over her nipples until they grew hard and taut. Words came from deep inside her, and she knew they were for naught, these words of hers, yet they spoke themselves anyway. "I beg of you, please don't do this to me, please, please no, no—"

His hands left her breasts, and in the long, silent moment that followed, she knew he was looking at her, not at her breasts but at her face. She sensed a hesitancy in him. If only she could see! Her eyes strained, but there was only blackness.

He came down over her body and enfolded her in his arms, burying his face against her neck, holding her so tightly that she couldn't breathe.

She knew in that instant she had lost.

Finally he lifted himself off her, and his hands traveled quickly, urgently, back to her breasts. She felt his mouth upon her, kissing and nibbling her throat and shoulders, until finally his lips and hands played together over her breasts. There was no pain from his hands, just something infinitely worse— warmth, strength, and a skill that knew her flesh, knew what to do and when to do it. She cried out, trying to twist free of his hands, of his mouth. His hands moved to encircle her waist, and as she tried to arch and wrench away, he eased them beneath her to stroke her back.

Tears scalded her eyes and dampened the black cloth that blinded her. She heard her own voice, begging and pleading with him to stop, but her words broke from her mouth only as meaningless sounds, helpless sounds.

His hands left her back and tugged at the material about her waist. In a swift motion he slipped the shift cloth from beneath her hips, stripping it down her legs, leaving her naked.

There was a sharp intake of breath from the man, and Kate knew that he was staring at her, examining her body. She had never been so aware of her body, of its purpose and its meaning to men.

She was rapidly growing exhausted. The futility of her struggles, her fear, were sapping her strength. She stilled, her body tensed. The damp cloth, salty from her tears, burned her eyes. She turned her head on the pillow and clamped her jaws together, waiting, waiting— for what, she didn't know, but deep down, somehow, she did know.

His weight came down on the bed and his naked shoulders pressed against her body. Not only had he taken off his mask, he'd also stripped off all his clothes. His flesh was hot and smooth against hers. His lips touched her waist and roved downward to her belly, his tongue scalding against her skin. She pushed her hips down into the softness of the bed, but it seemed to excite him only more. His mouth was sweet and gentle and insistent, yet it burned her, and she hated his mouth and those hands of his that seemed to know just where to touch her, where to caress her, where to press and stroke. She hated herself, for in the next instant, she felt a tiny shock of sensation that was like a pain in her belly, low and deep, but there, and she yelled against it, cursing him, her voice giving her back to herself, but just for a moment, for he didn't stop touching her, his fingers almost pleading with her flesh to respond to him. She cursed him and cursed him again and again, but there it was again, that shock of sensation, that near-pain so intense, so urgent, and she knew it was pleasure, a woman's special pleasure, and she fought with everything in her to deny it, to deny him, to save herself.

She could picture him, now balanced on his elbow gazing down at her. His fingers played over the softness of her belly, and paused, ever so slightly, before closing over the curly auburn triangle of hair. His touch was feather light, never more than feather light, but so knowing, always knowing, searching and learning her.

Why? Why wasn't he savaging her? She knew it was rape, yet he wasn't acting the rapist. His gentleness, his quiet exploration, his insistence that she respond, didn't fit, and she was lost in confusion and fear and the growing feelings he was arousing in her.

His fingers continued their exploration, pressing and probing the softness between her thighs.

She cried out in shock, the humiliation of it burning deep inside her, and she cursed him again, then begged him to leave her alone, please, just to leave her alone for a moment, just for a minute. But slowly and rhythmically he stroked her, his other hand roving upward to stroke and learn her breasts.

Impossible to struggle free of him, for his hands seemed to touch and probe every part of her body, the gentle pressure of his fingers burning deeper and deeper. Exhausted, she ceased her struggles. She heard her own sobs, felt her body, and knew that he was learning her as she herself was learning to fence, learning her, studying her, knowing her. She tried to detach her mind, but she couldn't. She was aware of his every touch now.

A gasp of shock broke her sobs when his fingers ceased their rhythmic caressing and she felt his mouth upon her. Shock held her rigid for a moment, then she jerked her hips from side to side, but he only slid his hands under her and lifted her upward. His tongue flicked over her lightly, tentatively, gently tugging, possessing her.

She lay stiff and unyielding, her body and mind outraged, when suddenly an intense sensation, an almost painful searing, exploded in her loins. Her mind plummeted and merged with the feeling, consuming her with its strength. The searing sensation faded, leaving her weak and uncertain of what had happened. She tensed every muscle and held her breath. But his mouth was burning her, white-hot and deep.

Julien's face rose sharply in her mind. Dear God, she was betraying him. Her body was responding and she couldn't stop it, couldn't even slow it now, for the man knew, he knew exactly what to do and how to do it. She didn't know him, couldn't see him, yet his hands and his mouth were becoming part of her.

All the words her father had screamed at her were true. She was a slut, a whore. Dear God, she was no better than Julien's lustful mistresses.

She felt the sensation building again, fanning throughout her body. Her mind screamed for him to stop, but only low, feverish moans came from her mouth. Frenzied waves of the exquisite inflaming pleasure swept through her body. Somehow, in the distant recesses of her mind, she felt that if he were to stop, she would die. She lost her will to fight him and strained her hips upward toward his mouth, urging him, becoming one with him. She trembled uncontrollably as shock after shock of ecstatic pleasure shot down her legs and up into her belly.

Slowly the waves of pleasure lessened, and a soft glow of warmth spread through her body, leaving her weak and shaking. The man's mouth left her.

Julien shifted his position and lay his full length beside her, his hands now moving over her belly and breasts more urgently. He couldn't wait longer, he had to have her now. He'd brought her to pleasure, despite her struggles, and he knew she'd fought him with everything in her. Yet he'd brought her to the edge and eased her over it, and it was because he knew her, knew she was part of him even though she'd denied it. Perhaps even her body recognized him. He wanted to believe it so. Ah, but he couldn't wait.

He straightened over her and gently parted her. She gave a cry of surprise as he slowly entered her. Blood pounded in his temples, yet he knew he must control himself, for she was a virgin and he didn't want to hurt her. She was soft and yielding, her body still shivering from the small aftershocks of the release he'd given her. No, he had to be controlled, go slowly. He pushed deeper into her, feeling for her maidenhead.

She suddenly screamed, her voice hoarse with terror. She struggled frantically, wildly, to free herself of him. He drew back quickly in surprise, for he knew he hadn't hurt her. But his own desire was now an insistent throbbing. Though he felt her fear, he refused to withdraw from her. Slowly he allowed himself to ease deeper inside her. In the next instant he realized with undeniable certainty that she had no maidenhead.

His wife wasn't a virgin. He jerked back, dumb-founded. No, he thought frantically, he must be mistaken. But her fear, her wild struggles, seemed to betray her. She had deceived him. Savage, uncontrolled fury swept

336

over him. She'd given herself to another man, or was it to other men? God, how very gentle and careful he was, seducing his innocent, virgin wife.

With no further thought, he thrust deep within her, oblivious of her cries of pain. He tore through the small, tight passage, ripping her in his frenzy. He gripped her hips in his hands, his fingers digging into her flesh, and forced her body upward to take all of him. He pushed until he was touching her womb, and still the fury pounded deep within him, angry betrayal, such a sense of hopelessness that he couldn't help it, couldn't help himself, the hatred he felt for his own blindness, for her perfidy, for her mocking of him, which was what her coy denials all were, naught more than a harlot's teasing. He wanted quite simply to hurt her, to punish her.

He cried out as his own release clutched at him, holding him in its grip for a brief moment. He drove into her with all his strength, spewing his seed deep within her body. Finally spent, he let himself fall on top of her, his head next to her cheek on the pillow.

As if from a great distance, he heard her crying, low ugly sobs. His fury slowly receded, and with it the cruel, animal savagery. Slowly he eased himself off her and stood staring down at her, his mind hollow with blank despair. His wife. His innocent young virgin wife. God, what a mockery. She was no longer crying, and he thought her unconscious, so quietly did she lie, until she tried to bring her legs together in a weak, futile gesture.

He gazed bleakly at her exquisite body, wanting to laugh at his own folly, his overweening pride. Bitter laughter mixed with despair in his throat and he turned abruptly away from her. Now he knew why she hadn't wanted him to touch her. It was not fear as a frightened virgin or a misbegotten desire to thwart him as her husband, but rather her dread that he would discover that he wasn't the first man to be her lover. His hands clenched at his sides. He wanted to shake the truth out of her. Who had been the man to possess her? God, not that bumptious ass Bleddoes, surely not him. Kate herself had laughed at his tenacious courtship of her. But who? *Who*?

Julien was shaking. Never before in his life had he so completely lost control of himself. He turned back, almost unwillingly, to look at his wife, suddenly sickened with himself. He'd raped her, Jesus, he hadn't intended that, no never that, but he had. He'd planned so carefully to teach her pleasure, to force her to realize that she was a woman with a woman's passions, and he had, he'd given her immense pleasure. He'd planned to reveal himself to her afterward. His jaw tightened in renewed anger at her. There had been no need to teach her passion. God, she had forced him to go to such lengths because of her lies, her deceit.

For a long moment he cursed her silently, trying to counter the nagging disgust he felt at his own actions with her unforgivable perfidy. Suddenly he became aware of the time. He thought it now impossible to reveal himself to her. He must get her back to the villa. Yes, he had to do that first, then think, then decide what to do.

Julien removed the vial and cloth from the pocket of his coat, doused the cloth thoroughly, and walked to the bed. As he bent over her, she thrashed her head wildly to avoid the cloth. He grasped her firmly and brought the soaked material over her nostrils. In but a moment she was quiet. He held the cloth against her face for several minutes to be certain that she would not awaken too quickly.

He lifted the cloth and let it drop to the floor. Quickly he untied the blindfold and pulled it away. He stopped short, realizing that it was wet with her tears. His proud Kate. Her long, thick lashes were wet spikes against her cheeks, and her pale skin was blotched with the streaking tears. There was a small drop of blood on her lower lip, bitten in her pain.

Julien forced himself to look away. With shaking fingers he untied the silken bonds from about her wrists, wincing at the dark, mean red welts. His eyes traveled to between her thighs. Mingled with his seed were dark traces of blood. He'd used her fiercely, but why would she bleed? She wasn't a virgin, there'd been no maiden-head. He didn't know.

He quickly bathed her and placed the cover over her body. He shrugged himself into his clothes and drew out his watch. A sense of unreality seized him. He'd had her with him but three hours. It seemed unbelievable that his life could so change in such a short period of time. And he'd been the author of all the change, he himself, no one else.

He quickly dressed her in her riding habit, not bothering to confine her masses of tangled hair with pins. It didn't matter now that she looked disheveled.

He lifted his unconscious wife in his arms and walked quickly from the room and out of the small thatched cottage he had secured for this one day. He lifted her over his shoulder, untied their horses, and mounted, taking the reins of her horse in his free hand. He eased her down into the circle of his arm, wheeled his horse about, and rode away.

27

"Oh, thank God you have found her ladyship, my lord! What ever has happened? James searched the grounds and all of the meadow where her ladyship rides."

"She's all right, Maria. She must have fallen from her horse. I found her on my return from the village." He strode past Mrs. Crayton into the villa.

"James, quickly, you must fetch a doctor immediately!"

"No!" Julien said sharply. "That is, it's not necessary, Maria. I've examined her ladyship and there are no broken bones. She merely struck her head, and there's nothing a doctor could do that we cannot." Seeing that the Craytons were unconvinced, he added with a curl of his lip, "Would you that the village doctor, a foreigner, attend her ladyship?"

"No, certainly not. What shall I do, my lord?"

"Fetch hot water, cloths, and laudanum," he said with cool authority. He turned abruptly and carried his unconscious wife to her room. She moaned as he laid her on the bed and began to pull off her riding jacket. He set his jaw and didn't look at her face, but he found that his hands were none too steady in carrying out their task. She seemed so very fragile, and he hated that because he knew she was strong and independent, so very sure of herself, but not now, not after what he'd done to her. He quickened, not wishing her to awaken until he'd gotten her into bed. He reflected inconsequentially that women wore too many layers of clothing. He ripped off her shift in his impatience, and as he looked down at her naked body, he felt no desire, only intense despair. Another man had possessed her, had caressed her soft white skin. With a deep moan of animal pain he wrenched himself away and strode to the armoire. He fetched a nightgown, the one she'd worn on their wedding night.

He crumpled the soft material in his hands, remembering all too clearly how he'd been so gallant, so caring of her and her virginal fear. With jerky movements he slipped the gown over her head and smoothed it over her body. He turned at an urgent tap on the door.

It was Mrs Crayton with the water, cloths, and laudanum he'd told her to fetch.

She moaned again as Julien eased her between the covers, this time turning her head slightly. Mrs Crayton took a quick step forward, but Julien blocked her path. "As you see, Maria, her ladyship will be fine in but a moment. I will attend her. Don't worry, I shall call you if I need your help."

Mrs Crayton cast a final glance at her young mistress, turned slowly, and walked from the room. She couldn't help but feel that his lordship was reacting too calmly to his young wife's accident.

Julien pulled a chair next to the bed and sat down wearily. It seemed that nearly a lifetime had passed in this one afternoon. He gazed at his wife's pale, beautiful face and felt a numb coldness sweep through him. How he wanted her to suffer, to feel the deep, scarring humiliation he now felt. His rape of her was not sufficient revenge, for that pain she would soon forget. God, what a ludicrous bargain he'd made. He refused to accept that he'd practically forced her to marry him, that she'd never wanted to have him. No, he wouldn't think about that, not yet anyway.

She slowly opened her eyes and blinked rapidly to sharpen her blurred vision. She saw her husband sitting next to her, his face buried in his hands. She frowned in confusion for one brief instant before her memory righted itself. She cried out as every moment of what had happened to her roared through her mind.

Julien schooled his voice into false concern. "My dear, are you all right?"

She turned wild eyes toward him. Her lips moved and she said in a strangled whisper, "How am I here? Oh, Julien, is it really you? You're here with me? There's no one else, no stranger, no other man, no one else?"

Julien leaned over her and said firmly, "You had a riding accident. I found you unconscious beside Gabriella on my return from the village. You will be quite all right, I swear it to you."

"Riding accident?" she repeated vaguely, his words making no sense to her.

"Yes, attend me well. You had a riding accident. You were thrown. Nothing more."

She didn't notice the hardness of his voice and quickly turned her face away from him. Dear God, he didn't know. The man must have left her to be found, not caring. At least he hadn't killed her.

But it wasn't right, simply wasn't right. "Julien." She struggled up on her pillow. "Oh, God, I must tell you, there wasn't, that is, I didn't have—" The words died a quick death. Her story would sound utterly unbelievable. She knew that even if he were to accept what she had said had happened, he would know that she was no longer a virgin, that another man had taken her. She choked back a sob and fell against the pillow.

"Kate, no, no."

She cried silently now, tears coursing down her cheeks, no sound coming from her throat. Her eyes were tightly closed. Oh God, his voice was so very gentle. If only she hadn't scorned him, fought him, but now it was too late. What had happened to her was real and she would never forget or forgive herself.

She felt her head being raised from the pillow and a glass touching her lips. For an instant she relived the cloth being held to her face, the bitter fumes plummeting her to unconsciousness. She struggled frantically, jerking her head back and forth.

"No, hush, it's only laudanum. It will make you sleep, nothing more."

She quieted at the sound of his calm voice. Sleep, yes, she welcomed the opportunity of forgetting, if for only a while. She opened her mouth eagerly and swallowed the water.

"Oh, God," she whispered, really but a shadow of a whisper, so low did she speak, "please let me never awake."

He jerked back at her words. With trembling fingers he set down the empty glass. He wanted her to suffer, to know regret and shame. But that she could whisper with such hopeless despair of death tore at his very being. The burden of guilt that he'd fought against consumed him relentlessly, and try as he would, he couldn't dismiss the enormity of what he had done.

He watched her fall into a deep sleep and settled back in a chair to keep silent vigil.

It was shortly before dawn, as he was building up the dying fire, that he whirled around at the sound of a low, piercing scream. He was at her side in a moment. She was writhing, her body tangled in the covers, in the throes of a nightmare. Julien grabbed her shoulders and shook her, but the effects of the laudanum seemed to hold her from consciousness, and she cried out again and again. In desperation he slapped her face until a tremendous shudder passed the length of her body and she opened her eyes and stared up at him, her pupils dilated with fear.

She threw her arms around his shoulders and hurled herself against his chest. She was trembling violently, low sobs racking her body. Julien froze for a moment in shocked confusion. Without conscious thought he closed his arms about her and held her tightly against his chest. He scooped her up, pulling her covers with him, and carried her to a chair beside the fireplace. He could feel the strength of her terror, so tightly did she cling to him. He whispered low, comforting words, words that scarce made sense. Slowly the racking sobs diminished and she loosed her grip, as if exhausted from the effort. She lay against him quietly, her head lolling against his chest.

He said her name softly, again and again, smoothing damp tendrils of hair from about her face. She opened her eyes and met his gaze. He struggled with himself to speak to her of the nightmare, knowing full well what it must be, and realizing that to do so would encourage her to pour forth her story. He held back, suddenly aware that if she were to speak, he would be unable to hold the truth from her. She broke the long silence. In a voice vague from the effects of the laudanum, she whispered, "God, I can't bear it. Surely I'm going mad, surely."

"Mad?" he repeated blankly, his mind arrested at her strange words. "What is it? What can't you bear?"

"The blackness, the voices."

He tightened his arms about her in silent comfort and waited for her to calm. She spoke again, her voice cracking, the words jumbled. "The blackness, it's never been so strong, so real. It covers something horrible, something evil, but yet I can't see what it is, it was so very long ago. There is just such pain, such pain, and the voices, cruel, jeering voices, ugly grunting voices, men's voices. They want me dead."

He tensed, his mind almost refusing to work. Long ago, not today. What was so long ago? "You must tell me what happened? What is this blackness, the pain, the voices? What did you dream?"

"I can't be sure, but it's there, always there, but I don't understand it." Suddenly she stiffened.

She looked toward the fireplace, focusing upon something he didn't see, couldn't see. In a high, hysterical voice—a child's voice—she cried, "Mama, why did those men hurt me? They ripped off my clothes, Mama, and there's so much blood. Why am I bleeding? It hurts so very much. Why, Mama? Please make it stop. No, Father, no! Don't hurt me! What have I done? Father, what have I done? No, no! *Stop!*"

Her voice stopped in a cry of pain. She winced and cowered, jerking her arms above her head as if to protect herself from blows raining down upon her.

Julien grabbed her arms and shook her until the cries ceased and the dull, glazed film dropped from her eyes. She looked up into his set face, and in a voice of great weariness she whispered, "Julien, I'm so very glad you're here with me." She nestled her face against his chest. "Please don't leave me. I couldn't bear it if you left me." But a moment later he heard her even breathing and knew that she slept.

Early-autumn sunlight poured into the room before Julien raised his eyes from his wife's still face. His arms ached but he didn't move, not wishing to disturb her. She was in a deep sleep, a healing sleep. He was aware that he felt extraordinarily humble, his bitter anger and wounded pride stripped from him. He understood her fear of him now, why she hadn't wanted to marry him, even though she herself hadn't understood her reasons. He remembered the day when they'd ridden to the small copse, and the look of blank terror on her face. A place of evil, she had said. She had not been able to fathom her reaction, and he hadn't considered it important, so intent had he been on his gentlemanly offer of marriage.

How could he have been so damned blind? He felt the hair prickle on the back of his neck at the thought of Kate as a small child being attacked. Good God, what kind of man would rape a child? His hands clenched and unclenched in black anger as he pictured in his mind a small, helpless girl at the mercy of men who cared for nothing and no one. All too clearly he saw Kate's father, cursing at her, blaming her, beating her.

She whimpered softly and he tightened his arms about her. It occurred to him, as he gazed down at her peaceful face, that his life had been singularly uncomplicated up to this time. He tried to weigh the enormity of the problems he now faced. Although he couldn't explain why, he felt certain that she wouldn't as yet remember her nightmare, even though his rape of her had penetrated the cloak of forgetfulness that had protected her all these years. He could well understand how a child's instincts for survival had forced her to lock away what had happened to her, to bury it so deep that there were only vague shadows, images that faded quickly, blackness that vanished with the blink of an eye. But now it could be only a matter of time until she remembered, and, he thought bleakly, such devastating knowledge could easily be too much for her. And it was his fault, all his fault.

He rose slowly, careful not to disturb her, and gently laid her in her bed. Then his own physical exhaustion overtook him, and with a deep sigh he stretched out in the chair and soon fell asleep.

Kate awoke, her mind alert and clear from the long hours of sleep. She sat up in her bed and looked about her. She was startled to see Julien sprawled in a chair beside her, his clothing disheveled and his head resting

349

against his hand. She frowned in confusion, vaguely remembering being held by him. He had comforted her, had soothed away an awful fear. She shook her head to focus the jumbled images, but they melted away from her. She slipped out of bed and felt a sharp pain between her thighs. She stilled. All that had happened to her came rushing back. Her eyes flew to her sleeping husband. He'd told her that she'd had a riding accident. Her mind clung tenaciously to this fact. No one, save her and that man, knew what had passed between them, and she grimly resolved that Julien must never know. She walked to where he slept and shook his sleeve to wake him. Somehow it didn't seem important that she was dressed only in her nightgown.

He awoke with a start and bounded out of the chair. He stared down at her, silent and pale. He pulled her gently against him. How very strange, she thought wonderingly, that she found his closeness and strength comforting. They stood thus for some time, until Julien drew back and with a gentle hand smoothed back her tangled hair from about her face.

"You are all right?"

She lowered her eyes, and he wanted to cry out at her look of anguish. Oh, God, he couldn't bear it. "Kate," he began. He felt so bloody helpless.

She looked up at him, her face now impassive, and interrupted him quickly. "I'm quite fine now, Julien. I wasn't gravely hurt in the riding accident. Gabriella must have been frightened again. It's over now. Yes, all of it is over now."

He was relieved at her decision not to tell him the truth. If she were to tell him of her rape, he wouldn't be able to keep silent, and what he told her would destroy her newfound trust in him. Somehow he must find a way to banish the terrible fears from her childhood before telling her.

He smiled at her and said lightly, "I fear, my dear, that if the Craytons were to witness the countess and earl of March in such a state of disarray, our consequence would be in dire straits." He ran a hand through his own messed hair. "Do you feel like a bath?"

She mustered a tentative smile. She raised her hand to her tangled hair and said, "Oh, dear, it will take Mrs Crayton at least thirty minutes to brush out the knots."

He admired her greatly in that moment. Without thought, he pulled her against him again, gently brushed his lips to hers, and released her. She didn't recoil from him, but rather stood silently gazing at him, with a confused look on her face.

"Would you have breakfast with me? In an hour?"

"Yes, my lord, I should like that very much."

She stood unmoving for some moments after he had left her room. She thought of his kindness and of his gentle, undemanding kiss before leaving her. It touched her deeply.

Julien found that his fondest hope, that Kate would learn to trust him and willingly wish to be in his company, was granted. In the days that followed, she became like a shadow, not allowing him out of her sight. On several occasions he found himself ruefully explaining to her that he had to leave her, for but an instant, to relieve his physical needs. Her face would flame with color, but she remained where he left her, doggedly awaiting his return.

It didn't occur to her that Julien would think her behavior odd, for her constant fear prevented her from understanding how much she had changed toward her husband. Somehow it didn't even seem strange to her when, the night following her riding accident, Julien gently informed her that he would no longer pressure her to consummate their marriage, that he wanted her to have as much time as she wished. From that evening on, she no longer wished to escape her husband's company as the hour grew later. Her bedroom was no longer a solace against him, but an empty, lonely place where her guilt and fear mingled with terrifying clarity, keeping her from sleep.

A week had passed when, near dawn one night, she awoke to the sound of her own cries. Vague, menacing shadows crowded about her; hands tried to grab at her, and ugly, crude voices dinned in her ears. In panic she threw off the tangled covers and ran terror-stricken to Julien's room.

He heard her screams and had just thrown on his dressing gown when she burst into the room, looking like a white apparition, her hair streaming about her face and down her back. He caught her up in his arms and held her fast against him, feeling her heart hammer against his chest. "There, it's all right. There's nothing to fear. I'm here, and I'll always be here for you."

"It was so awful, Julien, yet I can't seem to remember. Why can't I remember? It must be the same nightmare as before. I'm sure of it. I just can't grasp it and hold it, it slips away from me, but it's horrible, horrible—"

"You must trust me. Everything will be all right. I give you my promise."

She looked up at him, a small frown furrowing her brow, as she weighed his words. "Please let me stay with you, Julien. I can't bear to be alone."

28

Even a week ago he would have been gape-mouthed with surprise to hear her say that, but now, no, he wasn't shocked or surprised at all. He cupped her face in his palms. "Of course you'll stay with me. I won't leave you. You're safe with me. Do you believe that, Kate?"

She nodded slowly. He picked her up in his arms and placed her in his bed. He lay down beside her, pulled the covers over them, and gathered her to him. He felt a long sigh pass through her body, and in but a moment she was asleep, her head on his chest.

Sleep didn't come so easily to Julien, and he lay staring at the ceiling even as gray shafts of dawn filtered into the room. His promise to her to keep her safe rang hollow in his ears. How could he protect her from her own fears, fears that emerged to terrify her at night, fears she didn't begin to understand? During the day, she was living the guilt that he had forced upon her, and the misery in her eyes made him writhe with self-loathing.

Try as he would, he could think of no way to separate her rape as a child from his own rape of her. That's what it had been, despite

354

his bringing her to pleasure. Rape, pure and simple rape. Only rape wasn't ever simple. God, he'd been a fool, a conceited ass, so confident in himself and his ability to seduce his wife and then calm her into accepting him. Had he been utterly mad?

And thus he too had to remain silent. He couldn't speak to her of one because that could only result in her learning of the other. He had no doubt that if he told her now that he had been the man who raped her, he would lose her. And he feared she would lose herself, even more than she was now lost to what she was and who she was.

He closed his eyes and enjoyed the warmth and softness of her body. He stroked her thick hair, feeling the soft waves spring in his hand, as if alive.

When he awoke some hours later, she was gone. He wasn't the least bit surprised. He could easily picture her embarrassment upon waking in his bed. Nor was he overly surprised to find her pacing outside his bedroom door, waiting for him to emerge, dressed in her breeches for their daily fencing lesson. Neither of them mentioned her wild flight to his room the previous night.

There were changes Julien saw in Kate that day. She hurled herself into physical activity, extending their fencing lesson until finally Julien dropped his foil, seeing her face white with fatigue. In their riding in the afternoon, she pushed Gabriella to a frenetic pace, until again Julien was forced to pull her up so that her horse would not drop under her with exhaustion.

She tried to maintain a flow of light, inconsequential chatter that evening, as if to prove to herself that all was well with her. But she couldn't hide the haunted look that veiled her eyes whenever she slowed her frantic pace. Late that evening, after she had lost an imaginary two hundred pounds to him at piquet, he led her unwillingly to her room.

"I don't really want, that is, I'm truly not tired yet, Julien. I really don't think I can sleep."

He himself was ready to drop, but he didn't say anything about that. He looked down at her and smiled gently. "If you find you can't sleep, come to my room and we'll talk until you're drowsy. All right?"

She turned her face away quickly, and he could feel her weighing her trust in him against her fear of being alone.

"It doesn't matter. Whatever you wish, my dear. Why don't you think about it? I'll be in my bedchamber. Whatever you decide, I'll be there for you." He gently pushed her into her room, not wishing to press her for an answer.

He had just eased his tired body into his bed when there was a light tap on his door and she slipped silently into his room. She stopped and stood in awkward silence, her fingers plucking nervously at her nightgown.

"Come, sweetheart." He patted the place beside him. "I don't want you to take a chill.

Come and get into bed. We'll have a nice talk or whatever you wish."

She walked slowly, hesitating every few steps, and with a visible effort climbed into bed beside him. She was trembling. He made no attempt to take her into his arms; he only pulled the covers over them and lay on his back beside her. After a long moment of strained silence, she said, "I don't wish you to think, that is, you must think it odd that—"

He could feel her embarrassment, and so he cut off her pitiful explanation. "What I think is that you wore me to a bone today. Come, my dear, let's go to sleep."

He stretched out his arms and touched her shoulders, his movements slow and unthreatening. She tensed for only a moment and then allowed him to pull her against his chest.

During the next weeks, Kate felt as if she were slowly suffocating from her guilt and shame. Julien's unflagging kindness during the days and his gentle understanding each night made her all the more miserable. She could allow no excuses for herself. That her unknown captor had forcibly drugged her and ruthlessly bound her gave her no justification, no forgiveness for herself, because she had experienced pleasure at his hands and his mouth—oh, God, yes, his mouth, burning her, sending her outside herself, but making himself part of her even as she thought she'd surely die of the pleasure. Though he'd then forced her, she still thought herself guilty of betraying her husband. Her guilt ate at her relentlessly, and only her fear of losing Julien allowed her to keep her secret to herself.

Her only comfort was sleeping in her husband's arms each night. The terrifying nightmare had come to her two more times, but her low moans had instantly awakened Julien, and he'd shaken her to consciousness before the awful images grew strong within her mind.

She tried each time to understand the meaning of the fearful dream, but something deep within her jostled the images, as if to prevent her from grasping their significance.

She developed the habit of gazing at herself in the mirror whenever she passed one in the villa. She was certain that some change must have appeared on her face, some knowing sign, perhaps in her eyes, that would reveal her lost innocence. She felt she must see the signs before Julien did so she could hide them from him, anything so he wouldn't know, wouldn't guess. But each time she looked, she saw only a pale, set face, her lost innocence evidently buried in the depths of her eyes.

She thought occasionally of Harry, perfunctorily loving him, but his meaning to her was slowly changing. She was no longer his hoydenish little sister, spontaneously involving him in all her thoughts. She didn't know whose Kate she was.

The Swiss weather remained comfortably cool during those weeks, then it changed abruptly. The temperature plummeted, and on a Thursday morning they awoke to a light snow blanketing the ground.

Julien didn't blink an eye when Kate donned her riding habit to accompany him to the village to secure carriages for their journey back to Geneva. Upon their arrival in the village, she dogged his steps, oblivious of the curious stares cast her way by the local folk, and stayed at his side as he conducted his business at the tiny inn. Her only comment when they left was that the owner had a bulbous nose, obviously from too much drink, and years of grime under his fingernails.

Julien laughed. "Grime or not, my dear, he much admired you, and I'm convinced that I got a much better price because you were with me."

"Perhaps, Julien, I should have conducted your business. It is possible that I would have achieved even a cheaper price."

Then she gave him a wonderful gift. She smiled up at him, a small smile, gone very quickly, but still it was something.

Three days later, their luggage securely strapped to the boot of their chaise, Kate and Julien took their leave of the villa. The Craytons would follow at a more sedate pace in the second carriage.

How very different was their return to Geneva. As before, they stayed at the Coeur de Lyon, but this time, by tacit agreement,

Kate shared Julien's room. Happily, it occurred to Julien to have a screen brought to their room to ensure her privacy when dressing. He willingly played her lady's maid, buttoning and unbuttoning her gowns and helping her to brush out the tangles in her hair, teasing her, being as lighthearted as he could manage. He didn't say a word when she whisked behind the screen to complete her dressing.

"Do you recall, Julien," she said unexpectedly that evening over dinner, "when we were last here and you forced me to take that wretched walk with you to the lake? And I nearly contracted a chill because of your officious manners?"

"I find it very interesting that a female's memory becomes so quickly distorted. Why, as I recall, it was you, my dear, who was being stubborn and willful by refusing to wear that warm cloak I bought for you."

"Perhaps. But don't you see? It was *your* cloak. Somehow I felt that if I wore it, I'd be selling myself, that I would no longer be me."

He paused, an arrested look on his face. "I hadn't thought of it like that, ever. I'm sorry for that. I wasn't much of a good friend to you, was I?"

"Oh, yes. Never think you're not. You're my best friend. That is, I couldn't—" She stopped cold and he reached out and took her hand.

"Even so, let's forget about that now. Don't

you agree that it was something of an interesting argument?"

That did get a small smile out of her. "Yes,
I suppose it was, particularly since you gained
your ends in any case. Your wager in piquet
was, I admit, a master stroke."

"And you've shown great improvement. It's
been some three weeks now that I haven't
thrashed you quite so soundly."

"You damnable man. You'll see, I'm much
the smarter and will serve you your just
deserts."

"I admit it's a slim possibility, a bare glimmer of a possibility, if, in the dim future, I
manage to lose my wits."

She was suddenly as silent as a stone. She
simply couldn't imagine the future, dim or
otherwise. She counted her future only in
immediate days. She became aware that he
was looking closely at her, and so she quickly
spoke of the tastiness of the roast veal.

They journeyed slowly through France, enjoying the warmer weather, halting to explore
the Roman ruins in the south—particularly in
Nîmes, and making their way far to the west
of Paris. When they reached Calais, Kate was
surprised to find Julien's yacht, The *Fair
Maid*, moored in the harbor.

"Goodness, I'd forgotten that yacht of
yours, Lord March." There was laughter in
her voice, and he warmed to it, turning a very
real, very powerful smile on her.

"I hope I won't have to sling you over my

shoulder and carry you aboard." He would have done it before if it had occurred to him. Still smiling, he turned to wave to a small, portly man, uniformed in dark blue, striding toward them.

"I don't think you'll have to now," she said, looking with interest as the uniformed man bowed low to Julien.

"Aye, a pleasure to see you, my lord. The men were becoming a trifle restless." His voice was booming. He broke into a leathery smile and bowed to Kate.

"The countess of March, Captain Marcham."

"An honor it is, my lady," the captain told her, thinking privately that he was indeed fortunate that he and his men weren't left longer to kick up their heels in Calais. Lord, were he the earl, he would have extended the wedding trip another six months.

The *Fair Maid* was finely appointed, with small, elegantly furnished rooms and a deck and railing that shone to a high polish. During the nine-hour crossing, Kate spent the majority of her time contentedly bundled in fur rugs on the deck. As she sipped a cup of tea, offered by a shy young seaman, she remembered with some amusement her flight to France on the small, dingy packet.

"We'll dock at Plymouth within the hour, my lord," Captain Marcham informed them after what seemed to Kate an incredibly short time.

"Excellent time, Marcham. I hope you now

have a better opinion of my yacht, Kate," he added, turning to tuck the rug more closely about her legs.

"It's quite lovely, as you well know. It's just that we've come so quickly back, and I'm not certain—" Her voice trailed off, and she stared out over the whitecapped water, her mind in some confusion.

"Of what, my dear?"

She withdrew, giving a tiny shake of her head. "It's nothing. I'm being silly, nothing more." Suddenly he saw fear in her eyes, stark fear. She quickly added, "I promise you, it's nothing at all. I'm fine, more than fine. I swear it."

He would have howled at the moon if only there had been one. He felt sick with guilt and fear for her, even as he admired her more than he could say. She was brave, so damned brave, but she was hiding herself, hiding everything, and there was naught he could do about it, not yet at least.

When they stepped ashore at Plymouth, it was teeming with travelers, harried seamen, and many indigenous specimens lolling about on the dock. Somehow the touch of English soil beneath her feet and the hearty cries in the English tongue sounding on every side of her made her feel terribly alone. Though Julien stood not six feet from her, giving instructions to Captain Marcham and to the men who were removing their luggage, she had the unaccountable feeling that the man whose life she had shared for the past two months was now drawing away from her, returning to a way of life that was alien to her. Two months ago she wouldn't have cared—indeed, she would have welcomed it—but now she felt that what she wanted most was to return to the yacht and let Captain Marcham sail wherever he wished.

"Come, Countess," Julien said, taking her arm, "a hearty English meal awaits us at the Wild Boar."

Kate said nothing, for there wasn't, after all, anything to the point that she could say. She looked one last time at The *Fair Maid*, then moved into silent step beside her husband.

29

"Good Lord, George, you don't mean my mother is here? Now, at this moment?"

"Yes, my lord. Her ladyship informed me she'd had the 'feeling' that you would be returning shortly. She has been waiting in the drawing room not above half an hour, my lord."

"I had no clue she had such powers. Kate?"

"Oh, yes, it's very strange." She had a headache, and she still felt a trifle queasy after their long journey from Plymouth to London.

Julien looked down at her pale face.

"George, call Eliza. The countess is fatigued. I want her to rest now."

She didn't disagree, thankful that she wouldn't have to meet the dowager countess until she had had time to gather herself together and get rid of this wretched headache.

"Mother will, of course, wish to meet you, Kate. But if you do not feel just the thing, I shall take you to visit her another day. Eliza, escort the countess to her room." He patted his wife's hand, turned, and strode down the long, marbled hall, disappearing through a set of double doors.

"I will see to your luggage, my lady," George assured her, snapping his fingers in the direction of a footman, whose presence Kate had not even noticed.

"Thank you, George. My lord is right. I would like to go to my room now, Eliza." It didn't occur to her to question Eliza's presence as her maid, in Julien's house.

She removed only her cloak and bonnet before stretching out on her bed. She felt less wretched after Eliza placed a cloth soaked in lavender water over her eyes. Her stomach settled, and some few minutes later she rose up on her elbows and said, "It's the oddest thing, Eliza, but now I'm feeling much more alive than otherwise. Please fetch me a gown, for I would meet the dowager countess. Something modest, to suit a mother-in-law's taste, I think."

Eliza chose well, and not half an hour later Kate walked down the curved staircase, dressed in a demure, high-necked muslin gown of pale green, her hair brushed into a knot of clustered curls atop her head. She felt no particular trepidation at meeting her mother-in-law, for she really knew very little about her, save that the several times Julien had mentioned his mother he'd spoken with a sort of affectionate impatience.

The doors to the drawing room were slightly ajar, and Kate paused a moment to smooth her gown before entering. She stopped, dismayed, upon hearing a woman speak in a reproachful, complaining voice.

"Of course, I scotched any scandal, Julien, after you left in such unnatural haste for Paris. But how could you chase that girl in the most shocking way imaginable? I told you there was bad blood in the Brandon family, and now you have saddled me with this wicked girl. It is too much, and I fear I won't survive the winter. Perhaps I won't even survive until the beginning of winter."

Kate stood rigidly outside the door, waiting to hear Julien's response.

"Really, Mama, you've had two months to accustom yourself to the idea. I assure you that Katharine is a lovely young lady. You will see her for yourself soon enough."

"But even Sarah, my dear boy—"

"You forget, Mama, that Sarah is married. Surely you prefer a wicked Brandon to my running off with a married lady." Julien's voice was sharp. Kate wasn't privy to the gleam of sarcastic amusement on his face.

She dismissed her immediate cowardly instinct to retreat to her room, raised her head, and rather like a condemned martyr, strode proudly to her judgment.

She drew up short as she entered, her eyes fastened on the dowager countess of March. A small, dark-haired woman swathed in several fine paisley shawls, she sat on a sofa with her head pressed back against the cushions, her eyes tightly closed as if she were undergoing the most dire of upsets. One thin hand clutched a vinaigrette to her narrow bosom. Julien sat opposite her, his hands clasped between his knees, his look one of bewilderment.

Kate cleared her throat and forced her feet to move forward.

"My dear, do come in. Are you feeling more the thing now?" Julien gave her a smile and a wink before turning to his mother, who was now sitting bolt upright, her dark eyes open and assessing.

Kate made a pretty curtsy and said, demure as a nun, "I'm indeed honored to make your acquaintance, ma'am. Julien has of course told me much about you. Your kindness, your generosity, your immense understanding."

"Well, at least, child, you in no way resemble that impudent father of yours," the dowager said flatly.

"I'm said to resemble my mother," Kate said. She sat down beside her mother-in-law.

The dowager was silent for a moment as she searched her memory for a picture of Lady

Sabrina. She vaguely remembered bright-red hair set atop a rather pale, silent face. "Yes, perhaps you do, which has to be a blessing because Sir Oliver is a very homely man, so very unprepossessing, if you know what I mean."

"Oh yes, ma'am, 'unprepossessing' is the very word for him."

"Ah, Mother, Kate, would you care for a glass of sherry?"

"I suppose it would be a soothing agent to my nerves," the dowager said with a sigh. As Julien poured the sherry, the dowager turned back to Kate.

"You seem rather on good terms with my son now, young lady. Perhaps you would be so kind as to tell me why you refused my son two months ago and ran away in the most ill-bred manner possible and by yourself to Paris?"

Julien was annoyed and didn't hesitate to let it show. "Really, Mother, the past is in the past, and it's no longer of any import whatsoever. Any misunderstandings Katharine and I have had are over and done with, and are certainly none of your affair, in any case."

The dowager gasped and pressed her hands to her palpitating bosom. To Kate, Julien's measured words seemed only the mildest of reproaches, but it was not so, she perceived, to her mother-in-law. She quickly took one of the dowager's limp hands in her own and patted it.

"Of course you have a right to know,

ma'am. You must forgive Julien, for he is quite fatigued from our long journey. You see, my father was quite Gothic in his attitude, demanding that I wed your son before I knew my own mind. Indeed you are right, ma'am, it was most foolish of me to travel unaccompanied to Paris. I can but attribute my thoughtless action to my, er, confusion of sensibilities. I do hope that you will now endeavor to forgive my irregular behavior."

The dowager found herself in a quandary. She saw from beneath her lashes that Katharine's prettily spoken speech had found favor with her son, and there was a kindness of expression, a warmth in his eyes that she had never before observed. Having, however, cataloged a rather impressive list of complaints, she decided to take a nip at her daughter-in-law on another matter.

"My dear boy, your Aunt Mary informed me that Katharine was a lady of quality, and now I suppose that I must concur. But she also told me that you, Katharine, appear to be no breeder. Of course, I don't in general like to speak of such indelicate subjects, but I think it is a matter of great importance that an heir be provided quickly for the St Clair line—at least one, perhaps two or three, just to be safe, for life is so very uncertain, don't you think? Is it true, Julien? Does she have narrow hips?"

Kate couldn't think of a word to say. She sat there like a stick, her head down, wanting to cry, wanting to scream at her mother-in-law that none of it was any of her business and she was a witch. But she held silent and still.

Julien was at the end of his patience, his anger fanned by the misery in his wife's eyes. He stood over his mother. "All right, Mother, this time you've gone too far. It's obvious you mean only to make mischief. I won't have you badger Katharine with your tactless and altogether unnecessary comments. If you can't bethink yourself of any conciliatory words, then I would suggest that you take your leave."

"Julien!" the dowager shrieked, clasping her hands to her meager bosom and falling back against the cushions. "Oh, what a mother must bear, turned upon by her only dear son, to whom she gave her life, nearly her last breath. It was only by the veriest chance that I survived your birth, and now you turn on me. Oh dear, what else will happen before I must leave this earth, possibly even before the winter?"

"Now, Julien, surely—" Katharine said. Above all things, she didn't want Julien to have a falling-out with his hitherto fond parent, though the parent in question deserved a good kick.

She removed the vinaigrette from the dowager's unresisting hand and waved it under her nose.

"Come, ma'am, let us try to forget this unpleasantness. Julien, will you not apologize, please? One can see that your dear mother is upset, and her devotion to you is laudable."

She gave her husband a significant look.

To Julien's surprise, his fast-fading parent turned half-tearful eyes to Kate and uttered in a tremulous voice, "Dear, dear child, how well you understand the frailty of my constitution. Gentlemen do not, nay, cannot share the sensitivity of our feelings, even my beloved son who occasionally forgets himself and says things to wound me utterly."

Julien looked from his mother to his wife, gave her a wink, then threw up his hands as if in bafflement. He strode to the long, curtained French windows.

"You must forgive him, child," the dowager said sadly, leaning toward Kate and patting her arm. "I'm certain that you will coax him out of his masculine mood. Alas, a mother's influence wanes so quickly. As a new bride, you have all the power that I once had but obviously don't have anymore."

Kate hesitated to think of Julien's mother as a remarkably foolish woman, but the truth was the truth, and besides, Julien appeared to deal well with her. If not precisely well, the two of them together certainly did. Her husband was not only smart, he was also guileful. It was a good thing in this instance.

"I shall certainly try to bring him to his former good humor," Kate said, her voice calm, without a quiver.

The dowager looked rather soulfully at her son's back, and with the sigh of one sorely used, she began, with the assistance of Kate, to gather her shawls into a semblance of order about her thin shoulders. She even allowed her daughter-in-law to assist her to her feet.

"Julien, your mother is preparing to take her leave. Would you not like to bid her a good-bye?"

Julien turned about, a harried expression on his face, one manufactured, Kate knew, just for his mother. He walked to her and planted a light kiss on her thin cheek.

"My dear son, at least your father is not here to see what you've done."

"Mother, for God's sake, my father's misunderstanding with Sir Oliver has absolutely nothing whatsoever to do with Katharine. I would that you contrive to forget it, and now, or at least very soon from now. Do you understand me?"

Katharine added, "Dear ma'am, I would assure you that my father was always alone in his views regarding your esteemed family. My brother Harry and I have long been in disagreement with Sir Oliver in this matter. Indeed, after your acquaintance, ma'am, I am more convinced than ever that his actions were quite ill-judged."

"Ah, dear Katharine, how noble you are, so refined in your observations." The dowager's dark eyes grew bright, and the thin line of her lips turned up at the corners, albeit with some effort. She turned her face to Katharine and allowed her daughter-in-law to kiss her upon the cheek.

"I'll escort you to your carriage, Mother," Julien said, taking her arm. He wasn't about to risk a reversal of his parent's recently acquired good humor.

When he returned to the drawing room, he was obliged to smile, for Kate wore an impish grin, which delighted him.

"You're a baggage, my dear." He took her hand. "You speak of my turning Sir Oliver so sweet, and here you handled my mother like a master strategist. It was well done of you, and I thank you for it."

"Oh, you're quite welcome. Oh, yes, ah, Julien, who is this Sarah person? I couldn't help but overhear your mother speak of her, and I wondered. Oh, I'm sorry if it discomfits you, truly—"

"A beautiful, charming woman," he said outrageously.

She whipped her face up, her eyes darkening with sudden anger. "You wretched man," she began, only to pull up short as her own shame seared her mind. She drew a deep breath and planted a tight smile on her face. "I look forward to meeting this paragon." He was looking at her, and she quickly turned away. Sometimes she felt that he saw too much, that he could probe her thoughts.

Julien dismissed further provocative comments. "Well, my dear, what do you think of my humble establishment?"

She drew an easier breath and gazed about the drawing room. "It's quite elegant. Naturally, until I see the rest of the rooms I can't make a final judgment."

It didn't take her long to applaud Julien's excellent taste in the furnishings of the town house and to compliment the quiet efficiency of his staff. She was particularly drawn to the stolid butler, George, whose unruffled dignity she found comforting. It was he who eased her transition as mistress of the house, unobtrusively giving her advice on the management of the servants and the protocol of receiving visitors. In this matter, she was profoundly grateful, for in the next week the knocker was never still during the morning visiting hours. It appeared that all of London society wished to inspect the new countess of March. Because of her own inescapable abstraction, she was a great deal less nervous in the presence of her exalted guests, and many left the St Clair town house to spread the gossip that even though the countess was, unfortunately, from the country and a mere baronet's daughter, she did seem to know her way rather well.

Of all the ton who paid visits to the St Clair town house, it was Percy who found instant favor with Kate. After eyeing her for some minutes through his quizzing glass, he turned to Julien and blithely remarked that he was a lucky dog and quite unworthy of his good fortune. Kate felt a tightening in her throat at what she thought to be undeserved praise, when, but a moment later, Percy turned to her and asked what François was preparing for dinner. She blinked several times at this unexpected question, noted that Julien was grinning widely at her, and said truthfully, "Do forgive me, Sir Percy, I really have no idea. If, however, you will be patient, I shall ring for George."

"Not at all the thing, you know, Lady Kate, not at all the thing. I shall be over first thing tomorrow morning, and we shall plan the week's menus."

Indeed, Percy arrived punctually the following morning, and he and Kate spent a comfortable hour devising menus that would test François's culinary abilities. "After all, you pay the damned fellow one hundred pounds a year. You don't want to have him lazing about. Those Frogs take advantage, you know."

She could find no fault with this logic, and discovered after Percy took his leave that she had quite forgotten herself while in his company. She sought him out, and more often than not, it was Percy who accompanied her to Bond Street to do her shopping and to the park to ride at the fashionable hour of five in the afternoon. It was during one of these excursions that Kate chanced to see a very lovely lady dressed in the height of fashion raise her parasol in greeting. She was seated in an open carriage beside a gentleman who seemed to be remonstrating with her. Her piquant oval face was framed with blond ringlets, and her eyes were a startling blue. Kate raised her hand in a hesitant reply and observed a rather mocking smile pass over the lady's lips. She wondered whether she should turn Astrate and make the lady's acquaintance.

"Kate, dammit." Percy hissed, drawing his horse close to hers, "don't."

"What's wrong? The lady waved to me. Would it not be rude to ignore her?"

"No," was his clipped response. He click-clicked his horse into a canter, and Kate was obliged to do the same. After some moments, she drew up beside him and tugged on his sleeve.

"Percy, for heaven's sake, who was that lady?"

Percy stared doggedly between his horse's ears.

"Now, you're being quite cowhanded, Percy, you're jobbing your poor horse's mouth."

"Cowhanded?" Percy screwed his head around, incensed at the attack on his equestrian skill.

Kate chuckled. "Forgive me, my friend, but I had to get your attention. You're behaving quite foolishly, you know. There's no reason for you to be so very protective of me. It was Lady Sarah Ponsonby, wasn't it?"

As Percy regarded her in silence, she added in a flat voice, "She's quite lovely, is she not?"

"I suppose so, if one happens to like the china-doll variety."

"Don't try to cozen me, Percy. We both know that the china-doll variety is quite to Julien's taste. Oh, don't look at me so strangely and don't try to deny the truth. Perhaps I shouldn't know about her liaison with Julien, but I do, and there's an end to it."

"Exactly. It's ended. Julien dismissed her the moment he returned to London before your marriage."

"It appears the lady perhaps disagrees with you, Percy."

Though Kate quickly changed the topic and chattered with seeming unconcern for the remainder of their ride, Percy wasn't fooled.

After depositing Kate in Grosvenor Square, Percy repaired to White's, as was his habit. Although not one to let other people's concerns trouble him overlong, Percy found, quite to his surprise, that he felt it his duty to seek out Julien and inform him of what had occurred. He ran him to ground in the reading room, conversing with the portly, somewhat vacuous marquis of Halport. It was a good five minutes before Percy was able to detach Julien from the garrulous marquis. "Don't mean to be disagreeable, Halport," Percy managed to insert during a brief pause, "but I must remove March here. Need his advice on this nag up for sale at Tattersall's."

"Good Lord, not Otherton's slope-shouldered bay, I trust, Percy. He's a showy creature."

"Now, see here, March—"

"Devilish fine horse, if you ask me," Lord Halport said. Lord Halport turned to Percy and asked politely, "If you wouldn't mind,

Blairstock, think I'll take a look at Otherton's bay. As March says, he's a showy creature. I always like to maintain a full stable, you know."

"Not at all, dear sir. Don't mind a bit."

"Servant, Blairstock. My regards to your lovely countess, my lord March." Julien and Percy returned Lord Halport's creaky bow, and when the marquis was out of earshot, Percy said indignantly to Julien, "You, Julien, of all people, know that I would never consider that broken-down bay of Otherton's. Just couldn't think of another excuse to get rid of the fellow."

Julien grinned broadly. "Well, now that we've as good as sold Otherton's bay for him, why don't you join me in a glass of sherry?" Julien waved his hand to a somberly clad footman.

"Now, Percy, whatever is the matter? You're looking positively blue around your collar."

Percy rearranged his elegantly clad bulk into a more comfortable position and eyed Julien in profound silence. Seeing his friend so very calm and composed, he began to doubt the wisdom of poking his nose into the earl's affairs.

"Good God, Percy, it cannot be so bad as all that. Your tailor been dunning you?"

"Dash it, March, Kate has seen Sarah."

"She was bound to, sooner or later," the earl said mildly. "I see no cause for alarm. Don't excite yourself. It raises your color alarmingly."

"Easy for you to say, Julien, but you didn't see the look on Sarah's face or the way she waved to Kate. Like a cat with her claws curled. I swear she's up to mischief. You know as well as I do that she grows quite bored with Sir Edward. Wouldn't be at all surprised if she decided she wanted you in her bed again."

"You forget, Percy, that I spoke to her before Kate came to London. Just a woman's jealousy, no more."

"Well, Kate seems to think that you much admire Lady Sarah. Told me so, in fact. Tried to act like she didn't care, but you know Kate, she can't hide her feelings worth a tinker's damn."

Julien silently cursed Sarah but was obliged to admit upon brief reflection that he was not displeased that Kate was distressed. Could it be that she was jealous? A sure sign to him that she had truly come to care for him. He met Percy's gaze and said quietly, "Don't concern yourself further. I shall take care of the matter. And, Percy, I thank you for your kindness to Katharine. She is aware, I believe, what a very good friend she has in you."

Percy coughed. "I say, Julien, deuced nice of you to say that, but you know, well, Kate is such a trump, not at all like a woman, you know? She's like a comrade in arms, or I think that's what she'd be if I'd ever been in the army."

"That she is, that she is. Oh, by the by, Percy, what is François preparing for dinner this evening?"

Percy pursed his lips in thought before replying cordially, "Thursday, ah, yes, poached medallions of veal in Port wine sauce with mushrooms, you know, and served with spinach noodles. Beefsteak stuffed with chicken liver, with vegetables and roasted potatoes. Many other side dishes, of course. I approved all of them."

"Thank you. I trust that you will grace us with your presence."

Percy beamed. "Dashed nice of you to offer, March. Don't mind if I do."

After Julien and Percy had parted, Julien couldn't help but wonder if he was not living in a fool's paradise, pretending that there were really no problems at all, when in fact they were growing wildly in number. He knew that there had been no recurrence of Kate's nightmare, for though she slept in her own room, he quietly opened the adjoining door each night before retiring.

30

Lady Sarah Ponsonby let her vellum-bound copy of Lord Byron's *The Corsair* slide off her lap onto the pale-blue carpet, reached out for a sweetmeat on the table beside her, thought of her thighs, which were a bit too plump, and drew her hand back. She was bored, not only with her doting elderly husband but also with her lover, Sir Edward. Though his adoration for her hadn't diminished over the past several months, she found him unimaginative both in lovemaking and in his flattery—her eyes were bluer than the pale-blue sky of midsummer? She couldn't help but make comparisons between Sir Edward and Julien, and she found in all particulars that her portly lover was a decided second to the earl of March, who was not only a beautiful man but an excellent lover as well.

She felt a sudden knot of anger at the thought of the pale-faced girl Julien had wed. She was far too tall, in Sarah's estimation, and she found it altogether disagreeable that some considered the young countess to be quite beautiful. Well, beautiful or not, she thought, brightening, the baronet's daughter wasn't enjoying her good fortune, for all was not well between the earl and the countess. How fortunate it was that one of her lackeys was enamored of a talkative serving maid in the earl's household, for he provided her with a steady source of prime information. From her own experience, she knew Julien to be a passionate man, and she had first dismissed the careless bit of gossip that he didn't visit his wife's bedchamber. But then she had wondered why their wedding trip had been of singularly short duration. Now, since the St Clairs had been more than two weeks in London and many more bits of information were let slip by her lackey, she was convinced that something was definitely amiss with their relationship.

Her vanity tempted her to believe that Julien realized he'd made a shocking mis-alliance and was simply biding his time to again seek her out. It was an exciting thought, and she refused to dismiss it. After all, Katharine was but a girl—that rankled a bit—but she, Sarah, was an experienced woman, and a beautiful one, as she had been told countless times, by countless men, including Julien.

Her smooth brow furrowed in concentrated thought as she cudgeled her brains for the most expedient way possible to bring Julien to his senses. It didn't take her long to hit upon Lady Haverstoke's ridotto, which was but two days away. What better opportunity to show Julien that he'd made a mistake in his choice of brides? She would dress as Cleopatra, perhaps even paint her toenails, and wear the golden sandals. Dampening her petticoat to make the flowing white gown cling to her body was a bit uncomfortable, but it would serve only to make her the more alluring. With more energy than she was wont to show, Sarah rose from her couch and rang imperiously for her maid. She found that she was even looking forward to riding with Sir Edward.

"You're silent, Julien. Don't you like my costume?"

He remained silent for a few more moments, then said, "It's not that I don't like it, it's simply not quite what I expected you to wear."

Secretly, he was appalled. He had supposed that Kate would perhaps choose a shepherdess costume for the Haverstoke ridotto, or some such costume that wouldn't call attention to herself. Instead, unbeknownst to him, she'd attired herself as a courtesan of the last century. She powdered her hair and piled it high atop her head. Her gown was of a heavy dark-blue brocade, with full skirts worn over panniers, and cut very low over her white bosom, a narrow row of lace suggesting more than revealing the curve of her breasts.

Perhaps what shocked him most were her reddened lips and the small black patch placed artfully beside her mouth. She wore heavy sapphire earrings and necklace, and even to the least exacting taste, too many bracelets adorned her arms. He thought she looked the whore, albeit a very expensive one.

"Perhaps, Kate, you've become enamored of Madame de Pompadour's portrait?" he asked, trying to check his anger at her appearance.

It was her turn to be silent, and she turned the bracelets on one wrist before replying slowly, "Yes, I had the gown she wore in the portrait copied by Madame Bissotte. Of course, she was Louis XV's mistress, but still—"

"She was a trollop," he said more harshly than he intended. "I don't wish my wife to emulate such an example."

His anger died as quickly as it had come, for her face paled beneath the rouge and she turned quickly away from him. He realized with a shock that in some strange fashion, Kate was acting out the role of a whore because it was how she felt about herself. He wondered fleetingly if she herself was aware of what she was doing. He walked quickly to her and gently placed his hands on her shoulders.

"Do forgive me, sweetheart. It's just that I have no great liking for the Pompadour. It was said that my grandfather even visited her bedchamber a long time ago in Paris. Indeed, my dear, you look striking, the flamboyance of your costume serves only to enhance your beauty."

He was lying, and both of them knew it. But he also knew that the *Ton* would see nothing amiss with her appearance and would even applaud her daring originality. "Come, it grows late and the Haverstoke villa is several miles from London."

She turned to face him, a look of confusion in her eyes. "You don't go in costume, my lord?"

"My concessions are a domino and a mask. Had I but known that you so admired the dress of the last century, I would have dressed as Louis XV."

"Oh, no, you could not have. Madame de Pompadour was only his mistress. It wouldn't have been, that is to say—" She stopped abruptly and gave her head a tiny shake.

With a flash of insight he realized that she didn't see him as her lover, so in her eyes he couldn't be Louis XV. "I hardly think it matters, my dear. Ah, here's George."

"Your carriage is ready, my lord," George announced, unaware that he had rescued the count and countess from a trying scene.

"Oh, yes, indeed. I have but to fetch my domino." She turned on her heel and brushed past George.

Julien gazed silently after her before turning to his butler. "Thank you, George. Please inform Davie that we will be down presently."

He picked up his black-satin domino from the back of a chair and nonchalantly flung it over his shoulders. He fingered the soft black velvet mask before he slipped it into the pocket of his waistcoat. He thought grimly that he was indeed living in a fool's paradise, and it was crumbling bit by bit around him.

He'd believed the stay in London would help her, and it had seemed to help, but now ... He shook his head. When he walked past his butler into the entryway, his face was impassive.

Kate met him presently, an even more striking picture now, enveloped in her long dark-blue-satin domino. She had fastened on her blue-brocade mask, and not one auburn strand was visible through the white powder in her hair. If he had not known she was his wife, Julien wouldn't have recognized her.

Their ride to the Haverstoke mansion occupied the better part of an hour, and after many minutes of strained silence, Julien endeavored to ease the tension between them by describing the various members of the *ton* she would meet. He maintained a steady stream of anecdotes, which was interrupted only at rare moments by questions from Kate. She became animated only at the mention of Percy's name.

"I believe Percy plans to appear as a medieval lord of the manor, complete to battle-ax, so he told me."

"I do but pray that he won't drop it on his foot."

"Rather on his foot than on yours when you dance with him." Julien grinned into the dim light.

"And will Hugh be present?"

"Certainly. Like me, Hugh will relax his taste only to the point of domino and mask."

Kate didn't comment, for the swaying of the carriage was making her stomach churn uncomfortably. She leaned her head back against the white-satin squabs and closed her eyes.

The Haverstoke mansion was a two-storied pale-red-brick structure dating from the Restoration, set back from the main road by a rather rutted graveled drive. Lights blazing from every window and countless carriages lining the drive gave ample evidence of the success of the ridotto. As Bladen opened the carriage door for his master to alight, his eyes veered to the lighted servants' hall, where he was certain he and Davie would enjoy frothy mugs of ale and the smiles and teasing of some of the maids.

Lady Haverstoke had rigged out her entire staff in the formal livery of the last century, a startling yellow and white, and had insisted, much to their consternation, that each wear a wig of sugarloaf shape. Thus it was that her hawk-nosed butler was busy grumbling to himself and twitching at his wig when the earl and countess of March were ushered into the main hall. Elkins, his second in command, looked like an exotic yellow bird, a canary, the butler decided with a curl of his thin lips, for a canary sounded both exotic and yellow. And the way he was fluttering about, ingratiating himself among the guests—his strutting manner was simply not to be borne. The butler grimly resolved to put the little creeper in his place the moment the guests departed. He was obliged to cloak his violent intentions as the earl and countess approached. The butler's bow to the earl was of the perfect depth, though his knees trembled in complaint as he straightened more slowly than he had descended.

"If your lordship and ladyship will please to accompany me." The earl nodded briefly, and the butler smiled smugly as he conducted them up the winding stairway to the large ballroom on the second floor. Elkins, with his thin, high-pitched voice, would never be able to perform this duty with such a deep rich baritone.

He managed to gaze surreptitiously at the new countess of March and was disappointed that he couldn't make out her features through her mask and her powdered hair, as white as his sugarloaf wig.

"The earl and countess of March!" came his booming voice. He hoped that not too many more guests would arrive, for the assembled company was so boisterously loud that he was growing quite hoarse in trying to be heard over the laughing chatter and that wild German music—the waltz, it was called, Elkins had condescendingly informed him.

Kate had only a few moments to scan the startlingly colorful sea of guests for a familiar face before a large woman with a more-than-ample bosom, swathed in yards of purple satin, swooped down upon them. Her hair was tightly crimped, and a myriad of tiny sausage curls fluttered about her heavy face. Kate blinked at the two enormous purple ostrich feathers implanted atop her head, which swayed precariously as she walked.

"Ah, my dear March. And your new countess. So delighted you could come. Quite unusual you look, my dear. Marie Antoinette, I daresay. And you, my lord March, so disobliging of you not to come in costume. But no matter." She beamed at them, revealing large, protruding teeth.

"You look quite dashing, Constance," Julien said when the lady halted her monologue for a moment. "Yes, this is Katharine, my wife."

Lady Haverstoke favored Kate with a tap on the arm with her ivory *bris*é fan. "The hair creates quite an effect, my dear. So very white, ah, but you are in good company." Lady Haverstoke pointed her ubiquitous fan in the general direction of a small knot of elderly women, each attired more outrageously than the other. "Lady Waverleigh and that monstrous pink wig. That lady in the lavender silk, Elsbeth Rothford, how very youthful she would like to appear. And, of course, there's Lady Ponsonby, surrounded by her gallants—her court, as I call it." She looked expectantly to see some signs of agitation in Katharine, but seeing none, hid her disappointment and added for effect, "Scandalous, in my opinion. Cleopatra, she informs me, and garbed in that clinging wisp of material. And her toenails painted gold." Still observing no noteworthy response from

389

either the earl or the countess, she contented herself with the fact that the evening was far from advanced.

"My *dear* Lady Ranleigh!" And Lady Haverstoke was gone with amazing speed away from them, soon lost to view among a throng of guests.

"Lord Haverstoke must be either a man of great forbearance or deaf," Kate said, staring after their hostess.

"Lord Haverstoke had the good sense to depart this world some years ago." Julien wished he could see behind her mask to see what effect Lady Haverstoke's malicious and quite calculated words had on her.

"Come, sweetheart," he said then, taking her arm, "I believe I've located our lord of the manor, battle-ax and all."

"Oh, and there is Hugh, Julien. He looks terribly somber, does he not? All that black satin."

"Don't I look equally as somber?"

"How ridiculous—of course not. You look rather dignified, perhaps like a very young statesman."

"High tribute, certainly. If ever I take an active role in the House of Lords, my first act will be to condemn auburn hair."

"Then you will find that your bills for white powder will grow monstrously."

"Julien, at least have the decency to tie on your mask," Percy said, thrusting forward his hand and shaking Julien's heartily. "You look like some sort of hellfire parson bent on destroying the world."

"Kate tells me I appear more like a statesman," Julien said, smiling as he got the full effect of Percy's grandeur, his noble proportions encased in a jerkin of light-yellow wool. His battle-ax dangled from a large leather belt about his waist.

"How grand you look, Percy, so very impressive." She laughed in delight when he tried to favor her with a gallant bow. "Ah, good evening to you, Hugh."

"Katharine. If my memory doesn't fault me, you have copied Pompadour's gown. I must commend your originality and the skill of your modiste. An unusual lady the Pompadour was, to say the least."

Kate sensed more than observed a stiffening in Julien at Hugh's appraisal. She said quickly, "The portrait took my fancy, Hugh. But you know, the black patch is most bothersome. It itches excessively."

"Well, I would most willingly exchange your patch for this deucedly cumbersome ax," Percy said, shooting a look at Hugh. "Never should have let him talk me into wearing it."

Me talk *you*—"

"March," Percy continued, ignoring Hugh's astonishment, "you don't mind if I dance with Kate, do you?"

"If Kate doesn't fear for her toes, I suppose I can make no argument."

"Not at all."

Percy bore her off, and soon they took their places beside other equally colorful couples

391

on the dance floor.

"Well, Hugh, which do you prefer, parsons or statesmen?"

"Considering the Regent's problems with retaining statesmen of worth, I believe we should choose the latter and offer our services."

"And would you recommend our good Percy to command the army?"

Hugh tied on his mask. "'Twould give me great pleasure to see our dandy mount a horse in that getup."

Julien's deep laugh dissolved into a grunt of impatience as he chanced to look up and see Sarah beckoning to him in a most imperious manner. Hugh's eyes followed Julien's, and his nostrils quivered in anger. He frowned as he appraised her in her Cleopatra's costume, trying to remember if it was an asp or a viper that brought about the queen's demise. He became even more indignant when Lady Sarah blithely detached herself from her knot of admirers and calmly approached them.

"Don't be so obvious, Hugh, in your condemnation. Percy informs me that Sarah grows tired of Sir Edward, and if she chooses to seek out old quarry, it must be dealt with."

The two men's eyes met through the slits in their masks, and though Hugh was uncertain of Julien's intent, he was obliged to hold his peace.

"Do excuse me, Hugh. I hope this won't take long." Julien walked toward Lady Sarah.

"My dear Julien. Such a bore that you

didn't come as Caesar or perhaps Mark Antony. What a very attractive couple we would have made together." She raised wide, wistful eyes to Julien's face and sighed with soulful innocence. He thought it was a good act, one she'd perfected over the years, but it was getting a bit frayed now. He wasn't moved a whit. Indeed, he found it silly, truth be told.

"You have need of no one to further enhance your image, Sarah. Does your barge await you outside?" Though he'd been scandalized by Kate's costume, he was rather amused by Sarah's outrageous daring and was unable to prevent his gaze from traveling the length of her flimsy, clinging gown. "And the gold toenails—quite the crowning touch for a queen."

"Yes, are they not?" She was pleased at his masculine response, but not at all surprised. All men were alike, after all. Julien had just lost his way for a little while, nothing more. She laid her bare hand on his arm and said softly, "Won't you dance with Cleopatra, my lord March? I vow she's awaited your coming all this evening."

"If you wish, Sarah. It's just as well." He slipped his arm about her slender waist and whirled her into the throng of dancers.

31

Lady Constance Haverstoke watched with glittering eyes as Lord March led Lady Ponsonby to the dance floor. She turned to her companion, Lady Victoria Manningly, and remarked complacently, "What is the saying about moths flying forever to a flame?"

"Lord March should take care, I daresay," Lady Victoria said with pursed lips, "else he will find himself quite at odds with his new bride. That is she, is it not, over there?" She pointed to Kate's gracefully swaying form, rendered less so by Percy's ungainly costume. "She's a very proud girl, I've heard it said, but of course not unbecomingly so," she added quickly, remembering suddenly that for some strange reason Mrs Drummond Burrell—that terrifying officious old goat—had taken an unaccountable liking to the girl.

Lady Victoria judged from Lady Haverstoke's brazen attempt to draw attention to the earl and Lady Ponsonby that she wasn't privy to this bit of information. It would serve her right, Victoria thought, if the earl's bride were to cause a commotion. Certainly that cat Sarah Ponsonby wouldn't show to advantage in the eyes of society. She wondered if perhaps she should drop a hint in Constance's ear. She was surprised suddenly from her meanderings by the touch of Lady Haverstoke's hand on her wrist. "Do but look, Victoria, March and Lady Sarah are leaving the floor."

Both ladies watched in silence as the earl led Sarah to the large, curtained windows at the end of the ballroom, parted them, and slipped outside behind them.

"Perhaps it's not moths to a flame after all," Lady Haverstoke mused, with the superior grin of one who has accomplished her goal, "more like bees to the honey pot."

"Lord March is unwise," was all that Lady Victoria Manningly said.

"My dear Julien, how very thoughtful of you. It was growing so terribly close. I was longing for a breath of evening air, but only with you."

"Did you indeed, Sarah?" He was very much aware for one unwanted moment of her hand stroking his sleeve and the pervading odor of her musk scent. He said coolly, "I understand, Sarah, that Sir Edward has lowered in your estimation. Really, my dear, you are too fickle. He mounts a horse well. Does he not mount you as well?"

It was crude, but it didn't deter her. "I've missed you, Julien." Her lips were parted in the most provocative way. She felt the strength of him through the black satin of his evening coat and raised her hand to touch his face. "Ah, my dearest, how ever could you have tied yourself to that whey-faced girl?"

"Whey-faced, Sarah? Surely you can't have looked closely at her."

She tossed her golden curls. "Very well. Perhaps she is passable-looking in a provincial sort of way, but, Julien, she is but a girl, a green, ignorant, cold girl."

"A girl, yes. Indeed, my reputation would suffer were it otherwise."

"Come, you know very well what I mean. Why, it's common knowledge that—" She ground to a halt as Julien's hand gripped her wrist.

"Just what, I pray, is common knowledge?"

Sarah drew back at the coldness of his voice. "Well, it is not precisely *common* knowledge. I know, Julien. I know that she's cold. I know you don't sleep with your bride, that you don't even visit her bedchamber."

He said nothing.

She was emboldened to continue. "It's a mistake, my dear Julien, to have wed an inexperienced chit. Is she frightened of your passion? That is why, is it not, that you returned so quickly from your wedding trip?"

In the dim moonlight she couldn't see Julien's pallor, or the hardening of his mouth. She thought him to be struggling with himself, and she pressed her body against him and slipped her white arms up about his shoulders. "Oh, my dearest, can she give you this?" She stood on her tiptoes and pressed her mouth to his, her hands entwining in his curling hair and pulling him down to her.

Percy swiped his forehead with a fine lawn handkerchief that was oddly at variance with his woolen jerkin, and heaved a sigh.

"Lord, Kate, It will take me a bloody hour to regain my breath. Too deuced fast, that damned German music. Enough to send a fellow toppling early into his grave, or at least toppling onto his battle-ax."

"You were magnificent, Percy." As she spoke she was searching for Julien and Hugh. "Drat, how vexatious this patch is." She lightly rubbed her cheek around the offending black satin.

"Ah, there you are, my dear."

Kate and Percy turned at the commanding voice of Lady Haverstoke.

"How terribly feudal you are, Lord Blair-stock." She looked around her complacently. "It's such a sad crush, isn't it? I daresay we will have some ladies swooning if the space becomes too tight."

"Yes, indeed, ma'am," Kate said without a moment's hesitation. It was an expected compliment, surely.

Lady Haverstoke lowered her voice and said in a conspiratorial whisper, "How charming Lord March looked, dancing with Lady Sarah. Several of the ladies were disappointed when they left the floor."

"They left the floor, ma'am?" Kate asked, suddenly feeling nausea rise in her throat.

"For a breath of fresh air, no doubt," Lady Haverstoke said in a pitying way that made Percy want to slap her fat face.

"Well, it is deuced hot in here, Lady Constance, deuced hot." What the devil was the smug old tabby up to? It came as a bit of a shock to him that Julien would commit such a folly.

"Come, Kate, let us try some of that excellent champagne." Percy took Kate firmly by the arm, nodded briefly to Lady Haverstoke, and propelled her toward the punch bowl. "Don't listen to her. The old biddy's just trying to stir up some mischief, that's all."

"Is she, Percy?" Kate asked, stopping and gazing up at his perspiring face.

"Good Lord, Kate, don't be a fool. Julien is your husband, not some old roué to sport around with every pretty face."

"You're right, Percy, it is overly warm. If you will excuse me—" She felt the words choke in her throat as she sped away from him before he could form a protest.

"Damnation!" Percy accidentally bumped his battle-ax against a lady's elbow. "Apologies, ma'am."

When Kate broke away from Percy, she thought perhaps to seek out some quiet room where she could be alone. But somehow she found that her legs were quite at odds with her mind and moved her resolutely the length of the ballroom toward the long windows. She was beginning to feel quite ill, her stomach churning uncomfortably and a steady pounding growing in her head. She silently cursed her own physical weakness and stopped to press her fingers against her forehead. Her lacings were too tight, that was it. Eliza had tugged and tugged until Kate had gasped for breath. She smoothed the tight brocade about her waist, drew a deep breath, and wondered as she pulled aside the heavy curtains what was happening to her, what was so overwhelmingly compelling her to search out her husband. She found that she was quietly pleading to some divine power that she would find Julien alone. As she slipped through the narrow opening, she felt as though someone's fist had struck her hard in the stomach, for she saw Julien and Lady Sarah, standing very close, the lady's hand possessively holding her husband's arm. She heard Lady Sarah say with devastating clarity, "Is she frightened of your passion? That is why, is it not, that you returned so quickly from your wedding trip?"

Oh, dear God, Julien, she cried silently to herself, please, please ... She couldn't see her husband's face, but his continued silence dinned in her ears.

"Oh, my dearest, Julien, can she give you this?"

Kate pressed her face against the window-pane to blot out the picture of Lady Sarah locked tightly against Julien's chest, her mouth upon his. She was filled with sudden fury, and without thought she stepped forward, her hands balled into fists. Her long gown caught itself on the hinge of the window and pulled her up short. She bent down and gave the skirt a vicious tug and found that her anger was dissolving into a dim haze of misery. She looked down at her dress, a whore's gown, was it not? Nothing but a whore's dress. Good God, what right had she to rain down curses on Lady Sarah's head?

She pressed her hand against her mouth and turned about quickly. Hurrying back into the ballroom, she made her way to a more distant row of windows and slipped out quietly. She ran along the flagstone balcony, until, unable to help herself, she leaned miserably over the railing and lost her dinner.

She sat huddled against the railing until she was brought to her senses by voices quite near her. She panicked, thinking that it was perhaps Julien. He mustn't find her like this. Remnants of pride patched themselves together.

She rose slowly to her feet, pressing her lace handkerchief to her mouth and gritting her teeth against a new wave of nausea. With automatic motions she smoothed her gown and forced her face into an impassive mask as she sought out an antechamber to bathe her face and mouth. She felt strangely empty, as if nothing now mattered to her. She was grateful for the numbness, the feeling of detachment, for when Julien later approached her, as she chatted with the utmost unconcern with a young matron dressed in the acceptable shepherdess costume, she was able to greet him with a semblance of calm.

"Lady Ridgelow," Julien said with a slight bow before turning to his wife. "My dear, Percy is in quite a taking, claiming that you abandoned him at the punch bowl. Come, you must make reparations before we take our leave. A pleasure to see you again, Lady Ridgelow."

As Julien guided her through the now-thinning company, he said quietly, "Actually, Percy was in quite a taking over my behavior, not yours."

"Your behavior, my lord?" She looked up at him, striving for calm, for a show of indifference that he would believe. He saw too much always, and now she simply couldn't bear it if he saw her misery.

"Yes, and undoubtedly I owe you an explanation. By taking Lady Sarah to the balcony, I evidently gave the gossips a delectable topic of conversation. You, I am persuaded, must know my reason for doing so."

"Indeed, my lord, it isn't for me to question your actions." She wouldn't look at him, she couldn't. She kept her eyes straight ahead.

"Come, Kate," he said sharply, frowning down at her profile, "you've taken me to task on practically every one of my actions since the day I met you. That I perhaps chose an awkward place and time to set Lady Sarah straight is very much your affair. I am sorry for it, but at least it's now at an end."

Kate felt a deep bitterness invade the comforting numbness that surrounded her. Yes, she thought sadly, I saw just how well you handled the lady.

"I see I'm to judge by your continued silence that you either understand my motives or you are jealous. Which is it?" He grasped her arm and pulled her up to face him.

"As you say, my lord," she said finally, her voice wintry and far away, "I understand your motives perfectly. I assure you, there's no need to explain further. You're a man, after all."

"Just what the hell is that supposed to mean?"

"Are you not a man?"

"Damnation. No, this is quite ridiculous." He regarded her steadily and said at last, "It will be as you wish, at least for the moment. We haven't yet danced. Would you like to?"

"No. That is, I'm very tired. It's been a long evening, and so many people and all of them talking and talking. If you wouldn't mind, I would just as soon leave."

He studied her pale face. She did look exhausted and unhappy. Damnation, what was he to do?

Gray flecks of dawn penetrated the darkness of the room when Julien awoke at the sound of a piercing scream. He bounded from his bed, threw his dressing gown about him, and rushed through the adjoining door into

402

Kate's room. She screamed again, tangling herself among the heavy bedclothes.

He leaned over her and grabbed her shoulders, shaking her none too gently. "Kate, come on now, wake up, that's it, you must wake up. It's a nightmare. Nothing more, just that damned nightmare. Come, sweetheart."

A long shudder passed the length of her body, and she forced her eyes open. Julien was balanced over her, his face pale in the dim light, his hair tousled, beard stubble on his chin. She cried out in protest as he shook her again.

"It was the nightmare again. Oh, God, I hate it. It's so frightening because I can't see what's there, can't see anything, but the evil is there, I know it." She struggled up and pulled her hands from beneath the covers to push damp masses of hair from her forehead. She threw out her arms to clasp him to her, to burrow against him, but as she did so, Lady Sarah's face rose in her eyes. She fell back against the pillows and turned her face away.

Julien drew back, baffled. Always before, she'd wanted him to comfort her, to hold her. Slowly he straightened and automatically began to smooth out the tangled covers. He saw that she was trembling uncontrollably. "Sweetheart," he said quietly. She made no response, and he eased himself down beside her. Above all things, he didn't want to frighten her, and thus he contented himself with gazing at her averted face, satisfied, for the moment at least, that he was close to her.

Gradually the trembling lessened and her breathing became more regular.

She turned her head back to look at him. "I thank you, my lord, for waking me." Her voice was dry and crackling in the silent room, like fragile autumn leaves falling from branches.

"I'll stay with you now, all right?" He reached out his hand and lightly touched her damp cheeks.

She whipped her head away as if his touch repelled her or frightened her. "No! No, my lord, please. I promise you that I'm quite all right now. I'm sorry to have awakened you. Forgive me. I won't do it again."

"Bloody hell, that's quite enough." He sounded angry to her, and she closed her eyes tightly, turning back within herself. But there was only a vast, lonely emptiness there. She heard him rise from her bed. She could feel him looking down at her as he stood beside her. Dear God, what was he thinking? Would he go back to Lady Sarah? What would he do?

"Good night. You know very well you have but to call if you have need of me."

She didn't trust herself to speak, and so she lay in stiff silence until she heard his retreating footsteps. She opened her eyes, and unbidden tears welled up and rolled silently down her cheeks. She tried yet again to piece together the nightmare, but as always, it escaped her, drifting in vague shadows back into unknown depths of her mind, waiting there; she felt it would never be gone from

404

her. She took an edge of the covers and wiped the tears from her face.

Sleep didn't again come to her, and she pushed back the covers. She eased her feet into her slippers and padded to the windows. She curled up in the window seat, her face pressed against the blue-brocade curtains.

It was some hours later that Eliza found her, huddled and shivering, asleep in the embrasure.

32

"Dammit, Julien, you're a fool, and if you weren't my friend—and a better shot—I'd bloody well call you out."

Hugh looked just as angry, only his anger was cold and still. He said finally, "I'd be his second—if he were a better shot."

The three men stood outside White's, their overcoats buttoned high to their collars to keep out the blistering winter wind.

"You must have known that Constance Haverstoke would take the first opportunity to fill Kate's ears with Sarah. And you, damn your hide, you had to parade her in front of everyone onto the dance floor!" As a gust of wind threatened to whip Percy's beaver hat from his carefully pomaded locks, he momentarily shut his mouth.

405

"It's quite true, Julien," Hugh said. "Kate's so young, you should have realized that she would find out and what she would feel."

"Kate assured me that she quite understood my motives." But he knew it was a lie, he bloody well knew he'd hurt her badly, but he hadn't meant to.

"Besides being young, she is quite proud."

Julien threw up his gloved hands. "All right, that's enough from both of you." He raised haughty brows and added sarcastically, "You're acting as if Kate were your sister. I was on the point of telling you both, before Blairstock here ranted at me like a madman, that I intend to leave London with Kate on Friday. We go to St Clair. Does that satisfy your chivalrous meddling?"

"And Sarah?" Percy said, his eyes dark, for once undaunted by Julien's show of sangfroid.

"Neither of you has further need to trouble yourselves about that lady."

"Ah, so you came to an understanding with her when you took her outside to the balcony, is that what you're telling us?"

Julien jerked his head around. "It appears that my actions are quite common knowledge."

"Lord, Julien. You may be a fool, but Kate isn't. As I told you last night, Lady Constance gave her an earful. And enjoyed every minute of it, the old besom."

Julien's anger died as he pictured Kate in the dim morning light, silent and withdrawn from him. He raised weary eyes to his friend and said quietly, "The matter is settled. Do not, I pray, call me out, Percy," he added with a glimmer of a smile. "Now, I suggest, if you gentlemen are quite through telling me what a fool I am, let's go inside and have a glass of sherry."

It was strange, Hugh thought, as they were divested of their greatcoats in the cloakroom of White's, how very serious life had become since Julien had got himself wed. And to see Percy so impassioned over something that didn't involve his personal pleasures made him wonder uneasily if he knew more of the situation than he had disclosed earlier that morning when he unceremoniously burst in, most effectively dampening Hugh's appetite for his breakfast. He gazed from beneath hooded lids at Julien and noted the tense lines about his mouth and eyes. No, he decided, finally, Julien was too closemouthed and, like Kate, too proud to unburden himself to anyone.

They drank their sherry in silence, each feeling acutely strained in the others' company. Hugh thought the sherry tasteless.

"It's like you could cut the air with a blade," George said behind his immaculate white-gloved hand to Mackles, a young footman who had just received a blistering set-down from a usually polite, calm master.

"It ain't so much 'is lordship," Mackles said after ruminating over George's comment for several moments. "It's 'er ladyship. Like a ghost she's been, so pale and quiet-like, if you know what I mean." He glanced sideways toward the breakfast room, thankful that the door was firmly closed.

George knew very well what the footman meant, but he was suddenly aware that such a conversation, even though it be with a superior servant, was unseemly. "Well, just never you mind about all that, my boy," he said formally, bending a stern eye on the hapless Mackles. "You just help Eliza with her ladyship's trunks. His lordship and ladyship should be finishing their breakfast shortly and will wish to leave."

On the other side of the breakfast-parlor door, Julien was sitting across from his silent wife. "Do at least try some of your eggs, my dear. It will be a long time before luncheon."

She nodded, her head down. She didn't feel at all well this morning, and the thought of the eggs made her stomach churn. But as she didn't want him to know, she raised a morsel to her mouth, chewed with her eyes closed, and forced herself to swallow.

"Your gown is very smart. Madame Giselle?"

Kate nodded, thinking privately that the dove-gray dress emphasized her pallor and the dark shadows under her eyes. She looked dowdy and sallow. She'd pulled the gown from her wardrobe to the sound of Eliza's disapproving clucking.

"How long do you intend to remain at St Clair, my lord?" She asked, seeing her husband frown at her nearly full breakfast plate.

"If it pleases you, at least until the new year. You do have a say in the matter, you know."

She knew the look she shot him was disbelieving, but she only nodded. She could remember no occasion when any opinion of hers had affected his decisions. Indeed, she had learned but two days before that they would be leaving for St Clair.

Not many minutes later, the earl and countess of March said hasty good-byes to the assembled servants in the marble entrance way.

"Have a safe journey, my lord, my lady," George said in his superior butler's voice as he opened the front doors.

"I'll keep you informed as to the date of our return, George," Julien said.

Kate looked with something akin to dread at the open carriage door. "Maintain a smart pace, Davie," she heard Julien say to their coachman, "We'll stop at the inn in Bramford for luncheon."

"Yes, my lord," David said, giving the earl a smart salute. He shot a smug smile at the gimlet-eyed Bladen, who was not to accompany the earl on this trip.

Julien assisted Kate into the carriage and handed her two fur rugs to wrap about her legs. Then he swung in and after settling himself comfortably, tapped the roof with his cane. He briefly looked out the carriage

409

window to ensure that the other carriage, containing Eliza and Timmens, was also in motion.

Satisfied, he sat back and stretched his long legs diagonally across from him. "Are you warm enough?"

"Yes, my lord March," she answered, not turning her head to face him.

"So formal, sweetheart? Shall I call you 'my lady March'?"

She watched Grosvenor Square disappear behind them before saying with a forced smile, "If it suits your fancy. With all those servants at your command, it seems more natural for you to be a Lord March, and not a simple Julien."

"They're also your servants," he said, steadily regarding her.

"Very well. As you will, Julien."

Not a very auspicious beginning, he thought glumly, watching his wife from the corner of his eyes.

As the carriage rumbled through Hounslow Heath, Julien said, "It looks quite barren, does it not?" He directed her attention to the forlorn leafless trees set against a gray, fog-laden landscape. "Our most famous highwaymen have frequented this place, and still do, for that matter. I myself was stopped here some years ago."

"You were robbed?" she asked incredulously.

"Well, not precisely. I had to send the Bow Street runners for two of them, and the other

410

fellow managed to escape with a bullet in his arm." He chuckled. "You should have seen Davie. Foolishly brave he was, waving his blunderbuss about and screaming curses at the villains."

"You weren't hurt, were you?"

"Oh, no. Merely late for Lady Otterly's drum." He didn't add that the lady who was accompanying him flew into the most damnable hysterics.

"It must have been quite exciting," she said, her voice wistful. "I've never met a highwayman."

"They're a most unsavory lot. Not at all dashing or romantic, as the stories puff them up to be."

She shivered.

He leaned forward and tucked the rugs more securely about her. "Are you cold?"

She drew back. "No, no, I was merely thinking of Harry, and hoping he's unharmed."

The carriage lurched over an uneven stretch of road and Kate gritted her teeth against a wave of nausea. Even as she closed her eyes tightly and prayed that she wouldn't be ill, she was forced to say in a strangled voice, "Julien, please stop the carriage. Oh dear, I'm going to be sick."

He took one look at her strained, pale face and drove the head of his cane hard against the roof of the carriage. The carriage pulled to a halt, and Julien threw open the door and jumped to the ground.

"Give me your hand, quickly now."

She stumbled toward him, her handkerchief pressed hard against her mouth. He took a firm grip on her arms and swung her to the road beside him. She leaned heavily against him, the world spinning unpleasantly about her. He let her slip to her knees at the side of the road and held her shoulders as she retched violently. He silently cursed himself for forcing her to eat what little breakfast she'd had. The retching eventually subsided into dry-heaving spasms that shook her whole body. Julien ruthlessly pulled off her fashionable bonnet so she could rest her head on his thigh, and drew his greatcoat around her to protect her from the blowing west wind.

"My lord," Davie said quietly, "perhaps her ladyship would feel a mite better with some of my medicinal brandy."

"Thank you, Davie, the very thing." Julien took the flask from his coachman, wet his handkerchief, and gently wiped her mouth. "Come, sweetheart. This will make you feel much better." His calmness steadied her, and though she was now consumed with embarrassment, she slowly raised her head and allowed Julien to put the flask to her mouth. She took a long draft and felt the fiery liquid burn its way down her throat. Her stomach churned anew at the unwelcome intrusion, but to her profound relief, it quieted after a moment.

She felt too weak to struggle when her husband lifted her into his arms. Nor did she protest when, once inside the carriage, he held her firmly on his lap, her head resting against his chest.

"My lord, is her ladyship well enough to continue now?" Davie poked a concerned face through the carriage door.

Julien took quick mental stock. "How far are we from Carresford?"

"But a mile or so, my lord."

"Good. There's an inn there, The White Goose. I think the countess should rest there before we think of continuing. Drive slowly, Davie," he added, tightening his hold about her shoulders.

Kate burrowed her face against Julien's chest. Between bouts of the wretched dizziness, she felt there could be no greater shame than being vilely ill in front of someone else.

"Why didn't you tell me you were sick?"

"It's just a touch of something, I think. Nothing to worry about, truly."

He felt inordinately guilty that he hadn't guessed that her unnatural silence and pallor reflected more than her unhappiness. He frowned above her head, wondering why the devil Eliza hadn't told him.

"If you had only told me, we could have delayed our trip to St Clair."

"Oh, no. That is, I didn't want to stay in London." He felt her tense.

"Hush, sweetheart, it's all right. It doesn't matter." He let his chin rest on her hair. "If you're not feeling better this afternoon, I'll send Davie back to London for a physician."

413

"Please don't, Julien. I shall be fine, you'll see. I don't want to cause you any more inconvenience."

"It's not an inconvenience to want my wife to be in good health, dammit."

She sighed and was silent.

33

The White Goose was a staunch red-brick inn nestled amid elm trees across from the village green. The landlady, unused to Quality visiting her humble establishment, quickly wiped her large hands on her apron and bustled forward, waving imperiously at two of her sons as she did so.

"Be quick about it, Will. Open the carriage door." A large, ambling boy of about seventeen years hurried forward.

Not without some difficulty, Julien alighted with Kate in his arms. "Davie, stable the horses and keep your eyes sharp for the other carriage."

"Right this way, my lord." Mrs Micklesfield hurried to stand beside the open doorway for Julien to enter. He had to duck his head, for the smoke-blackened beams were perilously low.

"I require a bedchamber for my wife," he said, looking about him at the dim but cozily warm taproom. He hoped there would be no bugs in the mattress.

For a large woman, Mrs Micklesfield moved with amazing speed up the worn wooden staircase. She opened the door at the top of the stairs to a small but sparkling-clean bedchamber containing only a large old-fashioned tester bed and an ancient oak armoire.

Kate didn't particularly want Julien to put her down. She met his eyes as he laid her on the bed. She was a good deal surprised to see a frown of worry furrow his brow, for, in truth, she'd rather expected some sign of impatience at having his trip so disrupted. He leaned over her and plumped the pillow beneath her head. "Now, my dear, Mrs—?"

"Mrs Micklesfield, my lord."

"Yes, Mrs Micklesfield will undress you and tuck you up. I'll be back in a bit to see how you're doing."

"As you will, Julien. But you will see, I'll be fine in a few minutes."

"Stubborn Kate," he said, squeezing her hand, and walked from the room.

Soon Kate lay snug beneath a soft down quilt.

"Thank you, Mrs Micklesfield. That is indeed much better."

"I should think so, my lady. Now, you just rest and I'll fetch you some food and a warm chicken broth. It's just the thing to make you feel right as a trivet."

Kate felt dubious about the food, but she

415

was too weary to quibble. She closed her eyes and concentrated on righting her disgruntled stomach.

Julien stepped out of the taproom a few minutes later to see Mrs Micklesfield preparing to mount the stairs with a tray of covered dishes in her arms.

"Ah, my lord, quite knocked up, her ladyship is, but I've just the thing to make her feel better." She beamed at him in what Julien thought to be an uncommonly motherly fashion.

"But food, Mrs Micklesfield? Surely—she was quite ill but a short time ago."

"But of course, my lord. A lady in her condition must keep up her strength. All that racketing about in a carriage unnerved her. It is to be expected. Just a bit of food and she'll feel better."

"A lady in her *what*?"

"If I may be so bold as to wish your lordship my congratulations." Her leathery face softened. "But truly, my lord, as your wife is breeding, you really mustn't rush her higgledy-piggledy about the countryside, if you will allow me to say so."

It took a moment for her words to penetrate Julien's befuddled mind. Kate *pregnant*? He felt as if he had just stepped into some bizarre play in which he was the main character and Mrs Micklesfield his audience, and he had no idea of the lines he should speak.

As all the tortuous implications of this bizarre situation flashed before his eyes, he found that he was leaning heavily against the door, his eyes fixed dazedly on Mrs Micklesfield. There can be no greater irony, he thought. My wife pregnant by a wild German lord, who is I. Yet in the same moment he felt a certain sense of masculine pride. He remembered his blithely spoken words to his Aunt Mary Tolford. He'd promised her an heir within a year. It was his audience of one who forced him back to the complexities of reality.

"Shall I take the tray up to her ladyship, my lord?"

"No, Mrs Micklesfield, I'll take it up." It occurred to him that Kate might not know she was pregnant. "Mrs Micklesfield," he said very slowly, choosing his words carefully, "you didn't mention her ladyship's condition to her, did you?"

"Why, no, my lord, I assumed—"

"Excellent. I pray that you will not. You see, the countess isn't quite used to the idea as of yet, and her illness, it's upsetting to her and I wouldn't want to see her disturbed any more today."

Mrs Micklesfield nodded slowly. As the earl mounted the stairs, she shook her head, puzzled. Breeding was breeding, after all. Natural it was, she thought, remembering how her own five children had slipped so easily into the world. The Quality were peculiar, she concluded, and turned toward her kitchen, where a freshly plucked chicken awaited her ministrations.

417

Julien paused for a moment outside Kate's door. He felt convinced that she hadn't yet realized she was pregnant. After all, she had spoken so earnestly about not feeling just the thing. But, good God, how could she not know? Didn't women understand these things? Surely, when she missed her monthly cycle. No, he thought, it was entirely possible, nay practically certain, that she didn't know, caught up as she was in her own unhappiness and her dreaded nightmares. He made rapid calculations in his head back to that day, to that small cottage in Switzerland. It couldn't be much longer before she must realize that she was with child. Several days, a week perhaps. It didn't allow him much time.

He schooled his features into those of simple concern and tapped lightly on the door. He entered to see her struggling to pull the covers over her bare shoulders. He found that he was regarding her closely, perhaps expecting to see some change in her. But if anything, from the brief glimpse he was allowed of her arms and shoulders, she seemed more slender than before.

"Well, wife, Mrs Micklesfield has kindly prepared some food for you. It will make you feel healthy as a stoat, so she informed me."

He set the tray beside her and picked up a smaller coverlet. "Here, would you like to wrap this about you? I don't want you to catch a chill."

As she modestly wrapped the coverlet about her shoulders and pulled herself to a sitting

418

position, she turned to Julien and said with some surprise, "It's very strange, you know, but I find that I am really quite famished. I've never had this particular illness before, but it's quite odd the way it affects one."

Oh, dear God, he thought. He fought the urge to gather her in his arms and tell her that she was pregnant with his child, but he thrust his hands into the pockets of his breeches instead. He must first get her to St Clair; then, as much as he abhorred the notion, he must see Sir Oliver. He was convinced that he himself had first to know all that had happened to her; then perhaps he could help her to understand and forget.

Kate consumed every morsel of food on the tray and lay back with a sigh of contentment.

"Poor François would be positively unnerved if he witnessed the quantities of food you just consumed."

"He's forever burying the most delicious foods in those outlandish sauces of his. He could take a few hints from Mrs Micklesfield, I think." How very normal we're acting toward each other, she thought.

Julien walked to the windows and gazed out onto the gray afternoon. A light drizzle had begun, and raindrops were running down the glass in zigzag rivulets.

"Julien, you wouldn't want me to quack myself like your dear mother, would you?"

"I hardly think that resting after you have been vilely ill qualifies as quacking."

"Well, I feel quite marvelous now, and if

419

you wouldn't mind, I would that we continue to St Clair."

She did indeed look the picture of blooming health, color in her cheeks, her dimples briefly appearing.

"Please fetch Mrs Micklesfield. I can be dressed in a trice."

It wasn't beyond a half-hour later that Julien assisted his pregnant wife into the carriage and climbed in after her. Despite the drizzling rain, she waved her hand out the carriage window and smiled brightly at Mrs Micklesfield and her grinning son, Will.

It was Kate who urged that they push on to Hucklesthorpe before they halted for the night.

Though Julien would have preferred to leave early the next morning, he judged from his brief experience that she needed time after breakfast to settle her stomach. She didn't seem to notice that he ordered a light meal for her, nor did she take exception at their delay in leaving. They were both rewarded by his careful planning, for she didn't suffer a moment's illness throughout that day.

It was well after nightfall when their carriage finally turned from the main road down the long elm drive to St Clair. Mannering wasn't expecting them, but Julien knew there would be cozy fires in their rooms and a warm dinner ready for them within an hour of their arrival.

★　★　★

420

"My lord, my lady, how very grand to see you both." Mannering at first edged the great doors open and then flung them wide. "Ah, Lady Katharine, to see you here, as mistress of St Clair, such an honor, such an honor. Allow me to offer my congratulations, my lord. Dear me, how very late it is. If your lordship and ladyship will allow me to escort you to the drawing room, I shall inform Mrs Cradshaw."

"Whatever Cook has available, Mannering, will be fine."

"I do hope dinner won't be long in coming," Kate said as she stripped off her lemon-kid gloves and tossed them on top of her bonnet.

"On that score you needn't worry." Julien smiled. He knew that the mild-spoken Mannering, when confronted with an emergency, bullied, cajoled, and otherwise threatened mayhem on all his staff who didn't immediately perform in the most exacting and speedy manner possible.

After a footman had unobtrusively laid a fire, Julien seated himself opposite his wife next to the fireplace and stretched out his legs toward the crackling logs. As always, he felt a sense of deep contentment at being in his ancestral home.

"It feels so very strange to be seated in this room, as if I belonged here," Kate said, more to herself than to Julien. She ran her hand tentatively along the deep-red brocade of the armchair.

Julien shook out the ruffles over his wrists, pondering, it seemed, the great ruby signet ring on his right hand. "It would seem to me that you're far more at home here at St Clair than at your father's house."

"Perhaps. I certainly look more elegant now than that poor wretchedly dressed girl at Brandon Hall did." She paused a moment, a frown puckering her brow. "Julien, we don't have to visit Sir Oliver, do you think? I'm certain a genuine welcome is simply not in his nature, despite the amount of your guineas that now reside in his pocket."

Julien thought of his impending visit to Sir Oliver. Whatever the outcome, he himself didn't imagine that it could be in any way cordial. It was likely that Sir Oliver would be the one to sever all relations. He shifted his position in his chair and crossed one gleaming Hessian over the other. "Let's see what the next few days bring, all right? And as to that poor wretchedly dressed girl, as you so unkindly call her, I thought she showed a great deal of spirit and a goodly dollop of sheer nerve. I can't but remember your breeches with a certain fondness. The combination of your breeches, leather hat, fishing pole, and pistol were altogether irresistible."

A slight smile played over her lips, and he could very nearly picture the laughing dimples. "Well, at least in that instance, Julien, you must admit I bowled you over completely, quite left you stunned and speechless."

"Would you accept a challenge to duel with me? Breeches and all?"

"Only if I find my leather hat. But Julien, it's quite possible that your masculine pride may be hurt. Just think, you could be beaten by a mere female."

"Another dream in your sweet female's head," he said. "Just another dream."

"Your dinner, my lord," Mannering announced as he entered, followed by a footman staggering under the weight of several covered trays.

As Kate settled herself beside a small table to enjoy baked chicken and warm bread, she heard Mannering clear his throat and inform his lordship that the second carriage had succumbed to an unfortunate mishap. "The axle sheered clean through, so I'm informed, my lord. They're all stranded, my lord, in Tortlebend. It will be several days before the axle is mended."

Julien turned to Kate, who was in the process of wiping her fingers. "I hope you don't mind Mrs Cradshaw looking after you. It appears Eliza is enjoying a holiday."

"Not at all." She felt relief, truth be told. Sometimes it seemed that Eliza saw too much.

"As to the work you ordered, my lord, it was completed just last week. An excellent job the carpenters did, if you don't mind my saying so. One would never guess that the rooms did not originally adjoin each other."

"What work was Mannering talking about?"

she asked after Mannering had bowed himself out of the room.

"I merely ordered that our bedrooms be connected by an adjoining door, that's all." He chose to ignore the sudden flush on her face and made an elaborate pretense of eating his chicken.

34

"The earl of March is here, my lord, and awaits your presence in the drawing room."

Sir Oliver ceased tugging at his boot for the moment and looked up at Filber. "He is, is he?" The deep-cut lines that slashed down the corners of his mouth lifted, and to Filber's surprise, he gave a grunt of amusement. Then he wet his hands with his spittle and ceremoniously slicked down his frizzled gray hair.

Filber quickly dropped his eyes and looked down at the toes of his black shoes. He hoped that his repugnance at Sir Oliver's distasteful habit would go unnoticed by his master.

Sir Oliver rose, picked up a cravat from the dresser top, and carelessly knotted it about his neck. He peered at the result in the mirror, seemed satisfied with what he saw, and turned toward the door. "Let's go, Filber. After all, we wouldn't wish to keep my illustrious son-in-law kicking up his heels, now

424

would we? Such a proud young man he is, so very proud. But not anymore, huh? No, no more. He's been quite brought down by now." He gave a cackle of mirth and thwacked the stoop-shouldered Filber on the back.

There was an air of suppressed excitement about Sir Oliver that made Filber uneasy, that and his strange words about the earl of March.

It was barely nine o'clock in the morning, a time when his master was at his most dour and disagreeable. It was strange too, he thought, that Lady Katharine hadn't come with her husband—not that he blamed her, given how her father had always treated her, the poor little mite.

"It's gracious of his lordship to pay us a visit, don't you think, Filber? And such a gray, unpleasant day it is, too. Cold in winter, don't you know."

Filber quickened his pace in front of his master down the staircase. Now that he thought about it, the earl, though polite as always, had acted differently, rather too serious, perhaps even abstracted. Why wouldn't the earl be proud anymore?

Filber reached the drawing room and flung open the double doors. "Sir Oliver, my lord."

"My dear sir, how very pleasant to see you."

A common-enough greeting, Filber mused, as Sir Oliver brushed past him into the room and firmly closed the doors behind him.

Julien turned from the window to face his father-in-law. He nodded only slightly in

425

answer to Sir Oliver's greeting. He didn't move forward to take his outstretched hand.

Sir Oliver was not at all perturbed by his son-in-law's coldness. In fact, he grinned broadly, rubbing his hands together. "So cold, isn't it, my lord?"

He got no response, and continued, "Cut right to the chase, is that what you want to do? Very well, you're a long time in coming, my lord. If the truth were to be told, I expected to see you much sooner. Won't you be seated?"

Julien gave him an indifferent look, a look that took him a great deal of effort. Quite simply, he wanted to kill the miserable old man. "No, I think not," he said. "But perhaps it would be to your advantage to be seated."

"Don't mind if I do." Sir Oliver flipped up the tails of his coat and eased himself down into a thread-worn chair. "Well, how very well you're looking, my lord. What do you think of this cold weather?"

"I'm not here to discuss the merits of the weather, but I'm sure you already know that."

"And how is my dear, *dear* daughter? Is she well? Happy? No use shilly-shallying around, my lord. That's why you are here, is it not?"

"Katharine enjoys good health. And as you say, it is because of her that I am here."

Sir Oliver dropped his eyes from his son-in-law's set face and smiled, pretending to study his knuckles with rapt interest.

"Now, my dear boy, there was nothing in your most thorough marriage contract about the return of damaged goods, though I must say you thought of everything else. When you took her, you got quite a shock, eh? Not at all what you expected." He looked up and met Julien's gaze, a malicious gleam drawing his eyes more closely together. He chuckled. "Well stated, is it not, my lord earl? Actually, I'm surprised she's well. Didn't you beat her, at the very least? Demand to know who all her lovers were?"

Julien drew a deep breath and for the moment kept his anger in check. What the miserable old bastard said was exactly what he'd wanted to do. Was he such a shallow fool? He felt ill with guilt. But now it didn't serve the purpose. "Katharine's purity and innocence are not, I assure you, in question." A look of deadly contempt passed over his face. "I would add that I now marvel at this, considering that she sprang from your seed. Has it occurred to you that you're speaking of your own daughter? If your Methodist preachings allow it, I would suggest that you look within yourself, for if you have a soul, it is withered and rotted. God, but you're despicable."

"How dare you, you damned arrogant— Ah, don't tell me you haven't taken her, haven't realized she was a slut. I'll never believe that!" Sir Oliver jumped panting to his feet, his face mottled red with fury.

"Damn you to hell, sit down!"

Sir Oliver sagged back into his chair.

Julien planted himself in front of Sir Oliver,

gripped the arms of his chair, and leaned close to his face. "Now, you will listen to me, you filthy old man. It's quite obvious that you knew I would come, that you have indeed looked forward with a twisted delight to spewing your venom in my face. Did you honestly expect that I would return Katharine to you, spurned and disgraced?"

He straightened quickly, repelled by the closeness of this man. Sir Oliver's face was still blotched with his anger, but now his eyes were wary and he was licking his lips.

"Why are you here then, if not to return the little slut to me? To beg me to take her back?"

Julien nearly struck him then. He forced himself to be calm, for he had to find out what had happened. He made his hands unfist.

"At last we make progress." He walked to the fireplace and leaned his shoulders against the mantel. "You know, I presume, that Katharine has no conscious memory of her rape and your subsequent treatment of her. But did you know that it haunts her like an elusive specter, emerging with terrifying confusion in her dreams at night? She is close to unlocking the truth, yet it eludes her still, and she lives in a suffocating dread. And that is why I am here, to learn all of the truth so she can finally be cleansed of this ugliness."

Sir Oliver's pent-up hatred of his daughter took full rein. "My God, you blind fool! You defend her, you believed her a defenseless child. She's made a fool of you, aye, indeed, my lord earl. Well, I will tell you, she is a slut and she was a whore even then. Those wild green eyes, and that hair as red as all the sins of Satan hanging loose down her back. God, she shamed me, just her being born shamed me, and my doting wife, blind to the evilness of her own daughter, let her flaunt her wiles to the countryside. Oh, yes, I remember well that day, the lying little strumpet screaming that those men had hurt her. She deceived my wife with her tears, but I saw through her pretense. I beat her, yes, thrashed her to an inch of her life, to scourge the evilness from her, and I nearly succeeded, but my wife stopped me. Then the little harlot feigned illness.

"Lifeless she lay in her bed, those evil green eyes of hers just staring, only staring—at me, blaming me. And her damned fool mother, half-crazed, crooning over her, praying to God all the time to save her little girl. How I hated that, praying to God! And she trucked with evil, with the devil."

Suddenly Sir Oliver felt his voice choked off by a painful tightening in his chest. The blood pounded in his temples, and for several agonizing seconds he couldn't breathe. As quickly as the pain had come, it receded, and he gulped in the precious air, feeling his chest expand again with life. He tried to remember what he had been saying, and the image of Katharine as a child rose before him, her large, silent eyes staring at him, so much fear in those child's eyes, then that damned blankness that she had to be feigning. He heard himself give a crack of laughter.

"When she recovered, she forgot. But I reminded her, yes, I didn't tell her what she'd done, but I beat her, to keep the wickedness out of her, so she wouldn't do it again." Sir Oliver's eyes blazed again in sudden passion. "Don't you understand? All I tried to do was save her soul from eternal damnation, but I failed, I know I did."

He paused and looked up to see the earl still standing motionless by the fireplace, a curious, unreadable expression on his face. "She fooled you too, my dear lord earl, did she not? You believed her so very innocent, so guileless, indeed, you probably admired that evil red hair of hers, those green eyes that just stared and stared when she was lying there."

Julien didn't answer, just waited, for there would be more, and he wanted to hear it. Sir Oliver sat forward in his chair, a look of grim satisfaction marking his mouth. "Allow me to wish you much pleasure with your virgin wife, my lord. But beware that she doesn't cuckold you before your precious heir is born."

Julien looked dispassionately at the leering old man before him. He felt moved by a deep tenderness for his wife. He felt a helpless sense of pity and regret at her having spent so many years with this twisted man. If only it wasn't too late for her now.

"It happened at the copse, in the wooded area close to Brandon Hall?" He was pleased at the continued calm of his voice, but it was difficult, one of the most difficult things he'd ever had to do.

"Eh?" Sir Oliver looked with confusion at his son-in-law.

"The copse—the place where Katharine was raped," Julien repeated.

"One of her favorite haunts, that copse." Sir Oliver's voice rose suddenly. "It was her own private kingdom, I would hear her say to her mother. But I know why she went there, yes, to traffic with the devil, to learn the evilness of her body, to let those men come to her and play with her and defile her."

Oh, God, it was enough, too much. Julien pushed away from the mantel. He wanted now nothing more than to leave this suffocating room that held only twisted hatred. "I have no more to ask you. You have provided me with all the information I need."

Julien straightened and walked quickly to the door. He added softly as he turned the knob, "Of course you will understand that Katharine won't be paying you a visit. Indeed, I doubt you will ever see either of us again. And don't you, Sir Oliver, attempt to see her. What you've done to your own daughter—Never mind. You're beyond help, twisted and perverted. It's too late for you. But not for her. I won't allow it ever to be too late for her."

As he pulled the doors closed firmly behind him, he saw Sir Oliver gazing blankly down at his hands. He found that he didn't want to

431

kill the man or even strike him. He just wanted to get away from him and his venom.

"Your coat and hat, my lord."

"Thank you, Filber." Julien shrugged himself into his greatcoat and moved rapidly to the front doors.

"Is Lady Katharine well, my lord?" Filber asked, his voice softening.

"She will be much better soon, Filber." He couldn't prevent his eyes from straying momentarily to the closed drawing-room doors.

"If you pardon my saying so, my lord, all of us here wish Lady Katharine the very best. If you would be so kind, my lord, as to give her our regards."

Julien strode down the front steps and without a backward glance mounted his horse.

It was late in the afternoon when the sound of Julien's voice reached Kate through the half-open door of her bedchamber. She heard his sure stride on the staircase, the sound of his Hessian boots, and she stood rubbing her sweaty palms on her skirt, in an agony of indecision. Oh, dear God, she couldn't see him, not yet.

Her instincts for survival drove her into action. "Milly, quickly, go to the door and tell his lordship that I'm not well, no, that I wasn't well, but I am well now. Yes, now I'm asleep. Go, now, hurry."

She tugged off her dressing gown, threw it to the floor, and scrambled into her bed.

432

"Yes, my lady," Milly said, moving as quickly as her plump figure would allow to the door of the countess's bedchamber. She shot a furtive glance over her shoulder at her young mistress, now burrowed beneath mounds of covers, her eyes tightly closed. Milly gulped and stepped into the hallway, her nervous fingers closing the door behind her. Like most of the newer members of the St Clair household, she was completely in awe of the earl, and as he approached nearer and nearer to her, she began to feel almost incoherent, her tongue lying thick in her mouth. She couldn't lie to him, she couldn't. But what choice did she have?

"Good afternoon, Milly," the earl said politely. She bobbed in front of him, not once but at least three times. He motioned with an elegant gloved hand to the closed door. "Is the countess in her room?"

"Yes, my lord." As the earl made to move past her, she rushed into desperate speech. "Ah, but her ladyship isn't well, my lord, that's it, she's quite ill, at least she was a few minutes ago, but now she's sleeping, soundly, my lord, very soundly." Milly bore up rather well, she thought later, under the earl's close scrutiny, but at that moment she was aware only that her stays were much too tight. She shifted her weight to her other booted foot and looked at him hopefully.

"Very well," he said.

Milly breathed a sigh of relief, but to her consternation, the earl moved to the door and quietly opened it. She wondered frantically whether she would be able to secure another such excellent position as this.

He looked into Kate's room, now bathed in the somber gray late-afternoon light. A lone candle cast its withered light above the mantel, blending in curious patterns with the smooth orange glow of the fire. He could still picture his mother sitting on her favored spindle chair—a damned uncomfortable chair—remorselessly plying her needle into a swatch of material that never seemed to become anything. Only Kate's collection of hairbrushes scattered across the dresser top gave proof that another now occupied the bedchamber. He stood silently, hoping to see some movement from the bed, but the blue-velvet goosedown quilt remained firmly in place. He could make out only the general outlines of her still figure, the rich hair fanning out about her face on the silk pillow giving her Kate's identity. He stepped forward, stopped, and again retreated. Her dressing gown was on the floor. That was odd, surely. He frowned, started forward again, then halted. No, it would be better not to awaken her, he decided, pulling the door closed behind him. The maid, Milly, still stood where he had left her, like a small, plump pug, parading like a watchdog at his mistress's door. He raised an inquiring brow.

"Yes, Milly?"

Milly gulped. "Nothing, my lord. That is, if you wish me to remain with her ladyship—"

434

"No, let her sleep. She will undoubtedly ring if she has need of your assistance." He nodded dismissal, turned abruptly, and walked to his own room, his greatcoat swirling about his ankles.

Milly bobbed a curtsy to the earl's back, cast an uncertain glance at the closed door, turned, and fled down the hall to the servants' quarters. There was a prayer of thanks on her lips.

35

Although Julien forced the sniffing Timmens to go slowly in helping him to change into evening clothes, no word came from Kate that she would join him for dinner. Hunger finally drove him to the library, where Mrs Cradshaw brought him covered trays, doubtless piled high with every imaginable dish, enough to feed a battalion.

"Has the countess kept to her room all day, Emma?" he asked, uncovering a richly spiced lamb stew.

"Yes, she has, my lord," Emma said, comfortably, peering over Julien's shoulder to make sure the kitchen maid had put a salt shaker on the tray.

He swiveled about and looked at her sharply, but was greeted by only a bobbing of her head, for the girl hadn't forgotten about the salt. "Everything is quite nice, isn't it? Will that be all, my lord?" There was an odd smile on her broad face that crinkled up the wrinkles about her eyes.

A damned disturbing smile, he thought, searching her eyes for some clue, with no idea of what he expected to find there. No, she just continued to look at him with unnerving complacency. He felt irritation as he waved her from the room and turned his attention to his dinner. The tasty stew did nothing to alleviate his mood, which was brooding, just plain black brooding. Good Lord, to be faced with his lunatic father-in-law, a smug house-keeper, and an absent wife all in one short day was enough to dampen anyone's spirits. Still hopeful for a message from Kate, he endeavored to while away the long minutes by penning a letter to his fond parent. As no neutral phrases leaped from his quill, he gave up the attempt. With a sigh he rose and stretched, and cast an unenthusiastic eye toward the rows of leather volumes meticulously lined up on endless shelves. He finally selected a volume of Voltaire's *Candide*. He made his way upstairs, pausing a moment outside Kate's door. No light shone beneath the door, and there was no discernible movement from within. He raised a hand to the door, thought better of it, and continued slowly to his own room.

The hands on the mantel clock moved

inordinately slowly. It seemed an eternity before they softly chimed twelve strokes. He looked down at the few pages that his fingers had relentlessly turned, but couldn't seem to recall a word he'd read. He snuffed out a gutted candle and lit a new one. At least he didn't have to concern himself overly with his wife's health, since he knew the cause of her illness, which wasn't an illness at all.

But Sir Oliver—if only he could rid himself of the distorted, leering features, the twisted, damning words. He gave up the attempt to sleep and resolutely turned his wandering attention back to Voltaire.

He didn't know what caused him to look up, perhaps the veriest whisper of movement or a change in the soft shadows cast by the candlelight on the walls. His book dropped to the covers unnoticed.

She stood motionless at the foot of his bed, clad in a white satin gown that shimmered in the flickering light. Her hair was unbound and cascaded about her face and her shoulders, falling in shiny deep waves nearly to her waist. Her eyes rested calmly and steadily upon his face, the pupils so enlarged in the near-darkness that they seemed black.

"Good God, Kate? Are you all right? What's the matter?" He sat bolt upright in bed.

Her dark eyes widened, but she remained silent, her pale lips parted only slightly. She began to move stiffly toward him, her gown clinging to her in gentle folds, her eyes never leaving his face. If was as if she were willing

437

him to look at her face, not at her body.

"You had the nightmare again?" He pulled back the covers, realized that he was naked, and covered himself again. He had no intention of scaring her witless. But what the hell was she doing here?

She stood quite close to him now, and his eyes were drawn to her full breasts clearly outlined by the shimmery material. He felt desire stir strong in his groin. By all that was holy, he didn't trust himself to speak, or do anything else, for that matter. Damn her, what did she want?

"Julien, may I stay with you tonight?" Her voice was soft, a tantalizing whisper from deep in her throat.

He had to be dreaming, that was it. Never had he heard her speak like that. The nightmare, yes, she'd come in here afraid, that was all. He blinked away what surely must be an apparition, but the apparition that was his wife didn't move. He felt a gentle hand on his bare shoulder. "May I, Julien? Let me stay with you."

He drew a deep breath, knowing he was hard as a stone, but he wouldn't frighten her. What did she want? Why did she want to stay with him? She wasn't acting at all like she had when she'd had the nightmare. Slowly he took her hand in his. "Sweetheart, I don't understand you. You can talk to me, you know, about anything. Really, what's the matter? I will help if I can, you know that."

Then her fingers fastened about his hand,

and he forgot that he didn't understand anything.

Her lips curved into a smile, a gentle, tentative smile, yet one so provocative he jerked. She slipped her hand out of his and took a step back. Her white hands moved to the white ribbons about her throat. Slowly she began to pull them loose, one by one. There were six of them.

The gown parted in the wake of her fingers and revealed to him the full curve of her breasts. Her hands dropped to her sides, and she stood motionless for what seemed an eternity to Julien. She lowered her eyes from his face and in one long fluid moment shrugged the gown from her shoulders. The soft satin floated down about her waist and rested momentarily on her hips before falling light as a feather about her feet. Almost defiantly she tossed back her head, her long hair swirling about her face, and gazed at him. "You haven't answered my request, Julien. May I stay with you tonight?"

Somewhere in the back of his mind Julien dimly realized that he was being seduced, not an altogether new experience, but one that could not but be ironic, given that the lady who was doing the seducing was his wife.

What the hell did it matter? "Come, sweetheart," he said simply. He tossed the now-meaningless novel into the dark corner of the room and moved toward the center of his bed. "I trust, my love, that the pleasure will be both of ours. I surely intend to do my damndest to please you." He held back the covers, and without pause she slipped in beside him.

He balanced himself on an elbow above her, not yet touching her. He needed to savor the fragile moment, one that he had awaited for so long. His wife coming to him. It was almost too much to take in. Dear God, her body, her beautiful body, all of her here now, for him.

"You're exquisite, do you know that?" His hand smoothed waving tendrils of hair away from her face.

"I want to give you pleasure, my lord."

A discordant note sounded sharp in his mind, but dissolved as she lifted her arms and wrapped them about his neck, pulling his face down to hers. He kissed her, trying to keep it light, not demanding at all, but he couldn't help himself, for he wanted her, had wanted her for longer than he could remember, for longer than he'd even known her, perhaps. For an instant, his lust overcame good sense, overcame the excitement, the hope he'd felt to look up to see her standing there, wanting him, peeling that nightgown off herself, standing there naked for him to look at her.

He tasted the sweetness of her mouth and grew more demanding, probing possessively for her tongue. He felt her stiffen and slowed yet again. Damn, but it was difficult. He forced himself to release her. He came up on his elbow above her and simply looked down at her. He saw a flicker of fear in her eyes before she quickly lowered her lashes.

"Sweetheart, if you would rather not—"

He sensed a hesitancy in her. He gently touched his fingers to her cheek, and she raised her eyes to him again. With a fierceness that made him forget his own name, she arched her back upward, letting the covers fall from her breasts, and pressed herself against his chest. She held to him tightly, her hands sweeping down his back. "Oh, yes, Julien, please, please. This is what I want. You're what I want. No other man, just you, only you."

Her voice was breathless, somehow unnatural, but now he was aware only of her and his nearly savage need for her. Impatiently he threw back the covers and gathered her to him. He swept his hands down through her hair to her hips and pressed her hard against him. She buried her face against his shoulder, and he felt an exquisite rippling of pleasure as she dug her fingers into his back.

"Dear God," he whispered against her ear, "you don't know. You can't know. I've wanted you and wanted you for a very long time." He buried his face in her hair, savoring the rich softness.

He felt her fingers, feather light, touch his hair. "Don't you want me, Julien? You said you did, but you're not doing anything. Can't we just get it done? Truly, I want to very much."

He smiled, cupping her chin in his hand so that he could gaze into her full face. "I think the answer to your question should be fairly obvious." He grinned at her and moved gently on top of her.

She paled at the feel of him, pushing against her belly, moving down now so that his sex was hard against her woman's flesh. Her hips lifted. But he didn't move, just continued to hold her chin firmly. He kissed her lightly. "Don't be so impatient, sweetheart. I would give you pleasure first. That's the way of things, you know. I want to see your pleasure very badly."

"Oh, no, please, Julien, don't do that to me, please don't. I would that you take—" Her voice trailed off, and he sensed again that something was very wrong.

"Hush, sweetheart." His mouth closed over hers. He remembered her pleasure, oh, yes, remembered it all too well, the heat of her, the clenching of her muscles, her urgency. He drew up, and now his hands were on her breasts, kneading them very gently, for she was carrying his babe and surely her breasts were tender; perhaps they were even fuller but he couldn't remember. He looked down to see other signs of her pregnancy. Her waist was still slender, but there was, he saw, a slight fullness to her belly. She lay perfectly quiet in the crook of his arm as his hand moved at will over her body. She stiffened against him only when he closed his lips over a soft pink nipple. He felt exquisite delight as the nipple grew taut at the touch of his prob-ing tongue. He willed himself to go slowly with her. He had to do this right, he had to.

The quickness of her response surprised him, a long quiver that rippled the length of her body.

"Oh, no, Julien, no, please don't."

He looked into her eyes now, studying her. "Would you truly rather that I stopped?" She bit her lip and looked away. "Would you?"

"No." That single word, so great in its significance, nearly made him a wild man.

The silence of the room was broken at first by a low moan of pleasure that she couldn't keep buried. As she arched against him, her hands moving frantically over his shoulders and through his hair, she cried out once more and he thought he'd die with the pleasure of it. His fingers changed their rhythm, now stroking her soft flesh more quickly, more deeply. It was enough and too much, for she reached her climax in that instant, twisting beneath his hand, and he held her still, his hand on her belly. He gave her that instant, intensifying her pleasure to the fullest, before moving quickly astride her. His fingers parted her and he felt himself engulfed in the warmth of her body. He didn't hurt her, for she was ready for him and it seemed she wanted more of him, and thus he pushed deep, closing his eyes against the pleasure, feeling her arms tighten around his back.

She repeated his name over and over, arching her hips to draw him deeper into her. He found he couldn't control himself. It had been too long. He covered her lips with his and felt long-awaited release, moaning his own pleasure into her mouth.

"Am I crushing you, sweetheart?" He drew himself above her on his elbows. He was still deep inside her. He felt almost absurdly happy, a sense of warmth and caring for her that rivaled his release. He was held in the curiousness of the feeling, for he'd never before experienced with any other woman such deep satisfaction following sex. Perhaps that was it. This hadn't just been sex. This had been lovemaking.

Her lips parted, but before she could respond to him, he closed his mouth over hers.

"It would appear, my love, that I am quite unable to allow you conversation. Your lips are much too inviting." He kissed the tip of her nose and smiled into her eyes. He touched a finger to the corner of her mouth. "You may smile, however, for I wish to see my favorite part of your person—your dimples. God, how I've missed those dimples."

Slowly she curved her lips into a deep smile, and the dimples appeared as if by magic. He kissed each one solemnly.

She shifted her weight slightly beneath his body.

He'd believed his need for her sated, but at her movement, he felt himself grow hard within her once more. "I have a solution that both of us, I hope, will approve." He slipped his hands beneath her back and in a swift

444

motion pulled her over on top of him. Cas-
cades of auburn hair buried his face. He
smoothed her hair back and was tenderly
amused to see a flush of embarrassment on
her face.

He grinned. "Here I am giving you the
upper hand, so to speak. It doesn't please
you?"

She tried to slip away from him, but he
gripped her shoulders. "By all the laws of
God, if I were to let you go now, I would have
myself hanged from the nearest elm branch.
Don't you know how you feel to me? Sit up,
sweetheart, I would look at you."

She seemed to struggle with herself for a
moment before she slowly pulled her legs up
to straddle him, as he settled her atop him,
penetrating very slowly until he was high and
deep inside her.

"Do I hurt you?" He lifted up her hips
slightly with his hands as she tried to shift her
position. "Tell me, did I hurt you? I'm very
deep."

Masses of hair swirled about her face as she
slowly shook her head.

Suddenly she paled, her eyes darkened.
"Oh, Julien, I must tell you—" Her voice
broke off, strangled, and she stared at him
numbly, naked misery in her eyes.

He couldn't allow her to speak, not yet. He
could picture the horror in her eyes at what
she would think his betrayal of her, his animal
lust. No, not yet.

He pushed her hard down against him, and

she moaned, whether in pain or pleasure, he wasn't certain. He wound his hands in her thick masses of hair and pulled her face to his and captured her mouth. There were no more words between them. He possessed her body, as completely as if she were a part of him. With infinite patience he brought her again to pleasure, willing her, for the moment at least, to forget.

36

When Julien awoke the next morning, he reached out for Kate. She wasn't there. He was alone. For a brief instant he wondered if he had dreamed her coming to him, dreamed her standing there, looking at him, shrugging out of her nightgown, letting him love her and caress her—yes, a dream, a fantasy woven from his deep need for her.

Then he smiled a deep, satisfied smile, stretched to his full length, and brought his arms up behind his head. No dream. It had happened, all of it, and he'd given her pleasure, twice he'd given her exquisite pleasure. And now he wasn't overly concerned that she'd left him before he'd awakened. It was quite likely that she felt deeply embarrassed after having initiated their lovemaking. Just thinking of her now, naked in his bed, with him over her, made him hard, made his heart speed up. He quickly rose and rang for Timmens.

He took a long drink of hot black coffee and stared out of the morning-room windows onto the gray winter day. If only it wouldn't rain, today of all days. There was much to be done. There was a light tap on the door, and Mrs Cradshaw eased through the doorway.

"A good morning to you, my lord," she said, all bright cheeriness. He watched her gently lay several covered dishes on the sideboard.

"Such quantities of food would certainly make Sir Percy's eyes light up, Emma," he remarked, as he buttered a slice of hot toast.

She chuckled. "I daresay it would, my lord. Do you know that Cook has never enjoyed herself more? Despite the presence of the Frenchman, of course." She hovered near the table, as if she were unwilling to leave the room. Julien granted her the privilege of an old retainer and did not dismiss her, sensing that she wished to speak to him of other matters.

"The countess will be down presently," he said. Although she hadn't stayed with him, she wasn't a coward, and he didn't believe it in her character to purposely avoid his company. Well, perhaps he wasn't completely certain about that.

"Oh, that's natural, my lord, that she be a trifle late in the mornings."

Julien momentarily forgot the slice of crisp bacon on his fork and looked intently at Mrs Cradshaw. She looked back at him comfortably and smiled, saying, "But another two or three weeks and her ladyship will be enjoying an early breakfast again with you." Her look was placid, then she beamed at him like a damned mother who knew something he didn't know.

He forced a smile. She'd been fussing over him since yesterday, he thought, and that sentimental look—*Dear God, she knew last evening*.

He didn't know how he got the words out, but he did. "I suppose you have been giving her ladyship all sorts of good advice and time-honored remedies."

"Oh, yes, indeed, my lord. I'm so happy she's told you. Made me promise, her ladyship did, not to say a word to you, wanted to tell you herself. Such wonderful news it is, my lord. Fancy, opening up the nursery again."

He cursed himself silently for a blind idiot. That was why she'd come to him last night. Her motive wasn't to finally enjoy her husband because she wanted him, oh, no. He could imagine the hours she'd spent arriving at such a desperate and daring solution. But he realized he couldn't allow her to discover just yet that he too knew. He cleared his brow and his throat. "Emma, the countess doesn't need your assistance. Indeed, I expect her momentarily. I would much prefer that you meet with Nurse and inspect the nursery."

He spoke firmly, and she at once responded to the authority in his voice.

She brightened. "What a wonderful idea. Old Nanny is getting on in years now—so long it's been since you needed her—but her brain's sharp as a floor tack. Ah, she'll be so excited, my lord, so pleased." And she was gone even before he could nod dismissal.

He rose slowly and walked to the windows. Poor Kate. How could she have been so naive as to believe she could deceive him into believing the child was his? Did she not even realize that a man could tell whether or not a woman was a virgin? Evidently not, but why and how should she know?

He turned abruptly as the door to the morning room opened and his wife walked in as slowly as a person being forced to the gallows. With a palpable effort he said calmly, "Good morning, my dear. Do come and have your breakfast. Cook must have threatened the chickens, for there are mountains of eggs. As for the pigs, I dread to contemplate their fate. The bacon is crisp, as you like it."

He realized he was rambling on, but he wished to give her no clues as to his own thoughts, and to lessen her nervous embarrassment at seeing him.

Her eyes didn't quite meet his, and she mumbled an unintelligible greeting as she slipped into a chair.

He continued, all cheerful as a choirboy, "When you have finished, I would that we ride this morning. I don't think it will rain, and the fresh air will be invigorating."

He saw agreement register on her face before she spoke. Riding, she wouldn't be obliged to speak much with him. He wasn't a threat to her riding. "Yes, I'd like that, Julien."

"I'll leave you to your breakfast, then, my dear, and see to having the horses saddled. Would an hour be sufficient for you to finish your breakfast and change?"

"Oh yes, thank you, my lord." She couldn't prevent the look of relief that swept her features as he left the room.

Dressed warmly, a thick, lined velvet cloak buttoned to her throat, Kate ventured past Mannering out onto the front steps, where Julien held Astarte and his own powerful stallion.

"Stay, Thunderer." He released the stallion's reins to toss her into the saddle.

"They're restless and ready for a gallop," he said over his shoulder as he mounted. "Take care that Astarte doesn't get away from you." Although he didn't think riding at a sedate pace could harm her in her condition, he had felt a moment's hesitation about their outing on horseback.

"I suggest, my lord, that you see to your own horse," she said, eyeing the sidling and prancing Thunderer. "Astarte is far too much a lady to give me a moment's worry."

"Just so," he said mildly, and reined in his horse beside her to canter side by side down the graveled drive.

He was relieved that she wasn't paying any particular attention to the direction they took. It wasn't until their horses broke through the woods into the small meadow bordering the copse that she suddenly reined in Astarte. "Julien, whatever are we doing here? I don't want to be here. Let's go to the lake, all right?"

He pulled up beside her, and before she knew what he was about, he grabbed Astarte's reins from her gloved hands. He looked at her steadily. "It's time to bury old ghosts, Kate, past time."

"Whatever does that mean? Old ghosts? I don't know what you're talking about. Please, let's leave here now."

"Look around you. The copse, Kate. We must go there. That's where the old ghosts are, and this morning we will bury them. Trust me, please." He whipped the reins over Astarte's head and urged Thunderer forward.

"No, damn you, no!" She tugged furiously at the reins, trying to pull them from his closed fist. He quickened their pace, and she had to grab the pommel to retain her balance.

"Stop now!" He heard the rising hysteria in her voice, but held firm. Jesus, he prayed he was right in what he was doing. He drew in at the edge of the copse, jumped from Thunderer's back, and walked quickly to her side. She tried to pull away from him, but he grabbed her arms and pulled her down to the ground, holding her for a moment hard against his chest. He shook her lightly. Her face was growing more pale by the moment. She was beginning to look afraid. "Listen to me, please. You can no longer live in dread of this place. Haven't you guessed that your nightmare had its beginning here? Look about you. There is nothing for you to fear here, not now, not any longer. And you're not alone. I'm with you. There's nothing here. Do you remember the small girl who played in this copse? It was her fairy kingdom, her private world, a place of security, until that day when the men came upon her. Look, Kate, damn you, open your eyes. Look! Do you remember?" He gently pushed her away from him, into the depths of the copse. Her hands twisted at the folds of her cloak and she stared ahead of her, unseeing.

"Was it summer that day?" He asked quietly, moving to stand beside her.

She didn't answer him, and he saw that she was looking fixedly at an old tree trunk that was very nearly covered with thick ivy. She raised a gloved finger. "That was my throne," she said softly. "How overgrown it has become." She walked quickly toward the tree stump and gazed down at it, frowning.

He stood motionless and watched her in silence. She fluttered her hands about her, and she seemed to move more lightly, her step shortened.

"The mushrooms still flourish, that's good, and they're so very lush. The palace guards picked them for the queen. They should be flogged, the floor of the throne room is such a mess. All those brambles and that wretched encroaching ivy. And the queen's musicians, playing soft music through the green swaying leaves."

She sank down to her knees, her cloak billowing about her, and slowly began pulling away the tangled masses of ivy. She began to hum in a faraway voice, a child's lilting song, as she brushed away the dead leaves from the top of the tree stump.

"The men came, Kate?"

She became suddenly quiet and crouched over, turning on her heels to gaze through him. "Oh, no! Be quiet, all of you. Do you not hear the sounds, the strange noises? Heavy, wooden boots, strangers coming here. Quickly, stop your playing, your music will attract their notice."

She put a finger to her mouth and looked furtively about her. "Oh, no, they're here. Hide, all of you, quickly. Yes, that's right. Oh, I'm still to be seen." A hard, proud look froze her eyes into bright slits, and her mouth was a straight, tight line. "I'm the queen, I will be safe. Look, here they come." A spasm of uncertainty, then open fear, crumpled her features. She swayed back and forth on her heels, gazing mutely ahead of her.

"Kate, do you remember what happened? The men burst in upon you. They approached you, didn't they?" He moved silently to her and went down on his knees beside her swaying form. She shook her head slowly back and forth, as if willing herself not to remember. She closed her eyes tightly and averted her head, willing herself not to see.

"What did the men do? Did they hurt you? Did they laugh and mock and admire themselves for finding you?"

Her eyes flew open, and she thrust her hands out in front of her to ward off something he couldn't see. "No, no!" Her voice was a child's, shrill and loud. She was shaking her head violently from side to side. She tried to scramble away from him, but Julien clasped her shoulders and held her firmly. "What do you want here? This is Brandon land. You must go, do you hear me?" The fear in her voice, the pathetic defiance, made gooseflesh rise on his arms. Through her eyes, he could picture the men, rough, perhaps drunk, coming upon the beautiful child, their dirty hands clutching at her long hair, ripping at her clothing, savagely exposing her.

She stiffened suddenly, pain suffusing her pale face, and cried out, a shrill, terrified cry that rent the silent woodland. She crumpled forward, and he caught her against his chest. Julien was beyond words, helpless and impotent in a fury that grated on his very soul. No retribution, no reckoning; and now it was too late, years too late.

With shaking hands he pressed her against him, trying somehow to make her feel his understanding, his compassion. Over and over he whispered her name.

He was long aware of the damp, chill air creeping through his greatcoat before she stirred in his arms, pushed against his chest and raised her white, tearstained face.

"It's over now, love. There's nothing more for you to fear. Do you understand?"

The naked pain in her eyes made his belly cramp. "Listen to me. You've got to face it now. It's been over now, over for years upon years. The child's pain can no longer be your pain. You must banish it from you. The ghosts are dead, Kate. All of them. Put them in the past where they belong. Let them go."

"Ghosts ... bury the ghosts. That's what you said when you forced me here, isn't it?"

"Yes. They're no longer part of you, no longer a part of us. Let them go." He gently brushed the tears away with his gloved fingers.

She gave her head a tiny shake, her eyes narrowed in confusion. "But I don't understand, Julien. How did you know, for I did not. How?"

"The nightmare. You remembered and spoke in your sleep. To be certain, I spoke with your father."

To his surprise, she flung away from him and rose shakily to her feet. "Why didn't you tell me? Why did you force me through all this? Damn you. Why, Julien?"

"I wanted to, but I thought that if I told you, simply recounted what I knew, I couldn't be sure you would remember, or understand. There was so much that—"

"Well, now you have your confession, my lord. Did Sir Oliver give you every sordid detail? Did he tell you all about his slut of a daughter? Did he tell you how he would beat me for really no reason at all, just to purify me, how he'd yell as he wielded that damned whip of his, just to save me. Well, did he gloat and laugh and tell you everything?"

He rose to his feet. "Oh, no, sweetheart, you don't understand. All this drama, if you wish to call it that, I did it for you, to help you, to help you remember, so you could banish the past, so you could be free of it."

She sneered at him, her hands balled into fists on her hips. "For *me*? Dear God, how you lie to yourself, just as you've always lied. There weren't any nightmares until you forced me to wed you. There weren't any ghosts until you resurrected them. Did I play my part well, my lord?"

"Damnation, you're being ridiculous. You know I love you. You will listen to me."

"No, I won't. I have your full measure now, my lord. Do you intend a second visit to my father to tell him he was correct about his harlot of a daughter? Don't think he'll take me back. Or do you still believe my innocence? Do but recall how very passionate and abandoned I was in your bed last night. Come, Julien, was your precious Sarah ever more eager for your mouth caressing her body than I was?"

"That's quite enough. By God, you will stop this damned nonsense." He moved quickly forward to grab her, to shake some sense into her, but she evaded his outstretched arms and rushed to Astarte. She tugged the reins from the withered branch and threw herself onto her horse's back.

"Stop! Damnation, don't be a fool!" He yelled even as he was running toward her. He lunged forward to grab the bridle, but Kate jerked up on the reins and Astarte snorted in surprise and plunged backward. Kate wheeled the startled horse about and dug in her heels.

Cold, desperate fear gripped him. The child, dear God, she had to remember the child.

Astarte was galloping erratically, crashing through the undergrowth of the woods, naked winter branches ripping at both horse and rider. Kate's riding hat was torn from her head, drifting gently earthward, buoyed by the vivid blue ostrich feather, until it lay stark and helpless on the mossy floor of the woods, ground but an instant later into bright shreds by Thunderer's pounding hooves.

The woods ended, and both horses cannoned onto a narrow lane, beset with deep, treacherous ruts, gaping wide, an arm's length, many of them. Astarte veered off the road, as if sensing herself the dangers of those yawning holes, into a barren field.

Agonizing minutes passed as Thunderer strained to close the distance.

A long, low stone wall, for many years a meaningless boundary between properties, cut across the field to either side, its cold gray edges stark against the clouded sky. Surely now Kate would stop, she must stop.

"Kate, no! Astarte doesn't jump without command!" His yell filled the empty space. He made a last desperate attempt to reach her, but she evaded his outstretched arm.

37

"Astarte, over!"

The futile command hung about him, muting his hearing, a command shouted too late, perhaps a command Astarte wouldn't have obeyed in any case, for Astarte had been her horse since the moment she'd patted her nose and crooned words to her that he hadn't begun to understand. He watched in helpless despair as Astarte reached the stone wall, gave a frightened snort, and veered sharply, grazing the jagged stone edges.

Kate cried out as she lost her hold and was thrown, strangely huddled and small, across the wall to the ground beyond.

Julien whipped Thunderer forward, and the horse sailed gracefully over the stone wall. Julien leaped off his back and ran to where she lay motionless, on her back, the velvet cloak fanned out about her, a soft blanket of deep blue against the hard, rocky earth.

He fell to his knees beside her and quickly felt for the pulse that was beating steadily in the hollow of her throat. Thank God. He felt her arms and legs, then gently eased her into his arms.

Her lashes fluttered and she opened her eyes, filled with dumb fear. "Julien, the child."

He acted without conscious thought and quickly slipped his hand up underneath her riding habit to the soft shift that covered her belly. He had no practical notion of what he should do, but instinctively he gently pressed his hand against her belly. She was soft and smooth to the touch. "Do you feel any pain? Is there any cramping?" He continued to probe gently with his fingers.

"No, no pain." She sucked in her breath and gazed at him in consternation. In a voice devoid of emotion she said, "You knew of the child."

"Yes." He knew now that he couldn't keep the truth from her any longer. For better or worse, it was over now. "You remember when you were ill, the morning we left for St Clair. The landlady at the inn where you rested told me."

"Ah, Mrs Micklesfield. Then you also know that the child isn't yours." Her words were low and dull. The hopelessness in her voice wrenched at his heart.

"No, sweetheart. The child is mine."

"Damn you, no more mocking, do you hear me? Is there nothing you don't know?"

He gently shook her shoulders. "You must listen to me now. I know this will seem incredible to you, but it's true, I swear it. I was

459

the wild German lord who drugged you, who abducted you. It was I who forced you. I had foolishly thought to teach you pleasure, to make you admit to yourself that you cared for me, indeed, that you wanted me as your husband in every way."

"Oh, no." Even as she spoke, memory stirred deep within her. Memory of that man's hands on her body, his mouth against hers, against her breasts and belly, possessing her, and Julien's touch the night before, creating in her the same frenzy, the same urgency. That first time, it was as if her body had recognized him, but she hadn't, she'd been too afraid, too numb with memories that blanked her mind. "I was so frightened last night. I thought I was the most horrid of women to react so wildly. Oh, God." She pressed her fist against her mouth.

"No, love, don't think that of yourself, for I knew, as I knew why you came to me last night. I've hated myself for the deception, for forcing you to live with this misery. Please, perhaps you can forgive me for what I did to you. I didn't know what had happened to you, didn't realize—"

She seemed not to hear his words, and she searched his face with dazed anguished eyes. "But why did you hurt me?"

He drew a deep breath, and for an instant, he couldn't meet her gaze. The truth, he thought, it must be only the truth now. "When I entered you, I realized that you weren't a virgin. A virgin has a maidenhead,

460

you see, and you didn't.

"I thought your fear of me was a sham, that you had given yourself to someone else before me. I cursed you in that moment and sought only to give you pain. I wanted to hurt you as I thought you had hurt me.

"It was only later, that night, when I realized the truth. The nightmare, Kate. My rape of you made you remember, but only in that tortured dream. You spoke in fragmented images of the men, of the cruelty of your father. You became the little girl again and I saw it all through your eyes, saw it all through your pain. You remembered nothing of it the next morning." He saw in her eyes the gulf of misunderstanding that separated them, and he hurried to answer her unspoken question. "I wanted to tell you, but I knew I couldn't. Suddenly, you trusted me. I feared the consequences of speaking the truth. That's why I brought you back to London. I thought, foolishly perhaps, that you would forget."

"You couldn't tell me," she repeated dully, the woman struggling with the child's pain. She fumbled to grasp the child's horror, to bring her through the intolerable years, to somehow make her part of herself. As she opened her lips to speak, a long, sharp pain tore through her belly, and her words, jumbled and fragmented, tore from her throat in a jagged cry. She was held in senseless surprise as the pain dissolved, freeing her mind for a brief instant, then seared again through her, its force doubling her forward.

"The child, dear God, the child. I've got to get you back."

She looked at him blankly, her eyes dulled with shock and pain. He pulled her cloak closely about her and lifted her into his arms. The stabbing pain engulfed her once again, and she clutched at his arms, her cry muffled in his greatcoat.

She became aware of her hair whipping about her face, the loud din of horse's hooves pounding in her ears. The pain was becoming a steady rending part of her, and only dimly did she realize that she was crying aloud. If only she could ease the pain. She tried to bring her knees up to her chest, but couldn't move against the strong arms that held her.

Julien tightened his fierce hold on her, her cries of pain making his face set and grim. "It isn't much farther. You'll be all right, I swear it by everything I hold sacred. You'll be all right."

The words had no meaning to her. All understanding plummeted into a void of pain, dissolving shreds of reason. Incredible forces were tearing her apart. She screamed her pain, thrashing wildly against the arms that held her. Voices, loud voices, coming as if from far away, shouted, babbled, incoherent sounds. Suddenly a great lassitude numbed the agonizing pain, scattering it apart from her, making her once again at one with her body. She wondered, almost inconsequentially, if she was dying. How strange that death would be like this, a creeping, paralyzing darkness that closed so gently over her mind. She whimpered softly to herself, a sense of undefined regret, a brief, shadowy flicker blending into the darkness.

Her head lolled from his shoulder as Julien carefully dismounted from Thunderer. He cradled her in one arm, freeing the other to feel for her pulse. He blinked in dazed shock at his hand; it was covered with blood, her blood.

A sharp command burst from his mouth. His groom was running ahead of him, throwing open the front doors, quickly stepping out of the way, his mouth agape.

The set-down that automatically rose to Mannering's lips at the undignified impertinence of the groom was swallowed in consternation.

"Mannering, fetch Mrs Cradshaw immediately," Julien shouted over his shoulder as he bounded up the stairs. "The groom is off for the doctor. Send him up the moment he arrives."

"Yes, my lord, right away, my lord." For a moment Mannering stood staring after the earl, unable to remember where to find Mrs Cradshaw. In frustration, and for the first time in his well-ordered life, Mannering threw back his head and bellowed, "Emma! Emma!"

Julien passed the maid, Milly, on the upper landing. "The countess has suffered a miscarriage. Bring hot water and clean linen.

Quickly!"

He carried her to his bedchamber and laid her gently in the middle of the large Tudor bed. She was so deathly pale, too pale, so much blood, too much blood. He pulled off her cloak and cursed his shaking fingers as the small buttons refused to open. He ripped off her habit, his fear lending speed to his movements. There was so much blood, clots of dark purple, covering her legs, weighing down her shift and skirt. He threw the soaked clothing to the floor and stripped off her stockings and riding boots.

He heard a sharp intake of breath behind him. "Emma, bring me towels. She's still bleeding heavily." He didn't turn away from Kate, and only the rustle of Mrs Cradshaw's black skirt told him of her movement.

He could recall nothing, not a shred of information about miscarriage, a subject never spoken of in a gentleman's presence. The bleeding was now a purple pool, stark against the pale green of the bedspread. He had to stop the bleeding, he knew that, else she'd die. He ran to his armoire and grabbed several fine lawn shirts. With all his strength he pressed the shirts against her to stem the flow of blood.

"My lord, the towels."

"No, Emma, I don't think it wise to lessen the pressure. Bring blankets, we must keep her warm."

His arms were buried by the covers, and though they began to ache, he pressed his hands all the harder against her.

Mrs Cradshaw stood away from the bed, her gaze drawn to the bloody, torn clothing on the floor. "She lost the child. Ah, the poor lamb, she lost the child."

"Yes," he said, not looking up.

"I'll remove all the clothing," she said, leaned over, wrapped the soaked material in the towels, and rose, somewhat shakily. "Would you prefer that I remained, my lord?"

"No, Emma, it's not necessary. Take the clothing and burn it." The sharp command was cold, impersonal, but there was misery in his gray eyes, and she hated it, hated the finality of it.

She moved slowly to the door. "Dr Quaille should be here shortly."

He eased one hand from between her thighs and rested it briefly on her abdomen. It was an absurd gesture, for he had no idea of what he was probing for. He moved his hand to her breast and flattened his palm to feel her heartbeat. Though rapid, the beat seemed regular and steady.

He'd begun to despair of his actions, when the door was suddenly thrown open and the portly, red-faced Dr Quaille bustled forward, his stark black cloth suit proclaiming his profession.

He was panting from his exertion at running up the stairs.

"She's lost the child," Julien said. "I wasn't certain what to do for the bleeding. It wouldn't stop." He slowly pulled back the blankets. "As you see, I've pressed the cloth against her, hoping to stop the bleeding. There's been so much blood. Jesus, so much blood and she had such pain."

"Excellent, my lord, excellent." His voice was calm, reassuring, gentle even as he drew some frightening instruments from his worn leather bag.

"You've done just right. Now if you'll allow me to examine her, I'll fix it up, I swear it to you."

Still, the young earl didn't move. Dr Quaille said even more gently now, "You've done just as you should, my lord. I myself couldn't have contrived better, under the circumstances."

Julien slowly removed his hand. His shirts were soaked through with blood. He winced and said in a voice of despair, "It seems I've failed, for she still bleeds too much, doesn't she?"

"No more than I expected. Would you care to wait outside, my lord?" He saw the young man's pain, his fear, boundless fear and help-lessness, but he didn't want him to stay and witness what he was about to do.

"No," the earl said only.

Dr Quaille had no choice but to proceed. He removed the shirts from between the countess's legs. There was little new blood now. "As you see, my lord, your stratagem worked. The bleeding has nearly stopped."

Julien watched tight-lipped as the doctor plied some of the more unpleasant-looking

466

instruments of his trade. Thank God Kate wasn't yet conscious.

There was a sharp, insistent rap on the door, and Julien moved swiftly to answer. Mrs Cradshaw, Milly, and two footmen laden with tubs of hot water and mountains of clean linen stood in the corridor, their faces white and stricken. The mirror image, Julien thought, of his own.

"Ah, excellent." Dr Quaille looked up as Julien set the tubs on the floor beside the bed. To Julien's relief, he tossed the instruments aside and rose. "You need worry no more, my lord, for the countess will soon be on the mend again. In large measure due to your quick thinking."

"But the bleeding." Julien frowned down at the scarlet cloths.

"It's natural for the bleeding to continue, in fact, for several more days. And, I would add, my lord, that my examination indicates no internal problems. What I mean is," he amended, seeing the questioning look on the earl's face, "the countess is young and quite healthy. You will have as many sons and daughters as you will want. Of that I'm certain."

"My thanks, sir," Julien said simply.

"Now, my lord, I suggest that Mrs Cradshaw put the countess in her nightclothes. Then we shall awaken her."

38

After Mrs Cradshaw left the room with Dr Quaille in tow, Cook having prepared a light luncheon for him, Julien dragged one of the tubs of hot water into his dressing room, stripped off his bloodied clothing, bathed, and quickly dressed. He walked back into his bedchamber and looked up at the clock on the mantel, surprised that it was only early afternoon. There was no movement from the bed. She was still asleep, a healing sleep, he had assured Dr Quaille. Reluctantly the doctor had replaced the vinaigrette in his black bag.

Julien tugged his cravat into a more or less acceptable shape, drew up a chair, and sat himself beside his wife. For perhaps the fourth time, the morning's events made a tangled procession through his mind, violent emotions jostling against each other, so intensely destructive that he began to despair of a resolution that would bring about forgiveness.

She sighed suddenly, then buried her face in the pillow, as if loath to leave her dreamless sleep. Strangely, it was the total absence of pain that forced her to awareness. "How very odd. I'm not dead. At least I don't think I'm dead."

"That, Countess, I would never have allowed." He smiled, clasping her hand in his. "How do you feel, sweetheart? Is there any pain? Do you have any more cramping in your belly?"

Her mind planted itself firmly into her body. She heard his voice—soft and gentle, that voice—felt his warm hand holding hers. "No, there's no more pain." The question seemed foolish to her, but she'd answered, out of habit, she supposed.

What she felt was a great soreness, as if someone had battered at her, but of course, she couldn't speak of it. Her hand moved as if by purposeful design to her belly. It was smooth, empty. He watched her pale as she realized what had happened. He heard her voice break as she whispered, "The child?"

He squeezed her hand more tightly. "I'm so sorry, Kate. There wasn't anything I could do. Dr Quaille assures me that the accident hasn't harmed you in any way, that, if you wish, we can have as many children as you desire."

Odd, she thought, staring silently away from him, he speaks of children and yet I knew of the child for but one day. The poor wee thing, never really existing. She felt, somehow, strangely suspended in a vague present, where painful memories—ghosts, Julien had called them, and now the loss of the insignificant small being that was inside of her—didn't quite touch her. The future, the tomorrows that must irrevocably weave themselves into the present, were mercifully clouded. She looked at her husband and turned her eyes quickly away. The past was mirrored in his eyes—wrenching pain, deception, and misery. She didn't want to remember, to feel. She struggled to pull herself up on the pillow.

"Go easy, sweetheart, easy."

She gasped, fear suddenly filling her eyes. There was a warm stickiness spreading between her thighs.

"What's wrong?" He was leaning over her in an instant. "I think I'm bleeding."

"Lie still." Before she knew what he was about, he'd jerked back the covers. Small patches of purple stood out starkly against the white of her nightgown. He quickly slipped one hand under her hips and with the other stripped up her gown. His hands stilled. The pads of cloth had simply slipped away in her effort to pull herself up.

"Oh, no, please don't, Julien, please."

"Hush, don't be embarrassed. The bleeding is natural, and nothing for you to fear. Your sudden movement dislodged the cloths, that's all."

She tried to draw her legs together as he straightened above her.

"Hold still now. I'm going to bathe the blood from your legs."

"No, please don't. I can do it, Julien, please."

"After this morning's events, it's absurd that you should be embarrassed with me. Surely you wouldn't prefer a stranger."

She made a choking sound and lay tense and rigid as he gently bathed her. He seemed a stranger to her. All she knew were strangers; she felt alien even to herself.

"That wasn't so bad, was it?" he said, not expecting her to answer, and she didn't. As he tucked the covers about her shoulders, he let his fingers gently brush across her pale cheeks. "Would you like to see Dr Quaille now? He's been cooling his heels waiting for you to wake up, but Cook did feed him. After he's satisfied with your progress, then I'll fetch you some lunch. All right?"

He was another stranger, yet she had known him from her childhood. Why could she not be left alone? She wanted no more orders, no more gently veiled commands for her care. She raised bleak eyes. She wanted somehow to lash out at him, but she said only, "You take much for granted, Julien."

"You're wrong there. I take nothing for granted, at least not anymore. I wish only to see you well again. Then we will see what there is left."

Damn him, she didn't want his kindness. She watched wordlessly as he strode from the room.

"Ah, my dear Lady Katharine, there is color in your cheeks already. As I assured your husband here, you'll be much your old self in

471

a few days' time. One of the many advantages of youth and your glowing health." He clasped her hand and wasn't surprised to find her pulse rate still rapid.

"You are the most fortunate of women in your choice of husbands, let me tell you." Seeing her look of bewilderment, he added with a smile, "But for his lordship's quick thinking and intelligent actions, you might have suffered severe complications."

"Dr Quaille is overgenerous in his praise."

"His lordship's natural modesty, my lady. But in any case, I don't wish to overtire you." He patted her hand in a fatherly way and straightened. "I've given his lordship instructions for your care. No running up and down the stairs, now. I'll come to the hall tomorrow to see you. Daresay you'll be much more the thing then. Ah, and, my dear, there will be other children. Don't blame either yourself or your husband for this. It was an accident, nothing more, nothing less. These things happen. I'm sorry, but there it is."

Dr Quaille executed two swift bows, and Kate heard him exclaim to Julien as he passed through the bedroom door, "A most delicious luncheon, my lord. The ham slices—so wafer thin—a delight, my lord, a delight. Now, you're not to blame yourself either. It's just as I told her ladyship. These things happen quite frequently."

"Is it true, Julien, what the doctor said?" She asked when he returned some minutes later.

She wouldn't look at him. He said merely, "I acted as I thought best, that's all."

How calm he is, how very self-assured, she thought. "As you've always acted for the best in my regard," she said, her voice a blend of sarcasm and bitterness. "Perhaps in this instance, it would have been better had you not succeeded so well." There, it was said. Oblivion, she thought. Yes, I would have preferred oblivion to the pain of my gratitude to you, to the pain of your knowledge of what happened to me.

She'd finally pushed him over the edge. He leaned over her, his face close to hers. "Listen to me and listen with both ears, and your damned brain. Don't you ever say such a thing again, else I'll beat you. Whatever follies I've committed in the past, whatever pain I've brought to you—" He broke off a moment at her distraught face. "Perhaps you won't believe me, but yes, I've always acted toward you as I thought best, for both of us, for our life together."

She didn't move, simply stared up at him and said low and mean, "How glib you are, my lord. Deception? Why, it's nothing, an everyday thing, in fact. And forcing me, lying to me? Why, my dear, it was for the best, certainly you see that. But of course you're naught but a woman, and thus not privy to the mysteries of men's minds. All for the best, yes, that's it." She couldn't stop the sarcasm, the destructive words, they overflowed as from a cup full to brimming.

He straightened, his lips a thin line. "You're in no condition to speak of such things now. You're becoming overwrought. I don't want you to make yourself more ill than you already are. When you have regained your health and are capable of speaking more calmly—"

"Damn you, I'm not overwrought or hysterical or anything except bloody furious. Even though you don't want to face it, I just happen to be in full possession of my meager faculties. You've remained silent for so long now. Is it that you've forgotten the rational motives for your behavior? Must I give you more time to weave reason into your worthless arguments?" She fell back panting against the pillow, appalled at the rising note of hysteria in her voice. God, she was overwrought, damn him. "Oh, God, why didn't you just let me die?" Unwanted, scalding tears streamed down her cheeks.

"Here is her ladyship's lunch, my lord," Mrs Cradshaw announced as she came into the room. "Oh, dear, I didn't know—" She stood frozen in the doorway, the big silver tray balanced on her forearms.

It was with an effort that Julien tore his eyes away from his wife and walked to Mrs Cradshaw. "Give me the tray, Emma. Her ladyship will be all right presently." He added under his breath, "Fetch me the laudanum. It will calm her."

He returned to the bed and stood above her. "Are you hungry?"

"I'm not at all hungry. Give it to the dogs or the pigs. Give it to Dr Quaille. He was so pleased with the so very thin ham slices."

"Very well. You will take your medicine then and rest."

"I don't want your laudanum. I would rest quite well, were it not for your presence."

"You will have your wish as soon as you drink your medicine."

When Mrs Cradshaw reappeared with the laudanum, Julien dismissed her and carefully measured out the drops into a glass of water.

Kate took the glass from Julien's out-stretched hand and quickly downed the clear liquid. There would be forgetfulness in sleep, and that was something. For at least a short while, it was something.

"Now, as you wish, madam," he said flatly. "I shall relieve you of my presence." He turned and walked from the room, not looking back.

He returned some thirty minutes later, saw that she slept, and sat down beside her. He had lost her at last. The admission cost him dearly. There were no more plans, no new strategies to make her understand. At least with the secrets, the necessary deceptions, he'd been able to nourish hope.

"Deuced strange to think that my sister lives here," Harry said, all goodwill, stamping freshly fallen snow from his top boots. He whipped off his many-caped greatcoat, stood proudly a moment in his scarlet regimentals,

475

and clicked his heels together in grand military fashion.

"A fine figure you present, Master Harry," Mannering said fondly, removing the greatcoat from Harry's outstretched hand.

"I daresay I do look rather dashing," Harry said with a wide grin, looking to his brother-in-law for confirmation.

Julien had no problem rising to the occasion. "A regular rake in soldier's clothing. Have you left a score of broken hearts in your wake, Harry?"

"Not more than half a dozen." Harry stripped off his heavy leather gloves and gazed about him. "Always thought this place was like a tomb. But trust Kate to like it, always did, you know. She used to stand, mouth agape, mind you, staring at those ridiculous suits of armor. Claimed she would have been a fine figure of a knight, jousting and that sort of thing. Such a sweet little nit she was—and mouthy too—always wanting to do exactly what I did."

Harry pulled up short in his monologue. "Speaking of Kate, where the devil is she? Surely she ain't out fishing in the snow. Ah, I have it, I'd wager she's on one of your favorite stallions, careening all over the countryside."

Julien put a firm hand on Harry's sleeve. "No, Harry, Kate is here. Before you see her, though, I must speak with you privately."

"Eh, what's this? Is she brewing some new mischief? I warned you about that, my lord, before you married her. Never boring, my

476

sister. Ah, I know. She's got all sorts of grand treats planned for Christmas."

Christmas, Julien thought blankly. He hadn't given it a single thought. "Come, Harry, let's go into the library."

Harry shot his brother-in-law a puzzled look and said with an insouciance that Mannering readily forgave, "Do see that my hack gets stabled, will you, Mannering?"

"Certainly, Master Harry, certainly."

Harry followed in Julien's wake into the library and moved quickly to the blazing fire to warm his hands.

"Will you join me for a brandy, Harry?"

"Don't mind if I do. Hellish weather, but to be expected, I suppose, it being winter and all."

"No doubt," Julien said, handing Harry his glass. "When must you rejoin your regiment?"

"Not until after Christmas." Harry deposited himself with practiced grace onto a rather fragile settee, which groaned in protest under his weight. "Wanted to see what Kate is about, and then, there is my father, of course," he added with a marked lack of enthusiasm.

"If you prefer to stay with us, I'm sure Kate would welcome your company."

Harry sensed suddenly a tenseness in his brother-in-law's voice. Never one to tread warily, he demanded, "What of Kate? She's not ill, is she? Never been sick a day in her life, and the things she's done, they'd grizzle

477

your hair."

"No, Harry, not precisely," Julien said slowly. "She suffered a miscarriage three days ago. She is much better now, but is still confined to her room."

"Good Lord!" Harry jumped to his feet, forgetting for the moment the dignity he owed to his rank. "I had no idea that she was—well, she is your wife, after all and I suppose it's natural enough that—oh, my God, my poor Kate."

"She wasn't far along in her pregnancy, but as I'm certain you'll understand, it was quite a shock." He gazed at Harry speculatively from beneath half-closed lids. Unexpected though his visit was, it could not have been better timed. Perhaps Harry would succeed where he had failed.

"Damned shame." Harry brightened almost immediately. "I've just the thing to cheer her up. I brought her a present, you know. A trifle really, but I fancied she would like a real Spanish mantilla. All the ladies drape them over their heads in Portugal, you see."

"Doubtless she'll be delighted, Harry. Now, if you like, you can visit with your sister. Mannering will take you up. I won't intrude on your reunion."

Kate lay languidly on a sofa near the fireplace, a finely knit cover spread over her legs and a paisley shawl draped about her shoulders. An embroidery frame with only a few too large, uneven stitches covering its muslin surface lay precariously near the edge of the sofa. She heard a light tap on the door and quickly lowered her head, as if suddenly preoccupied with her stitching. It was Julien and she couldn't face him, she simply couldn't. She didn't move when she heard the door open.

"Well, I say, Kate, that's a fine way to greet your only brother, your *older* brother, who, I might add, you should honor and respect." Harry was the picture of cheer as he stepped into the room.

"Harry!" She struggled into a sitting position, her initial shock at seeing him giving way immediately to a tearful smile. "Oh, my dear, it's so good to see you again. How very fine you look, so handsome and dashing." She alternately clasped him tightly against her and pushed him back, as if to verify that it was indeed he.

"Ho, Kate," Harry protested after several of her fierce embraces, "don't want to wrinkle my coat, old girl." He patted her pale cheek, endeavoring to keep the worry from showing on his face. Lord, but she looked pale and drawn, and dreadfully thin. He'd never thought of a pregnant woman being thin, but she was. On the other hand, Julien had said she wasn't very far along. Still, it scared him witless.

To Kate, who knew her brother perhaps better than she knew herself, Harry's thoughts were mirrored in his wide blue eyes.

She forced a smile and said lightly, "Do sit down, my love. As you see, I'm still a trifle weak, but it will pass, Harry, and there is naught for you to worry about. Come, my dear, pull that chair closer, and tell me about your regiment and all your adventures."

Harry could find no fault at all with her suggestion, as it appeared she had no wish to speak of herself. He'd give her thoughts another direction, that's what he would do. "Deuced hot in Spain and Portugal," he said, stretching himself easily in the chair opposite her.

"Was there much fighting, Harry? I was very worried about you."

"Oh, no, just scattered packs of ruffian bandits. We routed the scurvy lot, let me tell you. No match at all for our men." He sat forward in his chair, warming to his story. "We had a couple of native guides, though of course we really didn't need them, just had them along to point us through the scrubby paths. Damned rocky terrain, you know, ground dry as a bone. But our men were hearty goers, rounded up the villains, no matter how cunning they were."

Kate sighed. "Oh, Harry, how I wish I could have been with you. I wouldn't have minded the heat, and goodness, all the excitement—"

"Now, that's not something for a countess to wish, old girl. Cursed rough work, you know." He paused and gazed around the elegantly furnished chamber. "Lord, I never thought to see you so regally placed."

"It does seem strange. I daresay, though, that Kate Brandon never wanted or sought such honors."

"Ridiculous, sister. Don't you remember we couldn't find a solution for you and Sir Oliver when I left for Oxford? Then the earl of March, dashed fine fellow, by the way, swoops down and rescues you, just like in those romantic novels."

She lowered her eyes and drew her lips tightly shut.

Harry eyed her with a frown. "I can see you've indeed fallen into a depression, and that isn't good for you. Now, my dear, trust me to cheer you up."

"Harry, you will stay here at St Clair, will you not?" she thought to ask, her voice pathetically eager.

"Think I very well might. The earl already asked me, you know. Sir Oliver won't quite like it, but I shall pay him a visit or two. Surely three visits to him would be overdoing it, don't you think?"

"You must call him Julien, Harry. He would not care for such formality from his brother-in-law." At the mention of her husband's name, she lowered her head and asked with forced lightness, "You've seen him, then?"

"He met me downstairs and told me of your accident. I'm sorry, my dear. Bound to have more children." He felt suddenly that he had stepped into uncharted land and was quite out of his ken. He could not unsay the words he'd already spoken, so he merely looked at

481

her hopefully.

"Of course, Harry," she said, her voice as dull and gray as the overcast day.

As he could think of nothing to say for the moment, Harry picked up a periodical from the table at his elbow and casually flicked though the pages.

Kate sought to divert his attention, chiding herself for making him feel awkward and uncomfortable. "It will be Christmas in but two weeks. If you don't think your military dignities will suffer, we could decorate the hall. There are holly and berries in abundance in the home wood."

Harry readily agreed to her suggestion, though secretly he thought it would be a dead bore. He suddenly remembered the mantilla carefully wrapped in tissue paper in his portmanteau. Kate loved presents. Surely it would be just the thing to cheer her up.

He rose and tried for a mysterious air. "Don't want you to move, Kate. I have a surprise for you."

He was rewarded, for Kate's eyes lit up, quite in the carefree manner of his hoydenish little sister.

"A present, Harry? Oh, how very kind of you. May I have it now?"

"Of course you may. Let me fetch it, and while I'm about it, I'll see if the earl—Julien—will now join us. Said he didn't want to interrupt our reunion, but we've had plenty of it by now, I'd say, and I'm sure he would enjoy seeing you. He's very worried about you, you know."

Kate said nothing to this suggestion, and Harry strode in his finest military fashion out of the room, feeling a bit more encouraged than he had only minutes before.

Dear Harry, she thought, so innocently does he step into the boiling kettle. She planted a smile on her lips, for Harry's sake.

39

By the time Christmas Day arrived, St Clair had undergone a magnificent change. Under Harry's very nominal direction, the servants had festooned countless bunches of bright-green holly, dotted with deep-red berries, all along the walls and beams in the hall, even going so far as to fasten clumps—most dis-respectfully, Mannering thought—atop the armored knights. Colorful paper strings of red and green garland were hung in deep scallops over the doors, and much to Kate's delight, Julien and Harry had hauled in a mammoth Yule log for the giant fireplace.

On Christmas morning, after Julien and Kate had ceremoniously dispensed gifts among the staff, they went to the library to join Harry. Julien presented Kate with an elegant pair of diamond drop earrings and a narrow gold bracelet dotted with small exquisitely cut diamonds that matched those of the earrings. She accepted them with a smile, conscious that Harry was watching at her elbow.

"Just the thing to go with your mantilla," Harry said, all innocent enthusiasm.

"You're right, of course. Thank you, Julien," she continued with pained correctness, "They are quite lovely. I'm sorry that I didn't have the opportunity to—"

"My birthday is in January, Kate. I shall expect two presents from you on that date. It's the sixteenth. Don't forget now. If you like, I'll even give you hints, perhaps write them down and put them under your pillow."

Harry gazed at them, baffled. He had felt acutely uncomfortable more than once during the past two weeks at being in their company. Several nights as he had made his way quietly to the kitchen, he had noticed a light shining from beneath the library door. He'd walked quietly to the door, cracked it open, and seen his brother-in-law sprawled in a large chair gazing fixedly into the dying fire. He had recalled Kate's aversion to marriage with the earl, quite inexplicable to him, and her flight alone to France. But, be damned, she'd married him and, for a while at least, carried his child. Certainly no aversion there. That wasn't possible, was it?

Late one night, as Harry gazed proudly at his scarlet uniform, pressed by Timmens's careful hands, he was drawn by the sound of loud voices coming from far down the hallway. Blessed with a lively curiosity, Harry quietly opened his door and looked down the darkened corridor. He realized with a start that the loud voices were coming from Kate's room. It came as something of a shock to him, for during the length of his stay Harry had never before heard Julien and Kate raise their voices to each other, much less argue, and in such an unrestrained way.

He retreated back to his room and closed the door, reflecting as he did so that perhaps marriage wasn't the divine state it was touted to be. It made him shudder.

Above all things, Harry disliked problems, particularly those he didn't understand. It occurred to him that staying with Sir Oliver might not be so bad after all. Certainly, at Brandon Hall, he knew exactly what to expect from his dour parent. But he didn't want to have to put up with Sir Oliver's endless and continuous sermons that touched on everything from the cleanliness of his linen to the number of girls he'd seduced. Odd that, such extremes in his father, who wanted everyone to see him as being a very holy, righteous man.

But Harry was totally unprepared the next morning, when he walked down the front stairs, to see his brother-in-law in the hall, his head bent in conversation with Mannering, his luggage stacked near the front doors.

"Ah, Harry, there you are," Julien said pleasantly, turning to face his flustered brother-in-law. "I've decided to return to London. There are pressing matters that require my attention. Kate has decided to remain here at St Clair a while longer before joining me."

He ignored the look of patent disbelief on Harry's face. "I'm driving my curricle. Would you care to join me?"

Harry would have liked very much to yell at the earl, to defend his sister with scathing demands as to the earl's reasons for such an abrupt departure. But under Julien's cool, inquiring gaze, he was made to feel that such an action would be grossly impertinent. He fidgeted with a gold button on his scarlet coat and said finally with stiff formality, "As you wish, my lord. I will accept your offer. Actually, I didn't really want to visit Sir Oliver anymore or stay with him."

He looked for the world like a ruffled bandy rooster, Julien thought as he turned his attention back to Mannering. He wondered if Harry would drop his reserve and question him on their journey. He really had no idea, at the moment, how he would respond to questions from a brother.

They ate their breakfast in strained silence. Julien carefully laid down his fork, drew out his watch, and consulted it. He transferred his gaze to Harry, at once amused and rather touched by his obvious agitation. "I applaud your sentiments, Harry, but you must understand that it is Kate's wish. I am certain that you have noted an atmosphere of tension between us."

"Yes."

"As a gentleman, you must know that I cannot divulge the reasons. To do so would be a great injustice to your sister."

"Is it because of her miscarriage?"

"Perhaps, in part." Julien turned the subject. "I've already said my good-byes to your sister. I will await you in the curricle. I believe Timmens has packed your bags and Mannering has seen them brought down."

Harry wasn't much relieved, but he felt that to persist would make him appear boorishly forward. He rose slowly and laid his napkin down beside his half-empty plate. He was taken aback by the hard glint in his brother-in-law's eyes.

He turned nervously and walked to the door. "Yes," he said over his shoulder, "I'll say good-bye to Kate." He wondered as he slowly mounted the stairs if he appeared mealy-mouthed to the earl. He knitted his brow a little over this, but by the time he lightly tapped on Kate's door, he'd managed to reassure himself. Julien was her husband, after all. It was in a heartening voice that he called, "It's I. May I come in?"

"Of course, my dear." As he walked into the room, she rose, shook out her skirts, and stretched out her hands to him. Harry pulled her rather gruffly into his arms and said in a low voice, "If you prefer that I stayed with you—"

"Don't be silly. You know very well that you

would pine away within the week for want of your laughing, gay companions."

"But the earl—Julien, Kate. He's offered me a place in his curricle to London. It doesn't seem the thing to leave you alone." He ground to a halt, seeing in her eyes the same hard look he'd so shortly before witnessed in his brother-in-law's.

"Oh, damnation, Kate. I didn't want to see you unhappy. God, to see you this way after all those years with Sir Oliver. Isn't there anything I can do?"

"This isn't a Greek tragedy, Harry. You just don't understand about people who are married, that's all. The earl merely journeys to London on business matters. There's nothing more to it than that."

"Your husband's name is Julien, Kate, not *the earl*. Don't take me for a fool." He would have said more, but he checked himself at the sight of her drawn face.

She looked up at him, the merest hint of a smile on her pale lips. "Never a fool, my dear, never. Now, I know you must be off. Pray don't concern yourself further about my stupid affairs."

He eyed her dubiously for a moment, and to her profound relief, said nothing.

"Take care, Harry, and don't wallow in too much mischief." She dropped a light kiss on his cheek, hugged him briefly, and drew back.

"You will write to me if there is anything you—"

"Yes, yes, of course." She felt quite calm at

the moment and didn't want to risk any faltering on either of their parts. Some moments later, from her vantage point at the window, Kate watched the footman strap the luggage onto the boot of the curricle. Julien and Harry, scarves knotted securely about their throats against the light flakes of falling snow, climbed into their seats. The groom handed Julien the reins, and Kate fancied she could hear the crunch of hardened snow beneath the wheels of the curricle. She maintained her vigil at the window long after new snow filled in the wheel tracks on the drive.

Although the household staff were astounded at the earl's abrupt departure without the countess, no word reached Kate's ears. To the casual observer there was no sign of disruption in the daily activities at St Clair. Privately, of course, there was endless speculation, even by the second footman and the Tweenie, a circumstance that Mannering heartily deplored but was unable to curtail. That the countess roamed through the various rooms, silent and aloof, was obvious to everyone, even those of little to no sensitivity.

Never sure how long the countess would wish to remain in any one room, footmen scurried to lay fires against the chill, only to discover not many minutes after their efforts that the room was empty again.

Luncheon and dinner trays were returned to Cook with scarce a morsel taken from the plates. A firm believer in the benefits of pork restorative jelly, Cook artfully hid spoonfuls of the thick gray substance beneath a cutlet or among the sauced vegetables. "The only one who's benefiting from my jelly is that miserable tabby," she said to Mrs Cradshaw, as she dished yet another uneaten plate of food into the cat's bowl.

Kate had no idea that she was unwittingly adding to the culinary pleasure of the kitchen cat, so closely was she locked into herself.

One afternoon, after wandering into the estate room, she returned to her room and huddled into a chair close to the fireplace, pulling a cover up to her chin. She had tried so hard not to think, not to remember, that she felt as if her mind was weaving itself into circular patterns. Finally, unable to withstand the onslaught of the bitter, shadowy memories, she allowed her mind to dwell upon them, each of them in turn. As once she had sought frantically to forget, she now forced herself to recall every detail, vividly re-creating the past five months, from the moment she'd fallen dead at Julien's feet in her duel with Harry.

She rose reluctantly sometime later to light candles against the early-winter darkness. As she carried a branch to a table near her chair, the glowing lights blended for an instant with the orange embers in the fireplace, creating a lifelike shadow that loomed upon the wall in front of her. She could almost feel Julien's presence near to her. It was almost as if she could reach out and touch him. She had but to listen closely to hear him speak to her. The large shadow flickered and flattened into an insignificant blur.

She sank into her chair and buried her face in her hands. With appalling clarity she remembered their last night together, when she'd taunted him until, finally, his calm, impassive facade crumbled. With a fury that matched her own, he had shouted at her.

"You speak so scathingly of *my* unbridled passions. But listen to yourself, madam, you rant like an uncontrolled, hysterical termagant. You can't say that you were mistaken in my character, for indeed you have never exerted the slightest effort to determine what sort of man I am. You have acted childishly, ignoring the needs and distress of everyone else around you. Your arrogance is amazing, your assumptions even more appalling. Damnation, woman, stop acting the shrew one minute and the victim the next."

"Damn you, how can you say such a thing, how—"

"How dare I what? Speak the truth? Make you realize that this mockery of a marriage is not only of my making? How many times you have hurled at my head that you dance to my every tune? I will tell you, madam, that the piper no longer plays."

She rushed at him with clenched fists. "You lie, just as you've always lied, just as you—" She raised her fists.

"Don't do it, Kate," he said in a voice of deadly calm. "Nothing would give me greater pleasure at this moment than to thrash some sense into you. You've quite nearly pushed me over the edge. Don't give me the excuse to do it."

"Ah, yes, your pleasure." She drew up, panting. "I've been naught but an instrument for your bloody pleasure, your token countess, whom your gentleman's code forbade you to seduce. You were forced to marry me so you could bed me, nothing more."

"Forced to marry you?" He looked at her thunderstruck. "Is that what you believe? You witless little fool. Hear me, Kate. I could have had quite an admirable selection of women for my wife. My choice of you for my wife, as the countess of March, had very little to do with the gratification of my sexual appetites. Only your irrational refusal of me caused me to act in the way that I did, that and the dreadful way you were forced to live by that maniacal father of yours."

"How very fortunate for you, my lord, that women find you so irresistible, else you would be forced to expend considerable energies staging your elaborate scenes."

"I seem to recall, madam, that it was you who staged our last so memorable seduction scene. And if my lamentable memory serves me correctly, your own passion rivaled mine."

"No, damn you, that's a lie. I didn't feel a thing, it was all imagined. No, I merely feigned feeling for you." She clapped her hands over her ears.

"No, I won't stop and I haven't said all that

I wish," he said, feeling like a savage now, nearly lost to control. He forcibly pulled her hands to her sides. "Damnation, listen to me. The young girl who was brutally raped no longer exists. You have seen her again, felt her misery. But now you must let her go. You are a woman, with a woman's needs and desires. You will destroy yourself if you do not banish that child's fears."

She wrenched herself free of him, her eyes grown dark and enormous. She gulped convulsively and the hated tears sprang to her eyes.

"Ah, sweetheart," he whispered, and extended his hand to her. "Please, come back to me." When she backed away from him, mutely shaking her head, he dropped his hands to his side, and his face hardened.

"Would that I never see you again, Julien."

"If that is what you wish," he said grimly, his eyes boring into hers.

"It is what I wish above all things."

"Then I bid you good-bye." Without another word he turned and left her bedchamber.

Kate raised her head from her hands, realizing inconsequentially that they were wet with tears. She rose slowly and placed more wood upon the dying fire.

The snowstorm ceased during the night, leaving a thick white blanket in its wake. Soft flakes fell about Kate as the steady pounding

493

of Astarte's hooves shook the low, snow-laden branches.

She didn't slow Astarte's pace until they'd crossed the small meadow that bordered the copse. She waited for the gnawing fear to come as she slipped off her mare's back and carefully tethered her.

Watchful of her footing, she walked into the small hollow and stood there looking about her. Several inches of fresh snow were piled high on the familiar tree stump. The small patch of mushrooms was buried. She bent down and swept the snow from the stump. It seemed so much smaller than she remembered, her two hands could almost span its surface. She felt nothing except a slight chill from the crisp winter air.

She sat down and pulled her riding habit and cloak close about her. She waited silently, still expectantly, but she could not recapture her child's excitement, nor her child's terror. There was nothing here for her, not the soft, sighing music woven from her child's thoughts, not the sound of the men's heavy wooden boots coming upon her, their glee at finding her there. The copse was simply a place, a small hollow of land, of no account really, not to her, not to anyone.

She rose finally and walked back to Astarte. She didn't look back as she retraced her steps.

40

"My lady! Oh my goodness, what a surprise! What an utter and complete surprise. We had no idea that you—well, you're here and isn't that something!"

"Good evening, George," Kate said brightly, sailing past the flabbergasted butler, waving as she did so to two lackeys. They staggered into the entrance hall under the weight of several trunks, portmanteaus, and bandboxes.

"I find myself without a guinea, without even a shilling," she said with a disarming smile. "Would you mind, George, settling with that excellent coachman, and, oh, yes, that very stern-looking fellow, who, I was informed, was an excellent outrider."

"Yes, my lady, certainly." He had sounded calm, even though to his own ears, his voice had risen a good octave. He motioned to a silent footman, who moved forward somewhat clumsily, bumping one of the countess's bandboxes. George shot him a look that promised retribution, and after giving the hapless fellow instructions and paying the coachman and the evil-looking outrider, he turned back to the countess. He took her ermine-lined cloak, her gloves, and a dashing bonnet.

"It's been a long time, George. I trust all goes well with you."

"Yes, indeed, my lady, so very well until just a moment ago. No, that's not really true, since you're here and that's an unexpected pleasure." A nervous tic had formed in the past few minutes in the corner of his right eye.

"Is the earl here, George?"

She followed his gaze up the long circular staircase and cocked her head to one side in question. He tugged on his cravat. "Er, yes, my lady, his lordship is indeed here, it's just that he—" George faltered and died.

"Yes, George?"

"That is to say, my lady, ah, his lordship is not alone, my lady."

"Well, no matter," Kate said kindly, patting him on his arm. "I'm certain his friends won't mind a visit from his wife, do you think?"

"It's not exactly his *friends*," George said in desperation.

"Oh, not his friends? How very curious. I wasn't aware his lordship admitted his enemies into his house. Come now, George, who is with his lordship?"

He realized that the countess of March wasn't the same young lady he'd known but a month before. *This* countess wasn't about to be put off. *This* countess was clearly in charge. He said, "Lady Sarah is with him. She arrived not fifteen minutes ago, demanding to see his lordship. Surely you see it's not his lordship's fault that she's here. Why, he would never admit a lady to this house, except you, naturally, but you're not a lady—well, you are, of course, but you're his wife, and surely that's more important."

"Yes, far more important." She smiled at him, and he started at the decided militant look in those eyes of hers. Then she gave the most sublime shrug. "Is that all? I dare say the *lady* who is not his wife is just this moment on the point of leaving."

Definitely the quiet, rather biddable young lady was long gone. No tears, just this calm indifference, this somewhat amused hauteur. It was astounding. He quite appreciated it. Perhaps, just perhaps, life would change for the better around here. It certainly couldn't get any worse, what with his lordship moping about, silent and withdrawn, drinking too much brandy, just sitting in the library, staring into the flames in the fireplace.

He got hold of himself. "Do allow me to inform his lordship that you're here, my lady." He had this sudden horrible vision of a scene that would make his own hair absolutely gray.

"Oh, no, George, that's not the way to handle this. Do trust me. I believe I shall surprise his lordship. He's in the salon upstairs?" He darted a look upstairs, gave her an anguished look, then just stood there like a dumb stick, at least that's how he characterized his own behavior to himself later over a glass of the earl's best brandy.

Kate turned and walked to the stairs, as bouncy as a child fetching a treat. She heard George say in a decidedly pettish voice, "Get about your business, my lads! Don't stand there gawking. Oh, yes, I must find some money for the coachman. No, no, I already paid them. Thank God for something, even a too-small something."

She walked purposefully up the stairs. Poor George's distress at Lady Sarah's tête-à-tête with the earl had, strangely enough, given her confidence. Trepidation is for fools, faint-hearts, and butlers, she decided, not for countesses, at least not for this countess.

Had she lost him?

No, she wouldn't consider that, no, indeed not. The door to the salon stood partially ajar, and Lady Sarah's repulsive voice reached Kate's ears before she actually saw the lady.

"Oh, Julien, let her stay in the country. She will be much more in place there. I always thought her awkwardly uncomfortable in society. She was always so pale and uncertain of herself, and our friends didn't know what to do with her. They were polite only because of you."

She waited, but Julien didn't say anything. Well, there was nothing for it. She marched in, head high. "How *very* kind of you, Lady Sarah, to have my welfare so much at heart. Do you really believe that everyone dislikes me? Is it because I'm such a bore? I don't believe I'm particularly pale now." She spoke

498

in the sweetest voice imaginable. She hoped it was as repulsive to Lady Sarah as her voice was to Kate. Actually she wanted to kill the lady, since her arms were around her husband's shoulders.

"Oh!" Lady Sarah jumped back, dropping her arms in stunned surprise.

"Good evening, my lord. I trust I find you well." She gave her husband a dazzling smile.

Julien was staring at her, not smiling back, not frowning, just staring, as if she were a specter. He said easily, "I go tolerably well, my dear, tolerably well."

"Now, my dear Lady Sarah, although it is perhaps comforting to think that one's husband is in such capable hands, I think it time to have a changing of the guard, so to speak. I daresay your own husband would much appreciate such a fond display of affection."

Although Sarah had never before been confronted by such a calm, contemptuous lady, she was made of sterner stuff than Kate imagined. Yes, she would quickly reduce Kate again to that pale, spineless chit that she'd known just a month before. The earl had been quiet since her arrival, attending to her every word with obvious interest, so it seemed, and had not appeared to be at all disinclined to accept her passionate embrace. Indeed, Sarah was emboldened to believe the earl had been on the verge of succumbing to her. Had it not been for the untimely arrival of his country mouse of a wife, she would have won. Perhaps she would still win.

"I don't believe you judge the situation quite correctly, dear," Lady Sarah said. "You speak so easily of fondness and affection. Why, everyone knows that you don't even sleep with your husband of three months, that you don't allow him near you."

Oh, God, she couldn't stand it. But she had to. Everything came down to this conversation, to his view of her now.

She stiffened almost imperceptibly as Lady Sarah continued smoothly, picking up speed in her growing confidence, "Doesn't it make sense to you that Julien would most certainly grow impatient with you, which I understand is usually the case when one forms attachments outside one's class. Don't you think it time for you to own up to the mistake? Don't you think it time to release him? Don't you think it wise, dear, to return to your quiet country life, where surely you will understand things better and be more comfortable?"

Kate wondered briefly how bunches of the lady's blond hair would look wrapped around her fisted hand.

"Am I more comfortable in the country? I do wonder about that. However, I'm touched by your obvious concern for my welfare. However again, I find you and your observations a dead bore, though I must admit to being a bit curious at your overly lively imagination. Now, if you please, I find your presence quite fatiguing, and must ask that you leave. I am here now. I am home. I wish to be with my husband, alone."

"Julien, tell her to go away, tell her not to talk to me in such a way."

"You intrude upon my comfort, Lady Sarah. Leave my house this instant, else I shall personally boot you out. I can too, you know, for I was raised in the country and I'm nearly as strong as my husband."

"You fool! *Your* house? I think the earl must have other opinions on that subject, don't you, Julien?"

"Well, half the house is mine. And indeed, this salon is in the very center of my half."

"Julien, would you cease this senseless charade and send her packing?" Sarah grabbed his arm and gave it a light shake.

There was a sudden silence, and Kate found that she couldn't meet his eyes. She had absolutely no idea what he was thinking, for he'd acted the interested but detached onlooker since she entered the room. She wondered with a sinking heart if the unmeasured words she had flung at him their last night together had finally driven him away from her, and if, indeed, he now viewed her as Lady Sarah had painted her. Did he now want to be free of her?

She forced herself to look up and saw that he was looking at her with an oddly keen expression that she couldn't begin to fathom. She wondered dispassionately if he would allow her a dignified exit.

"Sarah," he said finally, "I do believe the countess is in the right. The parlor is indeed in the very center of her half of the house.

Regrettable as it may appear, her logic is persuasive."

Kate blinked, thankful for once that no words were required of her.

"By God, surely you don't mean that, Julien. Surely."

"Yes, Sarah. Shall I ring for George?"

"No man dismisses me! How dare you? Just look at you, besotted by this provincial girl who has changed and I hate the changes, just as I hate her and always have." She was so angry, so outraged, that she couldn't move.

Julien turned to his wife, who was looking, to his amusement, quite bewildered.

He said softly, "Perhaps you're right, Sarah. I'm quite besotted and have been ever since the first time I saw her, dying dramatically in a duel at my very feet."

"I hope you will not live to regret this action, my lord. Actually I hope you will." She picked up her skirts and walked with what dignity she could muster from the room. They could hear her angry breathing as she stomped down the corridor.

"Close the door."

Without a word, Kate turned and pulled the door closed.

"Now, come here." He grinned at her. "Please come here."

"Perhaps I should ring for tea, my lord?"

"What happened to my protector, my mouthy wife who quite routed Lady Sarah— surely a novel experience for her."

"I don't know. It's different now. We're

alone and you're not my enemy."

"That's true enough."

"Surely tea isn't such a bad idea?"

"It's the very worst idea I've heard. What I would most prefer is to have my shrew of a wife in my arms."

"I'm not a shrew, curse you." However, she walked into his arms without hesitation.

He hugged her tightly against him, his hands sweeping up and down her back. Finally, he lifted her chin in his palm. She was staring up at him, as shy as a nun. He leaned down and kissed her.

She'd been so afraid, so very afraid, but the moment his mouth was on hers, she knew it would be all right, and she arched up against him, bringing his mouth closer, accepting his tongue, wanting more and more.

When he released her, her eyes darkened with disappointment.

He grinned down at her, absolutely delighted. "The servants, sweetheart, remember the servants. With Lady Sarah tearing down those stairs, doubtless hurling curses back at us, poor George must think we need him. Do you want him flying in here to see us making love?"

She gave him a look that made his hands clutch her shoulders. "Why not?"

"A very good point. However, before I have that lovely gown off you and throw you to the rug in front of the fireplace, I want to talk to you."

"I don't know if that's such a good idea."

"I'll kiss you while we talk. But it's important, love, don't you think so?"

"If you insist." She was silent a moment, then, to his surprise, laughed. "You should have seen poor George. I've never known him to be so bowled over. I quite marched all over him, you see. He must have believed that murder would be done in this house, for he knew I was capable of it, I know. And I was."

He sighed even as he kissed her again, and then again and again. "Being that my wife is a shrew, a very beautiful shrew, but there you have it nonetheless, I see I have to agree. Yes, murder at the very least, had I not intervened."

"Intervened, ha! You stood there like a stick. I didn't know if you would send me out or not. It was horrible. Oh, God, Julien, I was so afraid." She threw herself against him, holding him tightly.

"Shush, love, it's all right. Come now and sit down, else that rug will be under your back in a second flat and I'll be on top of you."

She sat beside him, actually, more on him, her cheek against his neck. "I treated you so badly at St Clair, so very badly."

She slowly pulled away, fixing her eyes on an elegant Dresden figure above the mantelpiece.

"You were speaking of the times you abused me," he said. "There were so many times. Could you be a trifle more specific?" Then he squeezed her hands, grinning.

"Ah, you jest with me, but it must be said. There was only the one time, really, and well you know it. Just that once. Well, the other times weren't all that well done of me, but those, I think, were very understandable, given what you did. German bandit, ha!"

"I would appreciate it if you would contrive to forget that man and what he did. He was a fool and stupid and altogether an idiot. I'm sorry for that, Kate, very sorry."

"But it made me remember, and even though it was dreadful and so frightening at first, well, you did help me, Julien. You got rid of the ghosts."

He looked at her closely. "Are you certain?"

She nodded. "Yes. Just three days ago, I rode Astarte to the copse. There was nothing there, Julien, nothing at all. It was just a place. There wasn't any more pain, any more terror."

"Jesus," he said, and pulled her against him again. "Thank you for coming back to me. You did it with panache. Now, tell me just one more thing."

"Yes?"

"Tell me you love me."

"I love you, Julien, more than anything I could ever have imagined feeling in my life. You're part of me, deep inside me. I'll never let you go away from me again."

"And I will have to cock up my toes and pass to the hereafter before I leave you, sweetheart. Sarah was right, you know. I'm utterly besotted with you."

505

"That's good. A man should be besotted with his wife."

"Excellent. Now that we've cleared that up, let me kiss you again. Lord, I love your mouth and your ears and your shoulders and your breasts and—" She laughed, then sighed softly when his mouth covered hers. Then he kissed each smiling dimple. He kissed her until she pulled away, gasping for breath. "By all that's foul, you don't know how to kiss. All right, I can see that you need me more than you can begin to imagine. Shall I teach you how to kiss properly now?"

"Do you really want your wife to kiss you with as much skill as your many mistresses?"

"Ah, all those charming females—a thing of the past. Since they are, then you will have to oblige me, don't you think?"

"Yes, but first I must ask you something. The Haverstokes' ridotto. I know it wasn't well done of me, but I couldn't help it. Why did you take Lady Sarah out onto the balcony and make love to her?"

"Who are we talking about?"

"Lady Sarah at the Haverstoke ridotto."

"Ah, you saw that? You really were eavesdropping on that most affecting scene. No, that wasn't well done of you at all."

"I'm thinking of fetching a pistol, Julien."

Although he didn't let her out of the circle of his arms, he was silent for a moment, frowning thoughtfully. "Then I guess I don't understand. How could you have ever doubted me if you overheard what I said to Sarah?

506

Given, she did wrap herself around me, but that was over quickly. You were a witness, weren't you?"

"But I saw her kissing you, I heard her speak so meanly about me and our marriage. I wanted to kill her and you, but most of all I wanted to erase myself. I didn't do any of those things because I got vilely ill. That was humiliating too."

"So, you got sick, did you? Then you didn't see how I handled the situation."

"No, I didn't. But I would say that your splendid tactics didn't carry the battle. After all, the lady seemed most sure of herself this evening."

"Alas, I have this fatal charm." He laughed and kissed her. "I'm relieved that I now have such a fiercely faithful wife to protect me from such temptations. Women—they're always throwing themselves in front of my curricle, fainting on my doorstep, dropping their handkerchiefs at my feet or on my boots—

"Ah, be quiet, you toad! You believe yourself so irresistible, do you?" She paused and studied his face. Her fingertips traced over his mouth, his cheeks, smoothed his eyebrows. "You are, Julien. You please me very much."

"Does pleasing have to do with pleasure, as in what I'm doing to your earlobe right now?"

"Perhaps it does," she said, her hands caressing his neck and shoulders.

507

"Will you forgive me for all the pain I've caused you?"

"Yes."

"I didn't know of any other way."

"But there was my anger, so uncontrolled, so unfair, and I lost our child, Julien."

"That's quite enough about that. Look at me. Your miscarriage was an accident, Kate. If there is to be blame attached, it must rest upon my shoulders. Do you understand me?"

"Oh, no, that isn't right."

"Do be quiet, Katharine. No more guilt for either of us, all right? We must both of us bury all the ghosts, else we'll spend our days in silent recriminations. I'm sorry for the child, but my first concern was and always shall be with you." He touched his fingers to her mouth to silence further protests and added in a lighter voice, "If you wish a future earl of March and many beautiful daughters, you may be certain that I shall most willingly oblige you."

"Will you really?"

"You know these things take time, Kate, many times, all of them fun, all of them filled with joy and laughter and pleasure. Shall I give you your second lesson?"

"What lesson?"

"Breathing, so you may kiss me properly without swooning from lack of air. Or at least if you do swoon, it will be from the pleasure I give you." He pulled her against him and kissed her. When he released her a few moments later, she looked at him and said with a sigh, "Oh, dear, it seems I'm so very slow to learn some things. Perhaps, in this instance, you won't find my backwardness a trial?"

"With your lovely mouth, soft and warm? No, I think not, sweetheart." He traced the curve of her lips with his fingertips.

"All right, Julien. Now, you must answer my question. You really didn't, you know. You just went ahead with your kissing lessons."

"What question?"

She kissed him and began to busily unbutton his white shirt. "I hope you won't think me too much a hussy, if I remind you of your promise to most willingly oblige me?"

"Oblige you in what exactly? I can't seem to remember."

"I must ask George for a pistol, my lord. Now, I want you obliged for many times. We have a duty to perform and I think we should begin to attend to it."

"Ah," he said, as he helped her unbutton his shirt. "The future earl of March?"

George chanced to look up and see the earl and countess of March emerge from the parlor and stroll arm in arm down the long carpeted corridor, his lordship's fair head bent close to the countess's cheek. If he wasn't mistaken, his lordship's shirt was unbuttoned.

A slow smile spread over his face as he watched them disappear from his view. He decided that he should inform François that the succulent sirloin of beef, so lovingly basted with herbs and red wine, would undoubtedly not be called for this evening by the earl of March.